Second Love

"Whisks from scandal to scheme, piling on the suspense."
—*Publishers Weekly*

Too Damn Rich

"A wedding of Krantz and Sheldon. Judith Gould is a master."
—*Kirkus Reviews*

Forever

"Mouthwatering . . . just the thing to chase away the blues."
—*Chicago Tribune*

Never Too Rich

"A romp . . . a smash success."
—*New York Daily News*

NOVELS BY JUDITH GOULD

Sins

Texas Born

Love-Makers

Second Love

Dazzle

Never Too Rich

Forever

Too Damn Rich

Till the End of Time

Rhapsody

Time to Say Good-bye

A Moment in Time

The Best Is Yet to Come

The Greek Villa

The Parisian Affair

Praise for the novels of Judith Gould

The Greek Villa

"A fascinating read." —*Romantic Times*

"An engaging contemporary romance that has a touch of mystery." —*Midwest Book Review*

"Wonderful twists and turns. . . . Devour a bite at a time, to truly enjoy and experience. . . . An outstanding work." —A Romance Review

"Will keep the reader in suspense to the final page . . . thoroughly enjoyable." —Roundtable Reviews

The Best Is Yet to Come

"An exciting relationship drama. . . . Readers will take pleasure from Judith Gould's inspirational tale."
—*Midwest Book Review*

"[A] page-turning plot and deliciously evil villains. A delight." —*Publishers Weekly*

"A fun, glitzy summer read filled with titillating sex and tidbits about upper-crust Manhattan, the trademarks that delight Gould's many avid fans."
—*Booklist*

"Another of Judith Gould's surefire pleasers."
—*The Sanford Herald* (NC)

continued . . .

A Moment in Time

"Gould's steamy tale about the lives of the rich and troubled is perfect for a read on the beach."

—*Booklist*

"Gould applies complex characters, steamy sex scenes, and a fast-moving plot to a popular premise. A modern day *Beauty and the Beast* . . . sure to please her many fans." —*Affaire de Coeur*

Time to Say Good-Bye
A *People* Beach Book of the Week

"Tugs seriously at your heart. . . . Fueled by a speedy . . . plot, delicious Dynasty-style details and some lusty sex scenes that will surprise—perhaps even shock—the earthiest of readers, this yarn delivers." —*People*

Rhapsody

"Cavort across the continents . . . with Gould's diverting tale." —*BookPage*

Till the End of Time

"This novel has all the right components: romance, a beautiful setting, deceit, and strong-willed, independent characters." —*Booklist*

JUDITH GOULD

The GREEK VILLA

A SIGNET BOOK

SIGNET
Published by New American Library, a division of
Penguin Group (USA) Inc., 375 Hudson Street,
New York, New York 10014, USA
Penguin Group (Canada), 10 Alcorn Avenue, Toronto,
Ontario M4V 3B2, Canada (a division of Pearson Penguin Canada Inc.)
Penguin Books Ltd., 80 Strand, London WC2R 0RL, England
Penguin Ireland, 25 St. Stephenís Green, Dublin 2,
Ireland (a division of Penguin Books Ltd.)
Penguin Group (Australia), 250 Camberwell Road, Camberwell, Victoria 3124,
Australia (a division of Pearson Australia Group Pty. Ltd.)
Penguin Books India Pvt. Ltd., 11 Community Centre, Panchsheel Park,
New Delhi - 110 017, India
Penguin Group (NZ), Cnr Airborne and Rosedale Roads, Albany,
Auckland 1310, New Zealand (a division of Pearson New Zealand Ltd.)
Penguin Books (South Africa) (Pty.) Ltd., 24 Sturdee Avenue,
Rosebank, Johannesburg 2196, South Africa

Penguin Books Ltd, Registered Offices:
80 Strand, London WC2R 0RL, England

Published by Signet, an imprint of New American Library,
a division of Penguin Group (USA) Inc. Previously published in a
New American Library hardcover edition.

First Signet Printing, October 2004
10 9 8 7 6 5 4 3 2 1

Printed in the United States of America

PUBLISHER'S NOTE
This is a work of fiction. Names, characters, places, and incidents either are the product of the author's imagination or are used fictitiously, and any resemblance to actual persons, living or dead, business establishments, events, or locales is entirely coincidental.

Urania. 1. One of the Muses.
2. Title of the goddess Aphrodite, describing her as 'heavenly', i.e. spiritual, to distinguish her from Aphrodite Pandemos, 'vulgar' love, as in Plato's *Symposium.*

The Oxford Companion
to Classical Literature

Chapter One

Coconut Grove, Miami, Florida

Wednesday, at the crack of dawn, Tracey tapped the button on the bedside alarm clock a full twelve minutes before it could emit its persistent high-pitched wail. Flinging aside the covers, she bounced out of bed, surprisingly not feeling the least bit nervous—despite the fact that her future hung in the balance. Today she would learn the dream to which she had devoted these past three years would finally come to fruition.

Either that, or she would be informed that those three long years had been for naught. If that was the case, she would be doomed to leave the project unfinished, shelve it, and start all over from scratch on a new book she had been mulling over—which would take yet more years of dogged work to complete.

However, optimistic as she was, Tracey Sullivan refused to consider anything but a positive outcome. *They like my novel,* she told herself. *That's why they're considering it for publication.*

Or, as her agent, Mark Varney, had put it, "I think it's going to happen."

Stretching her long, lean limbs luxuriously, Tracey

breathed in the salty air. A look in the dresser mirror confirmed that her beautiful ash blond hair was ruffled in an unintentional punk do. Her peridot green eyes looked perky, she decided.

Going over to the window, she raised the Bahamian shutters. As her hands moved, her jumbo sparkler—a six-carat whopper of an engagement ring—caught the slits of liquid sunlight which cast zebra-striped shadows across the room.

Outside was a lush jungle of palms, banana trees, ficus hedges, wisteria heavy with bloom and riotous bougainvillea. The morning sky was hazy and without a cloud. The air was heavy and oppressive with humidity, typical for August in sedate, secluded Coconut Grove. It was a haven of greenery close enough to enjoy the heady lust and ultra-chic stretch of playground that is South Beach, where celebrities and models flock year-round and, come winter, the moneyed elite from the world over converge to party the nights away.

As if on cue, the air pulsated with the Latin percussion of a celebrity DJ's remix of a tango with a throbbing disco beat. Tracey leaned out from under the slanting Bahamian shutters. On the tree-lined road, a finned '57 Cadillac convertible, filled with club kids heading home to crash, surged past like a mint-green-and-chrome land yacht, six pairs of arms raised skyward and pumping the air in time with the beat.

Where else but Miami?

The multicolored flash of wild parrots, descendants of long-escaped pets, shrieked from the midst of the foliage, and a solitary female jogger, wearing all white—T-shirt, shorts, sun visor and running shoes—ran along the side of the road. Also tuned in to the Latin beat, but through the headphones of her Walkman.

Tracey turned away from the window and concentrated on getting to work. She had her morning routine down pat, and this morning she followed it as religiously as on any other.

One: Wake up just after the crack of dawn.

Two: Head down the narrow hall of the little Florida cracker house to the kitchen, where she'd switch on the coffeemaker that she'd filled the night before.

Three: Shock her system wide awake with a brutal ice-cold shower.

Four: Pour herself a steaming mug of strong black café Cubano.

Five: Clad in nothing more than a man's extra-large white T-shirt, and her hair pinned up, sit down at her corner desk. She stuck pencils through her hair like chopsticks and booted up her computer. Then sipped super-charged caffeine to jump-start her system while taking a fresh gander at the pages she'd run off the night before.

Discipline, allied with a firm belief in her talent, made Tracey reserve both the first two and the last two waking hours of every day for working on her novel.

Tracey was determined to make a successful career as a commercial novelist. Well, to be honest, a bit more than merely successful. For Tracey's idea of success was to become a superstar novelist. Right up there alongside the likes of Danielle Steel and Jackie Collins and Anne Rice.

Like that.

Of course, she was well aware of the odds of ever reaching that summit. They were about the same as an aspiring actor's chances of hitting stardom. But daunting though they were, these odds did not discourage her. If anything, they gave her the impetus to work that much harder. *If nobody bothered to try, then there would be no stars.*

On this, the first day of the rest of her life, Tracey spent the first two hours at her computer. Then it was time to get dressed and go to her day job at WMAI-TV, an independent television station serving greater Miami and the Metro-Dade area. A minor television station, to be sure—but hey, she was working in TV.

"Morning, Dad," Tracey said brightly.

She'd headed down the narrow carpeted hall and, popping into the 1940s time warp of a kitchen, planted a noisy smooch atop her father's thinning pate. He was seated at his usual spot in front of the window, at the white, gold-speckled Formica-topped dinette table, a vintage piece of gold-tone metal that had been around twice as long as his daughter.

"Well, hello yourself, Sunshine."

He looked up from the crossword puzzle in the *Miami Herald* and smiled indulgently at her.

"You're chipper this morning," he added, observing her from above his Ben Franklin reading glasses.

"What do you mean, *this morning*?" Tracey huffed, pretending to take offense. "I am always chipper. Got that?" She put her hands on her hips and faked a glare.

"Yep. Read you loud and clear."

Tracey poured herself another mugful of caffeine. After taking a sip, she wiped her mouth with the back of a hand, unintentionally smearing Viola Mist Lipcolor across strategically applied Ripe Plum blush.

Her father chuckled.

"And what," inquired Tracey, "do you find so amusing?"

"Well, here you are, in your working girl getup. Splendidly combed and perfectly groomed. And what do you do? You rub your makeup around and turn yourself into Pocahontas on the warpath."

"Oh," Tracey exclaimed in genuine distress. She sprang to her feet.

"It's nothing a few minutes of repair won't fix."

"A few minutes!" Tracey automatically glanced up at the chromium-rimmed Seth Thomas ticktocking faithfully on the wall above the big white enamel-and-chrome Buick of a stove, another perfectly preserved relic from the forties. "Now I'm going to be late," she muttered.

Grabbing her bag, she hurried to the bathroom to survey the damage. Switching on the light, she recoiled. The face in the mirror looked ridiculous from the nose down. Like a child playing with makeup. Or a Karel Appel portrait.

Swiftly unlatching her purse, she got busy. She was still fixing her face when her father called out, "What's a ten-letter word for 'They rest on bridges'?"

"You're looking right through some," Tracey responded without having to think, but trying not to move her mouth as she leaned into the mirror and judiciously applied liner to her lips.

"Eyeglasses! That's it!" Tom Sullivan exclaimed. "Bless your heart. You are a genius. What would I do without you?"

"Well, you'd never finish your crossword puzzles, that's for sure," Tracey responded tartly. "I really don't know why you torture yourself with those damned things."

With a sharp click, she capped the lip liner, dropped it into her bag, and gave herself the kind of five-second perusal every woman learns to trust. Besides being aware of her every flaw, Tracey was pleasantly surprised by her choice of outfit. Today she was wearing a T-shirt-weight, turquoise cowl-necked sweater with the sleeves pushed up, a teensy black postage stamp of a miniskirt, black tights, and plain but fashionably chunky, shiny black shoes. Third World Prada rip-offs bought from a street vendor—but hey. Who could afford the real thing?

Certainly not moi, Tracey thought. *Not on my salary.* However, when the first check for her novel came, the very first thing she vowed to splurge on would be some really decent shoes.

Rushing out of the bathroom, she flicked an anxious glance at the wall clock.

"Dad, I'm off," she announced, leaning down and depositing a hasty kiss on her father's stubbly cheek. "And don't worry about dinner. It's my turn to cook, remember?"

"Wait a moment," he called after her. "What's a ten-letter word for 'Tragically inaccurate adjective of 1912'?"

Tracey already had both the front door and the screen door open. "Unsinkable," she flung back over her shoulder. She raced down the creaking steps of the front porch, car keys jingling in hand.

Her wheels were parked directly up front, on the other side of the bougainvillea-covered lattice that screened the house from the road. As transportation went, the car barely sufficed. Her once white, much pocked, and severely dented rust bucket was one of the few surviving Chevy Corvairs still on the road, with over 187,000 miles on the odometer.

Parked directly beside it was her dad's 1976 Oldsmobile Ciera. The Florida sun had leached the once shiny black paint job to a dark lusterless gray. As far as wheels went, it was no golden oldie either. But considering its age, it was surprisingly dependable.

Crossing her fingers, Tracey sent up a silent prayer to the god of motorcars, in hopes that both sets of wheels would last a little while longer.

Just another year or two, Lord, that's all I'm asking. . . .

Brushing aside knife-edged palm fronds, she walked around to the driver's side of the Corvair and glanced at the house that she called home. Like the cars, it too had seen more prosperous times. Set back a ways, the one-story bungalow had been built lengthwise on the narrow lot, its widely bracketed gable end and sagging front porch facing the road. It was an anachronism, particularly now that everything else on the entire block had been torn down, the neighbors or their heirs having sold out to one of the big developers.

Unlike the stretches of trendy, rehabilitated Art Deco hotels and apartment houses in South Beach, this particular block of Coconut Grove had, since the forties, been bungalow row—each building squeezed side by side, virtually against the next. On quarter-acre lots so long and narrow you could practically reach out of the windows along the sides and shake hands with the neighbors in the house next door.

No more, though.

The other houses were all gone, save for her father's lone bungalow. Because he had been one stubborn, solitary holdout. One man who'd bucked the trend and refused to sell. Except for him, construction on an expensive gated community would long have been completed.

Tracey remembered seeing the proposed building plans. Where the bungalows had stood would be overly large McMansions—vinyl and stucco châteaux with more gables than you could count. A high-end planned community which would banish the live oaks and banyan trees in favor of tiny manicured front lawns. Leviathans costing a million bucks and more. All in all, not much better than the high-rises already encroaching upon this oasis of green calm.

The day her father received the first offer for their house, the sweet, gentle man she knew and loved turned out to have another side to him. Because for once, Tom Sullivan's soft-spoken demeanor was missing.

In its place was iron. Cold, unbendable iron.

"I've lived here half my life, dammit, and nobody's going to force me out," her father told a reporter. "I don't care how much money they wave in front of my nose, it won't be enough." Over two years had gone by, and Tom Sullivan still hadn't budged from his position. Not when a quarter of a million dollars had been dangled in front of him. Not when they upped that offer to half a million, and then three quarters. Most recently, he'd even turned down a cool million—*after* taxes. That was when his lawyer, who worked pro bono, finally decided to wash his hands of him. "You're not only unreasonable," he told Tom Sullivan, "you're nuts. I can't work with a guy who's crazy."

Tracey thought about her father's stubbornness as she raced to work, pumping those old cylinders for everything they were worth. The Corvair got her to the television station with two minutes to spare. She angled the car into an empty slot in the employee parking lot behind the station. Climbing out of the car, she leaned back inside to snatch her bag off of the passenger seat, slung it over her shoulder, and slammed the door. Then, pivoting smartly, she cut across the half-full parking lot. Through the cyclone fence, she barely noticed the WMAI "News Chopper," a Bell Jet Ranger helicopter boldly emblazoned with the station's logo, parked smack dab in the middle of the big painted letter H inside the even bigger yellow-painted circle. Low heels clacking on oil-stained concrete, she had eyes for only the rear entrance of the building. There, five concrete steps and a pipe railing rose beside the wheelchair-friendly ramp for the handicapped, and a red sign with white lettering warned:

FOR EMPLOYEES ONLY
TRESPASSERS WILL BE PROSECUTED

The front entrance wasn't any fancier. WMAI occupied a pink cinder block rectangle three stories high, notable mainly for its absence of glass. Precious few windows punctuated its stark, fortresslike walls.

Which was perfectly understandable. TV stations are not

designed to be light-filled and airy. They need to be utilitarian and soundproof. Cocooned from storm, riot, high noon or dead of night. As Tracey drew closer, she heard the steady drone drifting down from its flat roof, atop which the giant air-conditioning units did twenty-four-hour battle against south Florida's heat and humidity. Stopping at the reinforced steel door flanked by security cameras, Tracey dug inside her bag and produced what looked like a plastic credit card, complete with magnetic strip, and slid it into an ATM-like slot. She punched in a six-digit PIN on the recessed keyboard, and the door dutifully emitted a buzz. She pushed it open and crossed the threshold, stepping from hot and humid one second into a blast of arctic winter the next.

Behind her, the door automatically clicked shut.

"Brad," she said, stopping at the desk just inside, "back from the Bahamas already? What'd you do? Lose your shirt?"

"Trace!" enthused the uniformed security guard, as though he hadn't noticed her arrival on one of the dozen video monitors built into the slanted desktop in front of him. Beside him, a police scanner emitted a burst of static-filled chatter. A retired cop, Brad Noble liked to keep up with what went down on his former beat.

"How you doin'?" he asked her.

Tracey had to laugh. It was common knowledge that he often caught breaking news over the scanner that the news hot shots upstairs managed to miss.

"How am I doing? Why don't you tell me?" she suggested slyly, gesturing toward the scanner with her chin. "You're the one who's been on duty since midnight."

Pretending disgust with the criminal element as a whole, and last night's perpetrators in particular, he shrugged beefy shoulders and flapped a hand dismissively. "Aw, you know. The usual. 'Cept for a coupla gang-related shootin's and a drug sting, it's been pretty quiet. No brush fires, no cruise ship fires. No tourists gunned down. No plane crashes in the Everglades. Hell, not even an emergency landing at the airport. How you like that? Sound like a long hot summer to you?"

"You know what they say," she said. "No news is good news."

"Not in your business, it ain't," he pointed out. "You mark my words." He nodded knowingly. "Unless somethin' hits the fan, the local evenin' news is gonna need some puff pieces. The anchors are gonna ride you to dig up some kinda human interest stories."

If that was supposed to discourage Tracey, it had the exact opposite effect. Like most assistants, she was still far from jaded. The prospect of being assigned to research a story—any story—rather than being used as a mere secretary thrilled her.

She gave a little wave and sailed on down the concrete hall, her destination the stairwell by the bank of elevators. She climbed the concrete stairs two at a time and opened the fire door to the second floor, the newsroom. The pulsating heart where stories were born or died or occasionally killed.

Tracey strode down the carpeted central aisle. Behind the glassed-in wall to her left, row upon row of flickering television screens glowed brightly from desk height to ceiling. Techies worked on keyboards slotting in local ads during commercial breaks of syndicated sitcoms. The room was immense and, except for the concrete supporting columns and the fourteen-foot-high acoustically tiled ceiling, big enough to accommodate a passenger jet. Above was a glassed-in balcony, double-glazed for soundproofing, which overlooked the ground-floor broadcast studio. The sight of the blue-carpeted dais upon which, like an altar, the glossy, semicircular news anchor desk faced jumbo-size video cameras, never failed to stir her.

There were no offices for the general workforce. Instead, rows of space-saving hexagonal pods, each of which contained six cubicles, filled the floor. Tracey turned right at the fifth row, then swerved across a narrow aisle. She was one pod from her workstation when she was neatly cut off by a beautiful young woman who propelled her rolling desk chair swiftly backward.

"Aha! Thought you could sneak past me, eh, *amiga*?" she

accused good-naturedly. Her shiny black eyes, olive skin, and ever so slight accent confirmed her proud Spanish heritage.

"Maribel!" Tracey exclaimed in delight, eyeing her best friend. Maribel Pinales had been the one who showed Tracey around on her very first day on the job. One look at each other and they had connected. Soon they bonded like sisters.

"I can't believe it," Tracey said. "They've put you back on the day shift?"

Maribel laughed. "They had no choice. Someone's got to make sure you're not slacking off."

Tracey narrowed her matchless peridot eyes in mock anger. "*Moi?* Step-and-Fetch Sullivan? Just goes to show how absolutely shameless you are. You'd use any excuse to get off the night shift." Tracey smiled. "In fact, I actually recall you telling me you'd get off it. Right after they reassigned you. Remember?"

"Remember?" Maribel sighed. "*Por Dios!* I can't even remember whether I had two or three cups of coffee for breakfast this morning."

"Oh, right." Tracey grasped the back of Maribel's chair and gently rolled it, like a wheelchair, into her friend's pie-shaped workstation. "I've got to get to work. We'll chat later, okay?"

Maribel twisted around. "How about we have dinner together?"

Tracey frowned. "We'll see. That all depends . . ."

"Yes . . . ?" Maribel raised her eyebrows questioningly.

Tracey extended an arm and wiggled her fingers, setting the six-carat marquise solitaire flashing.

"Oh, him!" Maribel rolled her eyes and gave a long-suffering sigh. "I don't know how you do it. Who else would score a fiancé whose family is listed in the top half of the Forbes 400? All while your poor *barrio* sister here is doomed to settle for any old *chico* who happens along. Is that fair, or does life stink?"

"Ha! Any old *chico* indeed! You're the one with the Miss Universe looks," Tracey pointed out. "Correct me if I'm wrong. Were you, or were you not, among the top five finalists in the Miss Florida pageant a couple of years back?

And have you, or have you not, turned down no less than four marriage proposals?" She paused. "Well?"

"Five," Maribel corrected gloomily, holding up four spread fingers and a thumb. "Five proposals, not four."

"Yes, but four of them were filthy rich," Tracey pointed out.

"Yeah, but all five of them were ugly old trolls, and that's putting it nicely. Now, your Brian . . ." Maribel swiveled her chair around, those giant black eyes sparkling as she sighed. "There's a dreamboat of a hunk—young, rich *and* handsome. He could be a model or a movie star. No fat ugly old man for you."

Tracey laughed and rubbed a thumb and forefinger beside her ear. "Just so you remember, the grass is always greener on the other side of the fence. And when you get there? Sure enough, you find out it's the same old grass." She paused, then said, "Besides, I'd be willing to bet you've got at least two or three prospects chasing after you right now."

"Well . . ." Maribel replied with a mischievous gleam in her eyes.

"Aha! I thought so. Tell me about him?"

"Later, okay? I've got to get busy now."

"Sure," Tracey said. "See you in a while." With that, Tracey began to turn and head to the adjoining pod.

Maribel caught her by the arm. "Listen, before you hit the desk. I've got to tell you"—she glanced around and lowered her voice conspiratorially—"I discovered the absolutely greatest street vendor of all time."

"What?" Tracey's ears perked up. "All right, give." She wagged a stern finger. "No holding back."

"Have I ever kept anything from you?" Maribel pulled a wounded face. "Anyway, he sells Gucci and Prada and D&G rip-offs. Weekends only. I'm telling you, his stuff is to die for. Word is, it's so good that even the store clerks can't tell for sure."

Now she really had Tracey's attention. For among a host of other shared traits, both young women shared the same taste in clothes. Clothes which, unfortunately, were hopelessly out of reach of their budgets. Until Tracey was married, she could only dream of buying the real label. Ditto for Maribel. Ergo, the perpetual hunt for good knockoffs.

"Swell," Tracey said happily. "It's a date, and you'd better not fink out on me."

"But what about"—Maribel glanced pointedly at Tracey's engagement ring—"Richie Rich?"

"Brian Rutherford Biggs III is a big boy," Tracey said with a lofty sniff. "He'll just have to be content to see me Friday evening and all day Sunday. I guarantee you, no matter what the rest of this week may bring, we're doing some serious shopping come Saturday. And that's that."

"Cool," said Maribel.

"Tell me something," Tracey said. "You don't think we strike people as shallow, vain, and consumed by consumer envy, do you?"

"I sincerely hope so," said Maribel. "Oh, and just think, Friday's a payday—"

"—which," Tracey said, picking up the conversational thread and running with it, "means we can spend it all in one place."

Laughing, Maribel got back to work while Tracey breezed over to her own pie wedge of a workstation. It was outfitted with a computer, phone, filing cabinets, and a coat hook. A bulletin board mounted on one divider wall was personalized with a cat calender and a variety of thumbtacked snapshots of herself with Brian, as well as her favorite pics of her father.

Trust Maribel to come up with a new vendor, she thought happily as she plopped down onto her red, ergonomic, five-legged futuristic starship command of a swivel chair. She was barely seated when the phone rang.

"Newsroom. Sullivan," she answered in a businesslike tone.

The voice on the other end was soft and smooth and aroused a dozen pleasant sensations. "You've got to help me. I'm suffering from severe Sullivan withdrawal symptoms."

"Brian!" she laughed. "You just saw me last night."

"I did? It seems like a year ago."

"Listen to you."

"I wish you would. What do you say to a nice quiet dinner tonight? Real casual and romantic. No other diners. No captains and waiters and busboys. Just us two. Plus moonlight, candles, champagne . . ." His voice was filled with a thousand promises.

Tracey sighed. "It sounds," she said helplessly, "like an offer I can't refuse."

"Good. Remember, I said real casual. I'll pick you up at seven."

"But—"

"No buts." He cut her off with little kissing sounds.

She was meaning to ask what he meant by real casual, but he'd already hung up.

Chapter Two

Tracey was home from work and racing around madly to make dinner for her dad. She ordered him to go watch TV.

"I can make my own supper," he said. "I'm a grown-up and can fend for myself, damn it. You ought to slow down and take your time getting ready. A beautiful young thing like you going out on a hot date."

Tracey shooed him away. "First of all, it's not a hot date, it's just dinner. And second, I'm fixing you a TV tray and that's that." She was becoming bossy because she felt guilty about going out with Brian and leaving her father home alone.

Tracey microwaved the frozen lasagna, toasted the garlic bread, and served it on the TV tray with a chilled bottle of Bud. Then she showered, letting the humidity corkscrew her hair Hollywood-style. By the time Brian honked the car horn, she had finished dressing, playing it safe and taking casual to mean sporty yet dressy enough to get in most anywhere.

"Wow!" Her father whistled admiringly as she twirled for him. "My little girl, the knockout."

"You're just saying that. We both know you're prejudiced." She picked up her cell phone, made certain it was on, and slipped it into her pocketbook. Her agent, Mark, hadn't called her yet, but there was still a chance he might. With the three-hour time difference and his habit of working late, he often phoned at nine or ten o'clock Miami time.

"You don't believe me," he said. "Go ask the mirror."

Which she did. With her peridot eyes, ash blond hair, and soft tan, she looked state-of-the-art Floribbean. She'd put on a cotton aqua tank top, cuffless orange trousers, and purple suede sandals with heels and ankle straps. In case things got a bit formal, she'd draped a purple, red, and rust shawl made of some miraculously crinkled micro fiber—a treasured thrift shop find—over one shoulder. Her purse was a little square zippered number covered in aqua sequins with a shoulder strap of aqua raffia.

Appropriate, she decided, for whatever surprise Brian had in store. If there was one thing she'd learned, it was that with Brian, you never could tell. She might end up in a speedboat and have dinner in Bimini. Or go club-hopping in South Beach, dancing the night away at various places—Bash and Club Exile and Honey. Or he'd really surprise her and they'd stay in a single spot for everything, wining, dining and boogying at B.E.D., for instance, or Oxygen Lounge.

He didn't like to be predictable.

Which was one of the things she liked about him.

His unpredictability extended to the vehicles he drove. A real gearhead, he owned a growing collection of classic cars. This evening he was in a 1959 Corvette convertible that was the envy of any automobile collector. It had a grille like chrome shark's teeth and a curvaceous body of gleaming Roman red, with racy concave white side panels. Plus the requisite whitewalls, chrome hubcaps, and round dual headlights mounted side by side.

It was a real attention grabber, all right, particularly with the ragtop down.

The instant she stepped out onto the porch, he was out of the car. Not by opening his door, but by vaulting athletically right over it. Landing neatly on the asphalt, then coming around the front and holding the passenger door open.

A true gentleman of the old school. Would he, she wondered, also kiss her hand?

She didn't wonder for long. As she approached, he obviously decided, *The hell with it,* and let go of the door handle. Held his arms wide.

She rushed right into them, letting his lean hard body fold against hers. Laying her face sideways against his chest, she inhaled deeply. He always smelled so good and clean. Never of cologne, only of soap and man and freshly laundered clothes.

She could hear his heart thumping against his rib cage as the Corvette's engine growled softly in idle. She could feel his instant tumescence straining against his trousers and pressing against her hip. She gripped his arms and leaned her head way back, looking straight up into his topaz eyes.

The sun had yet to set, and golden light, filtered by the jungle of branches, burnished his skin, highlighting every plane and angle of his handsomely sculpted face. His lips parted slightly, not to speak, but to greet her without words.

"Brian? . . . "

Did she speak it? Breathe it? Think it? Tracey couldn't be sure, but whichever it was, he needed no prompting and leaned his head forward, at the same time tightening one hand around her waist to draw her closer, and using the other to hold the back of her head.

And then their mouths met.

In her ears was a roaring which sounded like a distant Niagara.

His lips were warm and soft and nipped hers playfully. But she responded urgently, greedily, uttering a muffled cry when his tongue glided past her lips and began exploring, at first teasing the sweet tender moistness inside her mouth. For a short while their tongues danced a delectably slow minuet, then picked up the tempo until it became a passionate tango.

In her ears, the roar of Niagara rose to a thunder. High-voltage currents shot back and forth between them. Scorching heat coursed from his mouth into hers and boiled through her body and limbs.

His kiss deepened and he sucked in the air from her lungs and took it into his, held it a long moment, and then slowly exhaled, breathing it back into her. The sexual resuscitation was more than she could bear. It was as if a tempest raged around the two of them, encapsulating them in a cocoon and isolating them from the rest of the world. She felt acutely alive as never before, and her hunger knew no bounds.

God help me, she thought. *I can't get enough of him!*

Proof of her helplessness was the seeping warmth moistening her thighs. Unable to control herself, she ground her groin lasciviously against his trapped arousal.

"Whoa," he chuckled, breaking the seal of their kiss and raising his head. He gave it a shake, as though to clear it. "Easy there. Are we, or are we not, behaving like sex-starved teenagers?"

Reluctantly she let go of his arms. "I was only," she murmured, "expressing my sentiments by saying, 'Hello.' "

"Hello!" He emitted an explosion of warm laughter. "Wow. If that's a 'Hello,' it makes me wish I'd been gone awhile, see what one of your 'Welcome Home's would be like."

Her voice was husky. "Actually, not all that different."

For a moment he looked disappointed, but then she held up her hand with the big sparkling rock on it.

He smiled and nodded.

She smiled, too. How well she remembered the night he'd proposed to her. They had been dining alfresco at Red Fish Grill in Coral Gables, at a table under one of the palm trees that had their trunks all wrapped in little white Christmas lights. Luau torches blazed at the edge of the terrace, and there was still plenty of daylight to see beyond the lush grounds, a vista of sea and sky that seemed to go on forever and ever.

Sometime between the appetizer and the entree, he produced a little red box stamped "Cartier" in gold script, opened it, took out the ring, and slipped it on her finger.

Needless to say, it was a perfect fit. But then, what didn't he do perfectly?

"You see," she told Brian softly, "we might not be married yet, but I'm yours all the same. Being separated from you for a day hurts as badly as it would if it were a week or a month."

"Ever the romantic," he said, gently running a fingertip down the side of her face. Then he stepped back and held the passenger door of the 'Vette open.

"At your service, princess." He deliberately said it like Gavin MacLeod: Prin-*cess*. Extended a helping hand. "If I may be so bold? . . ."

Tracey played along, holding out an imperious hand. He bowed over it, barely brushed it with his lips, and helped her into the car. He shut the door firmly.

As she settled in the white leather bucket seat and strapped herself in, Tracey watched through the windshield as he put a little extra strut into going around the hood of the car to the driver's side.

To hear Maribel tell it, Brian Rutherford Biggs III was God's gift to women. She might well be right. He *was* exceptionally handsome, and with his aquiline nose and angled forehead, he had the swept-back profile of an aerodynamically designed hood ornament. He had thick shiny black hair combed sleekly back, and he exuded money, power, and confidence. Small wonder he was being groomed to take over his family's multitudinous businesses.

But he was more than just tall, dark, and handsome. Brian positively glowed with virility.

Chucking open his door, Brian lowered himself into the driver's seat and turned to Tracey. Flashed her one of his killer grins.

"And where," she inquired, adjusting the shawl around her shoulders, "are we going?"

"You'll see."

Suddenly she had a disturbing premonition. "Not to finally meet your parents!" she said in alarm. She was curious about why Brian hadn't yet introduced her to them, but she wasn't looking forward to it, either. "Please, Brian, if that's it, you've got to tell me. I would have dressed more appropriately—"

"Darling, will you stop? You look scrumptious. And as for my parents, you needn't worry about them—yet."

"What do you mean, 'yet'?" she demanded.

He smiled. "Just kidding. Anyway, Dad's completed a business deal in Shanghai, and he's so pleased with it he decided to take a week off to celebrate. Instead of coming straight home, he had my mother fly to Mauritius to meet him. They'll be there for a week or so on a kind of second honeymoon."

"Praise be to my Higher Power," Tracey murmured.

"Oh, for God's sake," he said. "They're only my parents. I don't know why you're so nervous about meeting them."

"I'm not." She gave a little laugh. "Well, I am, and I do *want* to meet them. I just don't want to give a bad first impression, that's all. You've got to promise me that when the time comes, you'll give me adequate warning."

"So you can get out the pearls?" he teased.

She sniffed. "It just so happens that I don't own any," she retorted. "Besides, if you haven't noticed, I'm not exactly the twin set and pearls type."

"Thank God." Brian's dark eyes were staring deeply into hers. "Why do you think I was attracted to you in the first place?" He leaned toward her and gave her cheek a peck. "The last thing I need is another debutante. Christ, I've ODed on enough of them to last me several lifetimes."

Tracey permitted herself to relax. "So, since it's not to your parents', where *are* we off to?"

He said, "Like I told you, you'll see." And flashing a raffish grin, he glanced in the rearview mirror, shifted into first, and put the pedal to the metal.

After crossing Biscayne Bay on the MacArthur Causeway, Brian aimed that chrome-toothed grille down the first ramp. The instant they hit South Beach, he swung a hard right onto Alton Road, then hooked another sharp right at the Miami Beach Marina.

Slowing, he expertly maneuvered the 'Vette past the line of cars waiting for the parking valets who were scrambling to keep up with the seafood dinner crowd. With his typical disregard for authority, he pulled into an empty slot where the sign specifically stated NO PARKING. Tracey felt conflicted: her middle-class upbringing causing stress about getting into trouble; the rebel in her reveling in the way Brian disregarded rules, thinking how cool it was and wishing she could work up the same nerve.

He said, "Here we are." Switched off the engine and proceeded to put the top up.

After the exhilarating open-air roar of wind and traffic, the silence seemed unearthly. The ticking noises from the cooling motor under the hood sounded absurdly loud.

Locking the car, he put an arm around her waist and led her to where the yachts were moored. From the paved quay the piers jutted out into the water like fingers, some of them straight, others angling into L-shapes. On both sides of each, boats were tied up. They ranged from a few twenty-some-foot bow riders to big white monsters over eighty feet in length.

Tracey looked at Brian. "I thought you told me your family's yacht was too big to dock at this marina."

"Yeah," he said, pulling a face, "and with a permanent crew of fourteen you've got about as much privacy as at a cocktail party."

Tracey nodded. In truth, she was dying to see the floating palace, but didn't want to seem too eager. *I'll see it soon enough,* she told herself.

Brian walked her out onto one of the piers, past boats with names like *Loophole* and *Missy* and *Fancy Nancy* and *Artful Dodger* and *To the Max*. Finally he halted at the very end, where he eyed a glossy fifty-four-foot express cruiser admiringly.

It had aerodynamic Euro-styling and a swept-back radar arch. The entire aft seemed to be devoted to outdoor activities, from the Jet Ski mounted sideways atop the hydraulic swim platform to the cushioned sun beds just inside the transom, from the upholstered L-shaped settee and hi-lo table to the midships windshield with its twin bucket seats and ergonomic helm. The dash was studded with so many computer monitors it reminded her of the command center of a futuristic starship. The forward half of the sleek flaring hull was punctuated with four elongated, chrome-rimmed oval portholes; atop them, the front deck was padded with additional recessed sun beds.

Brian let go of her waist, stuck his hands in his pockets, and prowled the length of the vessel. After pacing back and forth alongside it several times, he asked, "Well?" Not looking at Tracey as he said it, as if unable to tear his eyes off the boat. "What do you think of her?"

What did she think? Well, the term *Upholstered Motor* sprang to mind, as did *Party Platform*, but for once Tracey decided to test the waters before plunging in. "I, ah, take it that it . . . I mean, she . . . uh, belongs to you?"

"Yep." He grinned like the proud father of a newborn. "Just took delivery of her today. Like her?"

With a wave he displayed the name stenciled boldly across the transom, fancy black letters outlined in gold:

COME ABOARD

And in smaller letters underneath that:

MIAMI BEACH

Come Aboard.

The double entendre was not lost on her. *Heaven help us,* Tracey thought, with an inward groan. *What is it about men and their machines?* she wondered. *Does everything with a souped-up engine have to bring out the worst of all that is sophomoric?*

"Well?" Brian prodded. "Do you like her?"

She took the easy way out: "What's not to like?" Never really answering his question.

Not that he noticed. He just grinned and kept on looking the boat over appreciatively, the same way he might eye a curvaceously built beach babe.

"Yeah, you're right." He spoke slowly. "What *isn't* there to like?"

Finally he tore his eyes off the streamlined fiberglass and gave her his full attention. Instantly she could feel herself getting lost in the depths of his topaz gaze. She didn't care about the boat, but about him.

His voice was soft, in keeping with his gaze. "What do you say we break out the champagne, give her a proper christening?"

Her eyes were still on his. "I've never christened a boat before. I'm not so sure I'd dare break a bottle over the bow. Or anywhere else, for that matter. I'd be afraid of damaging something."

He blinked at that thought. "You're right. This baby doesn't have a scratch on her. Tell you what we'll do. I'll pop the cork, hand the bottle over to you, and you do the honors. Only you pour the bubbly rather than smash the bottle. Okay?"

She smiled. "Okay."

"And after that," he murmured, nuzzling her neck, "we'll cast off and head out into the bay. Call it our mini maiden voyage."

She could feel the world shrinking, until they were the only two people on earth. "And then?" she asked huskily.

"Then we drop anchor."

"And? . . ."

He smiled and drew her closer. Her breasts met his hard chest, and she could feel his heart beating strongly. "And then," he whispered, "we'll christen her properly."

Brian dropped anchor outside the channel markers in Biscayne Bay. The sunset had come and gone and the sky was purpling. He'd switched off the engines and generator so all they could hear were little wavelets slapping against the hull. *Come Aboard*'s battery-powered running lights were on, so anyone boating outside the channel markers would see where they were anchored.

Tracey, arms spread wide across the cushioned back of the aft sun bed, had her legs luxuriously stretched out in front of her. She breathed the fresh salt air deeply as she stared at the Miami skyline, visible in the distance under a ribbon of causeway soaring high and black against the darkening sky. "From here," she murmured dreamily, "the high-rises glitter like pavé diamonds."

"And don't forget the occasional pavé rubies, sapphires, emeralds, and citrines," he added. He was spread out on his back at a right angle beside her, his head resting on her lap.

"I wonder," she mused, cocking her head sideways. "What color jewel would be appropriate for that magenta-lit building over there, on the right?" She pointed. "It's not amethyst, that much I know."

Brian lifted his head, craned his neck, then let it settle comfortably back down on her lap. He shrugged. "Beats me," he said. "I've named about all the gems I can recite offhand. If you're really interested, you can ask my mother sometime. She's the gemological expert. I expect she'll eventually make one out of you, too."

"Don't frighten me. I'm a total idiot when it comes to jewelry."

"I'm not trying to frighten you. Besides, I know you'd be a quick study. Before you know it, Mother will have you running around with a loupe in your purse. It's like her American Express card. She never leaves home without it."

"Don't tell me! Why? Just in case she runs across a bauble in some jeweler's window?"

"Exactly."

Holy Moses, Tracey thought. She couldn't begin to imagine such wealth. And marrying into it, she would no doubt be expected to follow the example set by his mother and her friends, who dined at the right restaurant here, wrote big philanthropic checks there, knew the ins and outs of bidding for fine art and antiques, could distinguish not only the difference in style between Louis XV and Louis XVI, but could tell the quality of each piece at a glance, and ordered entire wardrobes from the various trunk shows they attended unless, of course, they flew to Paris for fittings. . . .

It was a dizzying prospect, and Tracey suddenly felt a mounting sense of panic at the idea of having to fit into such an alien world. For courage, she plucked her champagne glass from the nearest built-in drinks holder. She gulped the contents, sighed with pleasure, and momentarily forgot what duties lay in store for the future Mrs. Brian Rutherford Biggs III. Carefully she replaced the glass in the holder.

"This Dom Pérignon sure is good," she said.

He laughed. "Dom Pérignon is always good." He grinned up at her. "Hungry yet?"

"Not really. I'm perfectly satisfied," she said, "although I must admit I *am* feeling a bit light-headed." Her smile was barely visible in the faint glow of the running lights. "But who needs food? I've got all this"—she lifted a lazy hand to indicate the spectacular view—"and I've got this boat, and I've got *you* . . ."

"In which case," he murmured, "we might wish to take nourishment of a different sort . . ."

Upon which he rolled over and pressed his head face-down in her lap. And there he remained for the longest time without moving a muscle. Just breathing in. Breathing out.

There was no need for him to do more to arouse her. His every exhalation exploded puffs of warmth against the thin fibers of her orange pants and filtered through to tease and tingle the flesh beneath.

Tracey uttered a soft moan. Her eyes fluttered shut and she let herself go. At first she was content to simply drift, the gentle rocking of the boat lulling her while the warmth emanating from his mouth heated her groin and sent exquisite spears of pleasure shooting through her.

Such gentle teasing could not go on indefinitely. Once ignited, wildfires of this magnitude raged unchecked, and it was inhuman to think she could control them. Her body ached to receive his—and if it did not happen soon, she would surely go mad. Yet still he continued to simply lie there, unmoving, his breath alone stoking her heat, testing her resolve.

Suddenly she could bear it no longer. She slipped down from her splay-legged sitting position until she lay flat on the sun bed. "Oh, Brian," she moaned. "Either stop it or *do* something—"

She raised her hips into the air, clutched his head in her hands, and pressed his face into her, writhing snakelike beneath him.

Slowly he managed to raise his head despite all her efforts to keep his face buried in the cleft of her legs. Reaching up, his hands found hers, pried her fingers loose, and intertwined them with his.

She fought spiritedly against him, but defeat was inevitable. With an anguished cry of surrender, her arms were forced down into a classic crucified position, and he held her trembling body captive as he drew himself up over her.

Her breasts rose and fell swiftly.

"Slowly, my sweet," he advised, looking down into her shining eyes. "There is no need for greed. Haven't you heard that all good things come to those who wait?"

She stared up into his face. "Wait? Waiting is torture!"

"If it be torture," he whispered, "we have all night." He lay atop her, the two of them still fully clothed. To keep from crushing her, he supported himself on his elbows and toes and dipped his head to kiss her.

She parted her generous lips in anticipation, but he stopped and looked into her eyes. The devotion he saw there lit a fire of desire within him, and he was incapable of teasing her any longer. He must have her and have her quickly. Kissing her passionately, he rolled onto his side and pulled her against his hard, lean body. His hands slid beneath her aqua tank top and began stroking her creamy breasts as his tongue delved the sweetness of her mouth.

Tracey gasped at the touch of his hands, and a shiver of excitement shot up her spine when his fingers began tracing circles around her nipples. Moaning softly, she clutched him closer to her, aware of the lengthening hardness that awaited her. Brian groaned as she sought out that hardness and stroked it with her hand.

He in turn slipped a hand into her orange pants and began massaging the cleft between her legs. When he felt its wetness, a bolt of pleasure shot through him, and he drew back. "Let's get undressed," he whispered. "No one can see us out here, and so what if they can."

She nodded and helped him as he drew the tank top over her head, then pulled her orange pants down and off her legs. Taking her silken panties between his fingers, he stared with open relish at her blond mound as he pulled them off and tossed them aside. She had taken off her heels when she'd boarded the boat so as not to mark its pristine finish. Brian got up and hastily dispensed with his clothing, throwing it atop hers; then, thick muscular thighs spread wide, he stood staring down at her beautiful body with a fiery gleam in his eyes. She returned his look, taking pleasure in his masculine hardness and the obvious pride that he took in his own virility.

In an instant he was on his hands and knees, atop her again, his lips covering hers, kissing her with renewed passion before he moved to her breasts, where the tip of his tongue flicked her nipples. Tracey reached for his throbbing manhood, encircling it with her hand. Brian's entire body quivered at her touch, and he let out a growl of pleasure before reaching down and taking her hand in his, removing it from his cock and kissing it tenderly. He began to enter her, slowly and gently at first, entranced by the look of wonder and desire that was in Tracey's eyes.

She moaned with pleasure, her body's hunger for him mounting, and when he could finally hold off no longer and plunged into her, she let out a gasp and trembled from head to toe as a bolt of passion swept through her.

Brian's lips covered hers then, and his tongue hungrily licked hers while he rhythmically began moving in and out, craving her feminine sweetness. Tracey gave herself up to him unreservedly, her body moving with his, her own urges no less powerful than his. As she clutched his shoulders, she thought that he must surely be the world's greatest lover and she must be his only love.

He began to move with more urgency, swept up in a vortex of unstoppable desire, thrusting himself in and out with abandon.

Suddenly the loud chortle of a cell phone penetrated the veil of carnal delight that surrounded them. Brian groaned aloud, and Tracey's body automatically jerked. It was her phone, she was sure of it.

Her manuscript. Had it been accepted?

"I—I've . . . got . . . to get it," she said reluctantly. It was probably Mark calling from Los Angeles.

Brian's head moved from side to side, even as he slowed to a near stop. "No," he whispered. "Forget about it."

"I—I have to," Tracey replied, one hand scrambling for her pocketbook.

"No," he insisted, pushing against her hard. "I said forget about it."

The phone continued to ring, its sound shrill in their ears.

"Brian," she said, struggling against him, "it's important! I have to get this call."

His powerful body went limp, and he drew back from her. "Shit," he swore. "Get the damn thing." He swung around and sat with his head in his hands, elbows on knees.

Tracey quickly located her sequined pocketbook and grabbed her cell phone. "Hello," she said in a breathy voice as she depressed the talk button.

"Tracey?"

"Yes?" It was Mark Varney, her agent. *Oh, my God,* she thought, sitting bolt upright. She felt a sledgehammer suddenly knocking around wildly inside her rib cage. Going *boom-ka-boom, boom-ka-boom, boom-ka-boom. The book!* She reached out a hand to Brian, and he took it in his, grudgingly, she thought. Then he gave it a reassuring squeeze. *Better.*

"How are you?" Mark asked.

She stifled a nervous giggle. "I think you know that better than I do," she said tremulously. "Why don't you tell me?"

"All right. Listen, I just had lunch with Lisette Alexander at Browne-Smeeks—"

Boom-ka-boom. Boom-ka-boom. Boom—

"She's the head honcho who was so crazy about your outline and sample chapters," he reminded her. "As I told you a few weeks ago, no one person at Browne-Smeeks can give the green light on a project anymore. It's all done by committee."

Yes, yes! She felt the overwhelming urge to give him a long-distance shake and shout: *I already know that! We talked that over a couple of weeks ago! Now get on with it!*

"Well, she finished reading it and discussed it during her editorial meeting this morning . . ."

"Y-yes?" Tracey ventured. She was beginning to get definite unsettling vibes about where this conversation was headed.

"Also, since we talked last, the parent company of Browne-Smeeks initiated a new corporate policy."

Aw, shee-it. Here goes . . . She shut her eyes against what was coming and steeled herself, the palm of her hand slick and sweaty around the cell phone. Brian, who had sensed the nature of the call, gave her free hand another squeeze, and she thought she saw him smile at her in the near darkness.

"Up until now," Mark continued, "Browne-Smeeks's commercial books helped defray the losses incurred by publishing prestigious, money-losing literary ventures. Not anymore. PubCorp P.L.C., the parent company, just handed down a new decree. Each book they publish will, from now on, be treated as its own separate entity. As such, it's expected to make money."

"But my novel *is* commercial!" Tracey interjected. "You said so yourself."

Mark said, "You know it is, and I know it is. But Browne-Smeeks is leery of new authors at the moment. Particularly those without a track record to promote."

Tracey could feel her comfortable little world spinning out of control. New corporate policy . . . not the publisher's, but the parent company's, which of course called the tune. Behind her shut eyes she envisioned a bound book, then watched it explode in slow motion into a snowstorm of fragmented pages. It was her book that she was seeing, her "baby." The project she had invested hundreds of hours in, and nurtured . . .

. . . and for what? Just to see it killed off?

"In other words," Tracey said tonelessly, "my manuscript has been rejected."

There was a heavy silence. Then Mark Varney cleared his throat. "Yes."

Tracey made a strangled sound of exasperation. Who the hell were these corporate jerks?

"But bear in mind," Mark told her, "that Browne-Smeeks isn't the only game in town. Sure, with all the consolidations and buyouts, there are only a handful of publishing goliaths left. But we haven't approached Bertelsmann or Time Warner or Simon and Schuster . . ."

Tracey let him prattle on with his pep talk, but she was barely listening. Granted, there were times when the glass was half full. However, there were other times when it was definitely half empty, too.

He was saying, "The important thing is not to give up. You're too good a writer to throw your talent away. Give it time."

Yeah, right. Like I can afford to wait.

"Oh-oh!" she said suddenly just to get him off the phone so she could lick her wounds. "I . . . I've got to get going. I'm with a friend. We'll discuss this further some other time. Okay?"

"Sure," Mark said. "But look, don't let this get you down. I still believe in this book, and so does Lisette. It's not the end of the world."

Tracey drew a deep breath. "Right," she said as she pressed the end button.

But she thought, *Wrong. For me, it* is *the end of the world. Rejected.*

With shaking fingers, Tracey flipped the phone shut and dropped it into her pocketbook. Then she snatched her hand back as though the telephone had scorched it. Numbly she sat there, staring blankly at the yacht's deck, seeing but not registering its pristine whiteness that shone even in the dim light.

Understandably, the expensive finishes on Brian's yacht did not register on Tracey at the moment. Nor did the other luxuries on the big boat. What *did* register was the place in which she found herself trapped—a hollow no-man's-land of pain and anguish.

So bitter was the pill of disappointment, so difficult was it to swallow after laboring under the glow of optimism, that she had to bite down furiously on her lip, all the while blinking back the threatening flood of tears.

Brian put a muscular arm around her shoulders and drew her to him. "What is it, Tracey?" he asked in a soft voice. "Come on. Tell me about it."

"It . . . it was Mark Varney," she said in a little voice. "They don't want my book."

He hugged her protectively. "Don't worry about it," he said. "It's not the end of the world, Tracey." He nuzzled her ear and neck, then flicked his tongue around them before kissing her cheek. When she didn't respond, he said, "Hey, come on. Pull out of it, Tracey. There's us to think about. Remember?"

She nodded without looking at him. "I . . . I know, Brian," she said. "I just need . . . I need to be alone right now."

Brian emitted an audible sigh. "Alone? Jeez, Tracey. Here we are out on my new boat, having a great time, then one stupid phone call and it's like I don't exist."

"I'm sorry, Brian," she said. "I . . . I can't help it." She was trying to fight back tears.

"I wish I could make you feel better," he said.

"I do, too," she replied, "but I . . . I really can't help it."

"I understand," he said, hugging her to him. "Do you want me to take you home now?"

She nodded. "I think that would be best, Brian."

He kissed her bare shoulder tenderly. "Whatever's best for my girl," he said, trying to hide the frustration.

"Thanks," she murmured. *I guess I should feel lucky to have someone who cares so much,* she thought, *but I don't feel lucky at all.*

Chapter Three

Maribel was dressed and ready to go by the time her date rang the doorbell. However, she wasn't about to make a lunge for the door just yet. From experience she'd learned that it did a man good to have to wait a minute or two.

"Un momentito!" she sang out.

Maribel was ready to paint the town red. She was wearing a slinky, backless red minidress with a bralike bodice and cross-your-heart spaghetti straps which looped around her neck. Her black lace pantyhose were the perfect foil for red patent-leather ankle-strap pumps with skyscraper heels.

She took her time answering the door, practicing a sexy, flouncing walk. She stopped at the hallway console to pick up her shiny red alligator-embossed clutch purse and, more important, take a final inventory in the mirror above it.

She pouted her lips, admiring the base coat of Electro Red lipstick and the second coat of wet-look translucent gloss. They showed off the snowy whiteness of her teeth. As for her eyes . . . she nodded to herself with satisfaction. The effect of her eyes, shiny as black olives, along with her sharply arched, peaked black eyebrows, was heightened by the liberal use of eyeshadow—Madina Milano Absolute

#46, a soft red which brought out the devil in her. Nor had she forgotten to color-coordinate her nails, which gleamed with a barely dry coat of O.P.I.'s Color My Heart . . . Red.

"Arrrrr-iba!" she trilled softly, assuming a flamenco stance. "Catherine Zeta-Jones, eat your heart out!" Then, tossing back her thick long black hair, she blew her reflection an air kiss and went to open the door.

Ramón Felipe Escolano stood, smiling, in the lamplight of her porch.

Dios mio! She drew in a sharp breath. The one and only time they'd previously met, when they had hastily arranged this date, he had been in full-throttle pinstripes: a conservative three-piece tropical weight suit, orange silk tie, French cuffs with gold links. He'd knocked her eyes out, all right, and had projected sex appeal out the wazoo. But what she *hadn't* expected, what she truly hadn't dared hope for, was that the suit could hide such delectably sublime assets.

Dios mio! indeed.

Ramón Escolano was tall and slender. His face was composed of planes and angles, with cliffhanger cheekbones, a square jaw, prominent lips which begged to be kissed, and what at one time were referred to as "bedroom eyes." Large, black, and liquid, they were tipped with long lashes, the kind of eyes you could lose yourself in forever. The short, conservatively combed black hair she remembered had been transformed into stylish after-hours spikes.

"Well, *ho . . . la!*" she drawled slowly, her eyes sweeping him appreciatively from head to toe while her fashion radar, switched to full alert, took note of the small details.

Details like his black silk T-shirt with a V-neck collar which showed off a pair of nicely muscled arms and just the faintest hint of an abdominal six-pack. His pleated, loose white linen trousers which left everything to the imagination—courtesy of Ralph Lauren Polo, she presumed—were cinched with a sliver of black alligator belt which, if her eyes did not deceive her, had to be by Barry Kieselstein-Cord. Plus there was the white sports jacket he'd slung casually over one shoulder (Armani from the look of it, and not AX, either), and a big Rolex which, though hideously expensive, was crafted of tasteful, understated stainless steel.

All in all showy, yes, but not too, *too*.

In fact, she thought with a glow of pride, *a man after my own heart. . . .*

It was hardly a secret that Maribel was partial to handsome, fashionably attired men. After all, whoever she went on a date with was a reflection on her. Also, since she put 110 percent into looking *her* best, surely she deserved a man who did likewise.

"*Hola* yourself," he said, flashing a wide white grin. From behind his back he produced a single long-stemmed pink rose and proffered it with a flourish. "Beauty for a beauty."

Granted, it was corny, but it was a sweet gesture all the same. She accepted the rose with a surprised little smile and held the blossom to her nose. Inhaled its delicate fragrance deeply.

"You ready for a nice leisurely dinner and maybe some dancing?"

"Bueno!" Her eyes sparkled. He was sounding better all the time.

"I've made reservations at Kiss Steakhouse and Lounge. That okay with you?"

Was that okay? It was only among her five favorite places on earth!

She hooked her arm through his. "Oh, I think I could live with that," she tossed off casually, not wanting to sound like it was too big a deal.

"Kiss it is, then."

Kiss, at Lincoln Road and James Avenue, was a steakhouse, lounge, disco and cabaret all rolled into one. Everything about the place was high-style Miami. Both indoors and out, the dining tables had sculpted pedestal bases and super-exaggerated, high-backed chairs that looked like postmodern thrones with pointy tops.

Ray had snagged a table outside, under palms and stars. "I highly recommend the margaritas," he suggested as the maître d' pulled out Maribel's chair.

She laughed. "Believe me, when it comes to margaritas, you don't have to twist my arm."

"Two margaritas," he told the waitress, making a V with his fingers.

When she brought the drinks, they toasted each other. "Here's to us," Ray said, holding his glass aloft.

"To us," Maribel echoed, her breath catching in her throat. Her hand was trembling as she clinked her glass against his, and she looked at him over the rim as she sipped.

He was staring right back at her. "You like the margarita?" he asked softly.

She detected the undertone in his voice and felt her face turning red. She wanted to say, *I like you. I want you to make love to me.*

What she said was, "Delectable," but her eyes conveyed the unmistakable message that she was referring to more than just the drink.

Thanks to the margaritas, getting acquainted came easily. They discussed everything and nothing, and were both surprised by the extent of what they had in common.

"I can't believe it," Maribel exclaimed, eyes shining. "You're wild about ice hockey, dance remixes, Ozzy Osbourne, *and* foreign films? Come on, someone must have told you Visconti's right at the top of my list, too."

He shook his head.

"You mean, no one did? Swear to God?"

He placed a hand over his heart and smiled. "Swear to God."

"Wow!" she said, watching him take a little sip of margarita and lick salt off his upper lip with the tip of his tongue. She thought: *I must be dreaming. They don't come any better.*

And, though she was forced to budget carefully, resorting to designer rip-offs and secondhand shops while he was Armani-ed, Polo-ed, polished, and Rolex-ed, she soon discovered that their backgrounds were not all that dissimilar.

He had been raised by a single mother. So had she. Both had family in Miami and Cuba.

They made some more headway with their margaritas,

then Maribel tilted her head to one side. "I want to know more."

"Then cross-examine me."

"Well, you're awfully young to be an *abogado*, aren't you?"

He smiled. "I'm older than I look."

"Get outta here!"

"Seriously. I came to this country from Cuba in 'seventy-eight."

Now she looked at him in amazement. "You're a Marielito?"

"That's right." He had another sip of margarita, another lick of salt from his upper lip. "My mother and I came over with the first boat lift." He toyed with the stem of his glass, then glanced up at her. "Why do you sound so surprised?"

"Because your English doesn't have any trace of an accent. Even mine does, and I was born here."

"Yes, but you grew up in the Hispanic community. I was eight when we came, and my mother insisted on finding a job inland, living among the Anglos just so I'd have to go to an all English-speaking school." He made a face. "The trouble was, they weren't just Anglos. They were Florida crackers."

"Ai-yi-yi." She made a face.

He shook his head grimly. "Christ, I hated it . . . and did the other kids hate me! I was forever the outsider."

She nodded sympathetically. "Kids can be so cruel."

"Tell me about it. Since I was a Marielito, they kept taunting me about whether I was a criminal or a looney who'd been let out of the asylum by Castro. I remember my first day at that school. I got into a fight and came home all beat up. When I complained to my mother, she showed me no pity. 'You'll just have to learn to look out for yourself,' she said. And when I asked her, Couldn't we move to a friendlier neighborhood?, guess what she told me?"

Maribel shook her head.

"She said that I'd eventually thank her for it. At the time, I thought she was nuts. *Thank* her? I thought. For what? Throwing me into the midst of a schoolyard of redneck sharks? But she was convinced that anglicizing me was the only surefire way for me to get a jump start. To really make something of my life."

"Let me take a wild guess. The kids who tormented you? Ganging up on you the way they did?"

"Yes? . . ."

"That's what really prompted you to study like all hell and get straight A's. Am I right? And your grades, of course, only made you that much more unpopular."

He gave her an odd look. "That's right. Now let *me* take a wild guess. I gather you've been in a similar situation yourself."

"Well, similar, but hardly the same. Luckily I grew up in Little Havana. But *por Dios*, did my mother ever ride me to excel, too! It certainly didn't make me popular in school, being Little Miss Goody Two Shoes, always the teacher's pet. But you know something? Today I'm thankful my ma was so tough."

He smiled. "I know," he said softly. "Same here."

He motioned to the waitress for another round, and they took time out to study the menu. When the waitress returned with two more margaritas, she took their orders.

Ray had steak, medium rare.

Maribel had rosemary-skewered Maine diver scallops.

Ray decided a Napa Valley Sauvignon Blanc 1998 would go nicely with both entrees.

Which it did, making the transition from margaritas to wine totally painless.

After dinner he suggested they go into the Kiss lounge. It was a high-energy club, a vast space with soaring columns and fiber-optic lighting where DJs were spinning the latest international hits, and a cabaret featured fire acts and belly dancers. It was just half past ten, still early by club standards; the action wouldn't really heat up until sometime around midnight. But they preferred it this way. There was something more intimate without the pressing crowds.

And so they danced and he ordered a bottle of champagne and they danced some more.

One thing led to another. Dinner to dancing. And now, heated up by the throbbing rhythm, everyone else in the club seemed to recede until they were the only two people on the dance floor. Though their bodies didn't touch, they both felt as if they were making fierce love right there on the polished boards.

Finally Ray took her arm and shouted something into her ear. She couldn't hear what he was saying above the sound of the music, but she didn't need to. Words were unnecessary. She knew what he'd suggested.

She stared at him for a moment, her eyes wide and luminous. Then she nodded and followed him out of the club. Prudently deciding that friends don't drive friends home drunk, he decided to leave his car and cab it.

He had a brand-new waterfront high-rise condo, just across the causeway on Brickell Bay Drive. Entry was via state-of-the-art thumbprint building access. The uniformed concierge behind a great rosewood and marble desk greeted them politely. So did an armed security guard. A private elevator, also using thumbprint security, hurtled them hundreds of feet above Biscayne Bay in seconds. The elevator doors slid aside with scarcely a whisper.

Maribel was agog. She entered the apartment slowly and did a 360-degree turn in place. She could scarcely believe her eyes. This penthouse duplex, with its loftlike spaces, was as close to a castle in the sky as you could get. The floors were of rare polished woods, and the walls of floor-to-ceiling windows offered unparalled views. There was a minimal amount of modern furnishings, but what there was showed exquisite taste.

Outside, an immense private terrace was planted like a Zen garden, and had its own rooftop pool.

If this wasn't living the American dream, she didn't know what was.

Ray Escolano had obviously come a long way. The distance from here to Cuba had to be at least five million dollars.

"Por Dios!" she whispered. "*Que rico!* I . . . I had no idea." She turned to him. "Tell me, Ray," she said, "I know you're an attorney, but what is it exactly that you do? Represent drug dealers?"

He burst out laughing. "Hardly. I'm an estate tax specialist. My job is to find loopholes for filthy rich clients who don't want half their wealth to vanish the instant they die."

"And that got you all this?" She gestured around with astonishment.

"It's a little more complicated than that, but I hate talking business during quality time." His gaze was intense. "And from where I'm standing, I'd say this is premium quality time."

She stared back at him.

Afterward, neither of them would be able to recall which of them made the first move. They were like two magnets inexorably drawn toward each other. Before they knew it, his arms closed around her and she found herself pressing herself against the solid warmth of his body, lifting her face to his.

For what seemed an eternity, they were frozen in that pose, he taking his time feasting on the sight of her thickly lashed eyes, her upturned nose and generous, voluptuous mouth with lips parted in anticipation, teeth gleaming; she in turn eating up the face hovering just inches above hers, with black velvet eyes in which she could see tiny twin reflections of herself. She could feel the strong beating of his heart, the acceleration of her own quickening pulse.

The moment stretched telescopically.

Suddenly she could stand it no longer. "Ray . . ." she breathed urgently, and twining her arms around his neck, lifted herself on tiptoe to meet him halfway.

A muffled cry escaped her as his mouth made contact with hers, his lips softer than she ever imagined they could be. And with that kiss a hundred exquisite sensations suddenly awakened and thrummed throughout her.

Before long, his sweet little nibbles gave way to deep, hungry kisses, and wild abandon gripped them both. Their tongues met and dueled; under her corsetlike bodice, she could feel her sensitive nipples swell and tingle.

But arousal was a two-way street, as she happily discovered. With her hips pressed against his, it was impossible to ignore his straining tumescence. It was all his trousers could do to contain it.

Her body responded, a flood of moistness welling up inside her loins. She swayed unsteadily on her feet. Her legs were weak and trembly, like a newborn colt's, yet at the same time she had never felt this intensely alive, this exuberantly buoyant. It was as if she had sprouted wings and taken flight, soaring up, up, up to ever greater heights—

The tips of his fingers traced exploratory paths across the landscape of her bare back. Then one hand drifted down to caress her buttocks while the other came around and almost casually slid behind the bodice of her dress.

The touch of his fingers against her bare breast seared like sizzling sparks, sent bolts of pleasure darting through her. "Oh, yes," she breathed, clinging to his neck and grinding her hips fiercely against his tumescence. "Yes!"

"Sh. Not so fast," he whispered, cupping the breast in his hand and gently rolling her nipple between his fingers.

She sucked in her breath, squeezed her eyes shut, and let her head loll back in gasping ecstasy. "Oh, that's good. Oh, that feels so good! Oh, Ray . . ."

Then his other hand slid under her minidress and probed.

That did it. Suddenly there was no restraining either of them.

Maribel frantically clawed his shoulders in an effort to tug off his jacket.

Ray struggled to loosen the neck strap of her minidress.

She grappled with his belt and fly.

He managed to peel the clinging stretch fabric up over her head.

Clothes went flying every which way.

At last, naked as Adam and Eve, they stood a few feet apart and stared at one another, both of them panting, catching their breath. Sizing each other up. Liking what they each saw.

Maribel ran appreciative eyes over the well-toned sleek body of a swimmer, albeit a swimmer sprouting a scimitar of throbbing flesh from a thick thatch of black pubic hair.

Ray's eyes drank in voluptuous young female curves—strong proud breasts, a flat belly, flaring hips, and a bikini-trimmed mound.

Time-out was over almost as soon as it began. Then that primordial force slammed them back together. Once again their mouths coupled furiously. He kneaded her full plum-tipped breasts. Her fingers dug into his buttocks and pulled him tightly against her, trapping his straining phallus between his belly and hers. There it twitched and throbbed urgently, as though it possessed a mind of its own.

At first Ray tried to pull away, giving his manhood room to maneuver, but it was as though her hips were glued to his. Next he tried to push her away, but her fingers dug even deeper into his buttocks and pressed him more tightly against her. His foiled efforts to free himself made him gurgle with laughter which surfaced from the depths of their passionate kiss.

He broke the seal of their lips. "Why, you . . . you *bruja*!" he accused, narrowed eyes flashing. "So suddenly we're playing hard to get, is that it?"

"Who's playing hard to get?" Her eyes mocked him playfully and her lips formed a pretty pout.

"You know who," he replied. *"You!"*

And without warning he let go of her breasts, reached down and, quick as lightning, grasped her by the underside of her thighs. Lifting her clear off the ground, he frog-marched her over to a U-shaped sectional. Coming on it from behind, he sat her atop the soft butterscotch leather back and let her go. "Now who's laughing?" he demanded.

She remained seated in place by looping her arms around his neck. "I am," she giggled.

Then, seeing his furrowed brow, she decided to stop teasing him and let go, allowing herself to fall slowly backward until she was upside-down on the sectional. Her buttocks rested against the seat back, her legs rose above it, and her feet were in the air. Her head nearly reached the floor, her long black hair fanning out over polished granite flooring.

"And what happens now?" she whispered up at him. Her eyes were round and luminous. "Is the Big Bad Wolf just going to stand there, or what? Little Red Riding Hood's waiting, you know."

He gave a lupine grin and growled, "What happens now is the Big Bad Wolf is going to eat you!" And grabbing her legs, he spread them apart in a wide V and dove headfirst into her groin.

His tongue was as moist as her opening, and he used it to probe her innermost secrets. She was soft and warm and welcoming. Her body writhed, but her soft cries were not cries of pain.

When he surfaced for air, she pushed herself toward him. "No, Ray!" she moaned. "Please don't stop!"

He glanced down at her topsy-turvy face. Her head was thrashing back and forth, whipping her hair into a frenzy, and her face held an expression of fierce concentration.

"Please, Ray, it's so *good*—"

He filled his lungs with air, held it in, and dove again. When he exhaled it inside her, she went wild.

She went wilder still when he glided two fingers up inside her and nibbled gently on her trigger. That was when it happened. Her eyes flew open, her body spasmed, and he felt himself drowning in a flood of nectar.

He lifted his moist chin and grinned down at her.

She stared up at him with reproach. "Why did you stop? I don't want you to stop."

"I'm not stopping," he replied softly. "Why are you in such a rush? Where's the fire?"

"Inside me!" she whispered intensely.

He smiled. "In that case, my sexy little *paloma*, you have nothing to worry about. I've only just begun."

Chapter Four

"Going to have a busy day?" Tom Sullivan asked his daughter as she started for the door.

"Who can say, Dad?" she responded. "I may work in the newsroom, but I sure can't predict the news."

He chuckled. "That I know. You just seem to be in a bigger rush than usual."

"No," Tracey said with a smile. "Just my usual hectic pace. Why?" In actuality, she was hurrying out of the house so she wouldn't have to tell him about the bad news she'd received the night before. She knew she would have to eventually, but as yet she was unwilling to do so because she knew that he would be deeply disappointed for her.

"I think you forgot something," Tom Sullivan said, looking at her over the rims of his glasses.

"Forgot something?" She lifted her brows in a question.

Her father tapped his cheek with a finger. "A good-bye kiss for your dad?"

"Oh, my God, Dad!" she exclaimed. She hurried to him and planted a kiss on his bald pate, then kissed his cheek for good measure.

"That's better," he replied with satisfaction. "See you tonight."

Tracey headed off toward the door. "Tonight, Dad. Love you."

"Love you too, Sunshine."

It is impossible to predict when or where breaking news may occur. As a result, a news center has to be flexible, to shift gears into overdrive within seconds.

Which explained why Tracey was kept hopping all morning. One moment, nothing seemed to be happening, yet the next instant, all hell broke loose.

Like much of the news, the latest incident was picked up over the police scanner. What triggered it was a frantic 911 call from a woman at Southwest Seventeenth Terrace in Little Havana. Apparently the distraught woman and her daughter had been attacked by the woman's knife- and hammer-wielding boyfriend, who then proceeded to throw himself and their seven-year-old son off the roof of their five-story apartment building.

The newsroom shifted into high gear. A team of reporters and video cam operators went racing to the garage downstairs to the WMAI news vans. This was the kind of high-octane drama that reporters lived for. And, though she kept the thought to herself, Tracey, too, secretly thrived on that whirlwind of energy. At times like this, she was tempted to give up writing novels for full-time broadcast journalism.

Less than fifteen minutes later, a second incident—a spectacular fire in one of the new luxury condo towers on Collins Avenue above Sixteenth Street—depleted the newsroom even further of personnel. The news chopper pilot on duty ran off to start up his whirlybird on the helipad. A reporter and video cam operator followed.

Before long, Tracey and a handful of others found themselves in a ghost of a building, a skeleton crew holding down the fort.

Tracey fielded a couple dozen phone calls, used her computer to retrieve the telephone numbers of key personnel who needed to be called in ASAP, and punched a code that automatically left urgent messages on their beepers. Also, it fell upon her to make the "beat calls"—

seeing what city hall, the fire department, and the police department were up to. And, as if all that wasn't enough, Tracey wrote one-line teasers for the anchors, who would tape them the instant they arrived—i.e., "Miami's towering inferno . . . details on the five o'clock news," and pounded out recaps, fifteen-second stories on a variety of subjects. That done, she popped into the sound studio and did VOs—voice-overs—to whatever film footage would accompany the recaps.

In fact, Tracey juggled so many tasks at once that she felt a shameless pleasure in being indispensable—if only temporarily—and had a vivid picture in her mind's eye of herself as one of those six-armed Hindu deities.

The phones rang. On-the-scene reporters beamed in their stories via satellite. The anchors arrived and snatched the teasers she held out. Then it was time to "rip scripts." A printer spewed out news updates and stories in five different colored copies, each of which had to be hand-torn and collated, hence the term. The white copy was delivered to the director, the green to talent, and the yellow, pink, and blue copies to other appropriate departments.

If that morning was any indication, it didn't appear as if the news hours needed any fillers. Plenty was happening.

Finally, as if the old adage that trouble always comes in threes needed proving, presto!, what should occur but a six-car pileup on South Dixie Highway? Several red-eyed new arrivals drifting into the newsroom, roused from their beds long before their assigned shifts by Tracey's activation of their beepers, executed an immediate about-face, heading out to cover the accident scene.

Perhaps all the activity was just as well: Tracey was kept so busy that she forgot to worry about the bad news Mark Varney had given her last night. Suddenly her telephone chirruped for what seemed like the umpteenth time. In the midst of tapping away at her keyboard, she stopped to pluck the receiver from its cradle and rattled off her staccato reply: "Newsroom Sullivan speaking how may I direct your call?"

"Trace? Trace, am I calling at a bad time?"

"Who—?"

"Trace, it's me. Brian? Your fiancé? Or have you forgotten?"

Brian. Involuntarily she glanced down at her hand and the obscenely large solitaire weighing heavily on her finger.

She said: "Oh. Brian. Sorry. I was totally rattled, and you caught me off guard."

"I was hoping I'd catch you in. It's almost lunchtime."

Brian Rutherford Biggs III's drawl was smooth and laid-back. Being born rich, Brian was always at ease.

Something must be up. Brian rarely called her at this hour. As a rule, he would wait until late, closer to quitting time. *Oh, God,* she thought guiltily. *It's last night. He wanted it to be a very special night by showing me the new boat and then I screwed it up.*

"Brian," she said, "I'm sorry about last night."

"Oh, forget it, Tracey," he replied. "I'm in your neck of the woods. Just around the block, in fact. So I thought to myself, 'Yo, wouldn't it be cool if we could take lunch together?' "

Lunch? . . .

How was she supposed to eat when she had no appetite? What she needed was the opportunity to let Mark Varney's bad news sink in, so that she might come to terms with it.

Plus, she knew good and well how Brian liked her best: perky, cheerful, and carefree. The last thing he'd want is her unburdening herself.

"Oh, Brian, I don't know," Tracey said dubiously. "You can't imagine what a madhouse this place is right now."

Brian laughed. "Lemme guess. You're going out of your mind listening to talking heads. Meanwhile, you have your hands full selecting snippets of sound bites, plus you've been saddled with rewriting the anchors' news reports *and* coming up with wildly dramatic teasers—'Fire Consumes Everglades. Details at Five.' That kinda thing. How am I doing?"

Despite herself, Tracey laughed. "*Will* you stop romanticizing this den of slavery? The way they work you to death, you'd think they'd never heard of the Emancipation Proclamation."

"Which is exactly why I've ridden to the rescue. Meet you in fifteen minutes. I'll be up front, waiting in the car."

"Brian!"

"Unh-unh-unh. Remember what I told you when we first met?"

As a matter of fact, she didn't. He'd told her so many things. Did he really expect her to remember everything he'd ever said?

"What?" she asked.

"Numero uno," he reminded her, a slight irritation coloring his tone. "I never take no for an answer."

"Okay, Brian," she sighed, "you win. Meet you up front."

"Atta girl!" he said cheerfully.

Then, before she could take umbrage at his obvious condescension, she quickly severed the connection. As she hung up the phone, something about the glitter of multiple carats caught her eye. She held up her hand with the engagement ring and moved it this way and that.

Tracey frowned. Was it her imagination, or had the carats lost some of their luster?

Tracey wondered which of his cars Brian would show up in today, then smiled when he screeched to a halt in a copper-colored 1973 Mercedes Benz 450SL in perfect condition.

"Hop in," he said.

Before she strapped herself into the bucket seat, she threw her arms around his neck and kissed him deeply. Brian shoved the gearshift into park, then put his muscular arms around her, hugging her to him, returning her kisses with abandon. She felt herself melt into his arms, savoring his masculine aroma and his powerful physicality. Even if they hadn't agreed on a lot of things, Tracey had always been thrilled by his distinctly masculine nature.

"I . . . I really am sorry about last night," she whispered softly as one of his hands began stroking her breasts through the top that she was wearing. "You know how I hate to disappoint you, Brian."

"Hmmm," he murmured, becoming aroused, his tongue tracing a path from the base of her neck to her ear. "It's okay." His hand moved from her breasts to her miniskirt and slid underneath it and up to her thighs.

"Ohhhh, Brian," Tracey breathed, her body responding to his touch with little tremors of excitement. She held on to his neck, oblivious to the spectacle they were making of themselves to passing traffic.

He kissed her again, pulling her close, before finally relinquishing his hold of her. They were both breathing heavily, and Tracey couldn't help but smile.

"I guess we'd better get moving if we're going to get there at all," Brian said, returning her smile.

"I guess you're right," she said, her love for him welling up from deep down inside.

Brian gave her another kiss, then put the car in gear and focused on driving.

Tracey wasn't surprised when he turned toward his number one favorite restaurant—the Capital Grille at 444 Brickell Avenue. Indisputably the single most elegant restaurant in downtown Miami, it was also very expensive, *the* spot to meet for power lunches. Steaks reigned supreme here—sirloin, Porterhouse, filet mignon, au poivre—the Cholesterol Grill was how Tracey wryly referred to it.

Brian left the Mercedes with the valet at the East Fifth Street garage. As usual he didn't cut through the building. Instead, he opted for the long way around, to make a grand entrance from the front plaza on Brickell, just behind the drawbridge and across five lanes of traffic from the Sheraton and its ever-present row of waiting yellow cabs. He got a kick out of the big bench-surrounded planters and geysering water fountains, the crisp black awnings over the door and windows, the polished brass signs. Not to mention the rows of black wall lanterns and the patinated pair of stately black lions standing guard at the entrance.

"Now this," Brian said with an appreciative sniff as they followed the menu-toting maître d' to their banquette, "is what I call a real restaurant. None of that pretentious Cuban cuisine around here."

Tracey laughed. "You're my meat and potatoes man," she said, squeezing his hand in hers. That was a dig at the last place she'd taken him, she knew—Las Delicias del Mar Peruano, which served an incomparable *papa a la huancaina*—but she found his love of strictly American cuisine amusing.

"Hey, Brian!" called a florid-faced, well-fed banker type who looked as though the half-raw T-bone on his plate might well be his last supper.

Brian grinned and added a little strut to his walk. "Hiya, Arnie. Good to see ya."

A man at another table flagged him down. "Brian! How's life been treatin' you?"

Another campaign-trail grin, a pointed glance backward at Tracey, a little more of a strut to his stuff. "How does it look, Mike?"

A lot better than you two shitbirds, Tracey thought darkly, *that's for sure.*

Despite her efforts to the contrary, she felt extremely uncomfortable and out of her element here during lunch. It was so obviously Brian and Company's turf. Sometimes she wondered why he had become so infatuated with her in the first place.

On several occasions Tracey had managed to talk Brian into going to a few of her favorite establishments, but she soon gave up.

"Too ethnic," he'd opined of Los Ranchos.

"I don't know about this place," he'd said suspiciously of Garcia's.

"I wonder when the department of health last inspected this place?" he'd grumbled about an inexpensive Thai restaurant.

Tracey was surprised when the maître d' led them to a corner table in the rear, where they would be offered the most privacy. This definitely was out of character for Brian. Usually he demanded to be up front and center where he could see and be seen.

What, she wondered, *is so different about today?*

There was no need for either of them to peruse the menu. At this point even Tracey could have recited it by heart.

Brian reached across the table and took her hand in his,

looking at her with devotion. "I bet I know what you're going to have to drink."

"My usual summertime drink," she said. "A strawberry daiquiri." He had his usual, a super-dry martini with barely a whiff of vermouth and three olives.

Brian ordered an extra-thick Porterhouse. "*Bleu* and then some," he said. "Seared charcoal on the outside, bloody and cold on the inside. Baked potato with butter and sour cream, and a small green salad with blue cheese dressing."

Tracey chose a Caesar salad for herself. "Without raw egg in the dressing," she added pointedly.

He held her hand in his until the drinks arrived, all the while smiling at her as he made small talk.

When the waiter brought their drinks, she raised her tall frothy pink glass. "Let me see. Who shall we drink to?"

"Why don't you decide?" Brian suggested, reaching across the table and taking her hand in his.

Her face creased in momentary concentration, then broke into a sunny smile. "I know! What do you say to toasting ourselves?"

She clinked her glass against his.

"L'chaim!" she toasted. "Here's to us!"

"To . . . us," he repeated with a smile. Then he took a swallow of his martini, while Tracey sipped her daiquiri.

She watched as Brian suddenly set his glass down a little too heavily, his eyes riveted on something in the distance. Tracey turned to see what he was staring at and was surprised to see an elegant, willowy blonde approaching the table with an enigmatic expression on her beautiful face.

Brian scooted his chair back and stood up quickly. "Georgina!" he said in surprise. "How nice to see you."

The blond beauty put her arms around Brian and kissed him squarely on the lips, where her mouth lingered far longer than was necessary.

Tracey could only stare up at them in disbelief. *Who is she?* she wondered. *If she's a business associate or relative or even an old girlfriend,* she thought, *their behavior is much too intimate.*

Brian withdrew from the blonde's embrace and turned

to Tracey. "Tracey Sullivan," he said, "I'd like to introduce you to Georgina Kaufmann. Georgina, Tracey."

"How do you do?" Georgina said in a cultivated, haughty voice as she extended a long, slender hand to shake.

"Fine, thanks," Tracey replied, taking the proffered hand. "It's nice to meet you." The woman's expensive perfume, a flowery, spicy scent, almost overwhelmed Tracey.

Georgina's blue eyes turned steely as she looked down at Tracey with an appraising stare. "And exactly *who* are you, Miss Sullivan?" she asked. Her gaze shifted from Tracey to Brian.

Brian opened his mouth to speak, but was interrupted by Tracey.

"Does this answer your question?" Tracey said. She proudly thrust out the hand on which she wore the huge marquise-cut diamond engagement ring, moving it from side to side, enjoying the sparkling light that the facets threw off.

The blonde's eyes widened in surprise, and the color drained from her face. Her elegant head jerked in Brian's direction, but he only stood there looking down at the floor helplessly. Then, recovering her composure, Georgina narrowed those steely blues into slits and thrust her hand toward Tracey. She cocked the finger on which an enormous diamond—larger even than Tracey's—rested against a pale, slender finger.

"And does *this* answer any questions you might have about me, Miss Sullivan?" Georgina snapped in a furious whisper. "I believe this is bigger than yours."

Tracey stared at the diamond ring in rapt fascination for a moment, then looked up from its cool white magnificence to Georgina Kaufmann's penetrating gaze. Veins stood out in bold relief against the pale skin on the blond beauty's now contorted face and neck, and her entire body trembled as she tried to contain her rage.

Tracey felt her heart leap into her throat and thought for an instant that she was surely going to be sick. Mustering all the self-control she had, she quietly replied, "I think you're right on both counts, Miss Kaufmann."

In one swift, fluid motion, Georgina turned to Brian and

slapped his cheek with a resounding smack. "You pig!" she growled. She turned on her heels and swept out of the dining room as if she were a virago bent on murder. Her perfume still lay heavy on the air.

Brian sat back down with a sheepish expression. For a while, they were both silent, as Tracey observed his reddened face and his downcast gaze and tried to ignore the stares from other diners.

"I . . . I can explain—" Brian started to say in a quiet voice.

"I don't think you need to explain anything," Tracey said, still trying to control the mixture of anger and heartsickness that she felt.

"No, really, Tracey," he countered, attempting a smile, "you've got to listen to me."

"You make me sick," she said.

He shook his head. "You misunderstand. This is all a big mistake. I love you, Tracey."

"You love me?" she snapped. "How naive do you think I am? You may have been able to pull the wool over my eyes for quite some time now, but no more, Brian."

"You've got to listen to me," he said, pleading.

"I don't have to listen to anything," Tracey said, her anger mounting.

"Oh, come on, Tracey." His voice was like that of a child who hadn't gotten its way. "Georgina's . . . she's just—"

"Just what, Brian?" she asked sharply. "Tell me that? Her engagement ring made it pretty clear to me exactly what she is, Brian."

"No, Tracey," he said, fumbling for words. "You've got it all wrong. It's not like that."

She couldn't bear to listen to any more futile attempts to explain away the obvious. She looked down at the sparkling diamond on her finger, then slid it off. She felt as if she were giving up a part of her very heart, and everything she had believed in up till this moment.

"Here," she said, sliding the ring across the table to him. "Take this back. I don't want to see it, or you, ever again."

"No!" he said. "Don't do this, Tracey. You can't do this to me."

"I already have, Brian." She pushed her chair back and rose to her feet. "Good-bye."

He quickly got up and came around the table toward her. "Come on, Tracey," he cajoled. "You don't mean it. You can't mean it."

"I said good-bye once, Brian," she snapped, "and I won't say it again." She turned and fled from the restaurant, hurrying out to the plaza on Brickell Avenue.

Through the tears that now blurred her vision, she could make out the usual line of cabs waiting at the Sheraton across the five lanes of traffic. Almost blindly, she started running across Brickell, ignoring the honks of car horns, the screeching of brakes, and the shouts of outraged drivers. When she reached the waiting line of taxis, she got into the first one she came to, sliding onto the seat and slamming the door behind her.

After giving the driver instructions, she dried the tears from her eyes with a Kleenex from her purse, then lay her head back against the seat. She wanted nothing more than to go home and cry her heart out, to rid herself of the awful torment she felt. That was out of the question, however, because she had work to do.

Work is the best medicine, she told herself, wondering at the same time how she would ever manage to get through the rest of the day. *Besides, it can't get worse than this. There's no way in the world it can get worse than this.*

Little did she know that the worst was yet to come.

Chapter Five

When she returned to the television station, the Enquiring Minds—mainly Maribel and a few cronies—were still at lunch. That was a blessing. Those who cared about such things wouldn't be aware she'd cut lunch short and returned early.

Now to keep her fingers crossed that nobody would notice the one dead giveaway: the engagement ring missing from her hand. Tracey wasn't ready to offer explanations about what had happened. Luckily, there were plenty of stories, creating more than enough work to keep Tracey's mind occupied. Even better, when Maribel and Co. breezed in from lunch, there was plenty to keep them busy as well. *With a bit of luck, I'll be able to slip out without anyone being the wiser about Brian.*

As the afternoon wore on, news broke faster than it could be processed. The dispatcher kept the crews hopping, using cell phones to communicate with the news teams, and keeping the vans of reporters and video cam operators speeding from one story to the next.

As news items went, they ran the gamut.

A phoned-in tip-off to the ASPCA resulted in a story of a woman sharing a mobile home with fifty-four unneutered cats.

A stray bullet shot by a person unknown wounded a three-year-old boy on a swing in his neighborhood playground.

Farther out on the fringes of Dade County, a kindly great-grandmother much beloved for her acts of kindness and charity was busted for having turned her garage, with the aid of two dozen Gro Lights, into a virtual greenhouse chock-full of a bumper crop of marijuana.

Due to the volume of news, the reporters were spread thin. That was always a danger with small independent stations like WMAI.

On this particular afternoon, someone was needed to cover the events the other reporters couldn't get to. Someone who, so to speak, just happened to be standing in the wings.

Thus are stars born.

It was the last thing Tracey Sullivan expected, particularly since the day's unusually high volume of local news required checking and double-checking all vital facts and statistics. Which was exactly what she was doing at her computer when Joel Zaidoff, the news director, tapped her to accompany him.

"Drop what you're doin', kid, and tag along."

Tracey swiveled around in her chair and stared up at him.

Joel Zaidoff was in his forties, a chunky, beetle-browed man in a blue-and-white-striped short-sleeved sports shirt. He had a receding hairline and a stomach that hung down over his belt. His clipped, efficient mannerisms were often misinterpreted for rudeness—as was his penchant for sarcasm.

"Are you talking to me?" Tracey squeaked.

Joel Zaidoff made a point of looking around him. "No. It's one of my seven invisible flunkies who follow me everywhere. Of course I'm talking to you!"

"But I'm in the midst of—"

"Never mind what you're in the middle of. We're shorthanded, and if my eye is any indicator, you're photogenic enough for our male viewers to appreciate. We'll soon find out. Right?"

Tracey was stunned. "Photogenic? Me?"

"Well?" he growled. "What are you waiting for? Christmas? Come on!" Without looking back, he headed to the bank of elevators, secure in the knowledge that she was following.

Tracey had to run to keep up with him, so swift was his stride.

"Here," he said, tossing her a laminated temporary press pass, attached to a dog tag chain, to wear around her neck. "You'll need this."

Tracey caught it without fumbling and slipped it over her head.

"The vans are all checked out, so we'll have to make do with one of the regular cars," he told her as they took the elevator down to the ground floor motor pool. "I'll drive and operate the video cam. Think you're ready to stand there, mike in hand, and report while the tape's rolling?"

"I . . . I haven't—" Tracey began.

The elevator doors sighed open, and they headed to the garage, Joel waving aside any misgivings on Tracey's part. "Easy as pie," he said. "Besides, it's not a major story. Just a routine accident. You know, one of those cars dropping off a drawbridge incidents? Old hat. But still, we gotta cover it."

Tracey's heart was pounding fiercely. *This is my big chance,* she thought. *If I don't screw it up, maybe they'll want me to cover other stories. Who knows?*

In Miami, drawbridges are to traffic what major intersections are to the rest of the country. Miami Beach consists of a cluster of seventeen islands, and depends upon its network of causeways and drawbridges to connect it into a cohesive whole and to provide major arteries crossing over to the mainland. Miami proper, across Biscayne Bay, is not island-bound, but nevertheless has the Miami River and its innumerable bridges to contend with. Consequently, the local driver is familiar with the elephant-like blast of Klaxons and the warning clangor which denote the raising or lowering of a drawbridge. Road traffic must, by necessity, share right-of-way with waterborne traffic.

It also goes without saying that an accident on any one of these bridges can play havoc with commuters, particularly as the afternoon stretches toward rush hour.

Joel, a longtime veteran of Miami streets, had the windows shut and the air-conditioning turned up to full blast as they zipped south along Interstate 95. Tracey gazed out of her window as they crossed the Miami River, her eyes following the progress of a Metrorail as it glided serenely in the opposite direction, seemingly sky-high on the stilts of its arching rail, as though on a ribbon of skyway. Then Joel swung the car onto Southwest Seventh Street and headed east. Four blocks on, he stopped, encountering the clogged traffic waiting to head north up—

Tracey dug her fingernails into her armrest and squeezed, unable to stifle a gasp.

Oh, dear God. Brickell Avenue.

Aware of her reaction, Joel snapped her a curious sideways glance. "Whatsa matter?"

Tracey shook her head and stared ahead. "Nothing," she murmured tonelessly, which couldn't have been further from the truth.

Joel let it go. He reached over in front of her and snapped open the glove compartment, took out the big card reading PRESS in prominent block letters, and shoved it atop the dashboard.

Tracey sat there, stunned and unmoving. The location of the accident made her dreadfully afraid. It had taken place right outside the very spot where Brian had brought her to lunch. The southern span of the Brickell Avenue Bridge was visible from inside the Capital Grille.

What if . . .

Everywhere she looked, uniformed policemen had their hands full. Directing traffic with curt gestures and shrill blasts of their whistles, they were diverting a portion of the clogged traffic into Fifth Street. They waved the majority of motorists into making U-turns to head back the way they had come, using the three southbound lanes of Brickell Avenue.

Thanks to the press pass, Joel's Cutlass was directed past the worst of the traffic jam and across the avenue, into the relative peace and quiet of the parking lot of the Sheraton Biscayne Bay. Here, at the foot of the arched ramp angling up to the stationary masonry section of the bridge, a motorcycle cop held out a gloved hand, palm facing outward.

The touch of a button and the window on the driver's side of the Cutlass whirred its barely audible descent. To Tracey, acclimatized to the chill comfort of the air-conditioning, the sudden burst of heat felt like a blast furnace.

Joel poked his head out of the window and looked up. "Yes, officer?"

"Your sign says 'Press.' "

"That's right." Joel had his wallet out, held it up to display his official press ID. "WMAI-TV," he said.

They were directed to an area which had been co-opted exclusively for the cars and vans belonging to the press corps. As Joel maneuvered through the densely parked space, Tracey stared out of the windows at the bridge. The two northbound lanes of the ramp were thick with cars and milling passengers, who had obviously been detained for questioning as eyewitnesses. From where the cars in the front had stopped at the multiple red lights, the candy-striped barrier barring the roadway was mangled and twisted. A hundred and fifty feet of empty roadway rose on up the incline. A little farther out, the two steel-grated and concrete-divided halves of the drawbridge reared into the sky. The nearer tower was decorated with giant Deco-style urns and a tall bronze column. Atop it stood a cast-bronze Tequesta Indian warrior, poised to shoot an arrow.

Yet below could have been the scene of an automobile accident anywhere. A variety of rescue units were parked helter-skelter inside a chain-link fence enclosing a parcel of bulldozed multimillion-dollar riverfront real estate. The vehicles ran the usual gamut: fire trucks, ambulances, a tow truck, police cars and motorcycles.

Except, Tracey thought, *if a car did plunge into the river, they're hardly likely to rescue anybody at this point.* Then it occurred to her that something was missing. The one essential ingredient at the scene of any accident—

Wreckage. There was none to be seen.

Which, under the circumstances, was not exactly surprising, since the tragedy took place in the water. Indeed, police and Coast Guard launches had already converged, several idling upstream of the bridge and others downstream, placed there to turn around all waterborne traffic. From another launch in the middle of the river, a duo of scuba divers, geared up to take the plunge, held face masks in place as they flipped neatly and in tandem backward off of the deck. There was a splash and they disappeared underwater, bursts of bubbles rising to the surface, marking their positions.

Opening her door and ducking out of the car, Tracey immediately took stock of the fleet of vans and cars belonging to the competition—WFOR (CBS-TV), WPLG (ABC-TV), WTVJ (NBC-TV), and CNN.

So much for exclusive footage, she thought sourly. And that didn't take into account the news crews from WSCV and WLTV, the Spanish-language television stations. Or the members of the press representing both the English and the Spanish radio and print media.

The *whup-whup-whup* of rotors filled her ears, churned up grit, and made ripples out on the water. The shadows of helicopters caught her fleetingly and rushed past. Tracey tilted her head back, shielding her eyes from the sun. Like aerial sharks, news and police choppers were circling overhead. Meanwhile, at the entrance to the bridge's pedestrian walkway, police were hastily erecting barricades to cordon it off from the growing crowd of gawkers.

Among that audience, a circus atmosphere seemed to prevail.

Tragedy doubling as entertainment, Tracey thought grimly. *Let the tumbrels roll.* All that was missing were the peanut and Cracker Jack vendors.

"Yo! Kid!"

Tracey turned in the direction of the voice. Joel had popped the trunk of the Cutlass. Without warning, he tossed her a wireless handheld microphone with the WMAI logo attached.

She snatched it neatly from the air.

"Good catch." He nodded. "Cheerleader in high school?"

"*Moi?* That popular?" She looked him up and down. "You've got to be kidding."

He shrugged. "Ya never know."

He lifted out a big professional video camera and shouldered it like a pro. "Used to be a cameraman," he replied to Tracey's raised eyebrows. "About a million years before your time."

He slammed the trunk shut with one hand, then scanned the area, trying to get a feel for it.

"Listen, here's what we're gonna do," he said. "For the time being, we'll split up. I'll go film whatever looks half promising and sniff around down here some, see what I can unearth. Used to have a nose for this sorta thing. Meanwhile, you take the bridge. Circulate. Use your ears. But remember, instinct's the most important thing. You get that tingly feeling? Follow it."

He glanced at his watch.

"We'll meet back here in fifteen minutes to compare notes. Okay?"

"Right."

She consulted her own watch, an old Timex given some zing with a new wet-look strap of yellow rubber.

"Oh," he said, "and one more thing."

She looked at him.

"Don't be afraid to be aggressive, know what I mean? We're press. People expect it of us. And don't be afraid to play dirty. In this business, nobody wins by being nice. They see a woman, first thing pops into their heads is, she's got egg noodles for brains."

She thought, *Translation: Forget being a lady. It's okay to be a shit.*

"Gotcha," she said.

They parted company, Joel heading to a spot where he could tape some overall footage of the entire scene, Tracey making the rounds of the uniformed cops on the bridge, all of whom clammed up as soon as they caught sight of her press pass.

They all told her the same thing. "Sorry, ma'am. You'll have to speak to the PIO. He'll be briefing you as soon as we have something concrete."

"C'mon, you guys," she cajoled, not above playing on their sympathies. "You can see by my temporary press pass that I'm a newf. Have some pity, huh? Give me something. Anything? It can be off the record—"

Emphatic head shakes all around. "Sorry, lady. We got our orders."

She kept moving, striking out until she approached the passenger cars parked directly behind the raised mint-green barrier to the drawbridge. She saw teams of uniformed police officers questioning the drivers.

Hmmm, she thought, gravitating toward the first two cars parked side by side. *Now, this looks a bit more promising. . . .*

The vehicle in the left lane was an old Trans Am that seemed to be constructed of Bondex rather than Detroit steel. The driver's door was open, and the woman behind the wheel was seated sideways, feet planted outside on the ground. She was sullen-faced and bored-looking and thin as a rail. Wore wrinkled lemon yellow short-shorts, blue zoris, and a ruched bright green halter top. Yet despite the tropical colors, she managed to look drab. Her hair was yellow and showed black roots and could have used a washing, and her bony elbows were on her knees, her chin resting on a cupped hand. Her cheeks became concave hollows each time she took a drag on her cigarette.

A real chain smoker needing her fix of tar and nicotine. At the same time waving her cigarette hand, as though inscribing smoky hieroglyphics in the air with a wand, gesticulating nervously as she talked to a pair of cops.

From the looks of her, she was obviously shaken. By the same token, she was not altogether keen having cops hovering around with their pads and pens out. No doubt ready to run her plates and check on the accuracy of her personal information. Or maybe they had done that already.

Yes, the woman's narrow-eyed suspicion definitely betrayed the fact that she was no great fan of law enforcement.

Aha, pay dirt, thought Tracey triumphantly. *Betcha anything she's an eyewitness.*

Being careful to approach the cops from behind so they

wouldn't see her coming, Tracey moseyed casually toward the Trans Am. She stopped short some ten feet away, loitering directly behind the uniforms. As yet unnoticed, and just within earshot.

So far, so good. . . .

This close, Tracey could tell that the woman in the car was a lot younger than she had at first presumed. Poverty and hard living had obviously taken their toll. Tracey wondered how many kids she had at home.

"Yeah, sure. I wish I'da paid more attention"—from her thick, guttural accent, Tracey placed the woman as a Florida cracker—"but I didn't 'spect him to floor the accelerator! Y'know?"

The woman sounded exasperated and paused to take another deep drag. Expelled twin plumes of smoke through her nostrils. Then raised her head and looked up at the cops. She shook her head slowly back and forth.

"Christ, who'd a thunk the guy was that crazy? Huh?"

One of the officers said, "So it was your impression that the driver . . . ah . . . acted intentionally?"

"What? You mean like, he set out to git hisself kilt?"

Giving the cop a dawning, wide-eyed look now.

The cop saying, "Yes, ma'am. That's exactly what I'm asking."

The woman frowned, turning that around in her head. You could see her trying to look at it from various angles. Then shrugging, her interest on the wane. "How should I know? I mean, shee-*it*!"

One last drag, and she dropped the cigarette butt to the pavement, grinding it out under a zori.

"Maybe he meant to hit the brake pedal but stomped on the gas instead," she said. "Or he coulda thought he'd beat the bridge acrosst. I seen people do that lotsa times. Kids, mostly. On a dare. 'Course, I'se just speculatin'. I mean, the bridge was already 'bout halfway up—"

"Did he have any passengers in the car?"

"Not that I could see, nah. 'Course, I din't give him no nevermind, least not till he took off like a bat outta hell and shot off the bridge the way he did." She sniffled like she needed to blow her nose and reached for her cigarettes. Fished around inside the pack with her fingers and came up empty.

"Aw, man!" Her voice rose, drawing out the "man" in falsetto distress. She balled up the empty pack and flung it to the ground in frustration, littering never crossing her mind. "Fuck!"

She raked a hand through her hair, fingers leaving greasy furrows. Getting antsy now. Twisting around in her seat, looking back the way she had come. Any interest in the accident negated by inconvenience.

"How about the make and model of the car?" one of the cops prodded.

She raised her hands, then let them drop to her thighs. "Look, I'm outta smokes and dead tired, awright? How long is this gonna take, anyway? I'm gonna be late gittin' home from work, an' my sister-in-law is watchin' the kids. Her work shift starts in an hour. I don't got time for this shit!"

"Ma'am?" The voice of authority soft and polite, yet at the same time firm and no-nonsense. "The make and model of the car?"

"Oh, I dunno," she mumbled. "Black. Maybe blue." Another shrug. "Could be it was gray. Medium-size, anyhow."

"Hardtop or convertible?"

She fidgeted. "Hardtop," she said irritably.

Tracey's sigh of relief was almost painful. *Thank you, thank you, thank you, Lord,* she offered up silently. *At least it wasn't Brian.*

"Look, either of you guys smoke?" The woman glanced hopefully from one cop to the other.

When they shook their heads, Tracey could see the woman's eyes reaching past them, shifting to her.

Oh-oh.

Tracey instantly shook her head and turned away, making a show of looking around. Playing the role of a tourist trapped in one of the cars who had decided to get out and admire downtown Miami.

Glancing over her shoulder, she waited until the cops had moved on. She decided that for her part, a businesslike stride would greatly behoove her. This was, after all, her very first assignment in the field. A real opportunity. It would be a shame to blow it.

The car next to the Trans Am was a sleek new Jaguar, all metallic bronze and tinted windows, dual headlights and ovoid grille. A different pair of cops had finished questioning its driver and were now preoccupied with a Latina in a white Hyundai which was next in line.

As Tracey approached the Jag, the tinted power window on the driver's side was in the process of sliding up. Despite that, she managed to catch a glimpse of the driver. A buffed man in his late twenties wearing spiffy Dolce and Gabbana shades. He had streaked, carefully tousled hair that was all the current rage. Corporate type? Day trader? Trust fund baby? These days it was difficult to guess anyone's occupation. You couldn't distinguish the hairdressers from the surgeons.

Well, Tracey told herself determinedly, *whoever he is, one thing is for sure. Nothing ventured, nothing gained.*

She rapped a knuckle against the tinted glass on the driver's side, then stooped down and smiled nicely. A nice smile, she'd learned from experience, could get you most anything.

With barely a whir, the window slid back down.

"Yes?" the guy asked.

"Hiya!" Tracey said brightly. Through his sunglasses she saw two dark, perfect miniatures of herself. She made an awkward gesture. "I was wondering if you could help a girl out?"

"Sorry," he said, his voice resonant and wry. "I'm clear out of fingernail polish." Being humorous, but at the same time not so subtly letting her know he was gay.

So what else is new? she wondered. *Just ask any girl and she'll tell you: about every knockout guy in Miami is gay.*

"You were saying?" the driver of the Jaguar prompted. "About needing help? . . ."

"Oh. Yes."

Tracey was suddenly overcome by a case of jitters. This was a first for her, and if experience ever counted on a job, this was it. On the other hand, how would she ever gain the necessary experience unless she was shoved into situations in which she could acquire it?

"I'm with WMAI," she explained, holding up the laminated press pass which she wore around her neck. "The TV station? Actually, as you can see from this press pass, it's only temporary. I'm new there. Turned out nobody else was available to cover this story, so . . . Well, to make a long story short, the news director grabbed me and . . . here I am! I realize this is an imposition, Mister? . . ."

"Riphenburg," he supplied easily. "Theodore Riphenburg. But there's no need to be formal, okay? My friends all call me Ted. You can even call me Teddy, if you like. Just don't call me late for lunch." He grimaced. "Ouch. Sorry." Then, as if it explained everything: "That line's from *Mame,* I believe."

"Not to worry, Ted. You're forgiven." She smiled. "Just for the record, I'm Tracey Sullivan." She stuck out a hand. "That's Trace to you."

They shook hands through the open window. "Honored to meet an attractive reporter," he said.

Tracey gave him a gimme-a-break look, then switched into work mode. "Ted, would you . . . would you mind telling me what, exactly, you witnessed here?"

"I take it you're referring to that car shooting up the bridge, off it through the air, and nose-diving into the water?"

"That's correct." She nodded briskly. "Yes."

"Sure. I don't see any problem with that."

"Thank God," she said fervently. "You may not be aware of it, but you might very well be saving my skin."

This time it was his turn to give her a look. Then, with little sweeping motions of his fingertips, he indicated for her to step back as he opened the car door. He unfolded long legs and stretched. He was tall and fashionably muscular, but without all the bulk. Very au courant. And all Gucci-ed up—from an ingeniously cut silver gray shirt to genuine python skin pants and futuristic four-hundred-dollar black slip-ons.

"Well?" He grinned, whipping off his sunglasses. "I'm all yours."

She cleared her throat. "Let's see. First of all, do you think it was deliberate? You know, someone committing suicide? Or could it have been an accident?"

He glanced over at the raised ramp and then down to the people from the various emergency services units. Her gaze followed his. The divers had surfaced and were signaling to someone onshore. An inflatable buoy floated on the water, marking the spot where they'd apparently located the car.

Ted Riphenburg sighed softly. Without taking his eyes off the activity below, he said, "Definitely deliberate." He nodded. "Had to be."

Tracey cut him a sharp sideways look. "You're sure?"

"No doubt about it. I mean, you could hear him waiting for the right moment as the bridge went up. Revving the engine. You know, like motorcyclists will do at a red light?"

She nodded. She knew exactly what he meant. "Can you tell me anything about the make and model of the car? And did it have Florida plates?"

"Sorry. Only thing I noticed was that it was old. Not one of those gleaming classics like you see around South Beach, just a sad, beat up, rusty old thing."

They both watched the tow truck back up as close to the water as possible, its hydraulic winch playing out a length of thick cable, a huge hook dangling at its end. One of the divers swam toward shore to grab hold of it and guide it underwater.

"Ted?" Tracey asked, sounding purposely uninterested. "Would you mind it terribly if I interviewed you in front of the camera?"

He took his eyes off the drama below and raised an eyebrow. "For the news? As an eyewitness?"

She turned to him. "Of course as an eyewitness. What did you think?"

He grinned. "Hey, did I forget to mention that WMAI is my all-time fave when it comes to TV stations? Or that I keep my remote switched to that channel at all times? Or how I hit the on button the instant I get home, even before I shut the front door?"

"Ted?" Tracey interrupted sweetly.

"What?"

"Could you do me one teensy little favor?"

"Sure. Name it."

"Cut the shit, okay? I know very well what our demographics are. And you, mister"—she jabbed a finger at his chest—"unfortunately do not begin to fit into that stodgy group. As for our ratings, well, perhaps 'dismal' is one way to describe them."

He looked sympathetic. "Poor you. Well, how did that Avis ad go? About number two trying harder?"

"Well, try number seven on for size," she said sourly. "That's after the three major networks—five, if you include FOX and CNN—*and* the two Hispanic stations. Pretty pathetic, huh? But hell, it *is* the boob tube and we *are* aired throughout Miami-Dade County, which amounts to some two thousand square miles . . ."

Aware that he was suddenly preoccupied, Tracey let her voice trail off. What was it about the power of television? Mention of his being on the tube, even if it was only on WMAI, had got him cracking. Spurred him on to lean down and check himself out in the Jaguar's rearview mirror. Had him brush splayed fingers expertly upward through his hair, adding to the tousled look. A hair burner by profession?

He turned and grinned. "Ready when you are, Ms. De-Mille," he announced dramatically.

But she was looking down at the empty lot swarming with activity, searching for Joel Zaidoff. Before long she found him.

I should have known, she thought. Veteran that he was, he'd insinuated himself in the prime spot. Right by the tow truck, from where he was taping footage of the divers, both of whom were tugging the hook and cable out to the buoy.

"There." Tracey raised her arm and pointed a finger toward the tow truck. "We've got to get down there," she told Ted. "Just follow me, though I can't promise I'll make you a star."

"Stars," Ted Riphenburg informed her grandly, "are born, not made. At any rate"—he gave a mock bow and gestured—*"après moi le deluge."*

Tracey hurried down toward the tow truck. It was getting on four p.m. The countdown had begun. She could sense it as a rising tension among the various television news crews. No one was more aware that the clock was ticking than Joel Zaidoff.

She wasted no time introducing Ted Riphenburg to the news director. As Ted stood by, Joel lifted the big camera off his shoulder and set it gently down between his feet. Then she and Joel put their heads together and compared notes.

"What have we got so far?" Tracey asked. She was holding a yellow legal pad in one hand and a thick felt-tip marker in the other. Ready to take notes, intending to scribble key words—her version of shorthand. A makeshift TelePrompTer in the field.

"What have we got?" Joel growled disgustedly. "We got zip, that's what we got. We got nada. Just that the divers reported one male body inside the car. That they've given the cops the license plate number, and Miami's finest have run it through DMV's computer."

"And?"

"And he died upon impact. Wasn't wearing his seat belt."

Tracey glanced at Ted, who was standing by as she and Joel hashed it out. "Interesting," she said slowly, tapping her teeth with the marker. "Lack of a seat belt corroborates what Ted said about the driver revving the engine. Apparently it must have been suicide."

Joel scowled. "Yeah, but in our business, 'apparently' doesn't hack it. Matter a fact, it means diddly squat. Or don't they teach you that in journalism anymore? In my day, disseminating news responsibly was the process of—can you believe it?—factual reporting. Not speculation."

The rough snideness stung, as intended. But Tracey cautioned herself against being baited. With a toss of her head, she snapped: "I know what reporting the news is, Joel. But let's face the facts. You yourself said we've got zip."

Joel sighed. "So what're you saying?"

"Well, without one of our news vans, we obviously can't do a live feed back to the studio," Tracey pointed out.

"Tell me about it," Joel groused peevishly, balefully eyeing the competition's vans emblazoned with the logos of ABC, NBC, and CBS.

A quick peek at her wrist confirmed that fifty-nine minutes was all that remained before *The Early Bird Special,* WMAI's pride and joy. An hour-long mixture of hard and soft local news, sports, and the weather, it was the station's single most popular show, consistently garnering the highest ratings and, thereby, bringing in the lion's share of revenues.

The competing stations would all be carrying live coverage of the drama unfolding here. All but WMAI.

No live feed. Somehow, there had to be a way to get around that.

What did they do before there were satellite hookups?

Suddenly Tracey had a brainstorm. "Listen, Joel," she said excitedly. "Say we live dangerously. Now, don't give me that look until you hear me out. Say you taped me interviewing Ted here? Okay?"

She pulled Ted closer beside her and held him by the upper arm, her prize in the flesh.

"Here's Exhibit A," she said. "Never mind that there's no Exhibit B."

"Go on," Joel said, intrigued despite himself.

"Well, if I were to phrase my questions a certain way, like asking his opinion . . . and he then repeated what he'd told me about the driver revving the engine . . . well, that wouldn't count as a factual statement on our part, would it? I mean, in a court of law it would be considered a leading question, sure. But this isn't a court. Nor would it count as speculation." She smiled. "Best of all, no one can accuse us of bad faith, especially if I faced the camera and repeated that Ted was an eyewitness and added that we're still waiting for official confirmation, yadda, yadda, yadda . . ."

Joel said, "Huh!" He hesitated for a moment, hands in his trouser pockets. Jingling change while rocking backward and forward on his heels. Then he said: "Well!"

Giving Tracey a strange, curious expression, as if seeing her, really noticing her, for the very first time.

Tracey waited, keeping her impatience in check.

"Huh!" Joel said again. Then he added, "Ye . . . ah," drawing the word out into one short and one very long syllable. "You know something? You're not such a dumb cookie."

"Gee," Tracey said tartly. "Thanks, Joel."

He grunted and flapped a hand back and forth, as if shooing away a cloud of pesky gnats.

She focused back on the business at hand. "Actually, we really lucked out, Joel. If we don't waste much more time, we can leave the other stations in the dust. Or at least the five o'clock local news. And here's why," Tracey said, playing down the triumph in her voice. "As far as I can tell, we've cornered the only eyewitness the cops haven't given a verbal gag order."

"Hmmm," Joel murmured. "A scoop."

"It's time we got taping," Tracey said briskly, letting go of Ted's arm and once again positioning the legal pad to take notes. "All right, Joel. What have you managed to find out? Any names? Gory details? The car model? Anything?"

Joel shook his head. "Only that the driver was alone. There weren't any passengers. And that identity is being withheld pending notification of next of kin."

Tracey wasn't surprised. That was par for the course, as it should be.

Mentally collating the rest of what she'd learned, she swiftly jotted down her version of shorthand notations:

FR VISTRS & RES OF M & MB, RUSH HR
THS EVE GRNTD T B NITEMARE. MOTRSTS
R CAUT AVOD BRICKELL AVE ABOVE S.E.
8 ST. 1 DETH IS CONFMD AFTR
OLDR MODL SEDN RORD UP RMP OF THE
OPNG BRICKELL AVE BRDG. ACCRDG T AN
I-WTNSS, DRVR SEEMD INTENT UPN SUCDE.
I HAV HRE CRL GBLS RES TED RIPHENBURG,
WHO WS 1 OF THE UNINTL SPCTATRS OF
THS TRBLE EVNT. TED . . .

Writing the rest of her notes, Tracey was pleasantly surprised. Meager as the information was, the story actually seemed more fleshed out and concrete on paper than it did in her mind.

She tapped her marker against her teeth and said, "Joel? You're the old pro. Any suggestions?"

"Only that I'm gonna try to hang around until they haul the car outta the water. But I'm not countin' on it. Plus, I need to give myself enough time to beat it back to the studio, quick-edit our tape, and have it ready to roll by air time."

"When you leave, do I stay or go with you?" Tracey asked.

"You're our reporter in the field, so plan on staying here. If I can, I'll send a satellite van. Otherwise, we go live the Stone Age way. By you phoning in any new developments as they occur. Catch." He took his slim cell phone out of his pocket and pitched it to her. She caught it easily.

"Speed-dial 01," Joel said, "and it'll automatically ring at my desk. Dialing 02 will connect you directly with the anchor desk. Which of those numbers you'll call depends upon what's cooking here, if a remote unit van becomes available so we can do a live feed, what time it happens to be, whatever . . ." He shrugged. "If it's getting toward air time, I strongly advise calling the anchor desk directly."

"In other words, I'll do a live call-in? Give my report via telephone? Get questioned by Shania and Ed?" Shania Landis and Edgardo Juárez were WMAI's star anchors.

"Yes, yes, and yes again. Along with an accompanying still shot of you right up there on the small screen. Imagine. Your mug beamed out all over Miami-Dade."

He bent over, picked up the video camera, and hoisted it back upon his right shoulder. He studied Tracey through the viewfinder. Frowned. Balanced the camera while making little curling motions with his left hand.

"Step a little to your left. No, that's too far. Another half step to your right. Gotcha! Now don't move. I've got you framed with the perfect background."

Out in the water, one of the divers surfaced. Raised an arm, signaling the tow truck operator to start. Then, with the thrust of a flipper, he disappeared back underwater.

"Okay, listen up. It's goin' to start gettin' noisy," Joel predicted. "Now remember, on the count of five, you're on. Speak directly into the mike. Don't worry about the tow truck or any other noises. Your mike is specially designed to pick up only close-up sounds. The worst of the background noises will be filtered out automatically."

He paused.

"Ready?"

Tracey drew a deep lungful of air, held it in, and let it out slowly. She was clutching the microphone fiercely. Tension jumped like an interrupted electrical current, twitching the flesh near her right eye.

"As ready as I'll ever be," she said.

If Joel was fazed, he didn't show it. "Great. Now watch my left hand." He clenched it into a fist. "I'll count to five, both aloud and on my fingers. Okay?"

She nodded, then gave a start as she heard a mechanical screech of the great yellow beast. It began to reel in the protesting, lubricated, silver-black cable, pulling it taut. Now the real noise began, and competed with the camera for Tracey's attention.

". . . and five."

She began: "Was it a tragic accident, or was it suicide?"

Her voice was newscaster perfect. Dispassionate and serious, but confident, modulated and clear.

"That is the question facing Miami police this afternoon, and the answer might be days, even weeks, in coming. For now, only two things are for certain. One man is confirmed dead, and commuters and visitors are in for frustration during the coming rush hour. All five lanes of Brickell Avenue, from Southwest Seventh Street to Southeast First Street, one of the city's major arteries crossing the Miami River, have been indefinitely closed due to an accident on the Brickell Avenue Bridge, and traffic is being rerouted via alternate routes.

"Meanwhile, police are awaiting the recovery of the submerged car so they can begin their investigation into the cause of this tragedy. As you can probably hear in the background, efforts are under way to retrieve the vehicle, which should surface at any moment.

"The big question on everyone's mind, however, is: Why? One eyewitness, who described the automobile as 'an old sedan,' is convinced that the cause was suicide on the driver's part. I have beside me Theodore Riphenburg, of Coral Gables, who was one car behind the one in question, and who witnessed the incident."

Tracey turned to Ted and leaned close to him, so that they were both within camera range. She spoke into the microphone. "Ted, you said you witnessed this terrible incident and are convinced it was suicide. Why is that?"

She tilted the microphone toward him.

He leaned into it. "Well, he just seemed to be parked there, as if he was waiting for the bridge ramp to go up. I mean, he was parked there, before the Klaxons sounded or the lights turned red or the red-and-white pole came down. I had to really hit the brakes, because I didn't realize he was stopped. It's a miracle the car right behind me managed to stop in time without rear-ending me. That driver, a lady, I think, started leaning on the horn, like telling us to get a move on. That was when the warning sounded and the lights changed. Not long thereafter, the ramp began to rise."

"At the time, did you attach any significance to the car in front of you being stopped at that very spot?"

"No." He shook his head. "There was no reason to. I guess I figured he'd seen an approaching vessel and knew the bridge was going to be raised. In that context, it made perfect sense. You know, like certain stop lights you're so familiar with, you can time the light change down to the second?"

Tracey nodded. "So what was the first indication you had that it was a willful act?"

"I suppose you could say it was when he began revving his engine. He started doing that right as the bridge started going up. You know, holding in the clutch but racing the accelerator? Really laying on the RPMs?"

"In other words, it sounded like a car waiting for the starting signal in a drag race?"

He said, "Yeah," and looked a little surprised. "That's exactly what it sounded like. But it didn't really register as anything being off. Lots of people rev their engines at stop lights." He shrugged. "I've noticed them doing it at drawbridges, too. Only not that often."

A sudden tidal wave of sensations swept from the

water's edge and gained momentum. All around, the increased excitement level and activity seemed directly related to the change of pitch in the tow truck's hydraulics.

Clearly something was imminent. But what? The resurrection of the submerged vehicle?

Tracey instinctively tipped the microphone toward her own mouth. "Just a moment, Ted." Then, moving a half step sideways, she faced the camera head-on again, and said: "From the change in mood here, it appears that we might have some breaking news . . ."

For the first time, Tracey fully understood the woeful inadequacy of having to be taped on video. If only she were able to report developments *live*, as they unfolded.

Like everyone else drawn to this spot, the spectator in her turned in the direction of the taut, greasy cable angled down into the watery depths. The scuba divers had surfaced again. Were bobbing in place, face masks tilted back on their heads. Staying well clear of the cable.

Where it met the water, Tracey could see a definite disturbance on the surface, concentric watery circles radiating outward. As the seconds passed, the ripples gathered momentum, grew more powerful.

On one level, Tracey was aware of being just one more rubbernecker. On another, she was conscious of her duty. As a reporter, she functioned as the eyes and ears of hundreds of thousands of viewers.

The submerged vehicle was ready to break through the surface. Displaced water rose all around it like an enormous ring, the concentric circles gaining in size and power.

Then came a mighty splash and what sounded like a massive downpour. Slowly the cable lifted the vehicle, heavy with water, nose first from the river. The subtropical sun refracted a blinding glare from the smooth chrome of the grille and bumper. Sheets of water sluiced down off the dangling, dark gray hood, the sun causing the sheet metal body to momentarily glisten, as if with a shiny new coat of paint. Only to run off and dry dull.

Higher and higher rose the car. Now came an explosion of bubbles: what air had been trapped in the passenger compartment was suddenly released, giving the impression the water around the vehicle was boiling.

Slowly but surely, the windshield and the forward portion of the roof—the glass surprisingly intact—slid into view.

Remarkably, the car looked little the worse for wear, a sure sign of age and quality. The chrome was obviously the real McCoy—chromed metal, not silvered plastic which would have shattered upon impact with the water; body and chrome were genuine heavy metal.

Ascertaining that the WMAI logo on the microphone was still facing the camera, Tracey reported, "And here it comes, the vehicle which, for one reason or another, was launched off the rising ramp, tried in vain to reach the sky, and instead plunged to the bottom of the Miami River. From what is visible thus far, it indeed appears to be an older vehicle . . ."

Despite the palpable thrum of excitement all around, Tracey kept up a calm running commentary. She was so cool and levelheaded that she could have been covering an artichoke festival, or describing the latest trend in swimsuits.

Niagaras of brown, silt-laden water cascaded out the open windows, along with a number of small flopping silver-scaled fish. From the driver's side window, a pale human head with an expressionless face lolled slackly from its body.

". . . from what I know of cars," Tracey continued, "it appears to be an Oldsmobile Ciera. This particular model probably dates back to the mid-seventies—"

And at that instant, a sledgehammer of shock slammed her in the gut. Tracey's earnest reporter's expression turned to one of personal horror. She stopped in mid-sentence, her face blanched of all color.

Oh, dear God, no!

She *knew* that car. Knew it as intimately as she recognized the mockery of its rag doll occupant!

Oldsmobile Ciera. Older model. Dull gray . . .

How could she not have guessed?

Dad? she thought in horrified silence.

No! everything inside of her shrieked. *It can't be! It has to be a coincidence!*

For one long, dreadful moment she listed drunkenly on her feet, her torso swaying perfect Chaplinesque circles. Another instant or two, and she was certain she was going to pass out.

Chapter Six

Joel kept the video cam aimed and running, but raised his eye from the viewfinder. His face was a study in concern. "Tracey, what is it?"

Beside her, Ted Riphenburg echoed: "Are you all . . . but of course you're not all right! Any idiot can see that."

"Oh . . . my . . . God . . ." Tracey's power of speech, however faint, had returned, but her mouth was suddenly so parched her words came out in a cracked whisper. She was aware of breathing hard and fast, as though she had been running.

Oh, she wished, *if only it were possible to run away from this waking nightmare! To run and run and keep on running. Perhaps if I pinch myself, or will myself awake—*

But Tracey knew better. There was no waking from this particular nightmare.

How obscene it was that, in the mere blink of an eye, her well-ordered existence should be so brutally shattered. It seemed impossible that tragedies of this magnitude were able to come straight out of the clear blue and slam right into you without giving you the slightest advance warning.

Ted's response from only minutes ago ricocheted madly inside her head like a bullet seeking escape: ". . . *definitely deliberate . . . you could hear him waiting for the right moment . . . revving the engine."*

No! Tracey wanted to scream. *Ted, you're mistaken!*

He had to be. Because it couldn't have been suicide, for one simple reason: the body was that of her father.

Nor was it just wishful thinking on her part. You could ask anyone who knew him. They'd tell you. Tom Sullivan was definitely not the suicidal type. He'd said he'd see her tonight.

On the contrary. He was a fighter who'd take on anyone, no matter what the odds.

Hadn't he proved that with his ongoing battle against Palm Coast Developers, Inc.?

Someone pushed past her, bumping her left arm. Someone else's elbow connected with her right arm, half jerking her around. All while she stood there, microphone at her side, only partially aware of officials trying to keep order, and journalists and cameramen jockeying for position near the car as it was hoisted completely out of the water.

The car. Not just any old car, but her father's car. With her father in it.

Movement on Joel's part caught her attention. He still had no inkling of what was going on, but he was beginning to get seriously worried. Enough to start lowering his camera.

The camera, Tracey thought dumbly, her brain short-circuiting, flickering on and off in spurts like a loose electrical connection in a lamp. It was as if she was vaguely aware that the camera might be of some help.

A single word kept pulsing in and out of her consciousness: *Fire . . .*

Of course! Sometimes you had to fight fire with fire!

"Joel." Tracey's throat was so constricted she had to clear it twice. Then, "Joel," she repeated more firmly, a fervent light blazing in her eyes.

He looked at her cautiously.

She said, "Get that camera back up on your shoulder." Her voice sounding hoarse and soft, yet at the same time level and adamant.

She saw Ted and Joel exchange glances. Surprisingly, it

was Joel, the old pro, who was more hesitant to continue. He eyed Tracey narrowly.

"You sure you're okay?" he asked.

Tracey's voice grew stronger. "Yes, I'm sure."

She held her head high—and why shouldn't she? She had nothing to be ashamed of. Accidents happened all the time. Plus, this way she could at least kill two birds with one stone. First and foremost, fend off most of the vultures before they had a chance to descend and, second and more important, vindicate her father, or, at the very least, publicly present a passionate defense against his having committed suicide.

"Joel," Tracey said vehemently. "You have to let me do this."

"That's just it. Do what?" he wanted to know. "You obviously recognized the driver—"

She cut him off. "For God's sake, stop wasting time! Let's get on with it."

Joel sighed and shrugged. "If you insist," he said reluctantly.

Still not convinced, he hoisted his camera back upon his shoulder. When its red light blinked back on, Tracey could tell he'd resumed taping.

The microphone shook violently in her hand, and she had to will herself to keep it still.

"That . . . that car they just pulled out of the river," she said, her eyes locked to the lens of the camera, "I . . . I know that car. The driver's name is . . ." Then she caught herself. "The driver's name was," she corrected huskily, "one Thomas Sullivan of Coconut Grove."

Holy shit! Joel mouthed soundlessly, his jaw dropping.

Tracey continued, "I can report the driver's name because, although his . . . his remains have not officially been identified, this reporter recognized both him and his car."

She paused to draw a deep breath.

"In a cruel twist of fate, and as yet unknown to the authorities, Thomas Sullivan's next of . . . of kin has already been notified. I can say this with utter confidence because Tom Sullivan is . . . no." She frowned and shook her head. "Let me rephrase that . . . Thomas Sullivan was my . . . my father!"

Her voice had risen in pitch on the last word. Suddenly overcome by emotion, she raised her hand to cover her face, but motioned with the microphone for Joel to keep on taping.

After a moment she regained her composure. Bit down so hard on her trembling lower lip that she left the impression of pale bite marks. Reset her face. Raised her head and looked resolutely into the lens.

"I understand that speculation and personal opinions have no place in reporting factual news events. However, in this particular instance I feel I owe it to my father's memory to break this rule and editorialize. In other words, I personally have every reason to believe that the Tom Sullivan *I* knew, the father who raised and loved me, and whom I love with all my heart, would never, ever have contemplated suicide, let alone have committed it. He had too much respect for life and believed in living it to the fullest."

Tracey paused, fortifying herself for the next installment of her unrehearsed, from-the-heart speech. Again she swallowed to lubricate her throat. "Dad was a fighter. Anyone who knew him will tell you that. And the last time I saw him alive? Just this morning? Guess what he was doing?"

She looked questioningly at the camera before answering her own question.

"Would you believe, the same thing he did every morning? That's right. Drinking coffee and working the crossword puzzle in the *Miami Herald*. Now, does that sound like a man intent upon committing suicide?"

She shook her head.

"Not to me, it doesn't," she added.

She stood there, soul stripped bare, projecting an image of strength which was as unreal as the nightmare she'd stumbled into. All that needed saying had been said. For the time being, there was nothing else to add. Even if there was, she couldn't have verbalized it. The intensity of the shock she had suffered, followed by the strain of her taped report, had sapped her of all remaining strength.

"That . . . that's it, I'm afraid," she apologized weakly. "I'm sorry, but I . . . I can't continue."

She held the microphone away from her, as though to thrust the tragedy as far from her as possible.

Ted, standing closest, quickly plucked it from between her fingers. Joel immediately stopped taping and set the video cam down.

"Christ, I'm sorry," Ted said to Tracey. "If I'd had an inkling that it was your father, I would never have shot my mouth off—"

Tracey stared at him and shook her head. "No, Ted," she said with supreme dignity. "You said it the way you saw it. Just as I, in turn, said it the way my heart feels it. I can't hold your version against you." She tried for a little smile, but she had no wattage left.

"Trace," Joel said. "We need to talk. Preferably in private." He nodded in the direction of where they'd parked.

Tracey instantly bridled at the idea. She shook her head violently. "No! Oh no, you don't," she said, her voice tight and strained. "Unh-unh. You're not weaseling out on me now, Joel."

"That's not what I—"

"I beg your pardon, but that's exactly what you're trying to do. So don't deny it. I know you're suggesting it for my sake. Still, the answer is no. N-O."

She stepped closer to him and grasped his arm in the vise of her hand. Her eyes were bright with delayed shock.

"For my sake, Joel, you have to do as I ask. I want you to run with this footage. I need you to!"

"But why? Don't you realize you're setting yourself up for the most miserable experience of your life? Trust me, I know. I've been in this business so long they call me Methuselah behind my back."

She shook her head. "No, Joel. You don't understand. This is the only way I can avoid being hounded by the rest of these vultures. Besides, someone has to speak up for my father. If I don't, can you think of anyone who will?"

He looked at her as her fingers dug deeper into the flesh of his arm, her young face shining with the fervor of the righteous.

"On top of which, we also have Ted's footage," she reminded Joel. "That's just in case you're worried about presenting a balanced report."

Joel Zaidoff shook his head. "That's not what worries me," he said.

"Look, Joel, forget that I'm personally involved with this, okay? Just think of me as a reporter. Any reporter."

He sighed. "Yeah. Right."

"I'm serious," she said.

Joel's pained expression was proof that he understood. But he had to give her one last chance to back down.

"You're sure?" he asked. "I mean, really, really sure? Once it's aired, there's no going back."

"Don't you think I know that?" Tracey whispered fiercely. "I'm not a child. Now go! Get that tape to the studio in time for the broadcast. And stop worrying about me. I'll get home in one piece. There are tons of cabs back there at the Sheraton."

"I don't think this is a good time for you to be alone."

"I won't be. If I need, Ted here"—Tracey looked questioningly at Ted Riphenburg—"can escort me home. Right, Ted?"

"I'll be more than happy to," Ted replied. "In fact, I insist. You're in no condition to go home by yourself." And to Joel: "I'll see that a friend stays the night with her."

Joel nodded. "Good idea."

"What is it with you two?" Tracey demanded. "Do you guys really think women are the weaker sex? Is that your problem?"

Joel stared at her long and hard, then came to a decision and scooped up the video cam. As he started to hurry through the pockets of press hounds and various uniformed officials, Tracey called out, "Joel!"

He turned and looked back at her.

She held his gaze. "Thanks," she said. "I owe you one."

Chapter Seven

Santorini, Greece

Oia is a picture postcard come to life. An improbable village of blinding white clinging along the sheer clifftop and over the sides like a cluster of spilled sugar cubes.

Above and below, everything is blue, the sea and sky. The domes of the whitewashed churches are blue. Bluish, too, are the hazy broken chain of islands encircling the four-by-six-mile water-filled caldera, or crater, the product of a volcanic cataclysm during antiquity.

And last but not least, blue—in this case azure—is the slightly trapezoidal lozenge of Urania Vickers's swimming pool. Precariously sited a thousand feet above the Aegean, its lipless rim gives the swimmer the illusion of infinity, as if it overflows directly into the sea itself.

Urania's compound consists of three floors, a meandering honeycomb of eighteen rooms built deep into actual caves in the cliff side, all with windowed, whitewashed facades, the whole connected by a network of steep steps, narrow walkways, and sun-drenched terraces. Indoors and out, the floors are paved with *krokalia*, stone mosaics of round natural white pebbles inlaid with black pebbles to make elaborate patterns and borders. Observing the island's tradition, cascades of bougainvillea, planters of oleander, and pots of bright red geraniums add startling dashes of color.

If there be paradise, this is surely it.

Yet even this, crown jewel of the Cyclades, is not immune to the ritual boardroom slaughter perpetrated by Manhattan philistines.

"Oh, for heaven's sake, darling, why on earth should I be upset?"

Urania paced the terrace as though on stage. Resplendent in a gauzy silk caftan printed with emphatic vertical stripes, parallel dots and dashes of blackish blue, and further embroidered with lush concentric swirls of golden thread reminiscent of Gustav Klimt, she was at her regal best, right down to the brown cigarette tucked into the telescoping ivory holder of astonishing length on which she occasionally drew, but without inhaling, and upon which she relied more as a theatrical prop than a vice.

"Fact is," she continued, the thespian in her adding a slyboots twinkle to her eye, "you've helped enormously, Jewel-ya. Finally put me on the right track. I'm grateful, darling. Really I am. I can't thank you enough."

With a flourish, Urania tilted the cigarette holder at a sharp upward angle and drew a puff of smoke—reminiscent of Gloria Swanson's Norma Desmond. For, dramatics aside, Urania was her own star in her very own, albeit gradually fading, constellation.

The exceedingly tall, bony, and humorless Julia Markoff frowned and exchanged sharp glances with her two underlings. The three of them had writhing hair like Sarah Jessica Parker's, but which on them came across as serpents waiting to strike.

Urania, drifting along the low wall of the terrace overhanging the sea, was silhouetted against the late summer sun, itself preparing to stage its own daily production, but seemingly reluctant to proceed until Julia Markoff and her undeserving acolytes had gone.

Julia responded to Urania's bravura performance with evident relief. "I'm so glad you're not upset, sweetie. I was mortified that you'd take it the wrong way, and you know how I like to stay friends with my authors. It's important that we get along. Now, are you absolutely certain you don't want a ghostwriter? Rache here, or Ruthie, would pounce at the opportunity to stay on and help pound your novel into shape."

She glanced at first one, then the other, of her two clones for backup.

"Well? Wouldn't you, dolls?"

From their faces, it was clear that neither of them would like to do anything of the kind, but both gave labored smiles. One said, "I'd be happy to," and the other murmured dispiritedly, "Yes, delighted." Sounding as if Julia had suggested they volunteer for the gas chamber.

The feeling, however, was mutual. Urania would just as gladly have submitted to having her fingernails pulled with pliers. She wasn't about to suffer either of them fiddling with her manuscript, making changes here, adding scenes there, stripping it of Urania's own inimitable "voice" and then, after publication, dining out all over New York on *How I, and not Urania Vickers, actually wrote the novel.*

The star's first novel had been a minor success due to its curiosity factor. People had bought it for one reason. To see whether or not Urania could write.

The answer was best not delved into. As a reviewer wrote in *New York* magazine: "We always knew she can't act, but watching Urania Vickers camp it up has always been fun and rewarding. Now we know Urania can't write, either. Unfortunately, reading her is neither fun nor rewarding. It brings a whole new meaning to the term 'excruciating.' "

"I really don't think it's necessary for anyone to stay here," purred Urania. "I'll be faxing you pages next week."

"Delighted!" Or so Julia pretended.

For a few moments Urania turned her attention back to the panorama. She struck a pose, hip cocked, while ostensibly studying the composition of blue caldera, deepening blue sky, and purpling semicircular string of islands across the great water-filled crater. A thousand feet below, a hydrofoil, miniaturized by distance, was making swift headway. The faint drone of its engines carried upward in the silence.

"Oh, darlings, do look," Urania cried. "Open your eyes and see!"

Upon which Urania flung out both arms dramatically, as if to physically embrace the view.

"Isn't it so painfully gorgeous it makes you want to cry? People can go on and on about Bora-Bora or Capri or the Lesser Antilles or what have you. But this—this is beauty and drama and history. And imagine! Out there, on that island in the center, the live volcano still lets off steam and sulphur and—I kid you not—actually heats the water."

Julia, born and raised in the Bronx, and a confirmed Manhattanite by choice, did not bother to suppress a shudder. "To be perfectly honest, I'd rather not," she said stiffly. "How positively frightful. How can you stand living on a live volcano?"

Au courant hairdo, bonded teeth, weekly facials, and a sophisticated urban wardrobe from Saks and Paul Stuart only went so far. Unfortunately, Julia Markoff had retained her Bronxspeak—and said "loy-ve" instead of "live."

"Oh, living here is a dream, darling," Urania fired back. "Delightful and without stress. Far less dangerous than—" She was tempted to say, "the bean counters in Manhattan," but stifled the urge and said instead, "the streets of New York."

With that, the star whirled back around, one hand cupping an elbow, cigarette holder held straight up and down. Having detected the sound of bare feet, she looked into the shadows beyond her audience of three. Past Medusa and her two cohorts, a man of uncommon good looks, in a natural linen peasant shirt and rolled-up white deck pants, was leaning languidly in the shadows of an arched doorway. Watching the proceedings with amusement.

"Ah, Mark, *fabu*! I was so hoping you could join us before Jewel-ya leaves." And to Julia: "He is one of your most adoring fans, you know."

Julia lifted her wrist, held her watch close to her eyes, and sighed. "Time does have a habit of vanishing. Well, then, we'd best fly if we're to catch the last flight out. I can't imagine the strings you must have pulled to get us on it. I had no idea it's so difficult to get a flight off this island."

"That, Julia darling, is because Tony Bennett's got it all wrong."

"Yeah?"

"Yes. One doesn't leave one's heart in San Francisco." Urania snorted at the very idea.

"No?" Julia stared at her.

"Absolutely not. Why, one leaves it on Santorini—where else? Oh! There's Stavros now," Urania said, referring to a stocky Greek with a thick black mustache who was signaling from two terraces above. "He'll take you up to the car and drive you to the airport."

Urania momentarily wished she hadn't been able to get Julia and her wannabes off this evening. If she'd only known about Julia's phobia of volcanoes. What sweet torture she might have extracted from her spending the night.

"Yeah. Off we go," Julia murmured, adding: "Y'know? I've never seen such tiny cars in my entire life. I nearly gave myself a charley horse getting out of the one this morning."

"Darling, but how awful!"

"Yeah, I didn't know they made cars so teensy. Who're they for? Midgets?"

"Then you'd best be careful, darling. It's the same car going back."

Julia deigned to smile brightly, so evident was her relief that she was about to leave this peculiar place in the middle of nowhere. Her blaze of horsy teeth was as blindingly white as the local walls in the midday sun.

"Well, we're off," Julia declared. "Lovely to see you, doll."

"The pleasure was all mine, Jewel-ya. Darling, you must come again and stay awhile."

"Yes, I must." Translation: *Over my dead body.*

A flurry of noisy air kisses followed, dead giveaways that Urania and Julia were acquaintances who could barely tolerate each other. The wannabes had to make do with Urania's little waves, the kind of "bye-bye" finger curls made for babies rather than adults.

From the shadows, Mark called out to Julia: "We'll talk once you're back in the office, Jewel. Either I'll get in touch with you, or vice versa."

Julia took pains to put Mark in his place. "I'll have my secretary call your secretary."

Mark waited until the editor in chief and her two clones left. Only then did he pad barefoot over and stand beside Urania. Together, they watched Julia and Co. labor up the several flights of outdoor stairs to the cerulean gate set in the high whitewashed wall above, a thick barrier which effectively hid the compound from oglers on Oia's single main street—which itself petered out at this point into a narrow winding pedestrian alley crammed with tavernas, outdoor restaurants, and high-end shops, most of them jewelers catering to the affluent cruise ship crowd.

"You know," Mark observed, "sometimes I wonder which of you is the bigger bitch. You or Julia."

Urania, nibbling on the stem of the cigarette holder, flashed him an amused sideways glance. "You need to wonder?"

His silence made it clear this was a subject best avoided.

Raising her eyes, Urania noticed that Stavros was shepherding Julia and the clones out through the gate. She waited until the weak engine of a small car coughed and started, and the doors slammed. Only then, once she heard it drive off, sounding more like a sewing machine than an automobile, did Auntie Mame morph into Cruella De Vil.

"Rrrrrrr! That . . . that twat!" Urania spat, letting loose with everything she'd kept stifled all day. "That hideous, big-jawed, culture-starved idiot of a Bronx-born twat! Who the hell does she think she is, getting off on trying to shove her coven of ghostwriters on me? Me! Imagine!"

She turned to Mark in outrage, voice warbling in anger.

"The nerve, coming here—here!—to my home, my getaway! And what for? To offer the services of a ghostwriter! As if I'm not capable of writing my own novel! God, what a bitch!"

In her fury, Urania broke the cigarette holder in half. Staring at the ragged break in the ivory, she flung the two pieces away from her. They landed on the pebble-inlaid floor of the terrace with a faint clatter, the remains of a cigarette glowing and winking out.

"From now on," she fumed, "Jewel-ya 'the shitbird' Markoff, that frizzy-haired frump, had better stay where she belongs—in her cutthroat office where she's the big cheese. Elsewhere, she definitely stinks to high heaven!"

From Urania, who believed she owed it to her public to never step outside unless she was dressed to the nines and groomed to perfection, and who anointed herself with Panthère de Cartier, her absolutely favorite fragrance, this was a far more stinging barb than any string of four-letter words. It was, as far as Urania was concerned, the ultimate insult.

Mark waited, letting the virago go on until she ran out of steam. Only then, after she quieted down and flopped into a blue-cushioned white chaise at poolside, did he try to get a word in edgewise.

For, young though Mark Varney might be in agent years, he was not without experience. Having trained under the best—notably the recently deceased super-agent Julius "Boom Boom" Mancini, many of whose celebrity clients Mark had inherited from his late boss and mentor—he had dealing with stars and their unpredictable temperaments down pat.

Hardly ideal working conditions, especially considering he had arrived only yesterday. He was severely jet-lagged, no surprise considering the thirteen-hour flight from LAX in order to "be there" for Urania when she crossed swords with her equally combative editor. As if, one wondered, Urania's hand needed holding.

Actually, and this might come as a surprise to the great unwashed public, it really did.

For proof, just strip away the role of star and rid it of its accouterments, then look beneath the highly buffed, high-maintenance facade. Toss out the expertly applied makeup and shimmering clothes, the $1,845 pair of ostrich claw sandals from Gucci, or the steeply angled soles which, with high heels and a few scant inches of red and turquoise leather straps, translated into $455 mules at Manolo Blahnik. Take away the essential accessories—the black-and-white zippered bag from Tod's, which ran a cool $950; the Epi bag from Hermès, which cost as much as four or five bags from Tod's; the fanciful animal- and insect-shaped minaudières from Judith Leiber.

Then there were the minor trinkets from Fifth Avenue jewelers, which didn't come cheap—gold and peridots, aquamarines and citrines—forget diamonds, rubies, and emeralds. Remove, too, those other essential props: the apartments and villas at the very best addresses, the suites at five-star hotels, the bottles of vintage Cristal, the iced bowls of Beluga. And, because she found them amusing, and they flattered her with undivided attention and had the ability to make her laugh, there was the entourage. Beautiful hangers-on; party creatures who were so entertaining and outrageous, darling, but who required so much wining and dining—strip away all of these and what did you get? Certainly not the dazzling, seductive siren who turned heads the world over, but, more often than not—

And Mark wondered: *Why is this almost always the case?*

—a frightened, lost, child-woman. A pampered being who, without her necessary props and lines of dialogue, was barely able to tie her own shoelaces and who, unless her ego was constantly stoked and her self-esteem fed and fed and overfed, was, at heart, lonely, vulnerable, and given to dark brooding bouts of self-pity and despair.

But Urania's problems were very real. Her lifestyle ate up money at a faster pace than it came in. The two-book, five-million-dollar contract "Boom Boom" Mancini had negotiated for her before his death was in danger of cancellation.

And then what? That was a question Urania had rather not address, for the simple reason that there was no soothing answer.

Acting parts calling for a woman of Urania's age were sparse, both in films and on television. Needless to say, she had long since spent the million-dollar advance she was paid upon signing the contract. For around Urania, money had a habit of evaporating.

At the moment she was feeling the pinch. She owed her fashion designers small fortunes, was behind on the rent of her Paris apartment, and hadn't paid her household staffs in Beverly Hills or in Paris in weeks. There were bills from florists, from restaurants, from five-star hotels, and from party planners. If not for the trickle of money coming in from foreign sales of her previous novel, the show that was Urania would be in danger of having to shut down. Indefinitely.

In short, Urania Vickers was in dire straits. Not exactly penniless, but down to her last sixty thousand dollars—the price of a decent couture gown.

God, she thought, if only she could get her hands on the money still due her for the two-book deal! Unfortunately, the next two installments were contingent upon completed manuscripts—one million dollars per book.

Sad to say, but most of that money, too, had long since been squandered—and no one dared even whisper that dread word, "taxes," in her presence.

And yes, she had been writing, and like a maniac. Urania had stacks and stacks of manuscript to show for it—and pages of nasty faxed and FedExed memos that denounced her efforts as "unacceptable," "immature," "over the top," and terms such as, "it won't fly."

Clearly, the honeymoon with her publisher was over. To make matters worse, Greenleaf Books, of which Julia Markoff was editor in chief, was itself on shaky ground. As a small division of a large publishing house, it had been a prestige imprint, and for that reason the red ink incurred was deemed acceptable.

Not any longer.

With all the mergers and buyouts occurring in the publishing industry, Greenleaf's parent company had recently been absorbed by InfoMedia, one of those hydra-headed, multinational conglomerates. The global publishing giant's powers that be didn't give a whistle about authors—celebrity or literary—and not even about books. The only thing that concerned them was the bottom line. Period.

Which, in a nutshell, explained Julia Markoff's visit. She had, in effect, been sent to Greece to deliver an ultimatum to Urania: Either deliver an acceptable completed manuscript within four months, or the contract would be canceled.

Worse news could hardly be imagined. It meant that Urania's future funds, upon which she had been counting, were in danger of being cut off. Worse still, InfoMedia was threatening Urania's pretty round butt with a lawsuit, intending to recover Greenleaf's initial million-dollar advance in full. The very advance which had long since been paid out and long since been spent.

In short, these were definitely not the best of times for Urania Vickers. It seemed that no matter how hard she tried, there was only one direction she could go.

And that was down.

Chapter Eight

Miami, Florida

The weather showed its respect by waiting to let loose with the thunderstorm. Maribel Pinales did the driving. Tracey, seated on the passenger side, was clutching the urn containing her father's ashes. The weather held until they were back at the cracker house in Coconut Grove. Only after Maribel parked her spiffy little red Corolla and the two were sheltered under the wisteria-laden front porch did nature's show begin.

As a prelude, the sky turned inky black and a powerful wind thrashed the palms and mimosas and live oaks; tore at the ficus hedges, bouffant Schefflera and bougainvillea; rattled the rotting, overgrown lattice which effectively hid the house from the street.

Maribel held open the screen door and got out the key Tracey had given her. She had barely opened the front door and clicked on the lights and ceiling fan when the main attraction began.

Bursts of lightning illuminated the slats of the half-open Bahamian shutters. Earth-shaking crashes of thunder reverberated through the boards and battens and shook the humble house to its foundation. Overhead, the first splatter of fat raindrops tap-danced on the tin roof, only to turn into a roar so loud Tracey could barely hear herself think as the rain came down in solid sheets.

Maribel left the front door open to catch the crosswind, but snapped the screen door shut, exclaiming: "Who-ee! Just made it. Barely."

Tracey remained silent. Hugging the urn, she stood there and looked around the front room like a lost child, trying to figure out what was so different.

Something was missing. And then it hit her.

Her father's presence.

This house is dead, she thought. It had taken her father to bring it to life. Now that he was gone, all that remained were lifeless objects and elusive ghosts. Especially in this front room, comfortable with the broken-in masculinity of recliners and ottoman, bookcases stuffed with well-thumbed volumes, unmatched rugs on the shellacked wide-board floor. Without him, what was the glass-fronted curio case containing his collection of ice fishing decoys from Minnesota? Here Tom Sullivan had been able to put up his feet and watch television or read or listen to Billie Holliday from his treasure trove of vinyl albums. Here he'd lavished untold hours teaching Tracey to love jazz and play chess and poker, and to lose herself in books, or just to appreciate that simple but most precious of all gifts: privacy.

Sadly, nothing could turn back the clock.

This haven of tranquility, Tracey now understood, would never again be the same.

So immersed was she in the past memories that she didn't flinch when—*BANG!*—like the report of a gunshot, one of the Bahamian shutters slammed loose in the back of the house and proceeded to flap noisily in the wind.

"I'll see to that," Maribel said, grateful for the opportunity to break away. Heels click-clacking, she hurried through the house, checking every window.

When she returned to the front room, she found Tracey standing in the exact same spot where she'd left her. Arms still pressing the urn to her chest.

Maribel could tell that the day had taken its toll. Indeed, the last few days would have drained anyone of energy.

There had been the ubiquitous well-meant condolence calls, the offerings of casseroles and fruit salads, the constant deliveries of floral tributes. Reporters to turn away, but with gracious politeness, in order not to make future enemies.

There was no end of arrangements. Getting the body transported from the city morgue to the funeral home. Then having the casket delivered to the grounds of the Hare Krishna Temple, the congregation of which, out of respect for a tolerant but nonreligious Tom Sullivan, had put their premises at Tracey's disposal. Plus, the cremation itself had to be scheduled, not to mention tracking down and alerting former neighbors who'd sold out and moved, in case they wished to pay their last respects.

Then, late this morning, the brief, nondenominational service held out of doors behind the porticoed temple. It had attracted a collage of people, for Tom Sullivan's circle of colorful local characters knew no bounds. For the most part, his friends and acquaintances were a creative bunch: artists and writers, poets, people who lived aboard boats, plus a handful of fishing buddies and all manner of other eccentrics. All dropouts from the harried life of mainstream clock watchers. Perhaps in deference to Tom Sullivan's easygoing, casual style, not a coat and tie in evidence.

Throughout, Tracey held up like the Rock of Gibraltar. Never showing how much it cost her to accept the outpourings of solace, or having to share her private grief.

The single most grueling moment came after the service was over and the last of the mourners had departed. Tracey had insisted upon following the hearse to the crematorium.

Maribel was aghast. *"Concha de madre!"* she swore. "For God's sake, why?"

"Because I have to be there and watch," Tracey replied simply.

"Watch? Watch what?"

"The cremation."

"*Jesús*, no!"

"By all the saints in heaven, yes." Tracey would not be swayed.

It wasn't that Maribel was squeamish, or a stranger to

death. She was, in fact, very familiar with the etiquette of mourning, and every detail of what it entailed. Hailing from a Cuban-American clan made her well versed in the art of bereavement. Among her battalions of aging aunts and uncles, armies of nieces and nephews, and a virtual horde of first, second, and third cousins—not to mention the gregarious extended community of friends, neighbors, and acquaintances—she had attended more than her share of funerals. She knew when to be gentle and consoling. And when to be gentle but firm.

Experience told her that right now, the latter was called for.

"Here," Maribel suggested. She reached out to take the urn from Tracey. "Why don't we set that down for now, hmmm?"

But like a child protecting its most precious possession, Tracey turned away and clasped the urn that much tighter against her. She was loath to give it up, as if by letting it out of her hands she would widen the chasm between herself and her father.

Correctly guessing Tracey's motivation, Maribel tailored her approach accordingly.

"Now, Trace," she cajoled, speaking just loud enough to be heard above the roar of the waterfall crashing down upon the tin roof. She'd decided to use her most potent weapon: gentle, inexorable logic. "It's not as if we're going to do anything drastic, right? Just setting it down for a while."

Tracey's brow furrowed.

"That way," Maribel continued, "there's no chance of your accidentally dropping it."

"Oh." Tracey took a sharp breath, her breasts rising as she considered Maribel's argument. Accidentally dropping the urn hadn't occurred to her, but now that the seed had been planted, the very real possibility of just such a blasphemy happening filled her with dread.

Maribel was holding out her arms. "C'mon. I'll put it down for you."

Tracey still hesitated.

Then, as if to settle the debate, strobelike pulses of lightning flashed brightly from all the three windowed walls of the room. Almost simultaneously, a deafening crash and *ca-rack!* followed as a nearby tree was struck.

Tracey jerked, the ear-shattering noise nearly causing the urn to slip from her grasp. *Perhaps,* she considered, *Maribel has a point. Maybe I should put it down.*

With all the solemnity of a ritual, Tracey offered Maribel the urn.

Maribel accepted it with equal solemnity. She used exaggerated care to place it atop the glass-fronted oak curio cabinet containing Tom Sullivan's collection of hand-carved ice fishing decoys.

"There." She clapped her hands and stood back. "Now it's safe. Doesn't that make you feel better?"

Tracey tensed as another throbbing luminescence lit up the Bahamian slats. But the lightning's intensity had lessened, and two seconds passed before the speed of sound brought the accompanying clap of thunder.

The worst of the storm was moving on.

Maribel hooked her arm through Tracey's. "Now, c'mon, girlfriend. What do you say we get you comfy, okay?"

Tracey looked at her blankly. All-encompassing grief had obviously inured her, if only temporarily, to any personal physical discomfort.

"First," Maribel said, pointing an Aqua Blast-lacquered fingernail accusingly at Tracey's shoes, "you can kick off those slingbacks. You've been wearing them since this morning, and your feet must be killing you."

Holding on to Maribel for support, Tracey dutifully reached behind her and lifted first one foot, removed that shoe, and repeated the process with her other foot.

"Great! You're doing good." Maribel nodded approvingly. Keeping her arm linked through Tracey's, she started to steer her toward the narrow hall leading to the back of the house, where her bedroom was located.

Tracey slowed down. "Now what?" she wanted to know.

"Now we get you out of that straitlaced suit and blouse and into something comfortable. Like an old T-shirt and shorts. Or maybe T-shirt and panties." Maribel shrugged. "Any old thing, it doesn't matter what. For the rest of today, I can guarantee you that nobody, but nobody, gets to see you. I'm not letting anybody into this house, and I don't care if it's the president."

Tracey was quiet for a minute, resisted walking any farther. Her eyes moved from Maribel to the hallway, then returned to her friend and she asked her what they would do after she got changed.

"Why, the obvious, of course." Maribel looked a little taken aback by the question. "We sit back and put up our feet and relax. The point is, we don't do anything. What did you think I'd have us do?"

Tracey became introspective and murmured, "I'm too wound up to relax." Her fingers made an agitated, fluttery little gesture. "I feel I need to be doing something."

Maribel glanced at her sideways. "Ooo . . . kaaay," she said slowly. "That's cool. Any idea what that something you need to do might be?"

"I should start getting Dad's affairs in order. You know, find all his paperwork? Make sure bills that need paying are up to date, subscriptions canceled, see if he had insurance. Those sorts of things."

Maribel's voice was soft. "Yeah, but aren't you forgetting something?"

Tracey looked at her without speaking.

"You told me how secretive your dad was. How he kept any important papers and stuff either hidden or locked away."

Tracey nodded. "That's one of the reasons I need to get on with it. I have to know where things stand."

Her frown deepened, her gaze roaming the front room, then out the screen door to where the porch roof was shedding a solid, silvery sheet of water.

"In fact," she added in a near whisper, "I have absolutely no idea of what's what. Not so much as a clue."

"In that case," Maribel, ever practical, replied, "it certainly wouldn't hurt to start looking, would it?"

"Fishing tackle! Nothing more than some goddamn rusty old fishing tackle!"

Tracey kicked the battered old toolbox and sent it and its contents flying.

"Why in hell did he padlock this crap? Nobody in his right mind would want to steal it."

She raked both hands through damp hair and went, "Rrrrrrr!" Then wiped her sweat-beaded forehead with her arm and, defeated, let her legs go limp. She slid down the wall into a sitting position.

"I give up," she announced to the room and then just sat there, head tilted slightly back, mesmerized by the rotations of the vintage ceiling fan's three mahogany blades.

It was nearly midnight, and humid as equatorial Africa. So far she and Maribel had spent hours searching the twelve-hundred-square-foot house, including the tool shed out back.

And the reward for their efforts? Nada. Nothing, zip, zilch. All their searching—which included checking for loose floorboards or wall panels—had been in vain.

Maribel, alerted by the toolbox hitting the wall, cautiously peered around the doorframe. Seeing no missiles headed her way, she entered and tossed the bent stainless steel knife she'd been using to jimmy various locked drawers of Tom Sullivan's Formica-topped dresser. Judging by her expression, she, too, was frustrated.

"I just don't get it," she moaned wearily.

Joining Tracey, Maribel also slid down into the same sitting position, but directly underneath the window.

Now that the weather had cleared, insects, attracted by the light from inside, had plastered themselves against the screen and buzzed intermittently. Cicadas trilled. A zillion tree frogs, brought out by the rain, were croaking up a storm.

Maribel let her head loll to one side, then straightened it and moved it around in a circle, and let it loll in the opposite direction. She squinted over at Tracey. "Not that I ever doubted you were telling the truth, but when you told me about your dad being secretive, I thought surely you were exaggerating. But now I can see you weren't. Everything that can be locked or padlocked *is*. Every nightstand and desk drawer. I've never seen anything like it. I mean, think about it, Trace. I ask you. Is this weird? Or is this weird?"

"It's weird," Tracey agreed, picking lint off the wall-to-wall broadloom. "Dad was the most wonderful guy on earth, the kind of dad every kid dreams of having." She knit her brow and expelled a long-suffering sigh. "But he had two major failings."

Maribel was silent, letting Tracey get it off her chest at her own speed.

"One was refusing to tell me a thing about my mother. I mean it, Maribel—not a single thing! The other was divulging anything about his finances."

Maribel strummed her lower lip thoughtfully. "Yes, but there's got to be paperwork of some kind somewhere," she insisted. "If not here, then elsewhere. Maybe in a safety deposit box, although I haven't run across a key." She raised her eyebrows. "Have you by any chance?"

Tracey rolled her eyes. "Wouldn't I have told you if I had? And I checked the pockets of all his clothes."

"Okay, then let's view this rationally and use our heads. We've searched everywhere. There's no place else to look, since this house has neither a basement nor an attic."

Tracey clapped a hand across her forehead. "Of course!" she exclaimed, the bloom of inspiration flushing her cheeks as she jumped to her feet.

"Of course, what?" Maribel demanded, frowning up at her.

"It's so obvious! How stupid could I be?"

Clutching the windowsill, Maribel pulled herself wearily to her feet. "What is so obvious?"

"Don't you see? Locking everything up like that was only a ruse. So I'd never suspect."

"Whoa." Maribel held out a hand, palm facing outward. "Slow down. You've completely lost me. Now. A ruse so you wouldn't suspect what?"

"Where he hid everything," Tracey said. "Naturally, he must have counted upon my finding it in case of . . . well, in case of something like now. But to do that, I'd either have to be clearing out the entire house, or searching like a desperate bloodhound."

Maribel was becoming irritated. "Will you speak coherently?" And as Tracey moved toward the door: "Wait! Where do you think you're going?"

"Out to the shed."

"But we've already searched it."

"I know. I'm only going to fetch a ladder."

"No. Don't tell me. We're going to have to climb trees?"

"Nothing that radical, Maribel. Everything fell into place when you mentioned basements and attics."

"Need I remind you, this house has neither?"

"I don't need reminding. But while it doesn't have an attic per se, it does have a crawl space. Reachable only through a trapdoor and by ladder." She gestured. "Come along, I'll show you."

Tracey led the way to the bathroom, opened the door, and once inside, pointed up at the wooden tongue-and-groove ceiling. "See that dark outline? That's the trapdoor. And notice how much varnish has been chipped off it? I bet you anything the papers were right above me all these years."

Maribel didn't look entirely convinced.

"I'm telling you, Maribel, they're up there. I can practically smell them."

Tracey was staring up at the ceiling with shiny eyes.

"As a matter of fact," she added, "I'm so sure they're there that I'll bet my newest pair of Manolo Blahnik rip-offs. The good ones."

"Not the red ones with the Lucite heels!"

Tracey took her eyes off the ceiling. "That's right. The red ones with the Lucite heels," she confirmed.

Maribel looked at her in awe. "Wow! You must be pretty sure if you're willing to bet those."

Tracey draped a companionable arm over Maribel's shoulder. "But put it this way, *amiga*. It's the only logical place left to look. Right? And if I lose those shoes—so what?" Tracey shrugged. "Without Dad's papers, I'm up shit's creek."

There it was.

Resting amid a velvety blanket of dust and mildew which had recently been disturbed, the footprints still visible.

There it was, trapped in the beam of Tracey's flashlight.

The object of her search.

An old-fashioned metal steamer trunk, relic of a grander era in travel. The kind of luggage they don't make anymore, and which took two people to carry. Huge and heavy, with a thick leather handle at each end and rounded brass shields protecting all the corners, the hardware verdigrised to a nice pale green. Jumbo latches, also of brass, and a king-size hasp with a combination lock of a startlingly more recent vintage secured the lid.

Tracey said, barely above a whisper, "Holy shit." She was hardly able to breathe, and not from the dust, either. Her heart was pounding so hard it felt like it was knocking against her rib cage.

"Well?" demanded Maribel impatiently from the foot of the ladder. "What do you see? Anything?"

Tracey clambered up the remaining rungs in an instant. It was a lot less than an attic, yet more than a crawl space, thanks to the patchwork of plywood her father had laid across the grid of two-by-fours. Still, the space offered little in the way of headroom, considering it was four and a half feet maximum in the center and sloped down to mere inches at each side. Tracey had to walk hunched over to get to the trunk.

Behind her, she was aware of Maribel clattering up the ladder to join her. Then she heard her friend's sharp intake of breath as she, too, first laid eyes on the steamer trunk.

"I don't know how it got up here, but no way is that ever going to fit through the trapdoor," was Maribel's verdict.

Tracey wasn't fazed. "So? We'll jimmy it open up here, and then we can take turns doing relays."

"Yeah, but you're operating under the assumption that it contains what we're looking for. Don't be surprised if we find nothing but moth-eaten old hats and little boxes of birthday candles."

Tracey eyed her friend pityingly. "Oh, ye of little faith. Why don't you make yourself useful and go back downstairs? That lock looks like serious hardware. Back then they didn't make luggage the crappy way they do now. At the very least, we'll need a hammer and the crowbar. I'll see about an extension cord and a lamp."

Maribel sliced the air with a smart salute. "Aye, aye, *ma'am!*" she sassed. But Tracey noticed she lost no time in jumping to.

Huh, what do you know! she thought. *Maribel may act cool, but she's as anxious as I am to learn what that trunk contains.*

Then Tracey corrected herself. *No. That's wrong. No one can be as anxious as me.* How could they be? *My entire future depends upon what we find in that trunk. It can affect the rest of my life. Maybe . . .*

Her heart beat furiously at the very notion. *Who knows?* Tracey couldn't help thinking. *Maybe I'll even discover the identity of my mother.*

The clamp light flooded the trunk with a hundred and fifty watts. The enameled blue panels glared like a quasar, morphed Tracey and Maribel into hunchbacked witches, their gigantic shadows mimicking their every move across the underbelly of the slanting roof.

Maribel scampered aside, out of harm's way. "Ready?" she asked.

Tracey inhaled a humongous breath and held it in her lungs. She nodded.

"Okay. On your mark. Get set. Go!"

Muscles quivering, Tracey put all her weight behind the crowbar and levered it to its farthest limit. Pain shot through her forearms and up her biceps, signaling her to let go.

No, she told herself. *Just a hair more effort, that's all it'll take. Just a hair . . .* And the hasp snapped like a tree limb. Screws shot into the roof and bounced back, skittering across the floor.

Tracey let the crowbar drop and stood there in that apelike posture, stooped and panting, aware of her weakened, trembling arms, raspy breathing, and racing pulse. The bent hasp dangled uselessly from the lock.

"All right," she said. "Let's get on it."

She unlatched one side of the trunk while Maribel busied herself by unlatching the other. Together they lifted the lid. From the creaking, it was obvious that the hinges could use some oil.

There. The trunk was open.

Tracey stared down, overwhelmed by disappointment. All she could see was an empty tray, divided into two halves, which could be lifted out.

"Don't give up just yet," Maribel said. "We're not quite finished." Grabbing hold of the tray, she lifted it out, let it drop, and—

—bonanza!

Tracey couldn't believe her eyes. There were fat, mildewed manila envelopes showing their age and literally bursting at the seams, once secured by long-rotted rubber bands. Stiff brown accordion files tied up with string. Several taped-up boxes. What looked like an old photo album. A faded, yellowed bunch of rotting tulle, apparently part of a long-ago corsage. And . . .

A frisson of gooseflesh breezed along her arms and up her spine.

. . . lying face up, centered above everything else, a clean, brand-new white envelope. With a single word—*Tracey*—scrawled across it. She immediately recognized the penmanship.

Tracey could only stare. The shock of finding this trove was far greater than her initial disappointment. She wasn't certain what she should feel. Seeing her name, obviously only recently penned, was like receiving a message from the beyond.

Maribel caught her arm. Tracey turned to face her. She swallowed hard. A choking feeling suddenly swelled her throat, and the tears which welled up in her eyes rolled silently down her cheeks, leaving pale streaks on her dusty face.

"You see, *amiga*?" Maribel said softly. "You were right after all."

Tracey covered her mouth with her hand. She had reached the point of emotional overload. For the moment, she was unable to produce a coherent sentence.

Maribel kept her hand on Tracey's arm. "Do you need some time alone?"

Tracey wiped her eyes with the palm of a hand. She nodded without speaking.

"Hey, no *problema*." Maribel trying for a light note. "When you need me, just bang on the floor. I'll be up in a jif. Okay?"

Another nod from Tracey.

"And there's no need to rush. Take your time."

That said, Maribel hunched her way over to the trapdoor, placed one foot on a rung, then the other, and quickly descended the ladder.

Without Maribel for company, the crawl space seemed emptier, and a lot less friendly.

As if they belonged to a stranger, her fingers attacked the envelope and tore it open. Inside was a handwritten letter on a sheet of lined notepaper torn from a spiral binder, along with a few pages of what looked like a legal document. All neatly creased, folded the Tom Sullivan way, like an origami fan.

She began to read:

My dearest Trace,

You most likely think me a fool and a coward for not confiding in you. Actually, it hasn't been easy, particularly since it means not having been totally honest with you.

My darling, judge me as you wish; yours is the only opinion that counts. But I beg of you: try not to judge me too harshly or hastily, my treasured daughter and sole light of my life.

As much as it pains me to admit it, this trunk is my only legacy, as the attached legal document will show. But before you go rummaging through the boxes and folders, take time out and think the potential consequences through. Heed your mythology, never forgetting what happened to poor Pandora. Remember always that curiosity and vanity (and especially vanity, as I learned the hard way that it was my stubborn vanity which was my downfall, and which, thanks to my thoughtlessness, will have affected you directly) always extract a heavy price.

I need not wish you well (although I do), because I

know that you shall succeed in all your endeavors. That knowledge alone will let me rest in peace.

Above all, learn from my mistakes and take better care of your own than I took care of you.

I wish I could have been as perfect a father as you are a daughter.

If cognizance is ours after we are gone, I know I will miss you terribly.

All my love forever,
Dad

Tracey's tears dripped onto the letter. Perhaps Ted Riphenburg had been right after all, she reflected bitterly. It sounded as if her father had committed suicide.

She sniffed and wiped her nose. Put the letter aside and glanced through the legal documents underneath.

And wished she'd waited, and been able to postpone the dreaded news.

A single glaring word summed up the legal jargon.

Foreclosure.

It was the last thing she had expected, and it came as a blow. Her head reeled, and she had to fight to keep from vomiting.

She was holding a notice of foreclosure on the house. If the mortgage and taxes weren't brought up to date within six days, she would be forcibly evicted—contents and all.

Her father had won countless battles.

But in the end, Palm Coast Developers, Inc., had won the war.

Chapter Nine

"Fifteen thousand, nine hundred and forty-seven dollars and sixty-eight cents," Maribel said mournfully as she and Tracey had lunch on the terrace of The Tides in South Beach. "That's the current default owed on the first mortgage, which would bring things up to date. However, that doesn't include another six thousand and sixteen dollars in back payments which is owed on the second mortgage. And then there's still the four thousand, six hundred and seventy-three dollars in back property taxes outstanding. Talk about triple jeopardy. If the house isn't repossessed by the first or second mortgage holders, it sure will be by the tax authorities."

Tracey pushed a forkful of seared grouper around on her plate. "Twenty-seven thousand, thereabouts. And all I've got is five more days to come up with it." She shook her head. "Let's face it, Maribel, it might as well be twenty-seven million. There's no way on earth I can produce twenty-seven thousand dollars."

"And there's no money? Absolutely none? You're sure?"

"I'm positive," Tracey said gloomily. "There's nada." She sighed deeply. "Oh, if I'd only known he'd mortgaged and second-mortgaged everything to the hilt just to send me to

Columbia! But Dad was so damn secretive. So damn proud!"

Maribel rested her chin on her fist and looked thoughtfully across Ocean Drive to Lummus Park. The merest hint of blue ocean was peeking up from behind the dunes. "Surely there must be something of value around the house."

Tracey stared at her. "You're kidding, aren't you? You've been inside. It's all junk. Why, there's not even enough for a decent yard sale."

She too gazed wistfully over at the dunes.

"We might as well admit it," she said. "I'm sunk."

Maribel wished there was more she could do. She had insisted upon taking Tracey out for an extravagant lunch, and the farther from Coconut Grove, the better. The whole point was to get her out of the house and away from her problems, if only for a few hours. Of course, it had also required some finesse on her part—such as avoiding Brickell Avenue and, above all, the Brickell Avenue Bridge.

Unfortunately, neither a change of geographical location nor food that melted on the palate could help distract Tracey from her problems. If anything, the sheer magnitude of her legacy—or rather, the lack of one—had yet to register completely.

Maribel said, in sympathetic tones but without pulling any punches, "You're not sunk yet, but the outlook is certainly not good. If you were a boat, I'd say you're taking on water, *amiga,* and that's a fact."

Tracey smiled without humor. "There's always the Brickell Avenue Bridge."

"No!" Maribel's eyes blazed with Latin anger. She brandished her knife. "If you even think of such a thing, even dream of such a thing, I'll save you the trouble. You hear? Because I'll kill you first."

Tracey was touched by Maribel's vehemence.

"Don't worry. I won't do anything rash." Then, seeing that Maribel wasn't entirely convinced: "I give you my solemn word. Okay?"

Maribel held her gaze for a moment, then she finally nodded. *"Bueno,"* she said. "Now, before we go back to your house and start sorting through the rest of what was in that trunk—"

"Not that we'll find anything," Tracey said gloomily. "I did an overall quick search. It all looks like personal correspondence and photos."

"Yeah, but that doesn't mean we won't find something useful."

"I wish."

"Well, anyway. Before we head back, maybe you can be so good as to fill me in on a thing or two?"

"Such as?" Tracey asked, puzzled.

With her knife, Maribel gestured at Tracey's ring finger. "Don't think I haven't noticed that the zonker's gone. Or that Richie Rich did not attend the service, did not send flowers, and did not even have the courtesy to call. Just because I held my peace for the last few days doesn't mean I'm not curious. So." She sat back and folded her hands on the table. "What gives?"

Tracey said, with studied flippancy, "I gave."

"That doesn't exactly enlighten me."

"Then let me put it this way. I did the breaking off. I gave him that vulgar rock back." Tracey paused before deciding to continue. "He was seeing someone else. He'd even given her a ring."

"What?" Maribel exclaimed. "That low-down son of a bitch."

Tracey nodded. "I can't believe he had me fooled. I feel like such an idiot."

Maribel smiled. "Well, if you ask me—and I know you didn't—I think you ought to be relieved."

"And why is that?"

"Because," Maribel said patiently, "now you won't need rescuing. From yourself or from him."

Tracey was puzzled. "And why do you say that?"

"Because he wasn't the guy for you, Trace. In fact, instead of Mr. Right, he was Mr. Wrong. Anybody could see that."

"Gee," Tracey said. "I thought you'd decided he was perfect. Why didn't you say something? I could have saved myself a lot of heartache."

"No," Maribel said softly, shaking her head. "In that kind of situation, you'd only end up hating the bearer of bad tidings." She reached across the tablecloth and squeezed Tracey's hand. "I preferred keeping my mouth shut—and our friendship intact."

Her honesty brought tears to Tracey's eyes.

"Aw, no," Maribel pleaded. "*Por favor.* Don't get emotional on me now, huh?"

"If . . ." Tracey swallowed. "If I'm a bit . . . well, *touched* doesn't really begin describe it, it's more like *overwhelmed* . . . it's only because it means so much to me. I don't know how I could have gotten through the past few days without you. I mean it."

"I know you do," Maribel said. "And I'm honored, truly I am. But that's what friends are for." Then eagerly, leaning forward and abruptly changing the subject: "What do you say we make an important decision?"

"Maribel!" Tracey protested. "What's the rush? It's all I can ever do to keep up with you."

"That's the Cuban part of me," Maribel said. "We Spanish live life faster than you Anglos." She laughed. "Anyway, this decision's pretty simple." She frowned at Tracey's plate. "I take it you've finished moving things around and pretending to eat?"

Tracey sheepishly laid her knife and fork in an X across her plate and nodded. She felt awful. She'd seen the menu, and didn't need to be reminded how exorbitant this lunch was.

"Here's what I was thinking," Maribel was saying. "Why don't we throw caution to the winds and forget about our waistlines for once? Let's order some heavenly dessert—and I know just the thing. They make the most divine, mouthwatering classic crème brûlée here—real crème brûlée, without fancying it up and ruining it with raspberries or chocolate or some such." She looked at Tracey with sparkly eyes. "Mmm? So, what's the verdict? Do we sin? Or don't we? C'mon!" she cajoled, tilting her head to one side. "Let's live dangerously and do!"

"I think I'll pass." Tracey smiled. "But you go on ahead and have some. Don't let me stop you."

Maribel made a moue and sighed. "No, you're right. My clothes already hate me," she grumbled. "I can't afford to gain a single pound, 'cause I can't afford a new wardrobe. Well, so much for that. Crème brûlée . . ." She rolled the r's on her tongue, as though tasting it, and sighed even more deeply. "It was a nice fantasy while it lasted, though. Wasn't it?"

Tracey agreed. "Yes, a lovely, calorie-laden, guaranteed-to-pack-on-the-pounds fantasy."

"Which, like good little martyrs, we staunchly resisted." Maribel dabbed her lips with the corner of her napkin, twisted around, and caught the waiter's attention. She raised her hand and with an imaginary pen scribbled imaginary numbers in the air.

He smiled and half-bowed.

Maribel turned back around and rested her elbow on the table, her chin in her hand. "He's kind of cute, don't you think?" she asked dreamily.

"Who? The waiter?"

"Of course, the waiter! Who do you think I've been making goo-goo eyes at throughout lunch?"

"Hey, I thought you and Señor Mysterioso—"

"He has a name, you know. Ramón. Ramón Felipe Escolano, but his friends all call him Ray. What about him?"

"Well, with all that's happened, I still haven't met him, but I was under the impression that you and this Ramón had a good thing going."

"So? Just because one doesn't have any money doesn't mean one can't window shop."

"Maribel?"

"Well, it's true! You can look, even if you're not buying."

Tracey shook her head. "You're really incorrigible, you know that?"

Maribel smiled, her eyes on the returning waiter. "Mmmm. I find black men in crisp white shorts absolutely irresistible. Of course, a nice white colonial pith helmet would only add to the sexy charm." She looked suddenly thoughtful. "Hey. D'you think that explains why I'm so crazy about the Bahamas?"

"Perhaps," Tracey allowed fondly, "but what do I know? However, I will vouch for one thing any day."

Maribel raised her eyebrows. "Oh? Such as what?"

"Such as that you're *loca*—period!"

Back home, in the house Tracey had grown up in, she and Maribel sat in the front room, where the television flickered silently, sound turned all the way down. The channel was set to WMAI's *Afternoon Movie*, some early seventies martini-and-bikini spy thriller. Not a Bond flick, but the imitation kind, made on a shoestring. Relying solely on an old-fashioned roof antenna, the reception was grainy.

Neither Tracey nor Maribel was paying attention to the television. They had both changed into knock-around clothes, Tracey into an oversized Miami Dolphins T-shirt which came down below her bare knees, and Maribel into pale frayed Levi's short-shorts and a scarlet halter top. The front door was open wide, the screen keeping out the hordes of insects, while the Bahamian shutters were raised in optimistic hopes of catching a stray cross breeze. Overhead, the ceiling fan made little progress, its paddles battling air as sluggish as molasses.

All around them were piles of mildewed manila envelopes and dusty folders she and Maribel had carried down in batches from the crawl space above.

"If only we knew what we're looking for," Maribel fretted, popping the tab on a can of caffeine-free Diet Pepsi. She tossed her head, flinging her mane of shiny black hair over her shoulder. "You mark my words. Whatever it is, it'll have been staring us right in the face all along. Without our even realizing it."

"Don't I wish."

Maribel sipped some Pepsi and made ecstatic noises.

"Forget money," said Tracey, seated cross-legged on a bare section of shellacked wooden floor between two mismatched area rugs. "My quickie search would have uncovered it. Could be we'll run across a life insurance policy, but I somehow doubt it."

"Yeah . . ." Maribel was momentarily distracted by the picture on the television screen. It showed a starry-eyed blonde with big hair flattening herself against a stucco wall, arm cocked, snub-nosed pistol held upright as she tiptoed toward an open doorway. One would have had to be blind not to recognize glamorous Urania Vickers, yesterday's movie star–turned television superstar–turned novelist, whose pale eyes and fine cheekbones popped up regularly on the covers of the supermarket tabloids. The last time Maribel had seen a photograph of her, Urania Vickers hadn't looked that much older than in the thirty-something-year-old film—thanks in equal parts to the combined magic of airbrushing, liberally slathered Kabuki makeup, and a wig.

Turning her back on the television, Maribel placed her can of Pepsi on the floor and sat opposite Tracey, a mirror image of the same squawlike position. Picking a bulging accordion folder off the nearest stack, she began to pluck at the knotted string with her beautifully manicured fingernails.

"Did you ever consider that you might be wrong? All we need to find among all this stuff is something worth twenty-seven thousand dollars."

"Yeah. Right," Tracey remarked dryly. "Maybe a thousand-year-old lottery ticket."

Maribel sighed. "That's not what I meant and you know it. But how can you be so sure we won't find old stock certificates or . . . or bearer bonds worth twenty-seven thousand smackeroos . . ." Hearing her own flight of fancy, she gave a quavering sigh and drifted off into silence.

For a while, they sorted without speaking, sounds like shuffled cards and the rustling and crinkling of paper keeping them company. Now and then they would pass each other papers, letters, photos, notes.

Nothing of consequence. Brittle bills for telephone and electricity and gas, all dating back several decades. The accumulated detritus of daily living.

Finished going through the first envelope, Tracey reassembled its contents and stuffed them back inside. She gargled a sound of frustration and shoved it away.

"No luck, I take it?" Maribel asked.

"Not in this batch."

And so it went.

Next, Tracey took a thinner envelope with a figure-eight string tie and unlooped it. Reached inside and took out a sheaf of papers. She unfolded one sheet, and then another and another, working in ever swifter succession—

—and gasped. "What in all hell?"

Something trembly in Tracey's tone alerted Maribel, and she put aside a stack of old papers and stood up, pausing to arch a kink out of her spine. She glanced over at the television. Now Urania Vickers was at the helm of a speedboat, a squadron of other boats with gun-wielding thugs in hot pursuit. The scene done on the cheap, obviously shot in a studio in front of a projected background. Urania, scarf tied around her head, wearing big dark glasses and doing her B-actress best to wince while dodging imaginary bullets.

Maribel dismissed the TV, moved over to Tracey's side, and squatted down beside her. She was intrigued by what looked like an official government document, one of several. "What is that?" she asked.

Tracey handed it over. She said, "Apparently exactly what it says at the top. A birth certificate."

"Yes," Maribel said, "but it's made out for somebody named Anna Reynolds."

"That's what's got me flummoxed." Tracey's brow was wrinkled with evident confusion. "Just who is this Anna Reynolds? Have you got any bright ideas?"

"I am looking, Tracey, looking."

Maribel scanned the document closely, ran a long-nailed, Aqua Blast-tipped finger along each type-filled space.

"Ah. Hmmm. According to this document, the father is listed as one Thomas Reynolds, and the mother . . . let me see . . . as someone named Victoria Ure."

She glanced at Tracey. "Either of those names ring a bell?"

Tracey searched her mind but came up empty. She shook her head. "None whatsoever. I swear, before today I never heard of any of these people. But Dad's first name was Thomas." With thumb and forefinger she plucked at her lower lip, as if that might help clarify the mystery. Then quietly, as if talking to herself she said, "Only Dad wasn't a Reynolds. He was a Sullivan."

"Yes, yes—" Maribel nodded. After a moment's silence,

something caught her eye and registered. "Trace?" she said very softly.

Tracey stopped plucking at her lip. "What?"

Maribel traced the birth date on the certificate with her finger. "Did you notice that this gives Anna Reynolds's birth date as February fourteenth?"

Tracey snatched the document back, gripped it in both hands, and stared at it. "My God," she whispered, "you're right. Valentine's Day. It's the same as mine."

"And," Maribel added in a hushed tone, "notice that it gives the year as 1980. See?" She indicated the spot with her finger and once again traded stares with Tracey. "That's the date you were born."

Tracey shivered. "But . . . I don't get it," she sputtered. "And look here." She poked the paper accusingly. "Born at two forty-seven a.m., exactly the same time as me."

"You know what that means?"

"I think I do," Tracey said, her mouth set in a bitter line. "This birth certificate is made out for someone born the very day I was born. Not only that, but for precisely the same time, right down to the minute. And this somebody is named Anna Reynolds."

"Yes? So what are you getting at?"

"Simply this," Tracey replied shakily. "If Anna Reynolds is someone else, fine. But say that Anna Reynolds and I are one and the same . . ."

"Y-yes?"

"Well, then what about me? If this is the picture, where do I fit in?"

Maribel continued to stare at her, unable to summon an answer.

Suddenly Tracey was very tired. She leaned back against the wall and closed her eyes. "And more to the point," she said, "who the hell am I?"

Chapter Ten

Tracey sat at one side of the dinette table, staring at the mounting evidence of—well, she wasn't quite sure what, only that the puzzle still lacked some crucial clues.

Maribel, seated directly opposite, was facing the television screen. Apparently WMAI was running a Urania Vickers festival: three B-movies back-to-back. The spy thriller, which was over, a biblical costume drama, which was nearing its end and, judging from the teasing trailers mixed in with the commercial breaks, a little-known flick from 1972 titled *Empire of the Amazons*, which was up next.

Tracey, facing away from the soundless flickering of the television, paid it no heed. Her mind was focused on the paperwork she and Maribel had discovered, which lay faceup on the gold-flecked Formica surface, the crinkled, smoothed-out documents lined up like a chorus of accusations. The glare of the floor lamp, its three-way bulbs switched up to their full 150-watt maximum, only served to reinforce the stark surrealism of the scene.

The top row consisted of four documents, each more incriminating than the last. Tracey had arranged them in chronological order, from left to right, and they told their own story in broad brush strokes.

First was a copy of the marriage license of Thomas Reynolds to Victoria Ure, stamped AUG 27 1979, along with the accompanying seal of the city registrar; the civil ceremony had been performed in Pine Bluff, Arkansas. One of the signatures was familiar—the "Thomas" scrawled in the inimitable fashion her father had always signed it; the "Reynolds" in the exact same, matching script.

Tracey had no reason to doubt the authenticity of her father's signature. She was not, however, familiar with the bride's spiky penmanship.

The bride. Most likely my mother.

Tracey touched the signature, traced her finger along the spikes. How strange that, after all the fantasies she had entertained about her mother, now that she at last had a name and a handwriting sample, she felt no closer to the woman who had given her birth. If anything, a potential bond seemed less likely than ever.

It was a disturbing and unexpected feeling, the exact opposite of what she had always envisioned.

The next document in line was the birth certificate of Anna Melinda Reynolds, signed by a Roger L. Joplin, M.D., in Charleston, West Virginia, and dated February 14, 1980. Duly witnessed by the city registrar and affixed with the official seal.

The third document showed that Thomas Luke Reynolds had legally changed his name to Thomas Joseph Sullivan. This had been granted in Galveston, Texas, on October 16, 1982.

And finally, the fourth document in the row. The one which stated that Anna Melinda Reynolds's name had officially been changed to Tracey Anne Sullivan. As with the other documents, this one heralded from yet another unlikely location: Sun Prairie, Wisconsin, and was dated May 9, 1983.

"Maribel," Tracey said slowly, "I know you've heard of Galveston, Texas. But what do Pine Bluff, Arkansas; Charleston, West Virginia; and Sun Prairie, Wisconsin, have in common?"

Maribel drew in her eyes from the TV set. "That's easy,"

she laughed. "They're all places I've never heard of, at least not before now, and never intend to visit."

"My thoughts exactly." Tracey nodded. "I think we've hit the nail on the head. It's as if Dad and Victoria, or Dad, Victoria and I, or just Dad and I, hopped around the country on a giant pogo stick." Her frown deepened. "Only I can't for the life of me figure out why. It just doesn't make sense."

"Hmm. You're right, there has to be a reason. Maybe . . . maybe he had to move around a lot because of his job?" Maribel suggested kindly.

Tracey flicked her one of her *oh, please* looks. "I sincerely doubt that. Remember, before his accident and disability, he was a commercial fisherman in Louisiana. Granted, Galveston's on the Gulf. But why on earth would commercial fishing take him to Arkansas, West Virginia, and Wisconsin?"

She paused and added slowly: "I guess the way I should put it is that Dad always *claimed* he was a commercial fisherman. And that I always took his word for it." She threw up both hands in despair, then let them drop heavily into her lap, where they squirmed uneasily, like small trapped animals. "At this point, I really don't know what to believe anymore."

"There is another matter which doesn't make sense, and which we haven't addressed yet."

"And that is? . . ."

"Why, if your father thought it necessary to change his name and yours, is there no paperwork for Victoria Ure? Has that crossed your mind?"

"Actually, no," Tracey admitted, "it hasn't. But now that you mention it, you have a point." Tracey searched her brain for various scenarios. "At any rate, one possibility we haven't considered is that Victoria Ure may have died. In fact, that would go a long way toward explaining Dad's reluctance to talk about her. Could be, he grieved until the end."

"Yes, but we didn't run across anything which indicates death," Maribel reminded her. "No copy of a death certificate. No obituary. Nothing. Nor, if she's still alive, anything to indicate a divorce."

Tracey said, "In other words, except for Victoria Ure popping up on the marriage license and the birth certificate, the lady vanished. It's as if . . ." Tracey frowned, then shook her head. "Naw. Forget it."

"Trace!" Maribel cried. "You cannot do this to me! That is unfair. You know how I hate it when somebody starts to tell me something and doesn't finish. Now come on. Give."

"Okay." Tracey sighed unhappily. "What I was going to say is, what if the reason Dad was so secretive was because he might have been on the lam? Like from the law?"

"Trace, Trace," scolded Maribel. "Now you're really reaching. Think about it. If that were the case, why would he have gone through all the headache and hassle of *legally* changing your names? Don't forget, if they wanted, the authorities would have been able to find him in no time. All they'd have had to do was punch his old name into a computer, and blink! Up'd pop the official name change."

"Perhaps," sighed Tracey. "You know as lovable as Dad was, he was really, really weird."

"You can say that again. We've all heard of family secrets, but this one really takes the cake—" Maribel stopped abruptly, feeling a frisson, as if she had blundered across something significant—but what, she had no idea. "Cake," she repeated under her breath, tapping her lip with a quickening finger. "Cake . . . cake . . . Why am I reminded of—eureka!"

She snapped her fingers and grinned triumphantly. "Because mothers bake cakes," she crowed, "that's why! And that's it! Trace! That's the answer!"

"Maribel, are you quite all right?"

"Never been better. Listen, *amiga*. Try this on for size. What if your dad was trying to hide from . . . no. Scratch that. What if, for whatever the reason, he was trying to hide you from your mother? Perhaps for your own good? Now, that makes sense."

Tracey was silent, giving Maribel's brainstorming some time to digest. "Something . . ." she managed haltingly, ". . . something about that—"

"I know, I know, don't tell me," Maribel bubbled happily, "just feels right! That is what you were going to say, isn't it?"

Tracey's head bobbed a reluctant nod. She couldn't help thinking how ironic this was. Over the course of her entire life, she'd longed for nothing as much as knowledge about her mother. Yet now that she was sifting through layers of clues and getting closer, she wasn't all that certain she really wanted to discover the truth.

When she spoke, Tracey's voice was shaky. "So how do you suggest we continue?"

"How?" Maribel glanced at her watch and stifled a yawn. "Why, we come down, see if we can relax, and then try to get some shut-eye. We still have an awful lot of sorting photos, reading the fine print on stuff, and all that to do. I say we call it a day, take a well-deserved break, and continue tomorrow. Start out fresh in the morning . . . or afternoon or whatever. I've totally lost track of time. Meanwhile, we can catch that movie that's starting on TV."

Maribel nodded toward the television set.

Tracey twisted around.

On the screen—sound still muted—Urania Vickers was regal on her throne of rough-hewn rock, surveying the worship of a crowd of beautiful, scantily clad beauties before casting her glance toward the dais upon which a muscular young Prometheus writhed, trying in vain to escape his bonds. It was almost possible to read Urania's lips as she clicked claw-length talons: "Your punishment is the same which befalls any man who dares trespass this land. For this is the land upon which no man may set foot. This is the . . . empire of the Amazons!"

Whereupon the title, *Empire of the Amazons,* flashed luridly across the screen in three rows of screaming yellow letters.

Tracey turned back around, a pleading expression on her face. "Maribel," she moaned, "no. Have a heart. This is torture. You know how I loathe these kinds of low-budget flicks."

"Oh, but this isn't just any low-budget flick, Trace. This is *Empire of the Amazons*. A cult classic. Seriously, we have to watch this. I caught bits and pieces of it several times, and each time I nearly split a rib, I was laughing so hard.

It's truly a scream. Best of all, the humor's unintentional, which is what makes it so great."

"And what about these?" Tracey asked, indicating the second row of papers on the table. Each neat stack represented a mortgage, or notification of the mortgage holder's sale of the mortgage to another party. One stack was reserved for late notices and various letters demanding payment, each more threatening than the last.

My real legacy, Tracey thought bitterly. *Christ, if I'd only* known . . .

"Come on, Trace." Maribel's tone was wheedling. "Be a sport. Ten minutes. That's all. If you can tear yourself away from it by then, we'll stop watching. Okay?"

"Oh, all right," Tracey said in a voice of pained resignation. "Ten minutes. You can turn the sound up, but I'll watch from down there."

And so saying, Tracey scooted out of her chair and seated herself cross-legged on the floor. "I can sort through these photos while I watch."

Maribel hurried over to the TV set and turned up the sound. Predictably, the soundtrack was scratchy at best, the music prone to melodramatic swells. But it was the dialogue, and the fact that it had been filmed overseas on a shoestring, in Eastern Europe most likely, and been atrociously dubbed, which added the crowning touch.

Everything was out of sync. Lips moved where they shouldn't, and didn't where they should have. At times, the set wobbled as characters walked by. And although the movie had been shot in the seventies, the dialogue was classic fifties, but spiced with excruciating doses of archaic pretension.

Example: *"Where goeth thou, my queen?"*

"Never you mind. The barbarians come and my scabbard is without its sword. Hurry and fetch it. You! Prepare my unicorn. And hurry!"

And: *"What are you standing around for?"*

"I await your order, Your Majesty."

"I give the order!"

Had it been an intentional spoof, it wouldn't have worked. But done seriously, and this badly, turned it into a work of comic genius.

"Isn't it in a class by itself?" Maribel crooned. "I swear, it's almost as cheesy as an Ed Wood movie—and twice as fabu as Zsa Zsa Gabor in *Queen of Outer Space*. Talk about another howler! What you need, Trace, is a cram session in truly outstanding trash."

Tracey kept her ears tuned to the plot while her gaze flicked from tube to photo, photo to tube. At moments she couldn't help giggling. Maribel hadn't been exaggerating. It truly was one of the funniest movies she'd ever seen.

Ten minutes turned into fifteen. Fifteen became twenty. And still Tracey kept watching. The stack of photos had been sorted and put aside; none of them rang a bell. Next, Tracey selected a scrapbook bound in olive green vinyl and embossed with faux gold. She flipped it open and gasped at the eight-by-ten color photo of her father as a young man. He was posed with a woman of indeterminate age who clung to his arm, holding a nosegay of tiny pink roses wrapped in white tulle. This against a backdrop of cinder-block walls and shiny, wavy linoleum. A no-frills government office building? In Pine Bluff, Arkansas, perhaps? Wherever it was, it certainly had that institutional look.

Furthermore, the picture went a long way toward explaining the tatty, mildewed bunch of tulle she'd run across in the trunk.

But what really captured Tracey's attention was the woman who was clinging proprietorially to her father's arm, cheek pressed against his, red lips parted in a studied blaze of white teeth with just the faintest overbite.

It was difficult not to recognize her—especially with the TV on. This despite the token disguise of big pale-tinted designer glasses and what was obviously a wig—a bush of black curls. It might have been enough to throw off the scent of anyone in Pine Bluff, Arkansas, because what would a world-famous celebrity be doing there?

Even Tracey found it difficult to trust her own eyes. The woman in the photo—if she was the Victoria Ure of the marriage license and birth certificate—was wearing a Rodeo Drive version of a cowhand's outfit, albeit one which couldn't have been farther from the range if you tried. White leather jeans tucked into hideously expensive, hand-tooled white cowboy boots with elaborate stitching. A white silk designer blouse. All topped off by no mere ten-gallon hat or smaller flat gaucho version—no siree—but a huge round platter of a Cecil Beatonish, silk-flower bedecked white straw picture hat.

Is it? Or isn't it?

Tracey's eyes snapped to the television. On the screen, the queen of the Amazons was seeking the advice of an oracle, a blind hag who apparently lived on the lip of an active volcano. Amid rumbles and puffs of smoke, a lot of shake, rattle, and roll of the camera was going on. And there, in living color, honey-haired Urania Vickers, she of a periodontist's retirement plan, with blinding Chiclet teeth and that inimitable slight overbite . . .

Tracey switched her gaze back to her lap and the picture of the woman with her father. Her hands trembled as she turned the thick page. On the verso, a close-up of the bride. Uncanny, the resemblance!

No, not uncanny: the real thing. Had to be.

Her, here in the photo album on her lap.

Her! Up there on the screen.

"M-Mari-bel?"

"Trace? Is something wrong?" Maribel perceived the note of gravity in her friend's voice. "What is it? What did you find?"

"Maribel, take a look at these, will you? Tell me if I'm imagining things?"

"Sure!" Maribel jumped up from the recliner, turned the volume down on the television, and came over to where Tracey sat on the floor. She looked down, looked away, and then did a classic double-take. Her eyes were as big as saucers. "Whoa! Is that who I think it is?"

"That's what I was going to ask you."

The movie forgotten, Maribel plopped herself down next to Tracey and reached for the photo album. She held it within the glowing halo of the floor lamp. Cocked her head sideways like a bird and peered closely at the photo. Said, "Humpf!" Then hurriedly, excitedly, began flipping through the rest of the album. There were pages of other shots, all obviously taken on the same occasion.

Maribel shut her eyes. She shook her head briskly, the way a dog shakes off water. She opened her eyes again.

She thought: *If you took away the glasses and the wig . . .*

Now it was Maribel's turn to flick comparative glances between the photos and the muted television set, her face screwed up in concentration. Silently she handed the album back and exhaled an explosive blast of air.

"Well?" demanded Tracey, searching her friend's face for an answer.

"Hang on to your hat," Maribel warned. "Everything tells me it can't be, but . . ."

"But what?" Tracey asked breathlessly.

Maribel stared at her in utter astonishment. "What do you mean, 'what'? You already know the answer. If that's Victoria Ure in the photo, and if, as far as we've discovered, your father only married once, well, unless there's a twin sister no one knows about, I'd say Ms. Ure and Urania Vickers are one and the same."

"It . . ." Tracey made fluttery little avian gestures. "It just seems impossible."

"Of course it does," Maribel agreed. "But you find a picture of the bride and groom. And what do you know? The groom's your dad, and the bride turns out to be a dead ringer for Urania Vickers."

"True, but—"

"Unh-unh. My turn to speak." She flipped pages in the album, found a particular close-up, and tapped a finger on a spot. "Did you notice this tiny mole here, on Urania's neck? I caught it on TV. And it's right here, in this picture, too."

She paused and held Tracey's gaze and added, "Need more proof?"

Tracey was too speechless to reply.

"Face it, *cariña,*" Maribel said. "The odds must be a hundred-million-to-one, but everything points to Urania Vickers. Could be she met your father—maybe on location, who knows?—and they had a thing. Plus, if you look at the birth certificate and do your arithmetic, you'll see that she was already pregnant when they got married."

"At least three months pregnant," Tracey murmured. "And then some."

"Uh-huh. I bet you anything they kept the pregnancy, wedding, and birth a secret for publicity reasons. Nor can we discount the possibility that, at first, your dad didn't recognize Urania for the star she was. We can safely assume she used fake ID, because we know she was using the alias Victoria Ure. Could be, she even had your dad fooled in the beginning."

Tracey sincerely hoped not. *Poor Dad. He'd been a sensitive man, and easily hurt.*

"Secrecy also explains why they would have chosen to get hitched in some backwater in Arkansas. Urania, no doubt, counting upon the fake ID and a dark wig to transform her. Also, ask yourself—as she probably asked herself—who in Arkansas would recognize her for who she really was? Would anyone expect an honest-to-God movie star to pop up in Pine Bluff, Arkansas, of all places?" Maribel gave Tracey an inquiring look and shook her head. "I don't think so." Then: "You still with me?"

Tracey tried to swallow the lump in her throat. "I . . . I suppose so."

"Good. Now, since we haven't run across any divorce papers, I'm willing to bet the marriage is still on the books, though I don't know whether it's valid or not, since she used an alias. One thing is a given, though. She was certainly not a minor, and unless she suffers from extended blackouts or multiple personality disorder (which I sincerely doubt), she knew what she was doing.

"I'd also hazard a guess that she and your dad split up because she couldn't stay away from the limelight for too long. Once you're a star, I gather you need regular doses of adulation . . . kind of like a junkie needs a fix, y'know? And please don't take this the wrong way, or hate me for it, but when she up and left? . . ."

Tracey waited.

"Well, it would not surprise me to learn that she did so without so much as a good-bye. To either you or your dad."

Tracey sighed aloud. The idea of that having occurred gave her the chills.

God, I hope that wasn't the way it happened, she thought fervently. *If Maribel's guess is right, then Urania Vickers truly did break Dad's heart. Small wonder he was so close-mouthed about the past!*

"I'll say one thing," she told Maribel. "From the way you talk, you don't sound like a big Urania Vickers fan yourself."

That earned Tracey a matter-of-fact shrug. "What's to like or dislike?" Maribel asked. "I enjoyed most of her movies. They're not like great art, but hey, they're campy. What you see is what you get. Admittedly, I was glued to that hit TV series Urania starred in during the early nineties. I mean, was she ever big! For a few years there, she was the hottest thing on the tube. But whether I like her or not? Huh."

Maribel turned introspective.

"To tell you the truth," she said slowly, "I never gave it any thought. Either one way or the other." She laughed softly. "I certainly didn't run out and buy her autobiography. Ditto that novel she wrote." She shot Tracey a questioning glance. "And you? How about you? What are your feelings? Or rather," she emphasized, making a careful distinction, "what were they before today?"

Tracey rubbed her temples. "I reckon I missed out on Uraniamania. In retrospect, most likely because Dad steered me away from her movies and TV show, but in such a way that I didn't suspect anything. Until now I guess my feelings were neutral. Sure, I'd see her picture in the supermarket tabloids. They're in every checkout line. But I never bothered to read any of that stuff. I just didn't . . . care."

"Which is probably for the good, all things considered."

Tracey nodded, thinking, *You can say that again.*

"Anyway," Maribel concluded, "we've filled in as many blanks as we could. I'm the first person to admit that a lot of them are educated guesses. But until proven otherwise"—she held up both hands—"they fit. They also explain why your dad took off with you and stayed on the move, living in odd, out-of-the-way places. I bet it's even the reason why he changed both your names. That way, if Urania ever changed her mind, she couldn't find you very easily. He was probably afraid she might wake up one morning, feel a maternal urge for about five minutes, and try to take you away from him."

Tracey nodded but did not speak. She was ruminating in silence, and Maribel let her be.

Soon Tracey's attention turned back to the television. On the screen, Urania Vickers was mounted atop her prancing white unicorn, reviewing her troops. A commanding, Wagnerian Valkyrie in full battle gear. Clad in a little bit of this and a little bit of that. There was the strategically studded, Xena-style bustier. The futuristic, clear plastic breastplate à la *Barbarella*. The Roman legion skirt, the Aztec feather cape. Plus the *Blond Ambition Tour* ponytail.

The same held true for the weapons. Sword. Ray gun. Ninja throwing stars. Crossbow.

It really was too, too much, and Tracey started to sputter laughter—when a sudden camera close-up seemed aimed at her personally. Urania's face, larger than life, filled the entire screen, her sharp, catlike green eyes reaching through the tube to inspect Tracey closely, her expression one of rebuke.

The laughter died in Tracey's throat. For one long, awful moment she was unable to breathe.

Common sense told her it was her imagination at work, that the close-up was simply part of the movie. Still, she couldn't shake the vivid sensation of having her privacy invaded. Of Urania's somehow being *right here*, in this very room. As if the television was actually a doorway linking two worlds—reality and fantasy—and that it was possible to move back and forth, from one into the other.

Of course, it was a ridiculous notion. Childlike, really. Yes. But—

—but it seemed so unsettlingly *real* . . .

Maribel was alarmed. While she had been skimming through the documents, a disturbing development had caught her eye. Rapidly she flipped through the papers another time, sorting them by date.

The papers consisted of various notifications concerning the late Thomas Sullivan and his mortgages. Although they originated from different sources and were worded a variety of ways, all covered the same general territory.

The oldest, which she placed on top, was dated over three and a half years earlier. It was from Golden State Savings and Loan, and informed Tom Sullivan that the mortgage he had applied for had been approved. He must have refinanced his old mortgage, Maribel guessed.

The second piece of correspondence came seven months later, notifying him that Golden State had sold his mortgage to another lending institution, Southern Mariner Bank and Trust, Inc.

Next was a form letter from Southern Mariner, officially welcoming him "aboard" as a new customer. Then came the paperwork from a firm called the Second Mortgage Store. This was from a year and a half ago, and served as official approval of Tom Sullivan's second mortgage on his property.

None of these transactions were out of the ordinary.

What set off Maribel's warning bells, however, was the rest of the paperwork. There was way too much of it—and many more transactions than was normal for such a short time span.

Maribel Pinales didn't work in banking, but she'd learned enough from her various relatives to know how mortgages worked. She knew, for instance, that it was a common practice for one mortgage holder to sell a batch of mortgages to another. In due course, the homeowners would be notified that, from a certain date on, the monthly payments were to be sent to the new company at the new address.

Fine. She had no problem with that.

During the past six months, however, the turnover of Thomas Sullivan's mortgages had sped up alarmingly. For starters, the first mortgage had been sold yet again, this time to a broker named First Lender Financial Corp., Inc., based in Exuma, the Bahamas.

Not two months later, the second mortgage had also been sold, to an outfit listed as Equity Partners, Inc., based in Grand Cayman. Not only that, but during the next eight weeks, ownership of that very same mortgage was snapped up in quick succession by no less than *two* other banking institutions, Global Investors Trust, Inc., based in Liechtenstein, which in turn sold it to New Directions Banking of Atlanta, Georgia.

That meant Tom Sullivan's second mortgage had been resold three times in as many months.

Things were definitely getting curiouser and curiouser.

Fast-forward to six weeks ago. According to the documentation in Maribel's hand, Tom Sullivan's first mortgage changed hands several times, too. The next owner of that paper? None other than the very same entity which had held his second mortgage for a few piddling weeks, Equity Partners, Inc., of Grand Cayman—which, in short order, resold it to (would wonders never cease?) Global Investors Trust, Inc., of Liechtenstein, which promptly turned around and resold it to (wonder of wonders!) New Directions Banking of Atlanta, Georgia.

Now both the first *and* second mortgages were among a single lending institution's portfolio of assets.

Under normal circumstances, the mortgages would have been no prize, considering how deeply Thomas Sullivan had been in arrears. But under special circumstances, such as taking into account how badly Palm Coast Developers, Inc., wanted to get their hands on the collateral, the humble abode had turned into one of the all-time prizes of Miami real estate.

Was it any surprise, then, that only ten days previously, both mortgages had been sold *one last time*? And both to the same buyer?

Oh, yes. Maribel smelled a rat indeed.

She asked herself, *With all the millions upon millions of mortgages floating around out there, what are the chances of one person's first and second mortgages, which originated at different sources, being sold separately but through the same complicated channel of buyers, and then, within the space of a mere two months, being snapped up not once,* but twice, *each time by the same financial institution? So that whoever held the paper on the first mortgage held the paper on the second as well?*

Answer: The chances of that occurring *without design* were surely nil.

Plus, that did not take into account the king rat of all skanky rats, Nationwide Equity Holdings, Inc., which had ended up with both mortgages, and which had lost no time proceeding to foreclose.

"I'll say there's something rotten in the state of Denmark!" Maribel murmured under her breath. "Someone has been playing tag with Tom Sullivan's mortgages."

Maribel didn't need to ask herself whose fine hand was behind it. She thought: *Dig deep enough, and sooner or later you're bound to come across Palm Coast Developers, Inc.*

Now, focusing upon the most recent notifications of mortgage transfers, she examined them closely. Something flitted at the very edge of her consciousness. She reached for the two notices of impending foreclosure, one for each mortgage. She held them side by side and compared the two. What was it?

Then suddenly—bingo! Not in the text, but on the letterhead of the stationery. In the subheading.

"Trace?" Maribel said tentatively.

Tracey gave a start, her eyelids fluttering, and she had the impression that she and the television were separate rubber bands snapping back into place. Urania and the television had had a mesmeric hold upon her.

"Y-yes?" Tracey blinked rapidly, then shook her head to clear it. "Sorry." She made a weak attempt at a smile. "I was in another world."

"There's something I think you'd better look at," Maribel said quietly.

"Okay."

Paper rustled as Maribel brandished a sheaf. Tracey scooted over beside her to see what she was holding. One look, and she recognized the property transfer notices from when they'd sorted them. "Oh. Those." Said with a wrinkled nose and a sniff, as if they gave off an offensive odor, which, in Tracey's case, they most definitely did.

Maribel gazed at her flatly. "Have you gone over them closely?"

"Not yet." Tracey shook her head. "I was going to, but I haven't had the chance to attack that stack yet. Why?"

"For starters, these." As though they were contaminated, Maribel picked up the two notices of foreclosure. "Let me draw your attention to the name of the company," Maribel prompted. "If you look at these closely, you'll notice the, er, little matter of the letterhead?"

After Tracey took them, Maribel sat quietly, hands folded in her lap, eyes on her friend's face. Watching for a reaction.

It wasn't long in coming.

First Tracey read the stylish big blue block letters:

NEW DIRECTIONS BANKING, INC.

Nothing unusual in that. She nearly turned back to Maribel—and suddenly noticed what had escaped her when they'd initially sorted through the paperwork. Underneath the corporation's name, and directly above the centered address, was a subheading in fine print:

A SUBSIDIARY OF THE BIGGS-DIMON FAMILY OF COMPANIES

It took a moment to register. When it did, she gave a start. At first she couldn't believe her eyes. Biggs-Dimon? The company cofounded and co-owned by the family of Brian Biggs, her ex-fiancé?

"Don't you see?" Maribel said softly. "We now know who pulled the plug on your dad." Her lips expressed her repugnance. "Richie Rich. Or his family, which is one and the same. I'm telling you, if I could only get hold of the bastard's *cojones* . . ."

"Perhaps . . . perhaps he isn't even aware of this," Tracey said, immediately coming to Brian's defense even as she realized she was reaching. "It's a humongous corporation."

Maribel's silence wrote the book on cynicism.

"Tomorrow," Tracey said. "First thing in the morning, I'm marching into his office. I know he can fix this—even if it is for old times' sake."

Maribel stared at her in disbelief. All she could do was shake her head mournfully.

"Don't look at me like that," Tracey snapped. "I'm not asking for the impossible. Under the circumstances, it's the very least he can do. The son of a bitch owes me, dammit!"

Her eyes leaked tears, blurring her vision, so she was unaware of Maribel's sadly skeptical expression.

"He owes me!" Tracey repeated, hurt turning to anger. "The bastard owes me!"

Chapter Eleven

Santorini, Greece

The sun was sinking, washing pink the sea and clouds and Oia's whitewashed jumble of clifftop houses. Urania was reclining on the chaise, pointedly facing away from nature's spectacle even as hundreds of people flocked to the northernmost tip of the island, where the ruins of a stone building, known locally as "the fort," jutted from the point like the prow of a ship, the better to savor the sight.

Mark, who occupied the chaise facing Urania's, was also blind to nature's spectacle. He understood perfectly why his most important client was in no mood for beauty: he felt exactly the same.

What else could Julia Markoff's visit have left in one's mouth but the foretaste of doom?

He recalled one of "Boom Boom" Mancini's favorite quotes: "The only thing as over as Christmas is yesterday's star."

"Well, we can discuss tactics, or we can keep putting it off," he said, his voice conveying a laid-back casualness he did not feel. "Either way, it's time we took some radical action. What do you think? Hmmm?"

But if Urania thought anything, her lips were sealed.

Meanwhile, beyond the island of Thirasia across the caldera, the sun slipped beneath the watery horizon, and the sky quickly darkened. The photosensitive outdoor lights, set at ankle level around the terrace and up the steps connecting the three floors, automatically clicked on. So, too, the lights in the swimming pool, which cast an eerie sheen of radioactive green.

"You know, don't you, that Julia was counting on you not accepting her offer of a ghostwriter," he said. "If you'd jumped at the offer, your contract would be safe and Info-Media wouldn't stand a chance of wheedling out of it. We all know that four months is no time to pound a book into shape. For Christ's sake, Urania, did you have to turn her down flat? Couldn't you at least have said you'll sleep on it and let her know?"

"Why is it that I can hardly believe what I'm hearing?" she retorted. Urania Vickers, as most actresses, could modulate her voice to suit any occasion, and on this one chose to take the high road, using the unlikely tone of the injured party. "Must I remind you that you're supposed to be on my side, representing my best interests? So what do you do? Why, you take up for the enemy, that's what."

"Referring to your publisher as 'the enemy,' " Mark pointed out with a sigh, "is counterproductive. It will only reinforce that idea in your head."

"As well it should," Urania retorted with smug triumph. "I didn't put it there, did I? You can thank your friend Jewel-ya for that. At any rate, that's all beside the point. Any shrink will vouch for the psychological importance of voicing one's genuine feelings. I know, because I'm living proof of it. Now that I've expressed my true feelings, I feel tons better, darling. Tons."

Mark Varney rubbed his hands through his hair in exasperation. Once Urania's mind was made up about something, there was no changing it. She always managed to have the last word.

"Tell you what, darling." Urania's snapping abruptly turned into a sweet, dovelike coo. "Why don't you be an absolutely super sweetheart and see if you can't scare up

Maria? Hmmm? Tell her to break out another bottle of shampoo."

"Why?" he asked. "Are we celebrating something?"

The comment earned him a sharklike smile. "If we need an excuse, we can always drink to Jewel-ya's departure. But that's a waste of good champagne. Suffice it to say that if anyone deserves a libation it's your poor trounced author . . . don't you agree?"

Urania fluttered coy eyelashes, well aware of the devastating effect it had on men.

For a moment Mark hesitated. Urania had been sipping champagne all afternoon long. But what the hell. For all her faults—and they were legion—the one shortcoming Urania could not be accused of was alcoholism. Oh, she loved her bubbly; in fact, she was famous for it—especially if it were expensive and free. But she was even more famous for her professionalism. During her entire career she'd never once reported to a set late or—perish the thought—while under the influence. And, though Mark had observed her tipsy on more occasions than one, he had never seen her falling-down drunk.

Naturally, the reason behind Urania's sobriety needed no in-depth study. All too aware that her primary bankable asset was her looks, she was as careful of preserving her face and body as a surgeon was protective of his fingers. And, just as she would never have dreamed of stepping outside without putting on full-throttle makeup and having dressed to the glamorous nines, so too was Urania not about to help speed up the inevitable. The ravages of time and gravity did damage enough on their own; they hardly needed help from substance abuse, thank you very much.

"Well, darling?" she coaxed, with a mock pout. "What are you waiting for?"

"Be right back," Mark said, with a touch of resigned asperity, and rose.

Urania watched him leave through half-lowered eyelids. She admiringly followed his progress as he got to his feet in one fluid, uninterrupted motion and then padded, pantherlike, barefoot around the pool and into an arched door from which spilled an elongated tongue of yellow lamplight.

Urania was all too aware of Mark Varney's unintentional sexuality. Of his tanned naked torso with its six-pack of abs, of the loose white trousers made from some miraculous new microfiber which kept them looking fashionably crinkled, and which rode low on his slender hips.

If only, she sometimes fantasied, *he weren't so damned career-minded. Or his IQ were half of what it is. What a perfectly marvelous gigolo he would make!*

Unfortunately, Mark Varney had been born with brains as well as good looks—a waste of male beauty, as far as Urania was concerned.

From within the lit room drifted the soft susurration of murmurs, and then again the almost soundless slap of bare feet on smooth pebbles embedded in concrete, the swish and rustle of high-tech fabric.

"Maria's kept another bottle on ice," Mark reported, settling himself comfortably back on his lounge. "Sometimes I swear she's psychic, at least when it comes to you and your bubbly."

"Well, she ought to be," retorted Urania. "She's only been with me since"—she flicked her wrist casually—"oh, since forever."

"Which reminds me. She asked me to tell you that you're down to a case and a half."

"Already?" Urania pretended surprise. "My, but Cristal does have a habit of evaporating around me. Oh, well. We'll just have to call that place in Kolonaki and have a few more cases shipped, now won't we?" As if sixteen-hundred-dollar cases of Cristal were as easy and cheap to come by as generic beer at a local discount outlet, of which Santorini, of course, had none.

But then, paradise did have its drawbacks. First and foremost among them was the lack of even that most basic of human needs: a source of potable fresh water. On this arid isle, what was not collected in cisterns during winter's rainy season had to be brought in by seagoing tanker, and then delivered locally by truck. For drinking purposes one had to purchase bottled water.

Mark and Urania fell silent in the velvety star-spangled night, the twin of the three-quarter moon shimmering in the calm caldera far below while the lights of Oia ranged, helter-skelter, along the cliff top. Their conversation was on hold while a tight-lipped Greek woman, tough as beef jerky and with a face like a withered brown apple, approached from the arched doorway carrying a tray.

From a majolica ice bucket protruded a clear glass bottle beaded with sweat, its neck sheathed in gold foil. Accompanying them were two slender modern champagne flutes and two white linen napkins neatly starched and folded.

The woman was Irina Stefanou, and she was the mother of Maria Stefanou, Urania's trusted housekeeper. Of hardy peasant stock, Irina wore the grim uniform of widowhood with pride. She was swathed entirely in black: long-sleeved dress, head scarf, apron, stockings, shoes.

Irina set the tray down on a low table beside Mark's lounge. Somehow, in performing that one simple act, she managed to convey a world of disapproval—of Mark Varney in particular, foreigners in general, imported goods, and, above all, anything which smacked of frivolity. Champagne, for instance.

She withdrew as she had appeared, dourly and without uttering so much as a sound. There one minute and gone the next.

Mark waited until he was certain she was out of earshot. Then he pulled a sour face.

"I don't know about you," he said, sotto voce, "but that old bat never fails to give me the creeps. Must she go skulking around looking like the grim reaper? Or, for that matter, why keep her around at all? Can't you just send her back to whatever remote mountain village she came from? Surely she'd be happier there."

Urania clucked her tongue reprovingly. "Now now, darling," she chided. "You know I couldn't possibly live without Maria. She has been the one constant in my life. Husbands and lovers have come and gone, and so-called friends and colleagues have stabbed me in the back. But

Maria was and is my anchor. If that means putting up with her mother, well . . ." Urania gave a small shrug.

There was the unmistakable tinkle and rattle of ice as he lifted the bottle out of its frosty nest. The scratchy sound of foil as he peeled the gold seal from around the slender glass neck. Silence as he untwisted the wire holding the cork in place. And, finally, a soft explosion as he popped the cork, neatly palming it in a napkin instead of letting it fly.

Champagne gurgled and fizzed as he tilted the bottle over one flute, filling it in tiny tips to give the foam a chance to settle and not overflow. Then he leaned forward and, with something approaching ceremony, handed the flute to Urania. It was a little touch he knew she liked, and which usually put her in a good frame of mind—which was where he preferred she be.

He poured two fingers into his own flute. Enough to make a toast, but not enough to really drink. He wasn't in the mood for anything alcoholic.

Urania hoisted her flute. "To departed enemies," she announced cathartically. And that said, she tucked her nose down toward her glass and took the tiniest birdlike sip. Moistened her lips with the tip of her tongue and sighed pleasurably. Said, "Yum yum. Now, this is the nectar of the gods."

"You say that every time you drink champagne," he pointed out.

She smiled agreeably. "That, darling," she said, dipping a finger into her glass and swizzling the bubbles, "is because Cristal always hits the spot. Anywhere. And for any reason."

"They should make you their spokesperson."

Urania licked champagne from her finger. "Don't I wish." Her voice was momentarily wistful. "Just think of the gobs and gobs of free cases I could get in exchange for publicity."

Mark tested his champagne. He let it roll on his tongue. Urania was right about one thing. It was great champagne. Smooth as silk and full of contradictions: voluptuous yet light, intense but discreet.

Still, he'd choose Scotch over the finest bubbly any day. Macallan in particular, and the longer it'd been aged, the better. However, in deference to the Cristal, he waited a few moments before resuming their conversation.

Finally he cleared his throat to indicate a change of subject. "I hate to spoil a fine vintage . . ." he began.

Urania knew what was coming. "Oh, darling," she pleaded, throwing a dramatic forearm across her brow, "must we?"

"The sooner we get this subject out of the way, the better."

Urania sighed. Ever the trooper, it was impossible for her to disagree. "Oh, I suppose you're right," she mumbled, but not without truculence.

"Good," he said. "Now then. What do you propose to do?"

"Do?" The razor-edged steel was back in her voice and she raked him with her eyes. "What do you mean, what do I propose to do?"

Mark had a way of keeping his voice mild. "This problem with the book isn't going to solve itself, you know."

"Tell me about it," she said gloomily.

"So?"

"So, I'll keep on writing," Urania announced loftily. Then she dipped her nose toward her flute for another birdlike sip. "What do you expect me to do?" Her eyes flashed daggers as she raised her head. "Throw in the towel?"

"No," he replied expressionlessly, and set his flute carefully down on the little side table. "As a matter of fact, I figured you'd do exactly as you just said."

Now he had made her cross. "And what, may I ask, is so bad about that?"

He decided to be truthful. "Because it's what I was afraid of."

"Afraid! I take it you're referring to my commitment to write my own novel?"

He did not reply but spread his hands as if to say, *You said it, I didn't.*

His silence did not sit well.

"You know," Urania said flatly, "when everything's said and done, you really are a first-class prick."

He shrugged. "I've been called worse."

"I'm sure you have."

He swung his legs over the side of the chaise and sat forward, so that he was leaning earnestly toward Urania, hands clasped between splayed legs.

"I'd hoped it wouldn't come to this," he said quietly. "But it's high time we accepted certain unpleasant facts."

"Ex-cuse me?" Urania's voice had turned to pure ice. "And exactly what are these facts you suggest it's time the royal 'we' accepted?"

His voice was quiet. "I think you already know the answer to that one."

Urania exploded, reprising her earlier role of a Klimt-draped Medea. Although she was only leaning forward, one had the impression that she doubled in size until she loomed overhead.

"That's just not good enough, sonny boy!" she snarled. "I want you to say it, dammit! I dare you!"

Urania had forgotten Mark Varney's greatest strength: he was almost impossible to intimidate. One of the first things "Boom Boom" Mancini taught him was to ignore the huffings and puffings of stars who'd had their egos bruised.

"Well, there's the matter of salvaging your contract," he said evenly. "That means delivering what Greenleaf contracted for."

Urania, stung by what she perceived as disloyalty by her agent, said, "Or what will happen?"

"Well, there's their legal department, which has it in for you already," he pointed out. "Those vultures won't hesitate to use every trick in the book so long as they recoup the company's money and show they earn their keep. Don't know why, but I get the distinct feeling they're planning to use you as a high-profile example, even if it means dragging your name through the mud."

"Just let them go ahead and try," Urania scoffed. "I guarantee you, they'll be sorry they ever messed with me!" She jerked her head grandly.

"Yes, but consider the fallout," he said reasonably. "Every publisher in the world—and we both know that with all the buyouts and mergers there are only a handful of global players left—will think twice before waving multimillion-dollar contracts in front of you. And that's just within the industry. Where your fans are concerned, the bad publicity could have deadly ramifications. What happens if they desert you?"

Urania's laugh was a harsh blurt in the night. "Desert me?" She stared at him in disbelief. "My fans," she declared pointedly, "are loyal."

The worst of her rage was subsiding, and she was settling back on the chaise. Whereupon she was able to appear to multiply in size at will, she could perform the opposite as well, diminishing in size from super villainess to mere superstar.

A moment's silence was spent licking her wounds and expressing her indignation by pinching the sleeves of her gold-embroidered silk caftan. Making a production out of giving the fabric a little tug here and making a minute adjustment there.

"O*kay,*" Mark said, trying another tack. "So you're not worried about your fans. But what about employment?"

"Mark, you'll have to be more specific. I honestly don't know what you're getting at."

"You know, those 'Very Special Guest Star' spots on TV? The ones which have become your bread and butter? The ones which, together with your book income, have kept the wolves from your door? Don't be fooled into thinking the producers and sponsors won't react negatively to bad P.R. They'd as soon get another actress for those parts."

What Mark didn't say was, *An actress who's a little younger. One the young generation of today can identify with more easily.*

"Yappity, yappity, yap." Urania used her hand like the mouth of a weary crocodile puppet. "They'll get over it," she assured him.

He waited a beat. Then softly: "Yes, but will you?"

That hit home; it was obvious he had startled her. "H-how do you mean?"

"Look, Urania, I'm not going to waste any more time by mincing words. We both know how badly you need the money that's due upon the book's acceptance. And you can't afford to buy yourself out of that contract. Hell, you can't even afford to return the portion of the advance you ran through. We both know you had it spent long before you ever got your hot little hands on it."

"You bastard." Urania's eyes bore right through his. If looks could kill, he would have been dead on the spot.

It was no secret that there are two subjects Urania loathed above all others: first, her age; and second, her state of finances.

Somehow, despite her heyday, when she was pulling in top dollar, there was precious little to show for it. While Mae West left behind a fortune in Los Angeles real estate, and Paulette Goddard was a whiz when it came to playing the currency market, and Elizabeth Taylor had over the years collected art and major jewels out the wazoo, Urania Vickers was forever teetering on the precipice of fiscal disaster. Not so long ago, she was leaping at any bit part that came her way from Eastern Europe. Then there was the time she was flown to Singapore (first class, of course), for the ribbon-cutting ceremony opening an extravagant new shopping mall, a one-day gig for which she was well renumerated. Ditto, the free penthouse apartment she received in Boca Raton (and turned right around and sold) for appearing in the developers' ads as their star "tenant."

Still, despite Urania's star status and her willingness to act, there were never enough parts—or cold hard cash. Nor were there stocks or convertible bonds. Not even a rich husband who would leave her a fortune.

Was it not fitting, then, that this was the woman who spent her summers on the lip of a live volcano?

Mark continued: "The way I see it is this. You've got one chance of pulling this off and saving your skin, Urania, and that's by turning the material you've got over to a pro. Someone who can pound that mother into publishable shape, and fast."

"So, Brutus," Urania said bitterly. "You're insinuating that I'm incapable of fulfilling my own contract. That is what you're saying, *darling*"—she pronounced the word so that it dripped poison—"isn't it? *Darling?*"

"I'm not insinuating anything, Urania. I'm trying to save your ass, remember? And if I don't get any thanks for that, well, what else is new?"

"You get fifteen percent of my literary earnings," she said tartly. "Off the top. Some would say that's plenty of thanks."

He shrugged. This lack of gratitude was not new to him. It came with the territory, particularly with celebrity authors.

"Like it or not, as your literary representative, it's my duty to pursue your best interests," he continued. "And if looking after your best interests means finding and hiring a ghostwriter, then fine. It comes with the job, so I'll do it."

"My, my, my!" Urania mimed soundless applause. "Hear ye, hear ye! Why, how awfully loyal, and how . . . how awfully professional of you, kind sir."

He ignored the sarcastic jab because it barely registered; he was too busy thinking aloud: "It'll take some scouting around to see who's available and amenable. Hmmm. And it's got to be someone who can work miracles. The tricky part is, it's got to be a writer who's not known to Julia Markoff and her clones. Ideally, someone who's unknown to any editor at any of the other publishing houses . . ."

His words trailed off. He was frowning at some spot in the distance and tap-tap-tapping the arms of the teak lounge with his fingernails.

Urania's voice barged in on his thoughts. "You're sure taking a lot for granted, aren't you!" she interjected acidly. "Did anyone hear me say I'd agree to it?"

"Urania, stop playing games." He stared at her for a long hard moment. "Julia made one thing crystal clear. The time for magic is over. Don't you get it? It's walk-on-water time. We need a goddamn miracle."

"I suppose you already have someone in mind for this . . . this ghosting business? Am I right?"

"As a matter of fact," he replied truthfully, "no, Urania, I *don't* have anyone in mind. But I sure as hell wish I did. It certainly would make the job a whole lot easier."

The word "job" did not begin to do the project justice. A far more accurate description might be: the hellacious task of making sense of Urania's so-called manuscript—that chaotic, bewildering soup of utter, mind-boggling confusion, missing scenes, dropped characters, inexplicable digressions, stilted dialogue, and abrupt plot changes. Tackling that mess and cobbling it together into something reasonably coherent, readable and, most important of all, marketable was, on a difficulty scale, about as impossible as expecting alchemists to turn ordinary metals into gold.

His voice turned introspective, as though he were thinking aloud. Which, in a way, he was.

"It's going to take some checking around. We need someone who works fast, is dependable and, above all, is the soul of discretion . . ."

Urania rose imperiously to her feet. Her caftan seemed to gather itself up of its own accord, flowing upward around her like a column of molten fabric.

"Well, just make sure you don't forget one thing," she reminded Mark sternly, wagging a finger. "Whoever you scare up better work cheap. I'm not about to agree to a six-figure deal or a cut of the royalties. I'm tired of being taken to the cleaners just because I'm a star."

She started across the terrace, then stopped in front of the huge bone-colored wheel of cheese that was the full moon, calculatingly using it to cut an Erté-like silhouette. "Oh. And another thing."

Mark's voice was guarded. "And what might that be?"

"Whoever you find better keep his or her goddamn mouth zipped, that's what. Marty's going to draw up the contract, and I'll have him put in a condition clause."

The Marty in question was Martin Schulman, her entertainment lawyer. A tough old bird, he had not earned the reputation of being a vulture through acts of kindness.

"So be sure and warn whoever you find that if word of this leaks out, there'll be hell to pay. One peep and they'll get less than zilch. Because I won't hesitate to have Marty sue whoever's pants off for everything they've got—and everything they're ever going to have."

Mark managed to keep his voice dispassionate. "I read you loud and clear."

"Good. Just so that we understand each other." She barely paused. "What time is it in L.A.?"

He consulted his wristwatch and subtracted ten hours. "A little past eleven a.m."

"Good. I'll go and call him right now. Marty never gets into his office until about then."

And off Urania swept. Regally—how else?—her train of glittery, embroidered art nouveau swirls and dots and dashes rippled like liquid gold across the mosaic of pebbles.

Chapter Twelve

Miami, Florida

Sullivan's Law: If something bad can happen, it probably will—within a stone's throw of the Brickell Avenue Bridge.

To Tracey, that spot seemed to be the epicenter from which all things ugly, sordid, and painful radiated. Taking that into account, was it not appropriate that the office tower of Biggs-Dimon should be located not two blocks from the bridge?

Tracey thought so. Enough to overrule Maribel's objections and insist they take the most direct route—across the very bridge from which her father had plunged to his death.

It was nine-thirty in the morning. The sun was already scorching, and the drawbridge was down. Tracey stared mutely out from the passenger's side of Maribel's red Corolla. There was an air of unreality to the steady stream of commuter traffic flowing in both directions across the Miami River, in the concrete barrier separating the automobile lanes from the pedestrian walkway, and the bridge keeper's cantilevered, three-story building clamped to the upriver side of the bridge. Tracey's gaze took in the dock far below, where the tourist pontoon boats with their cheerfully striped awnings were lined up, ready for business, and the jetties where the Aquaworld Party Boat and the tall, ugly white whale of a casino boat, with its white sides and lack of windows and daylight, waited to ferry passengers out into the gambling zone of international waters. Balconied high-rise blocks of completed condos and new construction receded into the heat haze of the distance.

Driving past the bronze column atop which the proud Tequesta warrior aimed his arrow toward the skies, Tracey noticed, for the first time, the detailed spiral of carvings encircling the column from top to bottom, depicting the life of the native Indians—all of whom were long gone.

Gone.

Just like Dad.

Maribel pulled up to the curb in front of a sleek black monolith of steel and tinted glass. Tracey got out, taking in the surroundings as she pushed the car door shut behind her.

The office tower was set way back, making a statement by devoting a few million dollars' worth of prime real estate to a big plaza up front, with a giant black-and-white Dubuffet sculpture in the middle.

The tall dark tower was impressive and important enough to have earned its very own address—One Biggs-Dimon Plaza.

"Buena suerte!" Maribel called out cheerfully.

Tracey turned around and leaned down through the open passenger window. Smiling tremulously, she held up a hand to show crossed fingers. "Thanks. I have a strong feeling I'll be needing it."

"Hey! Remember what we talked about? Just be cool and you'll do fine. Okay?"

"Okay," Tracey said, thinking, *Talk about easier said than done!*

"I'll be waiting in the parking lot across Brickell," Maribel reminded her, then waved. *"Hasta la vista!"* she called, and drove off.

Tracey stood on the curb for a moment longer. After the little red car was gone, she looked around, gratified to see that she had timed her arrival perfectly. Employees, arriving from all directions, were streaming into the building, keeping the revolving doors of the main entrance turning, turning, turning.

Tracey drew a deep breath. "Courage," she murmured.

Holding her head high, she clutched her briefcase in one hand, shouldered her olive green leather bag, and joined the throng. She found herself whisked through a set of revolving doors and into the lobby, cool and lofty and all shiny black marble. A crescent-shaped black marble reception desk fronted the banks of elevators. Behind it sat two exceptionally pretty receptionists. And to either side stood a couple of capable-looking, armed and uniformed security guards.

Heart pumping and heels clicking, Tracey was careful not to rouse suspicion by hurrying past too fast. With a purposeful gait she sailed on by, fully expecting one of the guards or receptionists to call out and stop her.

Her luck held. Whether it was her brisk businesslike stride, or her dressed-for-success suit blending in perfectly, or both, Tracey passed herself off as just another drone among the thousands in the hive.

No one stopped and questioned her, even as she dallied at the building directory to see on which floor Brian had his office. Only now that she needed that information did it occur to her that Brian had never once taken her up to his office, or even suggested that they meet down here in the lobby or outside on the plaza.

Had that been intentional on his part, in order to keep her away from this building?

Eyes scanning the alphabetized building directory, she found what she was looking for:

Biggs, B. R. II, Pres & CEO
Biggs-Dimon International, Inc. PH/40
Biggs, B. R. III, V.P., Operations
Biggs-Dimon International, Inc. 31

How appropriate, Tracey thought. *Daddy has the fortieth-floor penthouse. And Brian Rutherford Biggs III is stuck nine floors below, on thirty-one.*

She couldn't help but be amused.

Poor Brian, she thought. Knowing him, she could well imagine how that must rankle. Snob that he was, he'd be reminded day in and day out just how he stacked up. It was no secret that he had his eye on the number one spot. He'd told her so himself.

Just as she was about to turn and head for the designated bank of elevators, she decided to see if she could find a certain subsidiary of Biggs-Dimon on the building register. She moved a few panels to the right, to the Ns. And felt her stomach drop like a stone. There it was:

New Directions Banking, Inc., of Atlanta, Georgia
A Subsidiary of Biggs-Dimon Int'l, Inc. . . 18

She had half-expected Biggs-Dimon's subsidiaries to have offices in the building. Still, seeing the one that had sold her father's mortgages to the company which was actually proceeding with the foreclosure gave her a chill.

And then she felt her cheeks draw in at another familiar name, also starting with an N. At first she tried to tell herself it could not be.

Nationwide Equity Holdings, Inc.
A Subsidiary of Biggs-Dimon Int'l, Inc. . . 21

Tracey did not want to believe the full extent of the betrayal she had suffered, yet there it was.

So Nationwide Equity Holdings, Inc., was not just another mortgage company. Nor was it merely part and parcel of the greater corporation known as Biggs-Dimon International, Inc. Rather, it was a corporate entity in and of itself. One owned by Biggs-Dimon, but devoted exclusively to the acquisition of properties for no other purpose than foreclosure. An eminently lucrative business whose product, a never-ending succession of mortgages in arrears, was provided by various other subsidiaries of Biggs-Dimon.

That discovery inflicted a whole new set of wounds. For as if her feelings weren't bruised enough, they were further scalded because Brian Rutherford Biggs III—

The shit! The goddamn little shit!

—had what? Met her? Dated her? Wooed her, and gone so far as asking for her hand in marriage?

Had all of what they'd shared been nothing but a scam? Had she been nothing more than a naive young woman who needed seducing in order to fulfill a grand corporate scheme? She had fallen for the oldest lines in history.

"I love you," Brian had whispered under the stars.

"I want to spend the rest of my life with you," he'd professed on a deserted beach.

"We were fated to be together," he'd murmured over expensive lunches and elegant dinners.

Love and Kismet.

Yeah, she thought sardonically. *Right. Sure. Piss and crapola's more like it.*

Well, at least she had the answer to one nagging question. Why someone as filthy rich and as powerful and socially prominent as Brian Rutherford Biggs III would pursue her, a penniless nobody, when he could have his pick of the debutante litter or a runway of beauty queens.

Please, Tracey prayed. *Let me be wrong. Let there have been more to Brian's and my relationship than that.*

Well, one thing was for certain. Like it or not, she was determined to find out.

Palm Coast. The developers who wanted her father's land.

Unsteadily, she moved down to the next glassed-in directory panel. To the Ps.

And of course, there it was. In shiny white letters on black felt.

Palm Coast Developers, Inc.
A Subsidiary of Biggs-Dimon Int'l, Inc. . . 28-33

Seeing her suspicions borne out buffeted Tracey like an invisible fist. She could feel herself flinch, then stagger and double over. Wildly, she reached out, crablike fingers splayed upon cool smooth glass to steady herself.

"Ma'am?" The stranger's voice trespassed upon her private agony. Slowly Tracey twisted her head around. And sucked in her breath. It would have to be one of the crisply uniformed security guards. Silently she cursed her own weakness: she'd accomplished the very thing she had set out to avoid—drawing attention to herself.

"You all right, ma'am?" he asked, his mistrust evident.

Tracey nodded. "Yes, I . . ."

I . . . what? she hissed at herself. *Think, dammit!*

She struggled to compose herself, first straightening her legs, then her torso. Raising her head was the final movement snapping her into a semblance of normality.

"Sorry." An intended smile faltered on her lips. "For a moment there, I wondered whether I shouldn't have stayed home. But I'm fine, thanks."

He appraised her through experienced cop's eyes, and she guessed he was a retired policeman-turned-security guard. "Maybe I can be of help?"

She shook her head. "Thanks, but I'll be fine. Just a case of the new job jitters. You know how it is? That panicky feeling that maybe you aren't up to it?"

She could sense his eyes thawing. "As a matter of fact," he drawled, "I do. Been there a coupla times myself. Tell you the truth, I'm pretty new around here too. Name's Jake."

She made herself smile. "I'm Tracey."

"Well, see you around, Tracey. And good luck, huh?"

"Thanks. I can use it."

"Right." He nodded briskly, then sauntered off to continue his patrol of the lobby.

It had been a close call. If he'd asked her to cough up some ID, and had then called upstairs to check her out . . .

Quickly, beginning at the end of the directory with the Ys, she worked her way along the various panels. *There!* A familiar name joggled her memory:

Southern Mariner Bank and Trust, Inc.
A Subsidiary of Biggs-Dimon Int'l, Inc. 35

One of the financial institutions whose hands her father's mortgages had passed through.

Keep going, she told herself. *Don't stop now.* Anything else? Then:

Wham! Another familiar name slammed into place. And yet another . . . and another . . .

The Second Mortgage Store . . . Golden State Savings and Loan . . . Global Investors Trust, Inc.—*Of Liechtenstein, if I remember correctly!*—First Lender Financial Corp., Inc.—*Of Exuma, the Bahamas*—Equity Partners, Inc.—*Weren't they the ones based in the Cayman Islands?* Tracey would have to double-check, but she could almost swear to it.

Her mouth was dry, her breathing violent. She'd supposed that some funny business must have been going on, but good grief! Every single company that her father's mortgages had passed through was owned by Biggs-Dimon. Every last one!

Try to explain that, you son of a bitch!

Mentally she aimed her thoughts up, up, up to her ex-fiancé in his no doubt plush office on the thirty-first floor.

And as she did, a circuit in her head made a connection. *The thirty-first floor . . . the thirty-first floor.* What was it that nagged her about the thirty-first floor? . . .

She rushed back along the glass panels to the Ps to double-check.

Sure enough. There it was, behind hermetic glass: Palm Coast Developers, Inc. They took up floors twenty-eight through thirty-three.

And Brian Rutherford Biggs III worked on thirty-one—

—at Palm Coast, wouldn't you know it, damn the miserable bastard to an eternity in hell!

But she was damned if she was going to let him get away with it, especially since he and Palm Coast had driven her father to suicide. She was damned if she'd let him hide up there in his thickly carpeted executive suite on thirty-one after leading her down the primrose path, and then tossing her aside like something expendable. Above all, she was Thomas Sullivan's daughter.

So watch out, you sons of bitches, she vowed, stalking to the banks of elevators like a tigress. Her destination was the third bank, which served floors twenty-eight through thirty-nine. The fortieth floor, lair of the Big Goombah, deserved a keyed elevator all its own.

Watch out and don't fuck with me. I'm on my way, and I intend to draw blood.

Up the elevator rushed, a glass pod rocketing skyward along the south-facing side of the shiny dark office tower. Below, the Miami River and the Brickell Avenue Bridge fell away, swiftly shrinking in size while opening up an entire new panoramic horizon.

Tracey Sullivan, whose acrophobia was such that wild horses couldn't have dragged her into a three-story, interior glass elevator at a shopping mall—let alone a glass booth zooming smoothly up the outside of one of the city's tallest high-rises—clutched her briefcase in front of her. She had her back pressed flat against the only glassless surface, the elevator door, and her teeth were tightly clenched. The sheen of cold sweat gleamed on her forehead, and her peridot eyes contracted as she sought to stare straight ahead.

I mustn't look down, she repeated over and over to herself like a mantra. *I mustn't look down, I mustn't look down—*

Bing!

The electronic chime alerted her to her imminent arrival on the thirty-first floor. Tracey prepared herself for a sickening lurch as the elevator halted, but the cab slid to a smooth stop. Unprepared for the doors she was leaning against to sigh apart, she stumbled, all but falling backward into the plushly carpeted reception area.

Tracey pulled a face. *Way to go, Sullivan,* she growled silently. *Talk about making a lasting impression.*

But a swift perusal of the surroundings reassured her. Somehow, her ungainly entrance had gone unnoticed. The receptionist behind the slab of glacier-green glass was in muted conversation with a woman, and the two suits seated on butterscotch leather sofas, obviously waiting for appointments, were concentrating on work—the elder leafing through a printout while the younger skimmed his fingers across the keys of an open laptop.

With a sigh of relief, Tracey gathered up the remnants of her poise. Unwrapped her arms from around her briefcase.

Straightened her spine. Drew her shoulders back and raised her head high.

She mustn't flub this confrontation. Too much was riding on it.

For an astounding transformation had taken place. Gone suddenly was the Tracey Sullivan of a second earlier. This new Tracey Sullivan was a woman on a mission, and in her present mood, nothing seemed impossible. Especially with her senses attuned to the nearby presence of Brian, the little shit! Like a bloodhound on a scent, she seemed able to smell his proximity.

Don't cross me, her every stride forward seemed to warn.

The unmistakable vibes preceded her. The receptionist, a pretty blonde wearing a telephone headset with a thin curved mouthpiece, was instantly aware of her and looked over, eyebrows raised questioningly.

"I'm here to see Mr. Biggs." Tracey's voice was soft yet so authoritative that there was no question as to whether or not she had an appointment. Her attitude said it all: here was a woman who called her own tune.

"That's Mr. Brian Biggs the *third*," she emphasized, just in case there was any mistaking her quarry.

The receptionist's finger hovered over the telephone console built into the desk. "And who, might I ask, wishes to see him?"

Tracey smiled almost sweetly.

"Ms. Parker," she lied unabashedly, having decided beforehand to use the name of a young Palm Beach socialite. This way she would retain the all-important element of surprise. "Ms. Daisy Parker."

Tracey waited as the receptionist punched a three-digit number and murmured something into the mouthpiece. Then she smiled up at Tracey.

"If you'll please have a seat, Ms. Parker," she said, gesturing toward the arrangement of butterscotch leather sofas, "Mr. Biggs will be right out."

"You!" Brian Biggs's exclamation hung in the air like an accusation.

What followed was silence. At the reception desk, the hushed conversation had ceased. Two couches away, the bleep of the businessman's laptop fell silent.

Tracey went rigid. Her fingers clenched the flap of the olive green bag on her lap. It was all she could do to retain the businesslike composure called for by the smooth corporate interior with its deep plush carpeting, indirect lighting, and luxurious leather couches, reinforcing the fiction that this was a temple, that here serious business was conducted in a manner above reproach.

As if!

Tracey stifled a snort. The minutes spent waiting in this sleek, stifling atmosphere had only pumped up the RPMs of her barely checked rage. This was too public a forum; too many sets of eyes were trained on her. With all that unwanted attention tuned in to her misery, the result was a sharp spike in her anger.

"Do tell, to what do I owe the honor of your fucking presence?"

Tracey winced at the F-word, and her face went scarlet and felt prickly with heat. She picked up her briefcase and shouldered her bag and rose, maintaining a forced dignity. Fighting a visible tremor, she crossed the thick carpeting and stopped in front of him.

She looked at him searchingly. "Brian," she said, "let's go someplace where we can talk."

His breath was a hot furnace. "We are talking."

"I meant in private."

"Why? I've got nothing to say. You yourself said it's over between us. 'Member?"

"Yes, I remember. But you won't let it be over."

"Me?" He blurted a harsh laugh. "What a joke! Did I call you? Seems to me, you showed up here on your own. Under false pretenses."

"That," Tracey said icily, "is because you left me no choice."

"Oh, cut the crap and get outta here." He waved her away. "I got work to do."

He started to turn his back on her, but she gripped his arm firmly.

"Not so fast, buster." Tracey's voice was low but edged with razor sharp steel. "If you can write the tune, you should be able to face the music."

"Music?" He blinked in genuine confusion. "What music?"

"On the very day we broke up my father died. Not two blocks from this building. Right down at the Brickell Avenue Bridge." The reception area being windowless, she pointed a quivering finger in the direction of the elevator doors. "I gather you read about it in the newspapers? Or caught it on TV?"

"Oh," he drawled, "now I get it. You're trying to lay the blame for his suicide at my feet. That *is* what you're doing, isn't it?"

"As a matter of fact," Tracey replied, "yes. That's it precisely. Because here is what I found among my father's papers."

She let go of Brian's arm, unlatched the briefcase, and produced a manila envelope. With a pugnacious glare, she thrust it at him.

"Go ahead," she dared him. "Open it. See the evidence for yourself."

It might have been a basket of serpents, the way he backed away from it. "I still don't see why you're bothering me," he said huffily. "Whatever it is, it's got nothing to do with me."

"Oh, no?" she said tightly. "It's got everything to do with you."

Beyond his shoulder, the other people in the reception area were busy pretending either disinterest in her drama or deep concentration in some activity or other.

With trembling fingers, she untucked the flap of the envelope and pulled out a sheaf of documents. She began by holding high the stapled papers at the top.

"Exhibit number one—"

Instead of lowering her voice and only focusing on Brian Biggs, she expanded her theatrics to include everyone in the reception area.

"—a mortgage from Golden State Savings and Loan. Two guesses who the parent company of that financial institution might be." She paused. "If you surmised that it's one of the many cogs in the giant wheel that is Biggs-Dimon, Inc., bravo! Advance to Go. Regretfully, I'm not in the position of giving you two hundred dollars."

She relegated the mortgage papers to the bottom of the stack and picked up the next few stapled pages, again raising them high with a flourish.

"Exhibit number two. Here we have the paperwork generated by Golden State's 'sale' of that mortgage. Perhaps you might have heard of the buyer? Southern Mariner Bank and Trust?"

"That's enough!" Brian said. He was breathing heavily, his brow dotted with perspiration. "That's none of anybody else's business."

"Oh, isn't it?" Tracey's sharp gaze drilled through him like lasers. "I didn't notice any of these documents being marked 'Confidential.' Did you?"

He stared back at her with intense dislike.

Tracey, however, was just warming up. She was on a roll, announcing: "If the name Southern Mariner doesn't jog anyone's gray cells—especially yours, Brian—perhaps a quick elevator ride down to the lobby will. If anyone wants to check the building registry, you'll discover that—yep, lo and behold!—it's another subdivision of Biggs-Dimon!"

She shuffled these documents to the rear of the stack and held up the next batch of paper-clipped pages.

"Now, to continue along the paper trail to see where it leads. In my hands I am holding correspondence from a nationwide firm called the Second Mortgage Store. I'm sure you've heard of it. Well, it just so happens that that's the company which gave my father the second mortgage on his property . . . property which, incidentally, happens to be most inconveniently located. Why? Because it's smack dab in the middle of entire square blocks which Palm Coast Developers, Inc., have managed to accumulate in Coconut Grove. And to what end, you might ask, have they leveled every house and tree and shrub in sight except, so far, ours? Why, in order to build a brand-new, super-deluxe, super-expensive gated community, that's what!"

The reception area seemed unnaturally silent.

Tracey tried, but failed, to hold Brian's gaze. He kept averting his eyes, the ruddiness of his complexion and the cords on his neck standing out as she continued her blistering attack.

"Tell me, *Mister* Biggs." Tracey's voice dripped sarcastic disdain. "You haven't indicated whether or not the name, the Second Mortgage Store, rings a bell?" She rattled the pages she was holding high. "Or, better yet, why don't we stop shoveling the effluvia and cut right to the chase? For starters, you might tell us about your direct involvement in Palm Coast Developers, Inc. How about it? Want to clear your conscience? Hmmm?"

The mention of his part in Palm Coast hit home. Brian's eyes widened, as though he'd been sucker punched, and then cast around furtively, like a cornered animal seeking escape.

She said, "Again, if there's any doubt as to the veracity of my information, we all *could* take the elevator down to the lobby. And confirm that Palm Coast Developers is very, very near, seeing as how they occupy several floors . . . including *this . . . very . . . one*."

"Tracey, for Christ's sake," said Brian, "from where do you get these . . . these conspiracy theories?"

For a moment the ugliness in his face morphed into childlike denial. Then, within the blink of an eye, he was once again the snarling, spoiled crown prince.

She said, "Now let me see . . . where was I? Right . . . and what do I have here? . . ." Mock surprise colored Tracey's voice as she riffled through the papers again. "Oh, I see. Yes."

She held out another batch of documents, as if her makeshift jury of Biggs-Dimon clients was clustered around and leaning in close rather than being frozen in place in scattered spots of the reception area.

"This is the official paperwork confirming the turnover of my father's first mortgage from Southern Mariner to First Lender Financial Corporation of Exuma, the Bahamas." She smiled coldly, knowingly. "Guess in what building you can find First Lender's U.S. satellite offices?"

Again, complete silence, broken only by Brian's rapid breathing.

She said: "If anyone guessed this very building, you can once again pass Go."

"You quite done?" snarled Brian.

Tracey sailed right on. "Of course, this highly irregular shuffling around of mortgages within the company, this . . . this obvious *conspiracy* among Biggs-Dimon's subsidiaries . . . gets even more complicated. Which, I take it, is the whole idea. You know, confuse your customers, then do some corporate pickpocketing and grab their collateral while they're not looking? If you'll bear with me, I promise not to confuse you too much.

"Okay. We've established that First Lender Financial now holds the first mortgage on the property. Fine. But guess what? You won't believe this, but the *second mortgage* is also sold? And not just once, but *twice*? In what, in banking time, might as well be the blink of an eye?"

More rustling of papers as she sought yet other documents to back up her claim.

"If you don't believe me, come and see for yourself. First it was lobbed to Global Investors Trust, Inc., a Liechtenstein-based corporation, and then to New Directions Banking of Atlanta, Georgia. And who owns those two banks, you might well ask? Why . . . glory be! They, too, are subsidiaries of Biggs-Dimon!"

"Okay, that's it!" Brian exploded, nostrils flaring. "Get out. Now!"

He was really steamed up, his face scarlet, his cheeks blotched with rage. Tracey judged that she still had a little leeway. Not much, but perhaps a couple of minutes before he turned into a full-fledged maniac.

"Ah, will you listen to him? And to think that he's my ex-fiancé." She shook her head at her own foolhardiness. "Can you imagine he's capable of sweet talk? Or that I actually fell for it?"

"Hey!" Brian shouted, his hands clenched at his sides. "You fuckin' deaf, or what? I thought I told you to get out!"

Brian shifted his wrath to the receptionist. He pointed a trembling, accusing finger. "Well?" he shouted. "Don't just sit there. What do you think you get paid for? For Christ's sake, woman, do something!"

The receptionist flinched at the verbal assault. Snapping out of her near hypnotic state as spectator, she got busy punching numbers on her keyboard. Tracey could see her lips move, but couldn't hear the urgent whispers she mouthed into the headset.

Seconds later, two beefy men entered the reception area and filled it with their bulky presence. Tracey's heart sank at their appearance. They, too, were wearing headsets, but the tiny Secret Service kind, which clip to one ear and have a tiny microphone pinned to a lapel. Both men unerringly chose Tracey as the target for a speedy ejection.

The security men were at least six-foot-four, and towered over her. She looked up at them fearlessly. "Look, ma'am," she heard one of them drawl quietly, from between barely moving lips. "We can do this quietly, or you can go kicking and screaming and then we'll have to hand you over to the cops. It's your call."

Tracey stared up at him a moment longer, then glanced over at her erstwhile fiancé. The little shit was refusing to even look in her direction. Her lips curled in disgust. Christ, but he revolted her!

She considered resisting and making an even bigger scene . . . or perhaps going limp the way she'd seen nonviolent demonstrators do, so she'd have to be pulled along or carried out. But she realized that these were not viable options. One of the guards alone could easily subdue and lug her downstairs.

More to the point: did she really want to be delivered into the custody of the police?

The answer to that one was a big N-O. Common sense told her she would accomplish less from a jail cell than she could from home.

Turning away from Brian Biggs and hoping she'd never have to lay eyes on the bastard ever again, she looked up at the security man who'd done the talking. Then, reaching down, she picked up her briefcase and held her head high. "All right, gentlemen," she said. "We'll do it quietly."

Chapter Thirteen

"*Querida,* what am I supposed to do with you? You are, bar none, the most stubborn, infuriating, self-defeating, and brainless idjit I've ever had the misfortune to adopt as a sister," groused Maribel. It was late night of that same day, and the two young women were rocking on the porch of Tom Sullivan's bungalow. Time had blurred, thanks to the headway they were making through the bottle of tequila which Maribel had brought.

"You are," continued Maribel in an overburdened tone, "a shame to Womanhood since time immemorial. Forget the Women's Movement, bra burning, and the breaking through of glass ceilings. You and your idiotic sense of pride. If you'd have had the sense of a chinchilla, you'd have hung on to that bastard's ring. It must have been worth—what? Thirty grand?"

Tracey shrugged. She really had no idea what the engagement ring's value had been, nor did she care.

"You see?" Maribel wagged an admonishing finger. "That attitude is your worst fault. That ring would have paid off both mortgages and the back taxes. But oh, no. You had to play Ms. Big and be *estúpida* and give that ring back."

Tracey eyed her ringless finger and heaved a sigh. Even in the moonlight she could detect the paler band of skin where, until recently, the engagement ring had shielded that part of her finger from the relentless Florida sun.

"Or," Maribel went on dreamily, her imagination fueled by a fresh shot of tequila, "that ring could have been the start of something really big. Oh, you know, like what's-her-name?" She frowned, searched her mind, then clicked her fingers. "Right! Paulette Goddard, the movie star. Now, there was a smart cookie. She knew enough to never return an engagement ring. And she received plenty, believe you me."

"So what did she do with them?" asked Tracey, curious in spite of herself.

"Why, the only sensible thing a woman can do—she had a scalp bracelet made out of all the diamonds. You see? That was a woman who could have taught us both a thing or two."

"Speaking of taking care of ourselves, now that I'm primed with bravery, thanks to your excellent tequila, I better go in and place a phone call. *Before* the booze wears off and I chicken out."

"A call?" Maribel was intrigued. "At this ungodly hour?" She brought her wrist close to her eyes and squinted at the luminous dial of her watch. "I swear it says . . . twenty to one? Can that be right?"

Tracey consulted her own wristwatch, which lost six minutes per day. According to it, the time was thirty-two past twelve, which proved Maribel correct. "Yep. Twenty to one it is."

"But who're you calling? And what for?"

"I'll tell you what for," she said grimly. "To start taking charge of my life. You know, taking care of myself? That is, I believe, the gist of what we were discussing?"

"*Sí*. I mean, yeah." Maribel hiccoughed. "But what does that have to do with making telephone calls in the wee hours of the morning?"

"Simple. Remember when you dropped me off here after leaving that . . . that infernal tower of thieves this afternoon?"

"Yeah? . . ."

Tracey sighed. "Naturally, as luck would have it, the guy I called wasn't in."

"Guy?" Mention of men invariably took precedence over all else as far as Maribel was concerned. "What guy?"

Instead of replying directly, Tracey said, "According to his secretary, he's seven time zones from here."

"Seven? Where is this hombre? In Japan?"

"Wrong direction. Try Greece. But his secretary was kind enough to give me his cell phone number. Trouble is, because of the time difference, I had to wait to call. I figured I'd give him at least till midnight our time. Any self-respecting person ought to be up by seven a.m." She looked at Maribel, hoping her friend would second her opinion. "What do you think?"

"Seven, did you say? Seven a.m.?"

Tracey nodded hopefully.

Maribel frowned. "I suppose to us working stiffs it's a respectable enough hour for something urgent . . . like an emergency. But to anyone else? I dunno, *querida*. Somehow seven-thirty sounds awfully early."

"I realize that. But like I said, I've got to go ahead and call before I lose my nerve or the tequila wears off."

"Who is this guy? Do I know him? Is he cute? Is he rich?"

Tracey struggled to her feet and stood there a moment, testing the ground. It seemed surprisingly stable. "I'll fill you in on everything I know . . . once I know it. Okay?"

"Sure. It's a deal."

The bedside phone woke him up. Not the insistent bleats of the house line, but the familiar soft chirrups of his own wafer-thin cell phone.

He rolled over, let his fingers do the walking and felt around the nightstand. Found the teensy vibrating gadget and flipped it open. Without even opening his eyes he pressed the talk button.

"All right," he said with sleepy resignation. "Talk to me."

"M-Mark Varney?" asked a hesitant female voice. Almost whispering his name, as though afraid it might wake him.

He lay there on his back, eyes still shut. "Yeah, and who's this?"

"I apologize if it's so early over there . . . maybe I should try again later?"

"Might as well get it over with. I'm up now."

"You're sure?"

He was starting to get annoyed. It was way too early for running around in verbal circles. "Sure I'm sure. Who is this?"

There was a pause. "Tracey Sullivan?"

"Who?"

He could almost hear the effort the call took on the other end. "T-Tracey Sullivan. You know, your unpublished author? The one in Florida?"

"Sullivan . . . Sullivan . . ." He pinched the top of his nose between thumb and forefinger. Sullivan? Suddenly his eyes snapped open and he sat up straight, as if he been goosed. Which, in a way, he had been. "Hey," he said, his voice warming. "Sullivan. Right."

Well, I'll be damned, he thought. And felt like kicking himself. Last night he'd lain awake for hours, agonizing over who to get to ghost for Urania.

Not that there was a shortage of ghostwriters out there. What was a scarce commodity, however, were those who could keep their lips zipped and, of equal importance, not cost a fortune. And here, out of the clear blue, came a call from the perfect candidate.

He said, "You by any chance psychic?"

"Excuse me? But did you just ask me whether or not I was . . . psychic?"

"I believe I asked that. Yes."

"You've got to be kidding." There was a short pause. "But why? Whatever gave you that idea?"

"Because, believe it or not, you're just the person I wanted to talk to."

"I am?" She sounded skeptical.

"You are," he assured her.

"Well." Another pause. "I don't know what to say."

He had to smile. "You don't have to say anything. Just hear me out. Okay?"

"Sure. Shoot."

"All right, here goes. But you've got to understand that we're talking about a hypothetical situation."

"Fine."

"What it is," he began, "is this. Say some big-time celebrity—you know, the kind the supermarket tabloids feed on?—wrote a book. Or, more precisely, a novel. You with me?"

"Y-yes . . ."

"And say this novel has a few, er, minor problems. Things that could use a little work. You know, some rewriting, a bit of plot rearrangement, probably some dialogue changes, maybe clearing up inconsistencies about the characters. Keeping some of them and getting rid of the extraneous ones? Making the subplots more coherent." He paused. "All in all, I guess what I mean to say is, it requires a little more than, uh, what's usually required editorially."

There was silence from her end of the line.

"Now let's add another significant factor. There's a lot of money riding on this project. Not so much for the, ah, freelance editor, whoever it may be . . . although the pay is not at all bad. But there'd be absolutely no shared credit for working on this. In other words, the big-name celebrity gets to bask in all the glory. Makes the usual rounds. Does the talk show circuit. Goes on a book-signing blitz. Eats up the adulation. You still with me?"

"Yes. I understand."

"So my question is this. How do you think a person hired to work in such a situation, and having to remain an unsung hero, would feel?"

"You mean, about being a ghostwriter?"

He cringed. He'd been specifically trying to avoid using that word. He said, "Well, ah, yes. I guess we could call it ghosting."

"And why do I get the distinct feeling that there's a lot more than just a little work involved? From the sound of it, you're talking major overhaul. Aren't you?"

He had to hand it to her; she was sharp, all right. "Guess your mama didn't raise a fool," he said admiringly.

"Actually, she didn't stick around long enough to raise anything. It's Daddy who deserves the credit. But getting back to this . . . this hypothetical situation. You *are* talking major overhaul, am I right? The kind of thing for which they call in what's known as a 'book doctor'? The publishing equivalent of what out in Hollywood is referred to as a 'script doctor'?"

Obviously she was more savvy about publishing than he'd previously thought. "You got it." He cleared his throat. There was no use beating around the bush any further. Not with her.

"Also," he added, "while we're at it, let's throw in the matter of a rather, uh, tight deadline."

"Just how tight?"

"Four months, max."

Tracey's voice was soft. "This isn't a hypothetical situation, is it?"

He didn't know why he was taken aback, but he was. "You sure do catch on fast," he said, not sure whether or not he liked the way she cut right to the chase.

"What's more, this is a roundabout way of asking me if I'm interested in taking this on, isn't it? That's what this is really all about."

He said to her, "That's right."

There. The subject was out on the table, so to speak.

He said, "Before we take this any further, let me ask you one question."

"Certainly. Fire away."

"What," he inquired, "did you call me about? I gather it must have been something important, or else you'd have waited a few hours."

"Uh, I . . . I must have gotten my time zones mixed up. It isn't anything that can't wait."

This was the first sentence of hers that didn't ring quite true. *She's lying,* he thought. *Or at least covering something up.*

After all, he reminded himself, he hadn't called her. She had called him.

But he let it go for now. That could wait. Right now there were more important things to discuss.

"Then I guess it's time to pop the sixty-four-thousand-dollar question," he said. "You interested?"

He heard her quick indrawn breath. "In ghosting?"

"That's right."

"I . . . I might be . . . amenable. What are you offering?"

"Fifty thousand dollars. Half up front, the rest upon completion."

"Twenty-five thousand," she mused, and he had the impression she was doing quick mental math. "Hmmm. I wish I could." Tracey sighed. "But sorry. No can do."

"Then what would it take?"

"Thirty-five up front," she said without hesitation. "Thirty, minimum."

Mark Varney did some calculations of his own. Candy had e-mailed him from Beverly Hills yesterday; a check for thirty-two thousand dollars had arrived from Madrid for the Spanish rights to Urania's last book. Now, if he could only turn that money around, which meant bypassing Urania's business manager, and forgoing his own twenty-five percent commission for selling foreign language rights . . . and assuming that Urania was willing to go along with it . . .

"How soon could you start?" he asked.

"That all depends. Do I work long distance? You know, from here? Do we use Express Mail or e-mail? You're the expert on these things."

"Actually," he said slowly, "what I had in mind was you coming over here."

"To Greece?" Tracey squeaked.

"That's right."

There was a short pause. Clearly she was trying to digest this wholly unexpected development. He could imagine her surge of excitement. *She's probably thinking: Europe! Travel! Adventure!* And how disappointed she would be. *Knowing Urania, she'll lock Tracey in a room with nothing but the manuscript, a computer, and a cot.*

But if Tracey was excited it was impossible to tell. Her voice was thoroughly professional. "Whose book would I be working on?"

"I'll tell you in a minute. But first, a warning. Should you decide to undertake this project, you'll be required to sign a nondisclosure contract. That means you'll be guaranteeing that you won't ever tell anyone what you're working on—or for whom. Not now, not ever. And by anyone I mean your nearest and dearest. Your husband, your lover, your boyfriend, your father, your best girlfriend, even a total stranger. *No one must ever know*. The same holds true for this talk; I'm operating under the assumption that I can trust in your discretion?"

"Don't worry," Tracey said solemnly. "I won't disappoint you."

"I hope not. For both our sakes."

"You make it sound so ominous." She seemed more relaxed now, and let amusement color her voice. "Don't worry. I can keep a secret."

"I sincerely hope so. But trust me. It's for your own benefit. I gather you're not keen on getting your pants sued off."

"You've got that right."

"So," he said. "Now that you know where things stand, what's your verdict?"

She laughed softly into his ear. "Who wouldn't jump at the opportunity? It sounds like an offer I can't refuse. Now do tell. Who is this Señor or Señorita Mysterioso I'm supposed to work for?"

"Work with," he clarified carefully, "not for." Wanting to make this point perfectly clear from the outset.

For Mark Varney was familiar with Urania's modus operandi. Once the project was finished, Urania would reinvent her relationship with Tracey—until, that was, history was rewritten once again a little further down the line, and Tracey was conveniently demoted to something like, "Who? Oh, you must mean that secretary . . ."

He said, "So. Do I have your word that this won't go any farther than from my lips to your ear?"

"Yes," Tracey said levelly. "You have my word."

He paused a beat. "Urania Vickers."

He expected Tracey to exclaim, "Not *the* Urania Vickers!"—gushing and squealing and falling all over herself with excitement, which is what nearly everyone else in the same situation would have done.

Instead, Tracey started to blurt out: "Ur—!" and never finished the last three syllables. His ears caught the distressed intake of her hissed breath. Something was definitely odd, not to mention off, to have tripped that kind of response.

"Tracey?" he inquired with genuine concern. "Is something the matter?"

"No, of course nothing's the matter," Tracey said hastily, in an effort to recover. "Everything's fine."

But somehow her reassurance rang hollow. Whatever the reason, this was the second time within several minutes that he sensed she was not being truthful, or at the very least, being highly evasive.

His voice was gentle. "You can talk to me, you know. About most anything. Contrary to rumor, I don't bite."

No, he thought wryly, *I only throw innocents to the lions.*

"No." She cleared her throat. "Of course not." She swallowed and said, "Mark, if the money can be wired here in time, I'll sign any contract you or Ur"—she coughed and quickly backtracked—"the author's attorney can overnight me. I know it sounds melodramatic, but my life is in your hands."

Chapter Fourteen

Maribel had insisted upon taking the afternoon off and driving Tracey to the airport. "I have to see you off, *cariña,* and that's that. No arguing. I'm picking you up at noon sharp. So you'd better be ready."

Meanwhile, there were a host of last-minute details to see to, a zillion anxieties to put to rest. Not to mention wrestling with her overstuffed luggage.

Tracey tugged the zipper of the bulging black nylon suitcase with all her might, willing it to move along its thick black track. No luck.

"Concha de madre!" she growled, employing Maribel's favorite curse. "It's got to close. Got to!"

Pressing one knee down on the bag's water-repellent nylon, she pulled once more. Progress! Inch by inch, the big zipper finally began to move along its black-toothed track, then behaved and zipped quickly around the last curve.

"Whew," she breathed. "At last." Shoving the suitcase to its upright position, she unceremoniously pushed it over to a second, smaller version of the same style waiting by the front door.

There. All ready to go.

Besides her blue nylon carry-on, she would also carry her laptop, a titanium G4 that Brian had given her, on which a copy of her manuscript was stored. Hopefully, she might get a crack at it now and then, either before, between, or after toiling away at Urania Vickers's pages.

In the case containing her laptop were her three most treasured possessions.

First, the pewter-framed eight-by-ten color photograph of her father, which she had taken a year earlier.

Then, the manila envelope containing photocopies of vital papers—her birth certificate, her father's certificate of marriage, and both her own and his official documents proving he'd legally changed their names. Plus, and this she would gladly have done without, his death certificate.

And finally, taking up nearly the entire bottom of the case, the photo album. The one which contained Urania Vickers's photographs posed as the bride of a younger Tom Sullivan. And pictures of the woman holding a baby.

Me, Tracey thought. *It has to be.*

The carry-on and laptop case aside, there was one last and questionable piece of carry-on "luggage." Tracey only hoped that Maribel's generous bon voyage gift, a shameless rip-off of a Miu Miu shoulder bag in brown military canvas, with adjustable khaki web-belting for a strap and tan stitched-leather accents, which would fool any but the most discerning fashion cognoscenti's eye, would not be construed as a third piece of carry-on. Any halfway reasonable person could see that it was a practical alternative to the old-fashioned handbag.

She was free and clear, at least. With the advance Mark Varney had wired her, she had paid off both outstanding mortgages—to the tune of twenty-two thousand dollars.

She hoped her father would have approved of her actions. *God, how silly I am.* She felt like kicking herself. *Knowing Dad, he'd not only have approved—he would have applauded.*

Her thoughts flashed to the trunk he'd hidden all those years.

You understand, don't you, Dad, that I've got to find out the truth about my mother? I'm mature enough to realize that the reason you refused to discuss her was because the subject was too painful for you.

I respect that. Especially since you didn't destroy the contents of that trunk. You deliberately left it there for me to find, along with your letter about opening Pandora's box.

You wanted to give me the choice of whether or not to follow the trail.

She couldn't begin to imagine how difficult it must have been for him to live with the emotional freight of that trunk, that chest full of memories never more than a scant few feet overhead.

Well, you showed me the direction to take, Dad, and now I have to follow that thread to discover who I am, and why I'm the way I am. But isn't it ironic that becoming a real writer and beginning the search for my mother should be tied together?

She was aware of tears leaving moist tracks on her cheeks. *Not now, Trace,* she scolded herself. *For God's sake, pull yourself together. You're leaving today.*

A glance at her watch proved that the closer the time came to leave, the swifter time sped up. It was almost noon already.

Tracey put on a very au courant Galliano/Prada-inspired suit. It consisted of a lightweight cotton, cinch-waisted khaki jacket with epaulets and breast and hip pockets with flaps, plus a matching, short, bias-cut skirt. Completing the look were brown-and-beige, camouflage-patterned, low-heeled pumps.

Tracey was a firm believer in that it never hurt to dress up a little.

Her drab-faced visage frowned back at her from the mirror. Something was missing.

Ye gads! She was dressed, yes, but she wasn't finished yet. Not by a long shot. There was still one thing left to put on: a woman's single most important ally—makeup!

Tracey practically flew into the bathroom and attacked her zippered pouch of cosmetics. She wasn't about to fly from Miami to New York, and then all the way on to Athens, without putting her best face forward.

Swiftly she got busy, her hands a blur. Putting on your face, she'd long ago discovered, was like making the perfect soufflé. All it took was a harmonious palette, a light touch, and ten hideously expensive products.

First, a dab of vitamin E firming cream gently worked into the skin. Then the thinnest possible coat of semi-matte makeup, which dried to a soft and silky finish. A mere drop of undereye concealer to get rid of any shadows. A deft all-over dusting of bronzing powder. A mere touch of Ripe Plum blush to heighten her cheekbones. The palest luminescence of pearl mist around the eyes. The thinnest eyeliner to enhance the glorious peridot of her irises. A bold radiant gleam of Viola Mist lipcolor, muted slightly by closing her mouth on a Kleenex. And finally, a slightly darker shade of Viola expertly penciled around the perimeter of the lips, along with an overall softening of the entire mouth by whisking it ever so lightly with a brush—

Just then came the blast from a horn as a car pulled up in front of the house.

Time to leave? Already? Tracey consulted her wristwatch.

Sure enough. Trust Maribel. It was noon on the button.

Hurriedly Tracey stuffed her makeup back into the pouch. By the time she had it zipped and was back in the living room, the door of the front porch had already slammed shut behind Maribel, who abruptly stopped short and stared.

"Por Dios! Cariña!" she exclaimed softly, under her breath.

"What's the matter?" Tracey, alarmed, asked.

"What's the matter? Nada is the matter. You look . . . *fantástico!* Looove that suit. Thank God I'm familiar with your wardrobe, or else I'd have gotten you a metallic green leather bag." Maribel pulled a face.

Tracey held her arms out at the sides. "You don't think this is . . . well, too much?" she asked hesitantly.

"Too much?" Maribel narrowed her eyes suspiciously and planted both hands on her hips. "Will you stop trying to weasel more compliments out of me?" She glanced beside her and eyed the luggage lined up by the door. She nodded approvingly. "I see you're all set to go up, up and away."

She went to the screen door, put two fingers in her mouth, and let out an astonishingly loud whistle. Within seconds, a sturdy young Latino in a gray uniform strode in and tucked two of Tracey's three carry-ons under his arms, hoisted the two cases she planned to check, and carried them out.

Tracey could only stare. "Who in the name of—"

"Never mind that." Maribel swooped Tracey's Miu Miu bag from where she'd left it and handed it over. Then, hooking an arm through her friend's, she flipped the door lock so that it automatically locked, and proceeded to march Tracey outside.

On the porch, Maribel let go of Tracey's arm and took a moment to lock the dead bolt. When she turned back around, she found Tracey staring out at the street.

Tracey's jaw had dropped. A white stretch limousine waited curbside. This monstrosity was none other than a Hummer, with no less than seven tinted side windows. The rear door was open to reveal enough of the air-conditioned interior for Tracey to catch a glimpse of rich leathers, flickering television, and fiber-optic lighting.

She turned pleadingly to Maribel. "You've got to be kidding. Right? You know there's no way on earth I'm about to be seen in that . . . that thing, whatever it is."

"And you won't be seen, thanks to the tinted windows. You'll be able to look out, but no one else can look in."

"Have you lost your mind? Why, the cost!"

"Is nada. You heard me mention my cousin Hector? The one who owns a limousine service? Well, he owed me a favor, so I called it in. I mean, I couldn't let you start on this incredible journey in anything but style, could I? Certainly not in my measly little Corolla!"

Maribel paused. "I *am* sorry about it being the Hummer, though," she added apologetically, "and the fact that it's white. I asked for a tasteful dark or gray Rolls or Lincoln, but this was the only thing available."

Tracey could only stare—amazed, amused, or appalled; she wasn't sure which described her feelings—at the elongated, luxurious, over-the-top version of the army's humble Humvee. Finally deciding, *The hell with good taste,* she tossed back her head and laughed.

"I love it!" she squealed. "Why not ride around in the

epitome of bad taste? When you consider my rust bucket of a Corvair."

She threw her arms around Maribel and hugged her tightly. "How can I ever thank you?"

"Haven't you heard? Friends are friends. They don't have to say thank you."

"You're loco," Tracey said fondly, "you know that?"

"So I've been told."

Managing to extricate herself from Tracey's bear hug, Maribel held out a hand, palm up, as though demanding money.

"What?" Tracey giggled. "Now you want to read my fortune?"

A dismissive exhale of air put paid to that. "Your airline tickets, *por favor*."

"Oh, honestly, Maribel! Don't worry so much. I have them. They're safe and sound right in here." Tracey patted the faux Miu Miu shoulder bag.

"Well?" Maribel demanded, her hand still out. "May I see them, or not?"

"Oh, all right," said Tracey, with a touch of huffy truculence.

She reached inside and extracted the requested folder. Since it contained tickets for three separate flights each way—six tickets for round-trip travel—it was thicker than usual. And, instead of an airline's logo emblazoned on the cover of the folder, was the name of the travel agency, Los Viajeros, Inc.

Naturally, the tickets had been issued by an agency to which Maribel had steered her, and which was owned and operated by—was it any surprise at this point?—yet another of her friend's multitudinous Cuban relatives.

"Here. See for yourself. Everything's in order." Tracey handed the folder to Maribel.

"Gracias." Maribel immediately seized it and dropped it, two-fingered, into her own bag.

"Wha—?" Tracey stared at her. "Now I have proof that you really are loco!"

"Sí," Maribel replied unflappably. Then, faster than a magician, her hands flying like lightning—presto! What

was she holding but another, identical ticket folder, also from Los Viajeros, Inc.

Tracey stared at it suspiciously. "What did you do now?" she asked, giving her friend a narrow sideways glance.

"Oh, you know." Maribel gave a little shrug. "A little *mágico* something, that's all."

Tightening her lips, Tracey gave her friend a dubious look. With Maribel, she'd learned, a little magic meant major magic. You never knew what to expect.

Tracey took the ticket folder and opened it. Flipped through the pages of tickets. And almost lost her eyeballs, her eyes popped out that far.

"Maribel!" she hissed under her breath. "Holy shit! What do you think you're doing? These are round-trip first-class tickets! I only paid for economy."

"So? Ever hear of upgrades? They're done all the time."

"Yes, but I haven't accumulated nearly enough miles—"

"Miles!" snorted Maribel. "That just goes to show how little you know about the travel business. Take it from me, *amiga*. Miles or no miles, regular customers of travel agencies often get upgrades, so long as seats are available. The only way to fly. And, if you'll notice, none of the flights have changed," she added smugly. "The only portion of the trip that's not first class is from Athens to Santorini and back. That's because those puddle jumpers are one-class only. Now, shall we get you to the airport so you don't miss those flights? Or are we just going to stand here and argue?"

Maribel took her by the arm and led her down the porch steps and over to the rear of the stretch Hummer, where the chauffeur was holding open the door.

He took Tracey's hand and helped her inside, then did the same for Maribel.

"Awesome!" Tracey looked around, taking in the mirrored ceiling, the polished woodwork, the two moon roofs, TVs, VCRs, fax machines, liquor bar, and leather couch seating for twenty. "Why is it I'm beginning to feel like a Hollywood star?"

"Because you look like one, *cariña*."

The long white Hummer began moving, passing a long

stretch of the barren Biggs-Dimon-owned acreage before entering the leafy, sun-dappled tunnels which made up the majority of the Grove's small, delightful streets.

Maribel said: "Now, just sit back and enjoy the ride. Oh, and here's this morning's *Miami Herald*." She picked it up from beside her and gave it to Tracey. "I got it in case all they hand out on the plane is *USA Today*."

"You're spoiling me rotten," Tracey warned.

"I do what I can," murmured Maribel, who tried, unsuccessfully, to hide her pleased grin. "Well, admit it, *amiga*. Doesn't this feel great?"

"Mmm." Tracey, sliding down in her seat, kicked off her pumps and put up her feet on the opposite seat. She stretched luxuriously. "At the risk of giving atrocious taste my stamp of approval," she sighed, "I'd have to agree." Then she burst out laughing. "Yep! It sure is terrific. I love it!"

"Uh-huh. Just remember, *cariña,* life is too short to spend in the back of airplanes."

"I'll try to keep that in mind," Tracey replied, deadpan.

Obviously familiar with the Hummer's interior, Maribel slid around and busied herself. Opened a built-in mini fridge and produced a chilled bottle of Mumm Napa Valley Brut. Pressed a button on a console and an armrest slid aside and two crystal flutes and a round slot, presumably an ice bucket, rose up out of it.

Tracey could only stare.

Maribel set about popping the cork and pouring carefully as the immense vehicle turned a wide, gentle corner, zigzagging at a sedate pace through the Grove's maze of green toward Miami International, the airport everyone loved to hate.

Maribel stuck the champagne bottle into the slot, handed Tracey one flute, and took the other for herself.

"Here's to the land of super-rich shipping tycoons," she toasted, raising her glass. "Who knows? Maybe you'll luck out and meet some tall, dark, and handsome hunk. Like the son of a shipping magnate."

Quite frankly, I'd rather find out the truth about my mother, Tracey thought.

But she didn't voice it aloud. For one thing, she wasn't about to spoil the mood; for another, neither she nor Maribel had ever discussed whom she was going to be ghost-writing for—or, how it being Urania Vickers had first come as a shock, but had ultimately proved irresistible.

Nor had Maribel once asked. If she suspected, she'd kept mum.

They parted at the security checkpoint.

"I promise you that I'll try to get my friend to start looking into the Biggses and their scam while you're gone." Maribel sniffled, not bothering to hide her tears. "Just promise me you'll write."

Tracey held her at arm's length. "I really appreciate whatever your friend can do, and you know I'll write. You'll be inundated with postcards. I'll try to e-mail regularly, too, but that depends upon the setup at the other end."

Maribel hugged her tightly. "I'll miss you, my *loca amiga*. You know that?"

Tracey nodded. "Likewise, believe you me." There was a catch in her voice. "Jeez, I wish you were coming along."

"So do I." Maribel smiled wistfully, then consciously pulled away and toughened herself. "Well, you better work like crazy, that's all I can say," she said, trying for a rough tone. "You hear?" She wagged a cautioning finger. "Because that way, you'll be back sooner rather than later."

"I'll work like a maniac," Tracey vowed. "I'll work till I'm loco and ready to drop!" Then, her voice soft, she said: "How can I ever thank you?"

Maribel looked taken aback. "Thank me!" She drew herself up. "What for?"

Tracey stared at her. What for?

"For being there for me when I needed you most. Believe me, I would have gone to pieces if you hadn't helped keep me together. I could never have gotten through Dad's death without you."

"Oh, please." Maribel flapped a hand. "Will you stop making such a big deal out of nothing? That's what I did—nothing. Nada." Her dark gleaming black eyes held

Tracey's gaze. "Besides, what are friends for, but to share good times, and see each other through bad?"

Tracey smiled and shook her head. "You really are something else, you know that?"

"If you say so. But enough of this maudlin shit, okay?"

Maribel narrowed her eyes mischievously and took two steps backward. Tossed back her long curtain of silky black hair. Grinned, displaying a mouthful of perfect, pure white Chiclets.

Maribel lifted a hand, palm up, in front of her lips and blew Tracey an air kiss. Then, with a wink, she turned around and went sashaying off. Never once looking back, tight little buttocks twitching this way and that.

Suddenly every male's attention zeroed in on her. Parody of sex or not, it was impossible for the opposite sex not to look at Maribel without tasting *dulce de leche* and salsa. Sugar and spice. Everything nice that naughty little girls were made of.

Talk about incorrigible! Tracey thought, not quite sure which she was suppressing—half giggle or half frustrated sigh. But of one thing she was already absolutely sure: *Whatever will I do without Maribel?*

Her friend was still within sight, and already Tracey was feeling lonely and oddly bereft, as though she'd been set adrift in vast, uncharted waters, and she had yet to leave Miami.

Pull yourself together, she scolded herself. *Standing here like an idiot is no way to start a journey, Sullivan.*

And squaring her shoulders, she lifted her briefcase with its precious contents, slung her faux Miu Miu brown canvas bag over her shoulder, picked up her carry-on and headed to the gate.

On the plane, ensconced in the giant leather recliner in first class, Tracey had yet another glass of champagne, enjoying the novelty of great service and all that extra leg room.

She leafed through the *Miami Herald.*

It covered the usual beat, and contained the usual ads. All same-o, same-o. It might as well have been any issue on any given day. But then—

Suddenly it felt as if she'd been punched in the solar plexus.

On the third page of the Metro Miami section was a four-inch-long, two-column-wide social item. Accompanied by two very flattering smiling heads.

One was a stunning young society blonde wearing big diamonds on her ears and even bigger diamonds around her neck.

The other was an all too familiar, darkly handsome man in black tie. The headline read:

Georgina Kaufmann to Wed Brian Rutherford Biggs III

Tracey couldn't contain her shock. Caught completely off guard, she actually moaned aloud. The pain and anger were still too fresh and close to the surface.

The article was the usual fluff, except that it was obviously as much a marriage of two companies as two people: the heir to one of the biggest real estate fortunes around was marrying the daughter and heiress of one of the biggest shopping mall tycoons around. One particular paragraph, however, stood out among all the rest:

According to Kaufmann, 28, a native of Boca Raton and a former beauty queen, she and Biggs, 31, have been secretly engaged for over a year. "We're just happy as all punch that a date's finally been set for the wedding!" she effused.

A year. They had been secretly engaged for a year.

And meanwhile, Brian played me like a violin. And, fool that I was, I fell for it. Hook, line, and sinker.

Tracey folded the newspaper neatly and handed it to a passing flight attendant. "Could you please throw this away for me?"

"Of course. I'd be glad to," the male flight attendant told her. He looked slightly concerned. "Are you unwell? You seem somewhat pale."

Tracey shook her head. "I'm fine, thanks."

"Perhaps I can fetch you something? Another glass of champagne? A coffee or a liqueur perhaps?"

"No, thank you."

"Then how about a glass of water?"

"No to all of the above, but thank you all the same. I appreciate it."

The flight attendant nodded and headed to the galley. Tracey let her head loll sideways. She stared out the scratched Perspex at the sky beyond. They were rushing headlong at more than five hundred miles per hour toward Kennedy International, and then she'd continue on to sunny Greece.

Trust Brian Biggs to pop up again, she thought bitterly. *Why can't the past just stay buried? And why does seeing his name and picture still hurt so badly?*

She rationalized that at least she wouldn't be seeing his name in print for a while. If she was lucky, she might never see it again.

But something told her that he was like bad money. Sooner or later, he'd be bound to turn up again. She hadn't heard the last of him.

Then she thought of the blond beauty queen he'd been engaged to all along, even while she herself was sporting his engagement ring.

Well, Ms. Kaufmann, you're welcome to him, Tracey thought. *All I can say is good riddance!*

Chapter Fifteen

Santorini, Greece

Even the most seasoned travelers agree upon one thing: to approach Santorini by ship is to experience one of the most awesome arrivals in the world. Santorini seems tailor-made for tourists, because here is something that defies re-creation.

The drama of cruising into the caldera, the miles-wide flooded crater, is heightened by the fact that it is virtually landlocked. There is the protective crescent of the main island—Santorini proper—to the east, with Oia lending the embrace of a sheltering arm to the north, and the peninsula containing the ancient ruins of Akrotíri providing the same duty to the south. Three smaller, various-sized buffer islands create a semicircle to the west.

Thus there are, in effect, three mouths into the caldera proper, almost as though nature was guarding a haven. For what the four islands protect is a fifth island located in the center. This is the tip of the mostly submerged, and still active, volcano.

The main island's dark, thousand-foot-high cliffs are crowned by the blinding white icing of villages spilling down over the edge, as well as the 1,300-foot depth of water, creating an intensely and startlingly shade of deep blue. In such a setting, even the most impressive cruise ship is rendered small, inconsequential, and flimsily man-made.

Each year, a million visitors stream to Santorini, but it is the gods who have the last laugh. Lest any tour groups overstay their welcome, the waters of the caldera are too deep for ships to anchor, and there is no hospitable port. In daytime, depending upon weather conditions, launches shuttle day-trippers ashore from the love boats and fun-ships, while the vessels themselves are forced to drop sea anchors, and require constant maneuvering to stay in place.

This, then, clinches the cardinal rule of nature: The most beautiful spots in the world are, almost without exception, the most inaccessible.

As the turboprop descended, coming in low over the wine-dark sea, there was no indication of the breathtaking beauty to come. Placing her forehead against the vibrating window and looking straight down, Tracey saw something that seemed grimly lunar, with barely a touch of even olive green in sight. Sprouting up all over, in various stages of completion, were white villas. And everywhere, dotting this inhospitable landscape, were an incalculable number of tiny whitewashed chapels, many with blue domes.

The visual feast which lay in store for her wasn't evident from the flight attendant's warning. First in Greek, then followed in almost incomprehensible English, it was announced that the taking of photographs of the airport was strictly prohibited.

Not exactly a hearty welcome.

And here she'd always heard about that famous Greek hospitality.

So much for Zorba, Tracey thought dryly.

When the aircraft's wheels touched down and the plane taxied toward a spot away from the tiny terminal, Tracey could see why taking photographs was forbidden. Camouflaged mounds of open-ended hangars concealed gleaming fighter jets. Bunkers were mounted with big anti-aircraft guns. Obviously the Santorini airport doubled as a Greek military base.

She didn't know whether to laugh or gasp. The security measures seemed curiously odd to her logical, journalistic mind. If the Greek government wanted to keep this military installation a secret, why was everything so plainly visible to any civilian landing at the airport?

Being midafternoon, the hottest time of day, the switch from air-conditioned airplane to blast-furnace heat came as a shock. So did the light. Tracey quickly slapped on her sunglasses. The combination of cloudless skies and a fierce sun reflecting off so much water created a light which was as harsh in its intensity as the topography of the island was stark.

An airport bus transported Tracey and her fellow passengers the few hundred feet from aircraft to terminal. She was glad to get inside. The air-conditioning felt marvelous, as did being out of that relentless sunlight, the kind she expected not on earth, but on the rock closest to the sun.

Taking off her dark glasses, she glanced around the baggage claim area, which was none too large. There was but a single small luggage carousel, around which the passengers from her flight clustered, as passengers will invariably do. A pair of Greek soldiers in camouflage fatigues, berets, and jump boots patrolled the area, semiautomatics on their shoulders. Seeing her, they both gave her an odd look, kept on going, then stopped short and did a classic double take.

At first Tracey couldn't imagine why they chose to stare at her like that. And then a lightbulb clicked on in her head.

Aw, Christ, she thought, flushing scarlet and quickly turning away. Of course they would stare, decked out as she was in a chic designer version of G.I. Jane. If she'd known this airport doubled as a military base, she'd never have worn this outfit.

She heard the two soldiers exchanging comments in Greek, then they laughed good-naturedly. They walked on, shaking their heads and grinning at the folly of foreigners.

Well, that does it, she swore to herself. *I'm not wearing this outfit again until I'm back in the States.* The luggage carousel started up with a honk and a grinding noise. The crowd around it pressed forward, which was why she noticed him. He was standing in the back, removed from the cluster of new arrivals. He was holding a large index card with the name SULLIVAN printed upon it in laborious block letters. Obviously by someone more used to the Greek alphabet.

She studied the man covertly before approaching him. He was olive-complected, with a thatch of unruly black hair and a lean, pitted face. Thick black eyebrows met above his nose, and a big black mustache drooped like a giant frown.

"I gather you're looking for me?" she asked. "Tracey Sullivan?" She smiled and proffered her hand for a shake.

He lowered his sign with a grunt, but ignored her outstretched hand. She couldn't tell whether it was by design or that he simply hadn't noticed. Lest she embarrass him or herself any further, she let her hand drop.

"I am Stavros Poulianos. I am to take you to Oia." He pronounced it *E-yah*, his voice gruff and his English thickly accented.

"That's awfully nice of you," Tracey replied. "I'm sure I could have made it on my own, but this is really great. Is it far?"

"Far? Oia?" Stavros shrugged. "A few miles," he said vaguely.

She gestured toward the carousel. "Well, I'd better go see about my luggage." She gave a nervous little laugh. "Wouldn't want it to get dizzy going round and round."

Humor had absolutely no effect. His stony, taciturn countenance remained unmoved. She sighed to herself. *More of that famous Greek hospitality, I suppose.* As she squeezed her way apologetically through the throng to the edge of the carousel, Stavros barged through until he was standing beside her.

I sure wouldn't want to get in his way, Tracey thought, making a mental note. Then, leaning forward, she looked in the direction from which the luggage was coming.

"There! That's one!" she exclaimed. She pointed, waited, then reached out to take it, but Stavros was quicker. His arm darted out and he swung it off before she could even touch it. Within a minute, both pieces of Tracey's checked luggage were safe in Stavros's grip—a suitcase in each hand and the case containing her laptop tucked under an arm.

Thus he led the way. Out of the cool, dim terminal and back into the hot glaring sun.

Tracey quickly slipped her dark glasses back on and decided that her very first purchase was going to be a broad-brimmed straw hat.

"Over there." Stavros gestured with his chin, indicating some parked cars directly to their left.

Tracey wondered what kind of car Urania Vickers would have. This being Europe, a Mercedes, surely. Or would it be something statelier and more befitting a star? A Bentley? A Rolls-Royce Corniche? Or perhaps one of each?

Stavros stopped and put down one suitcase.

"And what is this?" Tracey squeaked in disbelief. She watched with growing alarm as he chucked open the unlocked driver's side door of a hatchback with his free hand, reached in, and popped the rear hatch.

"The car," he said, without a trace of irony.

She could only stare. *Car?* she asked herself. *Did he really say car? Surely he must be joking.*

It was, without doubt, the smallest car Tracey had ever seen, and although it was shiny and new, it made her own pitiful Corvair back home look like a full-size sedan in comparison.

And the tires! Why, they looked like they belonged on a child's toy. She was almost afraid to ask: *Does this have an engine, or do we have to pedal?* Stavros magically stowed all the bags and swung the hatchback shut. According to the name, she noticed, it was called the Smart car.

Stavros came around and held the passenger door open for her. Relieved her of her carry-on luggage and somehow shoved it into the back also. Then helped her in and carefully shut the door.

The window was rolled down, a tiny blessing, in that Tracey could stick one elbow out. She quickly flipped down the sun visor while she was at it, then scooted about, trying to make herself tiny and more comfortable in the cramped space, but accomplished nothing.

Stavros folded himself into the driver's seat without effort. After starting the engine, he floored the accelerator, laid on the horn at tourists who were crossing to the taxi stand, and sent them scattering like so many luggage-laden chickens. He returned the cheerful wave of an airport policeman—this was obviously a game they both found amusing—and drove swiftly, staying in the middle of the curvy road, as though the solid center stripe was designed to line up with the center of the hood.

Abruptly he had to swerve to the right to avoid colliding with a Mercedes taxi speeding around a curve. Tracey grabbed hold of the dashboard, shut her eyes, stomped her foot down on an imaginary brake, and started praying.

Stavros glanced sideways at her and roared with laughter, a gold tooth in the side of his mouth glinting in the sun. "Welcome to Santorini," he said.

Santorini airport is located just above sea level on the western coast of the island, almost exactly halfway down the outside length of its crescent. From there, the road climbs slowly but steadily uphill. Tracey looked out of the side window, trying hard not to think of what an accident in a tiny speeding car must be like. Downhill to her right sloped fields of volcanic soil where grapes were cultivated. The vines stretched, not along wire fences, as was traditional elsewhere, but coiled on the ground like so many individual giant snakes. *Probably because this is the windy side of the island,* Tracey guessed. Among these dry, sun-drenched slopes, all the way down to the sea, quite a lot of buildings were going up, substantial villas in various states of construction.

They entered Messariá, hardly the most charming of villages, where Tracey got her first taste of mass tourism. Suddenly exhaust-belching busses, compact cars, taxis, and dozens of rented mopeds, scooters, and bicycles converged on the narrow, two-lane road, all going hell-bent for leather in both directions, each driver obviously of the opinion that he or she alone owned the road. Small budget hotels lined the pavement on both sides, so close as to appear to be squeezing out into the traffic. She saw scooter and car rental centers and the ubiquitous gas stations and roadside cafés and souvenir shops. Amid all the chaos was a man leading a string of donkeys, each gaily festooned with bells, flowers, and ribbons.

In town or not, Stavros continued to drive like the devil. He let nothing, especially not a bicycle or scooter, slow him down. He had his own style of driving: when in doubt, step on the gas. And swerve if necessary.

It was how everyone else drove, too.

Three more miles of driving uphill and they reached the main town, Firá. Once the quintessential Aegean town, it had become a major tourist center. The road looped through the western edge of the town, a traffic-clogged area like that in Messariá. There were shops galore, currency exchange centers, bakeries, cafés with umbrellas, Internet centers where travelers could access their e-mail or surf the Web, newsstands, postcard kiosks, souvenir stands, handicraft shops, and no end of travel agencies.

But even from this commerce-oriented side of Firá—Firá the whore—she spied glimpses of magic. There was either the gleaming blue dome of a church or its stepped, multiple-arched white steeple, each arch containing a bell. A whitewashed wall enclosed an organically shaped house with a bright, emerald-painted door for a gate and matching wood trim on the window frames and shutters. A mysterious, marble-paved pedestrian alley led off into the shadows, haunt of exclusive boutiques and jewelers. Everywhere were unexpected, extravagant explosions of bougainvillea.

But this was but a taste of the wonders which lay beyond. On the other side of the long, narrow town, a jumble of buildings clung a thousand feet up on the cliff top overlooking the caldera, and café and restaurant terraces jutted out into space. Below, cruise ships gathered and launches shuttled the hordes ashore. Tracey decided she would have to come back for a visit.

The town petered out and gave way to country. Now, for the next eight and a half miles of hair-raising twists and turns, the road continued on like a magic gray ribbon of asphalt, all the way to Oia. Suddenly, the little car crested a hill and for a moment the sea was visible on both sides of the road.

"Oh, my God," Tracey whispered.

On her right, hundreds of feet downhill, were scattered white cubist villas and large flat parcels of land which met the choppy, white-capped Aegean. And to her left the striated cliffs plunged a thousand feet down to the calm of Santorini's great, water-filled volcanic crater, on which sunlight sparkled like golden sequins. Far ahead in the distance was the hooked arm atop which Oia perched like a sun-drenched mirage.

Stavros, stony-faced as ever, was silent, but he eased up on the gas pedal, momentarily bringing the little car to a crawl so she could have a longer look.

Tracey was awed. *If only Dad or Maribel were here!* she thought, feeling a lump rising in her throat. *A sight like this is meant to be shared.*

"It's . . . like, totally awesome! It can't be real!" she whispered, when she found her voice.

As though in reply, Stavros floored the accelerator and the little car shot unexpectedly forward, thrusting Tracey back against the seat.

They had barely entered the outskirts of Oia when the road narrowed into a solitary lane hemmed in by walls. It was shared by pedestrians and traffic alike. Vehicles going in one direction had to pull over at intervals and wait for those headed in the other direction to pass, while pedestrians flattened themselves against whitewashed walls, the luckier ones finding refuge in recessed doorways. These were seemingly sliced out of stucco, the closed doors painted various shades of blue or deep red or a strangely vivid but fitting shade of green. Oddly, it seemed that everywhere, and completely out of proportion with the population, were the porcelain-blue enamel of church domes and the striking white fantasies of their bell towers rising proudly above the flat or half-cylindrical roof lines of clustered houses.

Tracey was agog. She didn't know which way to look. Her eyes were wide and bright and tried to take in everything at once.

Of course, it was impossible. No one could ingest such a visual feast in so short a time.

To the right were charming, two-storied, whitewashed hotels, convenience stores, souvenir shops, and tavernas with flights of steps leading up to their rooftops, where thatched canopies offered shaded tables to the thirsty and the hungry.

To the left was a precipitous drop-off. Narrow concrete paths and steps zigzagged down past the flat roofs of hundreds of white buildings, all descending and piled, seemingly without rhyme or reason, against and atop one another like a series of open drawers. These steep terraces were evidence of the power of nature. During millennia of upheaval and eruptions, varying masses of vertical rock formations had been thrust up, each above and behind the other, leaving shallow, natural shelves, which man had then turned into terraces that he ingeniously improved upon.

As a testament to the cleverness of the human mind, the early inhabitants had come up with the simplest and most brilliant of solutions to the problem of housing. The result were the *skafta*.

As indigenous to Santorini as the yurt is to Mongols, these shelters were created out of the abundance that was volcanic rock and caves. A *skafta* was either a long, narrow, hall-like area dug out of the cliff face or one resulting from deepening existing caves. Like a railroad flat, it might contain a series of rooms reaching far back into the cliff.

As for the opening at the front of the cave, the inhabitants simply walled it in, leaving doors and windows for ventilation or, where the natural terrace made it possible, even built the front room out a bit, creating marvelous pieces of cubist architecture. Most of these were now either holiday villas or hotels, comprising any number of individual *skafta*.

Stavros backed the Smart car into a small parking area filled with cars, motorcycles, and scooters. Squeezing into a narrow space, he switched off the ignition and carefully opened the driver's side door just far enough to squeeze out. Then he went to the back of the car, opened the hatch, and began unloading Tracey's luggage.

Tracey opened her door a full eight inches. Twisting around in her seat, she retrieved her laptop, shoulder bag, and carry-on. She felt the car shake and heard the hatchback slam shut. A swift glance over her shoulder showed that Stavros had her checked luggage in hand and under arm. He was already starting toward the stone-paved lane ahead.

Stavros stopped beside a cerulean door set into a long high white wall. On the other side lay Urania's compound.

It wasn't so much a villa, Tracey saw as she came through the door. Rather, it seemed to be a village in its own right. Spilling down the cliff side on multiple levels, rambling and layered, the whitewashed cluster of structures jutted out of a honeycomb of caves and were stacked, terracelike, one above the other. The perimeter on both sides was defined by a high, round-topped white wall which alternately descended in steps or swoops and provided privacy from the most immediate neighbors while keeping the overall panorama open. The entire jumble—cubes and arched roofs and white domes—was presided over by the windmill on the topmost level.

The bottom of the property ended abruptly, at the lowest terrace with its infinity pool jutting out over the caldera. Beyond was a sheer drop-off.

But between that and the top, every roof was a terrace. There were giant olive jars in corners, splashes of fuchsia bougainvillea and blazing red geraniums. All of the woodwork—doors, window trim, shutters, balcony railings—were painted the exact same shade of cerulean as the entrance door from the street.

Being nearly vertical and multileveled, the entire compound was connected by a maze of sloping steps. Tracey hurried after Stavros down several steep sets of concrete steps to the lowest level.

Here, the single longest structure in the complex reared its colossal bulk, angling out of the volcanic rock like a blinding white fortress. A series of eight tall arches were cut into its face, and these were hung with white silk sheers which, owing to the complete lack of a breeze, did not so much as twitch.

Everything was in readiness for indulging in one's whim.

Underfoot, the long trapezoidal expanse of terrace was paved with *krokalia* in a black-and-white checkerboard, each square inlaid with contrasting dolphins. The border had also been copied from antiquity—a continuous frieze of stylized, curly black waves against a white background. Upon this hand-laid mosaic, a row of plump-cushioned chaises had their backs to the arches, and small X-framed stools at the near and far ends held stacks of identically folded, snow white towels. Providing small islands of shade, three beige market umbrellas were set at thoughtful intervals.

And there, splayed out tantalizingly right in front of the chaises, that most luxurious of all luxuries in Oia—the lipless forever pool, seemingly suspended high above the dreamlike blue which was the caldera.

In this pulsating, surreal heat, Tracey wistfully imagined diving in and cooling off. Then spreading out under one of the umbrellas and nursing a strawberry daiquiri while enjoying the ethereal silence.

Yes, silence. For silent it was; the noises of tourist hordes and tavernas blaring *bouzouki* were above and beyond. Nor did raised voices split the otherworldly tranquility. It was as though the spectacular setting demanded one to whisper.

A grunt from Stavros roused Tracey from further dalliance. His destination was the nearest arch, where he stopped, waiting for her to catch up. He held the silk sheers aside, allowing her to enter first.

Which Tracey slowly and cautiously did, not knowing quite what to expect. Her breath caught in her throat. She walked into a huge space, half building and half cavern. It was extraordinarily cool, and perfumed by dried wild thyme that overflowed from chased silver bowls.

Stavros set down her luggage and pointed to her feet, making a circular motion. Indicating that she should wait right there.

Tracey nodded, grateful that she didn't have to speak. For she was rendered utterly speechless. Standing in place, without moving from that spot, she did a slow 360-degree turn. Except for a huge giltwood Baroque mirror and the matching, elaborately carved gilt console squirming with putti beneath it, the furnishings were basically simple, a combination of dark wooden peasant tables and chests enlivened with the occasional ormolu clock or pair of pricket candlesticks or a Baccarat ashtray or round low tables covered in zebra skin.

Tracey looked up as well. The ceiling was a series of long, whitewashed barrel arches, and the entire back wall was partially composed of natural striated rock, which the architect had incorporated into the design of the house. Two smaller, mysterious alcoves, dug from the volcanic rock, stretched into the dark reaches beyond.

Between the alcoves, centered in the place of honor on a flat section of whitewashed back wall and carefully spotlit, hung the famous Warhol of Urania. The painting was rendered in nine different versions, but hung as a single huge one, so that there were nine identical faces on canvas, each face and plain background painted a different color.

Tracey stared at it, mesmerized, her eyes moving from panel to panel. The last time she had seen anything comparable had been at the Museum of Modern Art in New York.

"Be-*aw*-ti-fool, is she not?" The throaty-voiced accent whispered into Tracey's ear from behind, making her jump. "The most *wand*-der-fool star in the cinematic *have*-ens."

Tracey spun around, finding her face only inches from that of a tall woman with sharp dark eyes, brassy blond hair set in a lacquered, old-fashioned coiffure, and breasts that thrust proudly forward like the twin prows of a catamaran. She was wearing a spotless white acetate blouse, a lightweight black polyester suit shot through with silver thread, and sensible black espadrilles. For adornment she had a tiny, ornate gold crucifix on a thin gold neck chain, a gold wristwatch on a black strap stamped to imitate lizard, and a plain wedding band. Her makeup was simple but effective. A slash of melon lipstick on unsmiling lips and old-fashioned eyeliner laid on rather heavily. But the overall impression she gave was of a distant, imposing dignity.

Yet to Tracey's surprise, the woman wasn't even looking at her. She was staring at the multiple Uranias, the same as Tracey had. Then those huge dark-lidded black eyes honed in on Tracey like lasers, appraising her mercilessly from very close up.

"You must be Miss Sullivan." The last two words were pronounced "*Mees Sol*-lee-von," all the emphasis on the drawn-out, first two syllables.

"Yes," Tracey said neutrally, "I am."

"And I am Mrs. Stefanou. Maria Stefanou."

Tracey pasted a friendly smile on her lips. With formal politeness, she said: "My pleasure, Mrs. Stefanou," and extended her hand.

Mrs. Stefanou took the proffered hand in her own, which to Tracey felt curiously cold and lifeless. She was glad when the woman let go.

"Madame is expecting you, and I am to welcome"—pronounced "*val*-come"—"you on her behalf and to see that you are comfortable. Yes?"

"That is most kind," murmured Tracey.

Leaving Tracey near the spotlit multiple Warhols of Urania, she said, "Please have a seat. I shall inform Madame that you are here."

"Thank you," Tracey replied, and watched as Mrs. Stefanou was swallowed up by the alcove from which the indoor steps led upstairs.

Instead of sitting down, Tracey calmed her growing jitters by slowly meandering about the massive room. Admiring the way the sleek and the primitive had been deftly integrated. Stucco, iron, crystal, gilt, marble, silk, fur. The sheer profusion of *stuff* was only evident once she took the scale of the room into account. Her first impression had been of a refreshing spaciousness and almost Spartan minimalism.

Too, Tracey now noticed what hadn't caught her eye earlier. Antiquities placed here and there, but discreetly rather than for maximum dramatic effect.

She approached a small Cycladic figure of limestone, so

simply carved it could easily have been mistaken for modern instead of dating from the fourth century B.C.—and so casually placed atop a stack of coffee table books that she had almost overlooked it. She became aware of the sounds of thrashing water coming from outside. Someone was swimming laps. She glanced in the direction of the arches, where the motionless sheers blocked the view.

Then came a silence, followed by the unmistakable gushing noise of water sluicing off a body. The swimmer, whoever it was, had climbed out of the pool.

Stifling her curiosity, lest she be mistakenly branded as a voyeur, Tracey moved even farther away from the arches and found herself in front of the largest marble of them all.

Its beauty took her by surprise. It was a headless, armless, and legless torso of a life-size male mounted on a black pedestal. The chest muscular, the abs well defined, although the waist was thicker and fleshier than the bodies beautiful of today. An athlete or a soldier rendered immortal through an artist's chisel, she thought. Yet it was so lifelike she could almost imagine the complete body.

"Pity he's half castrated, don't you agree?" asked a masculine voice from behind her.

"Oh!"

Startled, Tracey whirled around, one hand poised over her pounding heart.

"Do you make a habit of sneaking up on people from behind?" she snapped accusingly, eyes glaring up from under her thick lashes at the man who'd addressed her in perfect American-accented English.

A second later, she regretted her tart reply. One look at him and her first befuddled thought was, *Lordy, Lordy! This is where that word* hunk *comes from.*

And her second thought, following directly on the heels of the first, brought on a bright scarlet blush. *Well, he certainly doesn't leave much to the imagination.*

The "he," in this case, was in his early thirties and wearing nothing but a revealing turquoise bikini, unless she counted the damp white towel that hung from around his neck. Since his black hair was slicked back and wet, and he was dripping water all over the place, it didn't take a rocket scientist to figure out that he was the swimmer she'd heard in the pool.

Also, he was barefoot, which explained how he'd managed to approach her so quietly.

She immediately pegged him as a visiting soap opera star. Not that Tracey had much time to watch the soaps, but working at WMAI-TV she'd caught enough of what the competition was broadcasting to recognize the look. For starters, a man had to be tall, dark, well built, and handsome.

And this guy fit the bill all right. He had it all. In spades.

The body without a spare ounce of weight, packed with enough muscle to make him a shirtless heartthrob, but not *über*-muscled, so he looked like a steroid freak. His kind of physique, slender, perfectly proportioned, and with almost nonexistent hips, would ensure he looked equally edible dressed as undressed.

His face was super-photogenic and with all the daytime soap and male model prerequisites: square chin, ruthless cheekbones, and killer eyes one shade paler than cobalt blue.

In fact, although Tracey drew a blank trying to place the face with a show, she could swear his voice sounded familiar. She'd heard it before.

On daytime soaps, she thought. *Yep. No doubt about it. Had to be.*

"I was talking about the sculpture," he was saying.

Tracey turned around and stared at it blankly. What only moments ago had seemed an almost living, breathing entity had been usurped by the real thing and been relegated back to the pantheon of lifeless chunks of stone.

"Y . . . yes?" she said, stretching out the word in an effort to cover her flustered state, as well as to keep him talking so that she might get an idea of what she had missed.

He tilted his head sideways and frowned at the statue, hands clasped behind his back. "It's strange about antiquities, don't you think?"

She frowned also, but because she had absolutely no idea of what he was getting at.

He caught her mystified expression right away and said, "Go to any museum or gallery or auction. It's invariably like this. Say you've got an authentic ancient Greek or Roman head, right?"

She nodded, still wondering where this was headed.

"Well, chances are it's missing its nose. And if you've got a torso, you can nearly always count on its missing its arms, legs, and head."

He shook his own head sadly and added, with a sideways glance, "But males seem to be particularly vulnerable. Don't you agree?"

"Are they?" she said, for want of a better response. She was still too rattled by his sheer gorgeousness to think straight.

"I'll say. Take this particular torso as an example. As is usually the case, the genitals are missing. The genitals are always the first thing to go, or haven't you noticed?"

Tracey was thrown for a loop. "I . . . uh . . ." she stammered, then swallowed and raised her head. "Actually," she said, aware that her face had reddened to an even deeper shade, "I haven't given antiquities and . . . and imperiled male genitalia much thought."

"No reason why you should," the man said, with a raffish grin. "Hell of a conversational ice-breaker, though, huh?"

He extended a hand and flashed Hollywood-perfect teeth. "Mark Varney," he said warmly. "And you are obviously the talented Ms. Sullivan. We meet at long last."

Too late, Tracey realized why his voice had sounded so familiar. She'd heard it enough times. She took the proffered hand and, in her agitation, shook it heartily. "Nice to finally put a face to a voice," she managed.

"*And* a body?" he teased, in amusement.

"That too," she admitted, her ears tingling, unaware that she was still pumping his hand up and down. "Listen, about my silly reaction. I guess I expected someone—"

"Older?" Mark Varney supplied, his eyes dancing. "Stuffier? Paunchy? Balding?"

"Those also, yes." Tracey gave a nervous laugh. Then, conscious that she was still shaking his hand exuberantly like some automaton that hadn't been programmed to let go, she snatched her hand back. "The thing is, you always sounded so . . . well, so mature on the telephone," she said lamely.

I certainly couldn't see *what you looked like,* she thought. *And who could have imagined us meeting under these circumstances, with you wearing nothing but a scant square inches of bulge-revealing spandex?*

Who indeed?

Her eyes flicked between the marble torso and him. It was impossible not to compare the ideal of classical perfection with the challenging reality of Mark's impeccably defined musculature. Both of them perfect in their own ways.

Except for the genitalia, of course. Mark's are obviously very much intact. And impossible to miss in that skimpy—

The theatrical clearing of a throat startled them both, severing their attention from each other as instantly and rudely as a thunderclap.

Tracey turned around and stared.

Leaning against one of the open arches, and tapping her teeth with one earpiece of her tortoiseshell sunglasses, was none other than glamour personified.

Urania Vickers. In the flesh.

"Before we start off on the wrong foot," intoned the star, "let's get one thing straight. Hands off the boss's boyfriend. If you're a smart cookie, you'll never, but never, forget that."

Chapter Sixteen

Urania Vickers was a pro at making an Entrance.

Having announced her presence for maximum effect, she now slowly drifted to center stage. One hand casually twirling her glasses by an earpiece, the other extended in a regal parody of welcome. As though she expected her audience of two to drop to its knees and pepper her rings with kisses.

Or perhaps receive a benediction from her blaring ruby talons.

"Well, well, well," she purred playfully from between intensely red and glossy old-Hollywood-style lips that matched her nails and accentuated her slight, sexy overbite.

Urania's famous emerald eyes never once left Tracey's, and her every move was gracefully, dangerously feline, as if she were some superior species of cat stalking a very fancy feast but determined to draw out the pleasure.

"Now, let's see what we have here . . ."

The tapping of the earpiece of the glasses against gleaming enamel teeth was faintly audible. *Click. Click-click. Click.*

"Mmmm," she murmured, assessing Tracey with interest while walking a full circle around her. Enveloping Tracey not only with her overpowering presence, but in a fragrant cloud of Panthère de Cartier as well.

Tracey in turn appraised her appraiser just as intensely. Most likely even more so, since she had a personal stake in this.

The matter of her maternity.

Not that there was anything remotely maternal about Urania Vickers. A less motherly figure was impossible to imagine. The woman hardly looked the nurturing type. Clearly, every ounce of Urania Vickers's energy was expended upon herself.

She was all Star—with a capital S. A world-class celebrity ready to face any camera: movie, video, or paparazzi.

She never left her suite before being ready for a telephoto lens. Even when she didn't plan on going out or was not receiving visitors—and strapped for cash as she invariably was—she applied herself diligently to playing one role to the hilt: herself.

Urania Vickers, Superstar.

It was a part she had down pat.

A gossip columnist once summed up, "Urania Vickers is a star, but what she definitely is not is an actress."

Harsh criticism, perhaps, but right on the mark. Urania played the role of real-life glamourpuss better than she'd ever played any part on screen.

This afternoon was no exception. Fully costumed as if for a final take, she exuded glamour from head to toe. Her makeup positively glowed.

Granted, it took work and dedication. Most people had no idea how much and, as some insensitive souls invariably pointed out, the Urania Vickers look relied upon an extravagance of makeup. Yet these very same tongues would be hard put to deny that Urania Vickers did not look her age.

This, without the help of a plastic surgeon.

Urania's secret for looking youthful was simple. Tan as a nut all over, she was careful never to let the sun touch her face. Had never allowed its cruel and harmful rays to prematurely ruin her smooth complexion and turn her skin into leathery wrinkles.

That was the reason for wearing the giant platter of a straw hat, its crown wrapped with pink silk chiffon. The rest of her outfit was built around that all-important, sun-screening hat. Her phyllolike caftan, virtual drifts of flowing, layered, lighter-than-air silk printed in a riot of bold pinks, white, and black. Giant hoop earrings in Shocking Pink plastic. Scores of bangles on both wrists, pink plastic mixed with half a dozen of 18-karat gold. And on her feet, pink satin mules adorned with tufts of white marabou. Not from Frederick's of Hollywood, though. Manolo Blahnik—who else?

Beyond the clothes and makeup, however, what instantly struck Tracey was how Urania Vickers was at once larger than life, yet physically petite and more delicate than she would have expected. However, the dog-eat-dog worlds of film and television had left their mark, as evidenced by Urania's cold-eyed appraisal.

Tracey reminded herself what everyone knew: in Hollywood nice girls finished last. Also that, according to Maribel, Urania Vickers was known as the ultimate survivor.

Her initial appraisal over, the ultimate survivor turned her attention upon Mark.

"Scram, Prince Charming," she told him. "Us gals need to establish some ground rules."

Urania wafted supplely to Mark, looped her arms around his neck, and pressed her pelvis against his. Her voice dropped to a purr. "Don't look so glum, darling." She made a moue. "You know I'll deal with *you* later."

Her talons walked an itsy-bitsy spider up his neck, then ruffled his wet hair, creating a fashionably spiky do. Strong whiffs of sexual promise hung in the air.

Mark smiled at Urania, then extricated himself. As he turned to Tracey, his smile became rueful, almost apologetic. "I'll see you later?" he said cordially. "Perhaps at dinner?"

Tracey nodded. "Yes. Perhaps at dinner."

"Don't be so sure," Urania murmured, playfully smacking his behind. She watched possessively as he left the room, then sighed wistfully. "He's got awfully cute buns, don't you agree?"

Tracey thought it politic not to reply and only smiled.

Now, with Mark gone, Urania started to slip her sunglasses back on, but paused in midpoint to give Tracey a significant, over-the-rims look. "Don't forget, darling," she warned in a deceptively sweet tone, "he's forbidden fruit. We straight on that? Because if we are, we'll get along just fine."

Tracey nodded, but didn't reply. It was difficult not to feel intimidated and unsophisticated in the sleek, self-assured, and pampered presence of Urania Vickers. She was undeniably the star, that bright sun which reduced everyone around her to mere orbiting planets.

"Good! Now that we understand each other where Mark is concerned, let's enjoy what's left of the afternoon and get acquainted, shall we?"

She slipped an arm through Tracey's and started to lead her toward the silk-dressed arches and back out into the sun. "After all, we're going to be *working* together, darling."

There was a cough behind them, and Urania stopped and turned. Maria Stefanou was beckoning to her. "Just a moment, darling," Urania said to Tracey. She airily glided to Maria Stefanou's side and listened as Maria whispered into her ear.

Tracey averted her gaze from them so as not to appear nosy.

"Oh, dear," Urania exclaimed, sweeping back over to Tracey. "You must be exhausted from your journey, darling. Why don't you go get settled and freshen up, then join me at the pool later." She paused and smiled. "In an hour sharp."

"Fine," Tracey said.

"Just go with Maria," Urania said, dismissing her and disappearing outside.

"There are several guest suites, but as you shall be living here for several months, Madame thought you would prefer privacy . . . both for your sake as well as hers. I am to let you have the windmill."

Three levels up, and near the street entrance, Tracey remembered, which suited her just fine. As a matter of fact, given the choice—so long as it had the rudimentary comforts—it was what she herself would have chosen. And for precisely the same reason—privacy.

Not for Urania Vickers's, though. But my own.

"Now. If you will follow me," Mrs. Stefanou said. Tracey made to pick up her carry-ons, which Stavros had set on the floor.

"You may leave those," Mrs. Stefanou replied. "Stavros shall be bringing them up shortly."

"In that case, I'll only take my laptop case," Tracey said quickly, swooping it up by its handle. She added apologetically: "Silly, isn't it? It's not that I distrust anyone. I just feel better if I don't let it out of my sight."

Mrs. Stefanou lifted one eyebrow and shrugged. "As you wish," she said coldly.

Without further ado, she briskly led the way. Not back out to the terrace and up the steep, sun-drenched flights of steps as Tracey had expected. Instead, Mrs. Stefanou headed past Warhol's *Nine Uranias* and into the recesses of the alcove to the right.

Tracey reluctantly followed. If truth be told, she would rather have taken the outdoor route. Back here, there was no mistaking they were in a cave. Tracey had never been a spelunker. She did not particularly care to become one now.

"Please be careful," Mrs. Stefanou said. "The steps are uneven and slippery."

With that warning, she hit the light switch. Tracey could scarcely believe it. The rectangle glowed with light from within. Diagonal tunneling on the part of busy human ants had resulted in a steep, and very narrow, indoor staircase chiseled out of solid rock, which had then been cemented, stuccoed, and whitewashed.

"Watch your elbows."

And they climbed the steps, Mrs. Stefanou in the lead.

Elbows, hell! Tracey cursed silently, belatedly wishing she had let the laptop be. The space was so narrow that she had to transfer her shoulder bag to her hands, holding both it and the laptop awkwardly out in front of her, and lugging them thus up, one step at a time.

The lights, she now noticed, were set in shallow recesses along the walls. They were cast bronze copies of oil lamps from antiquity, with chandelier bulbs screwed into the spot where the flames would have been.

The air was moist and dank and humid; the shadows thrown, stark and mysterious and menacing. She wasn't sure which was the stronger feeling. Fascination? Or unease?

Mrs. Stefanou drew Tracey's attention to the candles in tin holders and small white plastic boxes containing matches, which occupied the same recesses as the electric lamps. She picked up one of the little boxes, shook it, and put it back down. "Waterproof," she pronounced. "For when the electricity, it go out. These flashlights also." She gestured to them.

"Does it?" Tracey inquired, with more than mild alarm. "Fail? Often?"

"Often enough for us to be well prepared," came the reply.

Fifteen steps up, the claustrophobic stairs widened into a minor kind of landing. Mrs. Stefanou had already reached it, and she waited there, looking expressionlessly down, hands folded in front of her. She turned her head and nodded at the wooden door. "That leads to Madame's suite as well as to the second master suite. I would not advise setting foot in Madame's suite unless Madame specifically invites you."

Tracey flushed. That went without saying. She hardly needed to be lectured on etiquette. However, she squelched a smart retort. "I understand completely," she said quietly.

Mrs. Stefanou nodded. "Very well. Shall we continue up, then?"

Again, a narrow, all-but-coffin-width squeeze. And again, Tracey making tedious, uncomfortable progress on her very own Via Dolorosa. At last she reached the top. A much larger landing, obviously an anteroom, it had a floor of white marble squares and four doors, one in each wall. One of them was a set of double doors leading outside: it was next to an open window through which blazing sunshine poured.

After the tunnel-like stairs and the electric lamps, the daylight was blinding. It was all Tracey could do not to throw her forearm protectively up in front of her face. The open window let in burning heat that was stifling.

However, Mrs. Stefanou, despite her black suit, did not appear to suffer in the slightest. She was cool and composed, without a hair out of place or the slightest sign of perspiration.

"This, of course, leads outside," she said, throwing open both double doors to a terrace and the picture-postcard view of the caldera. "And this door"—she crossed several squares of marble purposefully and climbed up a shallow rise of four white marble steps—"is your study."

She opened the door and stood there, arm outstretched to hold the door wide so that Tracey could see past her inside.

Tracey's first sensation was of an icy blast from an air conditioner, which almost made her purr with pleasure. The second was that this room was fairly large, low-ceilinged but bright, and altogether not unpleasant. It was readily apparent that it had been set up as a serious workroom only recently.

For my arrival, she thought, not without a trace of pride.

"May I?" Tracey inquired. She was making little pointy motions with her index finger, indicating the interior of the room.

Mrs. Stefanou gave that implacable shrug which Tracey would learn was so integral a part of the woman. "Be my guest."

Tracey went into the study past Mrs. Stefanou, who continued to wait outside. *Here,* she thought, *is where I'm to spend most of my waking hours for the next few months.*

She was instantly drawn toward a door with two windows that had traditional Greek blue-and-white-striped curtains drawn across them. She opened the door a crack and peered out.

What she saw made her emit a little squeak of delight. There was a *krokalia*-paved terrace, with a cerulean-painted bistro set: a tiny round table and two slat-seated café chairs shaded by a buff market umbrella and, for worshiping the sun, a folding wood and buff canvas sling lounge facing the caldera. Plus there was an unparalleled bonus, a view down to the two lower terraces with their bougainvillea-draped pergolas, the pool suspended above the cal-dera and, above all, from left to right and straight ahead, that million-dollar panorama.

An office with a view, Tracey thought. Except this was more than just a view. *It's what people travel thousands of miles to see.*

Shutting the outside door, Tracey proceeded to make a slow circumference of the room. Not much International Style here. Simply your comfortable basics.

Several old kitchen tables had been pushed together in the middle of the room to create one giant work surface. Where Tracey presumed she was to sit and work were two modern ergonomic office chairs.

She kept moving. The computer, she noticed with approval, was a recent IBM Aptiva; the printer, a Hewlett-Packard DeskJet. *So far, so good.* A check of the keyboard confirmed that no, the letters were *not* Greek, but were indeed of the Roman alphabet.

"The computer," Mrs. Stefanou said from the sidelines, "has access to the Internet. It would be appreciated if you used it for business purposes only. For obvious reasons, we guard our e-mail address jealously."

Tracey nodded. "I won't forget."

Taking an inventory of the individual items on the tables which composed the "desk," Tracey discovered everything she might require. A telephone. The traditional tools of the writer's trade: reams of white paper, a stack of yellow legal pads, beautifully bound blank Italian notebooks in graduated sizes, all with different marbleized covers.

And, in what looked alarmingly like genuine antiquities: ballpoint pens in an Attic *oinochoe*, a small terracotta jug formed by a three-dimensional woman's head with painted features; a couple of freshly sharpened pencils stood in a *lekythos* with a delicately painted, winged lyre player; common, multicolored paper clips in a green glazed *skyphos* cup.

"Please. Tell me that those . . . well, that they don't happen to be the real thing," Tracey ventured, her index finger making vague circles in the direction of the items in question.

Mrs. Stefanou gave her a surprised look. "But of course they are," she said in a voice that sounded astounded Tracey should even ask. "And why should they not be? The *oinochoe* and the *lekythos* date to 5,000 B.C."

Holy Hannah Yarby! thought Tracey. *What if one of these artifacts should accidently get broken?* It wasn't as if she could run out to the nearest Staples and replace it. *Good heavens, whatever happened to the good old plastic pencil cup—or any old jelly jar?*

Off to the side on two wooden tray tables, the kind normally used for drinks, she saw three separate stacks of paper. Each had a smooth roundish gray stone atop it as a paperweight.

A quick thumb through the most worn stack proved it to be a much-marked copy of Urania's manuscript.

A second stack of identical height seemed a cleaner, newly printed copy of the first, perhaps with changes and additions already made.

The third, and by far the shortest pile, though still quite hefty, was on letterhead. A quick glance confirmed that it apparently consisted of editorial notes. Lots of notes.

"Miss Sullivan? Would you like to see your rooms now?"

Tracey nodded.

They walked up a last set of steps. The windmill could have been any windmill on any of a hundred Greek isles, whitewashed and thatch-roofed. Tracey knew that most people would give their eyeteeth for the opportunity to be afforded such splendidly unique accommodations. Yet as she stood inside the door, acrophobia struck in full force. So far, especially considering the verticality of this island, she had been remarkably unaffected by her fear of heights. But this windmill dredged up all her most deeply rooted anxieties.

Doing the best to hide her fears, she leaned her head almost straight back and looked directly upward. It was a mistake. She realized that the moment a shudder swept through her. It was impossible to shake the sensation that she was standing on the bottom of a twenty-foot-wide pasta pot, albeit one of soaring whitewashed stone instead of aluminum, and inset with small rectangular windows at various diagonal heights. A flight of wooden stairs jutted out from the masonry, *without any protective railing or banisters whatsoever,* and circled the perimeter walls in a single fluid spiral as they curved diagonally up those rounded walls to a loft, which looked like a pie from which a perfect slice had been cut to make a landing for the stairs.

Past that wedge, the rest of the windmill was visible, rising beyond the loft, higher and higher, until it reached a shallow-pitched cone of a spoked timber roof.

Tracey knew there was no way on earth she would ever be able to go up there. Bad enough if the stairs had banisters and railings. But steps simply jutting out of the walls like that? With nothing to hold on to?

"I trust everything is in order?" Mrs. Stefanou inquired.

Startled, Tracey stopped staring up and turned around with a jerk. She had been so preoccupied with her phobia that she had completely forgotten that she wasn't alone. *No,* she wanted to say. *Everything is not in order.*

Prescience told her that if she let her cowardice show, Mrs. Stefanou was likely to use it to intimidate her in the future. She wouldn't put anything past that cold fish.

"Oh. It . . . it's certainly unique," Tracey managed to croak, hoping she did an adequate job of hiding her dread. "I've never seen anything like it."

"Yes, it is unique, is it not?" Mrs. Stefanou agreed.

But from her unsympathetic expression and the calculating look in those dark eyes topped with lids outlined like cedillas, Tracey had the uncomfortable impression that the woman had already latched on to her greatest, most secret fear.

"Now let me show you where everything is," Mrs. Stefanou said brusquely. "The sleeping area is, of course, upstairs. So is an armoire and a chest. I believe Stavros has already carried the large pieces of your luggage up the stairs."

Tracey nodded dumbly, thinking: *Oh, God, please! What-*

ever you do, don't let Mrs. Stefanou try to get me up those stairs.

"Iliki shall be by shortly," Mrs. Stefanou continued. "She is one of the maids, and shall unpack your things and put them away."

"She doesn't need to do that," Tracey protested. "I've always done my own packing and unpacking."

Then, alerted by Mrs. Stefanou's raised eyebrows, she demurred. "I . . . I'm afraid I'm not used to such fancy treatment," she added awkwardly.

"Nonetheless, there are certain standards we must uphold. Yes? Also, it is one of Iliki's duties." Mrs. Stefanou's lips seemed to hold a suggestion of a smile touched with a hint of scorn. An indication, perhaps, that Tracey wasn't of the usual caliber of visitors?

But I'm not a visitor, Tracey reminded herself. *I've come here to work. I'm staff.*

Then came the dreaded words. "I suppose you would like to see the upstairs now."

A sharp pain lanced Tracey's belly and she felt an asphyxiating contraction in her throat. Oh, dear God—

And then came a sudden flash of divine inspiration.

"Upstairs," she murmured, in a tone she hoped would be construed as a reluctance to make waves. "Hmmm. Yes, well, that does present a slight problem."

"Oh?" Mrs. Stefanou had her hands folded in front of her, obviously her customary stance. "And what might that be?"

"I do hope you won't tell anyone. It's so silly, really. But I have a tendency to sleepwalk."

"Yes?"

Tracey wasn't sure whether or not the woman understood. "I sometimes get up at night and walk around," she explained. "Without waking up."

"You do this in your sleep? Extraordinary."

"Actually, it's rather . . . unnerving. And here, with those steps, combined with this stone floor . . ." She sighed. "I fear I don't dare sleep upstairs. If I should sleepwalk and somehow have an accident, I wouldn't want Ms. Vickers to be held liable . . ."

"How remarkable. But yes. I do see your point. In that case, we must change your accommodations."

"Oh, no," Tracey cried. "I can't trouble you to do that. I love this windmill," she continued, hoping she wasn't laying it on too thick. "I've never had the opportunity to stay in one before."

"Yes?" Mrs. Stefanou did not look entirely convinced.

"So I'll sleep down here, on one of these mattresses."

That announcement earned her a look of outright disdain. "But those are for lounging and sitting. See how narrow they are? That is because those are not made for sleeping. Surely you must have a proper bed."

Tracey gently but determinedly overrode her. "But Mrs. Stefanou, where I come from, these *are* proper beds. They're like my bed in the apartment I shared with other university students. I'm perfectly happy, really, I am."

Mrs. Stefanou looked put out. Clearly it wasn't often that she was forced to concede.

"Very well," she declared. "If you insist."

Alone at last.

Mrs. Stefanou had gone—praise all ancient gods. Stavros and another man had carried down the armoire. Without needing to be told where to put it, Stavros instinctively decided to place it where Iliki, the maid, had made a space by removing one mattress and piling it atop another, thereby making a fine, double-cushioned bed.

Tracey was delighted by the armoire, the paneled double doors opening to twice as much hanging space as required. As a bonus, there were two deep drawers on the bottom, and it stood on bun-shaped feet and had thick decorative crown molding around the top.

Tracey tipped the men five euros each—around five dollars. At first the men politely refused, but she gently insisted. Finally, after glancing over his shoulder at the open double doors to make sure they weren't being watched, Stavros swiftly palmed his, and the other man did the same.

"Efcharistó," they said in unison, and Tracey saw them out.

"Efcharistó," she said from the threshold, earning approving looks.

Shutting the doors behind them, Tracey decided to get set up.

She swung her locked laptop case onto one of the couch-like mattresses and fiddled with the combination lock. Pressed two little knobs under the handle.

Click! The locking mechanism popped and the lock hinges flipped open. She lifted the lid.

Starting at the top, she started emptying the contents.

When she reached her father's photograph, she took it out with reverence, unwrapped it from the protective tissue with which she'd packed it, and held the pewter frame in both hands, staring lovingly into his face. She had to smile.

By God, Dad, but you were a handsome devil. It's a wonder you didn't marry again. But of course, he wouldn't have. *You had me, the chain around your neck, to consider. You didn't want to dilute your love for your selfish little girl by having to share it with anyone else. You refused to traumatize me by bringing another woman into your life.*

She put the photograph aside and picked up the manila envelope which contained the photocopies of the official documents she'd brought. Her proof, as it were.

Then she lifted out the scrapbook filled with photographs which, hopefully, backed up her suspicions and proved who she was or, if the case so happened to be, perhaps proved who she was not.

Gathering up all these precious items, Tracey looked about for someplace to put them, a place where they couldn't easily be found. She paced the circular room, knowing she would rest easier if she knew these items of proof were safely tucked away somewhere. Under a mattress? Inside the carved chest with the embroidered cloth on top? Beneath folded clothes in one of the armoire drawers?

The link came to her instantly. The armoire Stavros had brought! It was too tall to see anything placed on top, and besides, the high crown molding functioned as a protective wall. Moreover, the armoire had, by happy coincidence, been placed so that no one going up the stairs was likely to see the top of it.

Grabbing a ladder-back chair, she carried it over to the armoire. Even from the height she'd gained from the chair, she couldn't see over the crown molding. Good. However, she could reach above its lip with one hand and feel behind it with her fingertips.

She transferred her treasures, one by one, to the top of the armoire. The picture of her father came last, and she kissed the smooth cool glass before depositing it on top.

It suddenly occurred to her that she should tuck away the disk with a copy of her manuscript on it. Just in case. In case of what, she wasn't certain, but she decided that she would err on the side of caution. She retrieved the disk from her laptop, and placed it atop the armoire with her other treasures.

As she climbed off the chair, she happened to glance up at the opposite wall and out one of the windows. Her postage stamp view was of nearby buff-colored stucco inset with a small arched window covered in blue-painted iron scrollwork.

She remembered the building quite clearly. The "tower," as she thought of it, adjoining the white wall which enclosed Urania Vickers's compound. The building had caught her eye on her way in because, despite its determinedly cheerful, geranium-filled window boxes, it nevertheless gave off a forbidding, almost prison-like air. Probably because it had so few, small, and well-protected windows.

But that was not what attracted her attention now.

She could see a pale face behind the wrought iron scrolls, and two hands gripping the ironwork. The window was too far away, and the light wrong, for her to make out the person's features. Whether it was a man, woman, or child was impossible to tell.

She glanced at the top of the armoire, then out through the window, but the face was gone. Or . . . might she have imagined it? Maybe it had never been there to begin with? Who could tell? It could have been a trick of light and shadows. Given how jet-lagged her eyes were, they could have played tricks on her.

She climbed down from the chair and carried it back across the room to the table where it had originally been. Snapped her laptop case shut and placed it on the floor beside the table. Took off her clothes.

Now then. Some freshening up was definitely called for. Hadn't Mrs. Stefanou mentioned something about coming by for her later?

Into the bathroom she padded on bare feet, where the shower beckoned.

She quickly showered, remembering the restrictions on water, and padded out into the main part of the tower.

She opened a suitcase and began grabbing clothes out of it. She pulled on a pair of lightweight men's gray suit trousers, which were purposely on the slightly baggy side and loose around the waist. Then she buttoned the lower front of the long-sleeved white shirt she'd slipped into, tucked the shirttails into the trousers, zipped the fly, buttoned the waist, and folded up the starched shirt cuffs several times. She wriggled into a pair of pointy-toed white patent-leather pumps and tucked a white clutch purse, based on a biker's wallet, into the waistband in the front of the pants and attached the clasp at the end of the gold-tone chain to the first belt loop.

Tracey had no idea what was deemed acceptable around here, and the best she could do was use her fashion judgment and wing it.

There came another series of sharp raps, followed by a muffled voice calling from outside. "Miss Sullivan?"

Damn the woman! She probably was arriving on the dot of the hour Tracey had been given. Makeup would have to wait. In the meantime, Tracey ran her hands through her hair and rushed to the double doors. Unlocking one side, she unthinkingly pulled it wide and stared head-on into the blazing sun.

"Whoa!" she said, averting her eyes, but not quickly enough. Then, making a visor of her hand, she blinked to clear the corona of light from in front of her vision and saw Mrs. Stefanou standing on the other side of the door, the sun right above her, looking up at Tracey, every brass-colored hair in place.

"Madame is waiting."

"Just give me one second and I'll be right with you. Oh. Don't just stand there. Please, come in."

Leaving the door open, Tracey hurried into the bathroom and flipped on the lights and leaned closely into the mirror. Half-blinded though she might still be, she wasn't blind enough not to notice that her makeup could definitely use some freshening up. Unfortunately, that took time, a luxury she could ill afford.

As an alternative, Tracey went the opposite route. Soaked a washcloth and scrubbed her face completely clear of any remains of everything—base, rouge, lip gloss, you-name-it. Daubed it dry.

"Mmmm," she murmured, looking this way and that. The result was rather pleasing, even if she said so herself. She gave the impression of being youthful, earnest, and having energy to spare.

Next, she wet her hair and ran her hands back through it, plastering it down and thrusting it behind her ears.

There. *Finito.*

Though in a rush, she lingered in front of the mirror for a critical last-minute inspection. Her reflection confirmed that she was perhaps rather unorthodoxly dressed but had undeniable chic. The man-tailored trousers and slim shirt actually accentuated her femininity instead of subtracting from it, while at the same time they permitted her to project both an innate sensuality and an authoritative get-to-work attitude.

Most important, she could not be accused of trying to out-glamour the star. She knew better than to even try. Striding back out, she felt how she looked: a hundredfold more confident.

Even Mrs. Stefanou had to rein in her usual expression of dour disapproval. Perhaps she had never confronted this particular kind of élan and didn't know what to make of it.

Mrs. Stefanou led the way. This time they used neither the outdoor steps nor the tunnels of indoor stairs. This altogether different route took them along a series of linked terraces at the topmost level, all the way to the far north-western end of the property, where it abutted another building.

As they walked, Mrs. Stefanou took the opportunity to fill Tracey in on the "traditions of the household," as she referred to the rules and regulations Tracey was expected to obey.

"First, Madame is a star of international renown. As such, there are endless problems with the paparazzi, the tabloids, bothersome fans, even dangerous . . . I forget the word the police use . . . crazy people."

"Stalkers, you mean?" Tracey supplied helpfully.

"Exactly. But perhaps worst of all, some former guests and staff have used their cameras to enrich themselves at Madame's expense. Since then, no one is permitted to take any photographs on these premises."

She gave Tracey a stern, significant look.

"Second. Ask permission before making any long-distance telephone calls. And never, under any circumstances, give this number out. To anyone—for any reason. That is understood, yes?"

Tracey bobbed her head again. *Do I need a pass to go to the bathroom, too?* she wondered.

"Three, you must keep track of this." She handed Tracey what looked like a blank white credit card with a magnetic strip on the back.

"It is your key to the gate, like in a hotel. It is electronic. You have used before? Yes?"

"Only in hotels."

"Yes. But house, gate . . . key is key."

Tracey slipped the white biker's wallet out of her waist, unsnapped it, and slid the card into a zippered pocket inside. Then she zipped up and snapped the wallet shut and tucked it jauntily back into her waistband.

"If you need anything, summon help by using the telephone system. Zero and two are my number. Stavros is zero and three. Iliki is zero and four. Madame, of course, is zero and one."

"That should be easy enough to remember."

Mrs. Stefanou motioned with her hand and they continued on their way across the terraces. A few yards before reaching the wall separating Urania's property from the one next door, they came to two double switchbacks of "flying" steps—narrow concrete staircases with low stuccoed walls. These led down to the two lower levels.

While descending, Tracey now and again caught glimpses across the wall of a two-level villa built directly behind and below the "street-level" building next door. Though constructed in the vernacular style, with white walls and domed roofs, it had modern sliding glass doors and terraces of white Dionysian marble as well as formal balustrades rather than wooden railings or low stuccoed walls.

"Whose is that?" she asked, out of general curiosity.

"Some English gentle—" Mrs. Stefanou's expression never changed, but the reproof was evident in her tight voice. "Well, shall we say, some English . . . *man*," she said, effectively putting an end to the subject.

Looking in the opposite direction, across the expanse of Urania's compound, Tracey suddenly noticed that the dividing wall at the other end of the property was connected to that of the buff-colored tower. The very same tower in whose window she had seen the ghostly face. Or thought she had.

The cerulean paint on a wooden door set into the whitewashed wall was a dead giveaway; it had to be part of the compound.

"And over there?" she asked, gesturing. "Who lives in that tower? And why does it have such tiny windows? And so few of them?"

"In many places, curiosity is considered an asset," Maria Stefanou lectured primly. "However, here on Santorini, where we live atop and beside each other, we prize our privacy and ask few questions. Besides, that place is of no consequence. Nor are its inhabitants."

But Tracey was too intrigued by the buff-colored tower, particularly since she'd noticed the door connecting it with Urania Vickers's compound, to let the matter drop. *If the neighbor is of no consequence, then why are the properties still connected?* she asked herself. Perhaps, once upon a time, it had been a single parcel of land which had since been split up. But if that's the case, why hadn't that doorway been filled in? Why was that door still there?

"But who lives there?" she insisted.

"I suppose somebody uses it every now and then," Mrs. Stefanou replied vaguely. "Mostly it is used for storage. I believe even Madame has boxes and excess furnishings stored there."

She stopped midway down the second switchback and reached into the side pocket of her black jacket. Producing a tiny black pager, she said, "This also is for you."

Tracey took the pager and frowned down at it.

"Whether you are within these walls, or you should find the time to explore the island, or perhaps do some shopping," Mrs. Stefanou said severely, "make certain you carry this on your person at all times. I am sorry, but these are Madame's orders. We must all carry one, even me. You see?"

She held open one side of her polyester jacket to display the pager clipped to her skirt.

Tracey nodded and attached the pager to the waistband of her trousers.

Then on they went, at a quicker pace, to the bottom level and its vast *krokalia*-paved terrace. Approaching from this angle, only the far half of the swimming pool was visible. At the bottom Mrs. Stefanou pointed. Urania waited.

Chapter Seventeen

By the pool.

In Sunbrella shade.

Urania was on one cushioned lounge, Tracey on the one beside it. Both chaises were in the exact same semi-upright position and lined up with military precision. Little slide-out trays built into the sides of both lounges were pulled out, Tracey's on the left, Urania's on the right. Sweating glasses made dark wet rings on the silver-weathered teak.

Tracey was having bottled water with ice. Urania had first asked Iliki for a Campari with champagne, but decided it was too early. "Make that a Campari and soda," she'd said, then changed her mind again and was now sipping a *café fredo* from a tall glass with a straw.

Urania picked up a vermeil cigarette case from the tray of her lounge, clicked it open, selected a thin long cigarillo, and snapped the case shut. The small sounds seemed amplified in the otherwise serene hush. Then something clicked: a brushed vermeil lighter.

Languidly Urania exhaled a stream of smoke. Tracey fought to keep from wrinkling her nose. Despite designer tobacco and designer flame—Nat Sherman for the former, Cartier for the latter—the smell of cigarlike smoke tainted the pristine air like a stain.

Urania turned her head sideways on the cushion and eyed Tracey through dark lenses. "Mark puts great stock in you. From what he says, you're awfully talented."

Tracey, alert for any cues as to whether she was expected to respond, decided this was not one of those times. Urania had apparently cast her in the passive role of audience rather than fellow conversationalist. Nonetheless, being only human, Tracey felt the sunny glow of praise warming her insides.

"Shall I be frank?" Smoke trailed from Urania's nostrils.

Tracey was momentarily thrown. "Er, of course," she said, thinking, *What else can I say?*

"Well, you're not exactly a knockout. That's a point in your favor, at least where I'm concerned. I've never been the type to invite the fox into the henhouse." Glossy lips drew on the cigarillo, and acrid smoke hung in the windless air. "Guess you've noticed that, darling. Hmmm?"

Tracey was stunned into silence. She couldn't believe what she was hearing.

"To give credit where it's due, sure, you've got a certain sense of style. And you're attractive enough in a homey sort of way. That, incidently, is another point in your favor."

Urania flicked an ash into an ashtray, faced forward, and gazed off into the distance, past the rimless pool toward the caldera.

"See that little island way out in the middle of the caldera?"

Urania was pointing with her cigarette hand, unintentionally sketching smoke loops in the air. Tracey looked. "Yes."

"That's Nea Kameni, an honest-to-goodness live volcano. Complete with steam and sulphur and hot springs. You can take a boat out there, and they let you swim at a certain spot. You can actually feel the water temperature rise the closer in you get. Meanwhile, even as it boils and bubbles out there, here we are. Believing we're invulnerable. Giving fate the finger, despite knowing full well it could erupt at any given moment."

From where Tracey was sitting, Nea Kameni looked the very essence of calm.

"So . . ."

Urania's voice became soft, but she was sitting up straighter, her head turned in Tracey's direction once more, the famous emerald eyes glowing from behind her dark glasses. Her attention was entirely focused upon Tracey's reaction. Whether toying with her, or testing her for weak spots, only Urania knew.

"What do you think about that, darling? Does living on the edge, constantly at Mother Nature's mercy, make you nervous? Or does it excite something deep down inside you? Tell me."

That's easy enough, Tracey thought.

Smiling slightly, she put her tumbler down and said, "I'm pretty well acquainted with the whims of Mother Nature. Don't forget, I'm from Miami. That's smack dab in the middle of Hurricane Alley."

"Ah, of course," Urania replied, playing it a mite dramatically. "How could I forget? Mark did say you were from Miami. Well. I'd say that gives us something in common . . . the both of us living in disaster-prone areas, I mean."

"Yes, I suppose it does."

"Were they awful?"

"What? The hurricanes?"

Urania nodded.

"Actually, I was a lot less scared than I should have been. In retrospect, I can thank my father for that. He was very practical in times of uncertainty."

Except when it came to dealing with Palm Coast Developers, Inc., Tracey thought grimly.

"What is it?" Urania asked. She looked genuinely concerned. "A shadow just crossed your face."

Tracey was startled by the woman's perceptiveness. "It did?"

"It most certainly did," Urania said flatly. "I'm always tuned in to these things. It's a professional hazard."

Tracey hadn't realized she was this easy to read. But then, Urania was an actress, she reminded herself. She would constantly have to be on the lookout for nuances and fleeting expressions, those subtle mood changes that most people would never notice, but that, in her case, would be filed away for future reference, and be resurrected when a performance required it.

"I was thinking about my father," Tracey murmured.

"Yes? . . ." Urania encouraged.

"He . . . he passed away recently. I think I have a long way to go before I'll ever get over it. I miss him terribly."

Urania's voice was soft. "It sounds as though the two of you were very close. You must have loved him very much."

"I did." Tracey smiled sadly. "I still do. Love doesn't stop with death, you know."

There was a moment of silence. Urania tapped a length of ash into the ashtray, drew on her cigarillo, and blew out smoke.

"And your mother?" she asked.

Tracey should have seen the question coming, but it still took her by surprise. Also, it was the perfect opening for asking Urania about any children *she* might have had. But now was not the time. It was much too soon, and would undoubtedly be construed as prying.

"I . . ." Tracey swallowed and stared out into space. "I never knew my mother," she said thickly.

"Oh. I'm sorry to hear that. I take it your father raised you?"

"That's right."

"Goodness! How remarkable—a single *father* household." Urania shook her head. "You know, I just don't get it. Things were certainly different when I was young . . . well, a bit younger," she quickly corrected herself. "Even divorces were rare when I was growing up. But now? It seems that in the States, single mothers have become epidemic. Someone told me recently that single-parent households now outnumber married ones. Can that be true?"

"I really couldn't say. I'm not up on the statistics."

"Aha!" Urania paused in the midst of drawing on her cigarillo, turned to Tracey, and pulled her sunglasses down her nose. "So you're one of those people who check before you leap."

"That's my newsroom training, I'm afraid."

"Newsroom?" Urania recoiled, as a vampire might from

a sunstruck cross. "Don't tell me you're a fucking reporter!"

"I'm not," Tracey reassured her. "But I majored in broadcast journalism, and I worked as an assistant at a Miami TV station. The one thing that has been drummed into me over and over, both at school and at the station, is no matter how good the source, you've got to check and double-check the facts."

Urania sniffed. She was slightly mollified, but past experience with the press had obviously soured her mood. Pushing her glasses back up her nose, she stared out at the caldera and exhaled a sigh along with a plume of smoke.

"Why is it I can't seem to get away from reporters? Huh? They're everywhere, behind every tree and under every bush. Christ, you wouldn't believe what I have to go through. The stories the tabloids concoct about me, or the lengths to which the paparazzi stoop just to get a blurry shot of me with a telephoto lens. The invasion of privacy is horrendous."

"It sounds horrible," Tracey commiserated.

"Horrible?" Urania gave an incensed laugh. "You can't begin to imagine just how horrible! Try this on for size—"

Urania didn't so much stub out her cigarillo as crush it to shreds.

"I used to have the loveliest house on Ibiza. Inland, not on the coast, so I'd be isolated and could enjoy some privacy."

"And did you?"

"Hell, no! Turns out one of those slimy, camera-toting bastards spent whole days and nights lurking in the ruins of a deserted farmhouse on a hill a few hundred yards away. And what did he do?" Urania expelled an angry breath. "Waited until I got undressed!"

Tracey's mouth dropped open. "He didn't!"

Urania raised her right hand. "I swear to God. He snapped topless pictures of me through the open window of my bedroom. My own dark bedroom, I might add—at night, Tracey!—using an infrared camera. What do you have to say about that?"

"But . . . but that's revolting," Tracey sputtered. "Illegal—"

"That," Urania said, smiling with humorless superiority, "is journalism for you."

"It's amazing you didn't kill him."

"I probably would have, if I'd known the little shit was there. But I went one better." Urania's lips curved into a smug scimitar of a smile. "I hit 'em where it really hurts. In the pocketbook. Sued the shit out of the tabloid that published those shots. You should have seen their team of lawyers. Oh, those stuffed shirts were just full of themselves. Talk about playing hardball. They wouldn't give an inch. Made a bigger production about First Amendment rights than the Founding Fathers. So I fought back the only way I could—by seducing the jury. Playing the injured party to the hilt. Well, the trial had barely begun when the owner of that rag sensed the way the wind was blowing and decided he'd better settle. Out of court, and fast."

"And did you?"

Urania expressed surprise. "You mean, you don't know?"

Would I have asked if I did? Tracey felt like retorting, but didn't.

Instead she said, "How could I know? Going to Columbia, burying my face in books, *and* holding down part-time jobs took up every ounce of energy I could muster. On top of which, I avoid those supermarket rags out of principle."

Urania's lips formed a pretty pout. "Aw, c'mon, Tracey. 'Fess up. Don't tell me you've never been tempted by the lurid headlines?"

"Well, of course it's difficult not to notice them if you've got to do your grocery shopping. They're plastered all over the checkout lines. But I'm proud to say I never bought one of those scandal sheets in my entire life."

To Tracey's surprise, Urania's reaction was the opposite of what she'd expected. The star looked downright disappointed.

Did I say something wrong? Tracey wondered.

After a moment, Urania brightened. As Tracey was discovering, it wasn't easy keeping up with the star's mercurial changes of mood. But these mood swings seemed of remarkably short duration, as her attention span was extremely brief.

Tracey crossed her fingers, hoping that this was the rule rather than the exception.

"You know something?" Urania said impulsively. "I'm going to share a secret with you, Tracey. Just between us girls. Okay, darling?"

She didn't wait for a reply.

"But first, you've got to promise not to tell anyone. Have I got your word?"

"I . . . well, I can keep my mouth shut, if that's what's worrying you."

"Okay, here goes. This is my deepest, darkest secret . . . my real weakness. Now, promise me you won't laugh."

Urania reached down and pulled a big, very low rectangular woven straw basket from underneath her chaise and lifted off the lid.

"Silly, isn't it, darling?" she confessed, with a girlish giggle. "But I'm positively addicted to them. I can't help myself."

The basket was full of tabloids. The very publications which Urania decried. All the familiar American supermarket suspects were represented: *The National Enquirer*, *The News of the World*, *The Star*, *The Globe*. Plus there was the crème de la crème of the gossip rags, the big European glossies—*Paris Match*, *Stern*, *OK*, *Hola*, *Hello!*

"I have them sent to me wherever I happen to be," Urania confided. "Would you believe I actually get infuriated if I'm not in one of them?" Her movie star red lips puckered into a childish pout. "In show business, you've got to keep a high profile, you know. Otherwise you disappear and—poof! You're yesterday's news. Buried and forgotten and unemployable."

Tabloids? Tracey couldn't get over it. *Too bad I can't tell Maribel,* was her first thought. It was all she herself could do not to squeal with delight. *A star who shamelessly thrives on tabloids! Awesome!*

There was something touching about Urania's revelation. This was the soft, human side of the tough-as-nails star, the side which the great unwashed public never saw.

Urania flipped the lid of the basket shut and shoved it back under the chaise. "There, darling," she said, lighting another cigarillo. "Now you've got the goods on me." She flicked Tracey an amused little sideways glance. "Are you surprised?"

Tracey swallowed. "Quite frankly, yes."

"Well, you know the old saying," Urania went on. " 'It doesn't matter what they print, so long as they spell your name right.' And you know something? It's true."

"But what about the lawsuit over the pictures? Did you settle?"

Urania looked exasperated. "Of course I settled. I'd have been a fool not to. You can drown yourself in legal bills if a trial drags on, and then, even if you win, there's no telling if and when you'll get restitution, what with the appeals process and all."

Urania's expression turned ugly and her voice became a hiss.

"Those creeps. Would you believe, at first they 'generously'—their term—offered me a consolation payment of twenty grand and a public apology? Can you imagine the nerve? I guess they decided they could get away with throwing me a measly twenty grand, and that I was so hard up I'd slobber all over it like a dog drooling over a bone. Hah! Let me tell you. I let them know where they could stick that offer—and in no uncertain terms."

"Then what happened?" Despite herself, Tracey was fascinated with the behind-the-scenes machinations.

"I had my attorneys demand a seven-figure sum. Of course, the lawyers representing that rag tried to play it cool and cover their shock, but you could tell they were apoplectic. When they finally got the message that we were dead serious, the dickering began. Back and forth, back and forth, both sides running up the billable hours. But I wasn't about to settle for a penny less than a quarter of a mil—after attorneys' fees, that is." She grinned like a shark. "And guess what?"

"You got it."

"You bet I did! Nearly double that amount. Had 'em by the ole *cojones*, as they say in Mexico. Then blew most of the proceeds buying this spread."

Urania indicated the compound with a grand sweep of

her hand. "What do you think of this place, Tracey? You likee?"

"Like it?" Tracey stared at her, barely able to put her reply into words. "What's not to like? It's magical. It's remote. It's drop-dead gorgeous. Why, this must be the most spectacular place in the world."

Urania was pleased by the enthusiastic reaction. "That's my opinion, too, and believe you me, I've been all over the place. India. Bali. Acapulco. Capri. The Riviera. You name it. For me, Santorini has them all beat."

"I don't doubt it. This is so—" Tracey's voice suddenly broke and she quickly looked away.

"Hey!" Urania eyed her with concern. "What is it? You were starting to say? . . ."

Tracey gave a sickly little smile. "I was going to say that it's incredibly romantic," she said tightly, "when the irony of the situation hit me."

"Oh, dear," Urania sighed, her eyes gleaming, her lips inhaling acrid smoke. "Why is it I sense the lyrics of a country-western song coming on?"

When Tracey didn't immediately reply, she added, "Had some recent man trouble, did we?"

Tracey unconsciously stared down at her ring finger, where the paler band of skin had yet to blend completely with the surrounding tan. She spread all five fingers wide. "Until very recently," she said slowly, as though addressing her hand, "I was engaged to be married."

"Are you saying this guy called it off?"

"No," Tracey replied. "I called it off."

"Why's that, darling?"

"My father owned some property that Brian's—my fiancé's—business desperately needed. I found out he was willing to marry me just to get hold of it, and he was even engaged to somebody else at the same time. Hideous, don't you think?"

"Hideous? I'd say it sucks. *Men!*" Urania shook her head. "You know, darling, I've been through at least a dozen engagements that didn't pan out, four marriages, three of which didn't pan out either and ended in divorce, and was widowed once. And what did I get out of it? I'll tell you what. Heartache and nasty publicity. Every single time. Without fail. Finally, I wised up and came to the conclusion that I was best off being single and playing the field."

Urania smoked in silence for a while, then she said, "Well, sort of single, anyway. But I'm done with marriage vows. The last time really did it. I don't know what got into me. It was one of those silly, spur-of-the-moment, 'Let's go to Vegas' kind of things, and we tied the knot in one of those horribly tacky wedding chapels. Vegas! I ask you! When the ring is from a pawnshop where some poor loser cashed it in, and the witness turns out to be, of all things, the most disgusting Elvis impersonator"—she laughed richly—"is it any surprise the marriage was doomed from the start?"

Tracey couldn't help but laugh along with her. She didn't know what it was about Urania Vickers, but it was impossible to dislike her. Particularly when she let down her guard. She reminded Tracey of the Wizard of Oz. Behind the elaborate facade and theatrics was just an ordinary person. A woman like any other, but one with an appealing, self-deprecating sense of humor.

"Getting back to you," Urania said. "I take it you were just as happy to leave Miami for a while?"

"The timing couldn't have been better," Tracey admitted. "First discovering my so-called fiancé was just using me for his own ends, then my father dying—" She blew out a deep breath and sniffed loudly. "Don't worry, I'm not going to break down or anything. I've pretty much come to terms with it. But the last thing I expected was to come here and find paradise."

Urania removed her sunglasses with slow deliberation and studied Tracey really hard for the first time.

"You know, you seem like a nice kid," she observed. "Smart. Well mannered. Good intentioned. Squeaky clean and with a sense of style yet. Tell you what. Let's forget what I said earlier. As long as you keep your mitts off Mark, what do you say we all enjoy a nice getting-to-know-each-other dinner together?"

Sipping her water, Tracey ignored Urania's scrutiny and stared out at the view. Dinner with Urania and her boy toy. *My agent.* It could be interesting, even educational. Or it might just as easily turn out to be filled with tension and all the wrong vibes. Urania had made it clear to whom Mark Varney belonged.

As if I'm out to encroach on her territory, Tracey thought. She didn't know whether to feel insulted, flattered, or amused. As if it mattered. She wasn't here to socialize or provide amusement or strike up friendships. She had a job to do, and a very limited time to do it in. Therefore, the simpler and more impersonal she kept their relationships, the better for everyone concerned.

"It's lovely of you to offer," Tracey said, "but I'm afraid I should take a rain check. I'm absolutely beat. What I need is a good long sleep. Don't forget, I have to be on my toes in the morning. Tomorrow's my first day of work."

Urania wasn't used to rejection, and didn't take it well. She put her glasses back on and sniffed haughtily. "Yes, of course." Her voice dripped ice. "You're absolutely right. I keep forgetting. You aren't here on vacation, are you? I'm paying you to help straighten out certain . . . well . . . editorial difficulties with my novel."

Realizing that Urania was miffed, Tracey said, "I didn't mean to sound rude—"

"I quite understand, darling. Now do be a good girl and run along. You need your rest. Like you said, tomorrow isn't just another day. It's your first *working* day."

Tracey stared at her. She was completely taken aback by the speed with which Urania could change moods. One moment she had you believing you were her new best friend; the next, she could freeze you out completely.

"Well, darling?" Urania was frowning. "Still here? What are you waiting for?" She clapped her hands, then made shooing gestures. "Go. Go!"

Tracey gathered up the remnants of her dignity, rose to her feet, and without another word left the terrace. She climbed the series of steep steps down which Stavros had led her earlier. Her face was red and stung with embarrassment and outrage as she returned to the windmill.

Talk about a first-class bitch! she thought. Hot, lukewarm, icy cold. That woman could switch moods as easily as she could spin the handles on a faucet.

Tracey thought of something else. *Maribel and I must have been dreaming. There's no way I could be related to that monster down by the pool.*

Nor did she have any desire to be.

And another thing. *Strange, but I didn't feel the slightest connection to her. There's no way she can be my mother. If she were, surely I'd have felt* something. . . .

Which was just as well. Tracey pitied anyone who had Urania for a mother. No one deserved such a fate. Not even her worst enemy. Well, maybe one person. Brian Rutherford Biggs III.

But no one else. Absolutely no one.

Chapter Eighteen

Miami, Florida

Seven o'clock was later than she usually got up, but Maribel Pinales wasn't relying upon a shrill alarm clock to suddenly jolt her awake. She much preferred this divinely slow and languorous method, which roused her with gentle sensations and allowed her to drift deliciously up from the dreamy depths without the least bit of urgency.

Really, she thought, her lips curving into a smile even before her eyes opened, *is there an alarm clock on earth which can compare with the succulent whorls traced by a lover's warm, moist tongue on first one nipple, and then the other? Especially nipples which were still swollen and slightly bruised from hours spent making love the night before, and so now received only the most tender ministrations?*

"Ahhhh . . ." She started to stretch and yawned blearily. The tongue, meanwhile, was now tracing a snail's trail down her flat belly, the muscles of which automatically twitched in response, and continued on to tease feathery spirals around her navel.

Slowly her eyes fluttered open. "Don't you ever get enough?" she mumbled happily, lying there lazily and staring up at the lacquered ceiling.

Ramón lifted his head long enough to say, "Is it my fault that you're such an irresistible sexpot?"

That made her burst out laughing, which brought her fully awake. "Ramón Felipe Escolano," she inquired, "did anyone ever tell you that you were full of *mierda*?"

"As a matter of fact," he said, "yes. You have. All the time."

"Hmmmm . . ." Maribel frowned thoughtfully up at the ceiling. *Have I?* she wondered. Then she smiled, pleased with herself.

"Why, yes," she acknowledged, "I suppose I have. But that's only because I care for you deeply, and therefore do my best to help keep your feet grounded in reality. You have it far too good, you know."

"I do?" His head popped up abruptly. "And just what," he demanded huffily, "is that supposed to mean?"

"Unh-unh. You don't have to stop what you're doing," she said. She shifted position on the California king, drawing in her legs and bending them, the better to splay her haunches and make her sex readily accessible.

"Right now," she added, "your tongue is much better suited to making love than conversation."

"Just why are you suddenly giving me such a hard time?"

"I thought *you're* supposed to give *me* a hard time," she corrected him smugly. "Just think of me as a . . . a vessel for your physical needs."

He almost, but not quite, gagged. "You are . . . my God . . . will you listen to yourself?" he sputtered. "Now who's full of *mierda*? Huh?"

She lifted her head from the pillow, leaned forward, and rested her elbows on her knees. "Well, Ray?" She eyed him narrowly. "Are you, or are you not, going to give me a hard time?"

There was no mistaking the challenge. And of course, he rose to the occasion.

"Sure," he said, and sighed in mock resignation. "Anything the vessel wants, the vessel gets."

"Now you're talking," she said sweetly.

He took a deep breath, admiring her luscious firm

breasts, dark strong thighs, and lasciviously inviting, exposed pink petals of her femininity. This was one of the things about Maribel which appealed to him so strongly. She didn't act coy or flutter her lashes like some uptight faux virgin. On the contrary. Maribel Pinales was straightforward when it came to sex, and wasn't afraid to show her enthusiasm for mattress athletics. She was one of the few women he'd ever met who called a spade a spade.

He knelt to get into position, his manhood rearin' and rarin' to go. But as he reached out to embrace her, Maribel balanced herself on one hand and, in a single fluid movement, lifted herself off the bed, tucked her legs balletically underneath her, and slithered smoothly sideways, just out of reach.

Instead of welcoming female flesh, Ray's arms, loins, and penis met air.

"Hey!" he exclaimed, in surprised dismay. "What the—"

Her voice was soft and husky. "Not so fast, *señor*."

His head snapped in her direction. "Maribel," he complained, "what in hell's come over you?"

Holding his gaze, she answered his question with a question of her own. "Tell me something, Ray. Since the very first day we met, have I ever once asked you for a favor?"

"Huh?" He blinked, suddenly confused. "Just what are you driving at, Maribel?" he asked, adding, "Please tell me you're not being a prick tease."

She said, "I'm not being a prick tease."

"Then what *is* it?"

Before continuing, she looked to make sure he was still hot and horny.

No problem there. *Good,* she thought. That was one thing about men you could usually count on, thank God.

"What it is, Ray," she said, stretching out lengthwise on her side. Reaching for his dangling testicles, she cupped them gently in her hand, as though weighing them.

Her touch had the desired effect.

His penis throbbed, like a heat-seeking missile searching for its target. He shut his eyes. Sucked in his breath between clenched teeth.

"What it is," she said again, gently tugging on his *cojones*, thus forcing him to move penitently toward her on his knees, "is that I have this friend. This very, very close friend."

"You mean, you're seeing someone else."

"Oh, for heaven's sake, Ray! Where *is* that mind of yours? In the gutter?"

"I guess so," he gasped hoarsely.

"Well then, get it out of there. I'm talking about my favorite girlfriend. We're like sisters. *Comprendes*?"

"Like sisters," he repeated, nodding his head rapidly, and just as rapidly closing the distance between his erection and her face.

"That's right. Like sisters. And don't forget it." Maribel tightened her grip on his balls, not enough to cause pain, but just enough to cause slight discomfort if he moved any closer.

"Anyway," she went on, "it just so happens that my friend has this problem."

"Yeah," he rasped. "Okay. We'll discuss it right after—"

"I'd prefer we discussed it right now," she cooed.

"Not fair!" he grunted.

"All's fair in sex and war," she misquoted. "Anyway, I don't mean discussing it in detail. But it is a legal problem, you see . . ."

As she spoke she fondled his heavy, pear-shaped scrotum.

". . . and I realize it's not your speciality, seeing that you're into estates and all, and she's neither ready to sing a harp solo, nor has a thing to leave to anybody. But I said to myself, Hey, Maribel. You know, with Ray being in the legal profession, he'll surely know *somebody* who can help, some lawyer or cop who maybe owes him a favor."

While he knelt there, as susceptible to Maribel's request as Adam to Eve's apple, she moved her head toward that organ in which, as any woman can attest, every man's brain really resides. Still caressing his testicles, she decided to provide some extra motivation by flicking her tongue around the enormous straining head of his sex.

Empires have been lost for less. As anticipated, his penis jerked and twitched mightily.

"Okay!" His voice was a tortured whisper. "You win. I'll help. I'll help!"

She glanced up at him, the tip of her tongue leisurely following a raised vein along the length of his shaft. "Deal?" she asked.

"Deal," she heard him breathe.

"And . . ." She paused as her tongue reached his nest of pubic hair "You're not going to try to wheedle out of it later on, are you?"

"No!" Clearly the man had succumbed completely.

She rewarded him by opening her mouth around the bulbous head of his penis, closing her lips firmly around it, and treating it to some especially strong and well-deserved suction. Still cupping his scrotum in one hand, she used the other to grip his straining shaft, massaging it in tandem with the movement of her lips.

As she worked on him, her mouth and hand picked up momentum. His penis seemed to have a life of its own, pulsating and straining in the warm wet cavern of her mouth.

She felt him tangle his hands in her thick glossy hair, sensed him bend his head impossibly low, felt the urgent kisses on the nape of her neck. His breathing was coming faster and faster. Then, feeling the heat threaten to rise from within, he quickly took her face in his hands and raised it. His body had gone absolutely still.

She uttered a cry as her mouth released his penis, and she stared at him in bewilderment. "Why did you make me stop?"

He waited a long moment, then let out a deep breath as the urgency subsided. "Because, my overeager little *puta*," he murmured, "I'll take it from here."

"Yes," she whispered. "Take me."

Still holding his gaze, she obligingly raised her hips to meet his. As he lowered himself into the lubricated petals of her rosebud, her eyes widened in a kind of wonder. He began lowering and raising himself until, by degrees, he filled her completely and they were joined as one, and the expression on her face underwent a transformation, became rapt with a primal kind of greed and possession which blazed like fire.

Now he began to thrust in earnestness and rode her with savage intention.

A sense of power such as she had never before felt suddenly took hold of her. This was not just any man. Not even just any man with killer looks. No, this was Ramón Felipe Escolano, first-rate attorney, pillar of the Anglo and Cuban communities, and adviser to the very rich and famous. A most eligible catch for any woman.

And for now, at least, he was hers.

"Oh . . . *Dios!* . . ." she gasped, raking her hands across his bare, perspiration-slicked back, feeling the torque and tension of each individual muscle, and marveling that such a thin, smooth veneer of skin could be wedded to such sheer brute strength.

If he felt her nails raising welts on his back, he either couldn't care less or was oblivious to them. On he plunged, his rhythm pounding and relentless.

Suddenly she tensed, her back arched clear off of the bed, and she cried out as agony and ecstasy merged. Her head thrashed back and forth on the pillow as mighty spasms seemed to shake the earth. One series of shudders after another jolted through her. She screamed.

Her screams only egged him on to thrust that much more furiously.

Now her fingers dug cruelly into his firm round buttocks, in an effort to press him as deep inside her as possible. She could feel his muscles contract and expand, clench and unclench, as he got caught up in the ever quickening pace of meeting her upward thrusts.

Harder and harder pumped his pelvis. Faster and faster. Harder and faster, and faster and harder, and—

"Argggh!" The scream rose from within the core of his being and tore, like an animal's howl, from his throat as the juices of life thundered up through his vitals.

Which set her off yet again. As the second wave of climax engulfed her, their combined cries and screams filled the room with an extraordinary harmony. Off-key musically, perhaps, but perfectly in synch.

It was her second orgasm of the morning, but by no means the last. And though it was his first orgasm since last night, he was by no means finished, either. In fact, he had barely gotten started. His cock, still buried in the wellspring of her femininity, hardly lost any tumescence before it was rock hard once again.

In no time at all, he was plunging exuberantly in and out of her, with even more savagery.

Finally, as they lay entwined together on the bed, their immediate passions spent, she waited for his lion to regain its roar. With a maniac like him, Round Three was, after all, perfectly possible. Most likely probable.

She lay there and smiled up at the ceiling. *Besides,* she thought, *a deal is a deal. You've got to give it your best shot if you expect the best in return.*

Not that she would have withheld her sexual favors if Ray hadn't been forthcoming about helping her with Tracey's problem. Even if he'd said, "No dice," Maribel would still have given him her all.

But that aside, she nevertheless had the distinct feeling that . . . well, not counting the sexual gymnastics of this morning, this was but the beginning of a beautiful thing—and the best was yet to come.

Chapter Nineteen

Santorini, Greece

Tracey slept for fourteen hours straight through. So deeply that Nea Kameni couldn't have woken her had it erupted. Yet when she finally woke up, she nearly jumped out of her skin.

Crash, bang!

The explosive noise brought Tracey from the depths of nourishing slumber to the verge of a heart attack. Jerking upright, she let out a cry and exclaimed, "What the hell?" while her eyes darted about wildly, seeking the cause of all this cacophony. After a moment, when her brain had time to kick in and absorb the evidence, it was obvious that she'd had two visitors while she'd been asleep.

The first—Iliki perhaps, or Mrs. Stefanou—had evidently let herself in sometime the previous evening without waking her. That much was clear from the wooden tray on a folding stand that now lay collapsed on the *krokalia* and rugs and that held the now dried-up remains of a dinner which had thoughtfully been left for her. Attesting to that fact were shattered pieces of beautifully patterned pottery, shards of glass, a broken bottle of table water, an unopened and intact split of white wine, a glittering array of crisp-fried sardines, thick slices of bread, some sort of mashed grayish-green matter, maroon-colored olives disseminated like an abandoned game of marbles, and a surprisingly intact piece of phyllo pastry with a variety of creamy fillings.

The second visitor, caught red-handed, had obviously been attracted by the victuals and stood there, its spine ridged and stiff from the unpleasant surprise of having the dinner tray collapse under it. The thief was a thin white cat with a black Rorschach test on its chest, black boots, and a bandit's mask around its large yellow eyes. It stared at Tracey, more to gauge her reaction than out of any feelings of guilt.

"And just who," Tracey inquired, using the indulgent tone reserved for children and animals, "might you be?"

Reading her gentle voice as that of a friend rather than a foe, the cat sat down, lifted one rear leg straight up in the air, and proceeded to lick itself in that delicate way cats have. Then it stood back up, stretched, sized Tracey up once more, and picked its way cautiously among the broken crockery and spilled food, pausing to devour several sardines in as many seconds. From the ravenous way it scarfed down the food, Tracey surmised the creature was more used to famine than feasts.

"Poor thing," she murmured. "Doesn't anybody feed you properly?"

Getting out of bed, she carefully picked her way barefoot around the mess and squatted down in front of the cat. A long-healed rent at the tip of one ear and several hairless scars along its sides attested to wounds suffered on the feline battlefields of Santorini.

Satiated, the cat licked its chops, purred, and began rubbing itself back and forth against her legs.

"Aw, you poor thing," she murmured, scratching it lightly between its ears. "Any suggestions about how we're going to explain this mess?"

"Psst!" hissed a voice just then, followed by a desperate whisper: "Miss!"

Tracey spun around, but did not see a soul.

"Miss!"

This time she pinpointed the direction from which the voice came, and she glanced up.

She sucked in her breath. He was a boy of ten or eleven, and he was about a third of the way up outside the windmill. From his red face and trembling hands, it was clear that clinging to the window ledge took every ounce of his strength.

"What in the name of—" Tracey began, then scolded, "Get down from there right this minute. Are you crazy? You're going to get yourself killed."

"I shall . . . knock on . . . door? Yes?" The boy sounded out of breath. "You let . . . me in?"

"For heaven's sake, yes," she said. "Of course I will."

"Please! Promise you . . . will not . . . let anyone . . . see Zeus. Okay?"

Zeus. *An appropriate name,* she thought. But her first order of business was getting the boy down.

"I promise," Tracey said. "But only," she amended sharply, "if you get down from there."

The boy grinned hugely. "Okeydokey," he said, and his little fingers let go. Tracey heard a thud. Shortly a series of sharp, urgent raps sounded on the double doors.

She ran into the vestibule and barely had one of the doors open before the boy wriggled in past her.

"What is it with—" she began.

"Ssssh!" The boy held an index finger to his lips and motioned for her to quickly shut the door behind him and lock it. His eyes were huge, frightened saucers.

Tracey was puzzled, but something about his sense of urgency rubbed off, and she did as requested. His first order of business was to zip barefoot into the windmill proper. Before Tracey could warn him to watch out for broken crockery and shattered glass, he was already in its midst. She watched as he bent over and gently scooped up the cat in his arms and held it against him. The creature relaxed and purred.

Tracey followed the boy and stood behind him. He was stroking the white fur and murmuring softly to the cat in Greek.

She tapped him on the shoulder.

The boy turned around and aimed those huge saucer eyes up at her.

"All right, young man," Tracey said. "I'd say you have some explaining to do."

Only now did she have the opportunity to take a good long look at him. He was a skinny little scamp, endearing in that urchin kind of way. He had large dark brown eyes and the thin, bony arms and spindly legs and scraped knees and elbows of most other boys his age. However, he was neither malnourished nor suffering from neglect.

Quite the opposite. His complexion was a healthy olive, his hair a curly, unruly black mop, and his features sharp, well defined, and intelligent. Someone had seen to it that he was neatly dressed. He wore a freshly laundered, striped-knit T-shirt with khaki shorts, and his relatively clean feet were evidence that he'd only recently ditched his shoes and socks—presumably to free his toes to facilitate climbing up walls.

"Oh, miss," he whispered in barely accented English. "Thank goodness I found him. When I discovered Zeus was missing, I searched everywhere for him."

Tracey was taken by the way his face became pinched with worry.

"Please, miss," he pleaded. "You need not tell anyone Zeus was in here. Do you?"

"W-well," Tracey said. "I'd prefer not to, but I'm sure I'll be expected to offer some sort of explanation for this mess."

The boy looked crestfallen, but nodded.

"Look, it isn't the end of the world," Tracey said, in an effort to cheer him.

"Oh," he moaned, "oh, but you see it is. This means Mrs. Stefanou shall make Zeus disappear."

"She wouldn't!" Tracey was taken aback by the vehement certainty in his young voice.

The child met her eyes directly and nodded. "I know she will," he said. "It happened before, with Demetrius. He was my last kitten. She warned me three times, and I tried . . . really I did, but you know cats. Well, now that she has warned me three times about Zeus already—"

His beseeching brown eyes brimmed with tears and he began to breathe asthmatically.

"And what?" Tracey prompted.

He clutched the cat tighter. "And his life will be worth nothing."

The words were nearly lost, hiccoughed as they were into the back of the cat's furry white head.

Oh, dear, Tracey thought. *What is it with me? Do I have "soft spot" written all over, or what?*

The boy's face suddenly brightened as something occurred to him. "Perhaps," he suggested, "if the two of us think hard enough, we can come up with some other excuse."

"I think it's pretty obvious what happened," Tracey pointed out drily. "The evidence speaks for itself. You can even see the paw tracks."

The brightness in his face dimmed, and he rocked Zeus sorrowfully in his arms. "Yes. I suppose you are right," he agreed glumly.

The sight of him hugging the cat tugged at her heartstrings. "I'm not promising anything, mind you," she warned, "but maybe, just maybe we can figure something out."

His face lit up like a Christmas tree.

"Ooo . . . kay," she said. "Since it looks as though we might become partners in crime, it's only right that we are properly introduced. So, young man, just who are you?"

"Oh. Pardon me. I did not intend to be rude." Cradling the cat in his left arm, he solemnly proffered his right hand. "Prometheus," he said, with no small measure of pride. "That is my name."

Tracey shook his hand with equal solemnity. "And I am Miss Sullivan. My first name is Tracey, but my friends call me Trace."

Prometheus eyed her hopefully. "Am I a friend?"

She smiled. "I'm confident we will be, else I wouldn't have shared my nickname." She eyed him a bit longer. "So. You're named for the mythological man who stole fire from heaven."

"Yes, the one who was punished by being chained to the cliff and eaten for eternity by the eagles. But I am not a thief. I do not steal."

There was a short pause, during which Prometheus bit down hard on his lower lip.

"Well, I don't steal much," he allowed, averting his gaze. "Not anything of value. Only food from the kitchen for Zeus. Also I used to for the other cats."

"What other cats?"

"Oh, they used to be everywhere," he said in an impassioned voice. "Anyplace the tourists ate they begged to be fed. But we went to the mainland in the winter one year, and when we came back they were nearly all gone."

"How odd," Tracey murmured.

"They were probably all drowned or poisoned, miss," Prometheus said, "so as not to bother the tourists."

"Not 'miss,' " she reminded him gently, not heartened by this bit of news. "Trace. You are to call me Trace. Remember?"

"Yes, of course." Prometheus smiled, but it faded as he cocked his head and frowned. He had evidently heard something, for Zeus's ears pricked up and stiffened also. "Oh, Trace," he cried wretchedly. "It is Mrs. Stefanou. I hear her coming. Please!"

He reached out and shook Tracey's arm. "You must help!"

"But . . . how?" she asked.

He glanced fretfully around at the floor, then back up at her with an imploring expression. Evidently he expected her to concoct a spur-of-the-moment story.

Without further ado, he said, "Zeus and I must hide!"

It was apparent that he was familiar with the layout of the windmill. He made straight for the stairs that jutted out of the circular perimeter wall and curved upward and around. Tracey watched him dash fearlessly up those dreaded steps. In a flash, boy and cat disappeared into the loft overhead. Tracey could hear the creaking of the old wooden floorboards, some other muffled scuttling sounds, then silence.

No, not silence. Now she, too, could hear what Prometheus and Zeus had heard—the unmistakable click-clack of purposeful heels approaching on the terrace.

She breathed deeply. No doubt about it. The gait was

Mrs. Stefanou's. No sound-cushioning rubber-soled espadrilles today; rather the dreaded click-clack of jackboots. In a few moments she would be here.

With increasing dismay, Tracey turned in place and gazed at the mess surrounding her. *The telltale cat paws. Unless those are obliterated, no story will hold water.*

Swiftly she used her toes to smear the spots where the cat tracks showed. It was silly—she *knew* it was silly—but all the same, she felt both the wild euphoria and the sudden panic of a juvenile truant, or a co-conspirator, which, she realized, she had unwittingly become.

Outside, the footsteps had stopped. Tracey braced herself for what she knew was coming. Even so, she flinched when it did:

Rat-tat-tat . . . tat-TAT. The sound of sharp knuckles against wood.

She stood there a moment, undecided, willing her jumpy nerves to calm. A bead of perspiration trickled down her forehead. She was conscious of holding her breath.

"Just a moment!" she called out, in time to halt a second barrage of knocks. Squaring her shoulders, Tracey picked her way through the detritus of the collapsed tray. She was barely past the perimeter of the mess when inspiration hit.

Make it convincing. Get some of it on yourself. Backtracking, she bent down, smearing congealed stew on her fingertips. Thought, *Why the hell not? It's for a good cause.* For good measure, she purposely smudged the front of her nightie. Thus armed, she marched out into the vestibule and angrily threw open the door.

There was no need to feign blinking against the sudden glare of sky, or the necessity of shielding her eyes with her arm. The cloudless blue seemed to vibrate with miragelike heat.

Silhouetted in front of this quivering background was the stately figure of Mrs. Stefanou. Spotless, creaseless, buffed, and shiny as a drill sergeant on her parade field. Brassy blond hair perfectly coiffed. Wearing a shiny navy blue suit whose synthetic fabric had mysterious oil field origins, the jacket with pointy lapels and worn open to accommodate her imposing, white-bloused bosom, the skirt reaching primly below the knee. It was a variation on a theme—her white-collar uniform—and she clearly wore it with pride. What had sounded like jackboots came from a pair of sensibly low navy blue heels.

Behind her, and a little off to one side, lurked another silhouette, this one in traditional, unrelieved head-to-toe black. It was an old crone who wore large, high-fashion Sophia Loren–style eyeglasses.

Mrs. Stefanou filled the conversational void.

"*Kaliméra,* Miss Sullivan." No matter how warmly the greeting was meant, Mrs. Stefanou managed to make it sound like a death sentence.

All that's missing is the bang of the gavel, Tracey thought.

"*Kaliméra,* Mrs. Stefanou," Tracey responded tightly.

Her tone earned her an inquisitively arched eyebrow. "My mother," said Mrs. Stefanou, by way of introduction, gesturing at the crone.

This was a cue. Why else would that withered face suddenly break out into an ingratiating, gap-toothed smile?

Now Tracey noticed that the old woman was holding a wooden tray by its handles. It was identical to the tray the cat had knocked off the stand, and from the looks of it, was laden with the accouterments of what Tracey judged was meant to be her breakfast. Pint-size silver coffeepot, matching creamer and sugar bowl, white china with the cup inverted in the saucer, a basket containing rolls, a butter dish, jams, a bowl of black oil-cured olives, a boiled egg in an egg cup, cutlery wrapped in a starched linen napkin.

"You must be hungry. I trust you slept well? Yes?" Mrs. Stefanou eyed her severely.

It was the opening Tracey had been waiting for. "I could have slept better," she answered tartly.

Her reply was unexpected, and the woman frowned up at her, as though a bad night's sleep anywhere in Oia, and especially in Urania's compound, was an unheard-of phenomenon. Then she peered curiously past Tracey into the windmill. It took a moment for her eyes to adjust to the cool dim interior beyond. Then she blinked rapidly, gasped with shocked disbelief, and balled up her hands into tense little fists that trembled at her sides. Red splotches burned on her cheeks.

"Óchi!" The word was expelled in a scratchy rasp and her huge, dark-lidded eyes narrowed into slits as they surveyed the mess inside. She stared accusingly up at Tracey. "That cat!"

Mrs. Stefanou charged past her into the room with all the fury of a tornado bent upon a single act of destruction.

"I am finished dealing with that cat!" she shouted hoarsely, waving her fist in the air. "By God, this time I am going to find it and kill it!"

"Mrs. Stefanou. Mrs. Stefanou!"

Tracey hurried inside after the woman. Mrs. Stefanou stopped at the edge of the mess created by the upturned tray. She was leaning forward, glaring around suspiciously, nostrils twitching like a bloodhound's on a scent.

Tracey arranged her features into an expression of impenetrable innocence. "What cat are you talking about?"

"What cat? You have to ask, 'What cat?' " Mrs. Stefanou's voice rose, and she quivered with barely contained indignation.

Swallowing guiltily, Tracey said, "If it's this mess you're talking about, Mrs. Stefanou, well . . . I'm afraid you're blaming the wrong culprit."

"Eh? Excuse me?" Again the woman's eyes blinked rapidly. A nervous reaction, Tracey gathered, rather like a tic. At the periphery of her vision, she glimpsed the old crone staring in agog from outside the door, her mouth open in a perfect O.

"Mrs. Stefanou, please. Just look at me. You see?"

Tracey held up both smudged hands and gestured at the smears on the front of her nightie with disgust.

"Oh," said the woman. "And such a lovely nightdress. A pity. I'm certain laundering will get it out."

"Yes, but that isn't the point. Remember yesterday? When I told you that I have a tendency to walk in my sleep?"

"Y . . . yes? . . ." Mrs. Stefanou drew out the word.

Tracey gave a deep sigh. "I really hate bringing it up, because it's evidently a case of good intentions. It's not as if

I'm ungrateful, you understand. But while I was asleep, someone must have brought in that tray of food and put it there."

"But of course!" Mrs. Stefanou drew herself up. "You did not have dinner, so I personally instructed my mother to bring it." Mrs. Stefanou glanced over her shoulder at the door, where the old woman stood, still staring in. "In case you were hungry."

"And I appreciate your kind thoughtfulness. But I'm afraid I unknowingly walked right into it. In my sleep."

"Don't tell me!" Mrs. Stefanou, clapping a hand to her cheek, looked aghast. "I did not think—"

"But why should you have? If anyone was remiss, it was me. I should have warned you in more detail. I just never expected such kindness."

Tracey decided it wouldn't hurt to lay it on a bit thicker. Play on Mrs. Stefanou's sense of self-importance. "It's not as though I'm a guest. I've been employed to work here. I certainly don't expect special treatment."

Mrs. Stefanou sniffed. "It is at Madame's specific request that you are accorded every courtesy."

"I shall thank Madame when I see her," Tracey said. "And I wish to thank you, also."

"You are welcome."

"It's such a glorious day out. If you'd be so kind as to tell your mother, I think I'll take my breakfast outside. On the terrace."

"Yes. Why not? I shall send Iliki to clean this," Mrs. Stefanou said, glancing at the mess. "Also, if you will give her your nightdress, she will see to the laundering."

"In that case, I better change out of this." Tracey touched Mrs. Stefanou ever so lightly on the arm and guided her slowly back outside. "Well, good-bye, Mrs. Stefanou. And please, do accept my sincerest apologies. I hate to be so much trouble."

"Trouble?" Heels click-clacking, arms half-raised, and waving her hands in frustrated irritation as if her quarry had escaped her, Mrs. Stefanou quick-stepped her way out. "Is no trouble," she said without a backward glance. "No trouble at all."

* * *

The instant the coast was clear, Prometheus's head popped into view upside down, like a bat's, from the loft above. "Awesome!" His sibilant whisper was filled with admiration. "You were awesome!" He sounded beside himself with excitement.

Tracey slumped against the closed door. She was shaking with relief and briefly shut her eyes.

Scuffling sounds came from above, then bare footsteps on wood, light as a dancer's. Prometheus all but flew down the curve of stairs two at a time, Zeus in his arms. The boy could barely contain himself. "Oh, Trace, how can we ever thank you? You saved poor little Zeus's life."

"Nonsense, Pro," she countered. "You can't take everything literally. Mrs. Stefanou could well have been speaking figuratively."

Prometheus shook his head stubbornly and cuddled Zeus tightly. "Trace, you were here. You heard and saw her for yourself. She would have killed him. I told you, it has happened before. I hate her! She's evil!"

That he believed this was evident from his earnestness.

"Then all the more reason for making sure Zeus stays out of trouble in the future," Tracey told him.

"Yes, you are right. I promise to see to it."

"Good." Tracey reached out and tousled his hair. "Because I don't think we can fool Mrs. Stefanou so easily again. I gather she's quite cunning."

"As are you," Prometheus said, with a huge smile. Then, wiping the smile from his young face, he suddenly became politely formal, a perfect little gentleman. He held out his hand and shook Tracey's.

"I am deeply indebted to you," he said soberly. "Zeus and I will never forget it. If you need anything, just tell Kathy at the Mini Market. She can be trusted to pass on any messages. But please, please, swear you will not talk to anyone else about me."

"Don't worry, you have my word."

"Or better yet . . ." His face shone with hope like the midday sun. "Perhaps . . . if I do not make a nuisance of myself, that is . . . I could visit you every now and then? See if I can help you in any way?"

Tracey was touched. He was a regular little musketeer. "I'd like that very much," she said.

"Really? You mean it? You're not just saying that?"

"I'm not just saying that," Tracey assured him, and smiled.

"Fan-tastic! I can't wait to show you some of my secret places. Spots here which no one else knows about."

"Now, shhh!" Holding a finger against her lips, Tracey opened the door a crack and peered out. The old crone was nearly finished setting the table under an octagonal umbrella.

Silently Tracey shut the door again. "Now, as soon as Mrs. Stefanou's mother—"

"That witch!" Prometheus exclaimed.

"Pro! Why, that is not a very nice thing to say."

"Well, she does look like a witch. Doesn't she? Although she really isn't. A friend of hers is one, though. Have you seen her?" He looked heavenward and rolled his eyes back so only the whites showed.

"You mean, she's blind?" Tracey asked.

He stopped his cruel imitation and quickly crossed two fingers. He shuddered. "Something about her frightens me."

She signaled for him to be silent, and again opened the door a crack and peeked out. The terrace was deserted. The old crone was gone. She opened the door farther and quickly looked both ways.

All clear. And her breakfast awaited. Suddenly Tracey realized she was ravenous.

She pushed the door, keeping it cracked. "All right, Pro," she said. "I think it's time you and Zeus skedaddled."

Adopting a mock swagger, he said, in a deep bass, "C'mon Zeus, you heard the lady. We're outta here."

Tracey stared. His command of the American vernacular was truly amazing.

Seeing the stunned expression on her face, he said: "What's the matter?"

"Your lingo. Where on earth do you pick it up?"

"I watch a lot of American movies on video," he explained. "They are almost always in English, and have Greek subtitles."

"I see."

Then he surprised her even more. He hopped on tiptoe. Pecked her cheek. Said, "*Hasta la vista,* baby," in a perfect imitation of Arnold Schwarzenegger. And he and the cat were gone.

Chapter Twenty

After breakfasting on the terrace, Tracey decided it was time she started earning her keep. She popped back into the windmill and changed into a comfortable working outfit of a sleeveless, cartoon-print T-shirt, baggy knee-length white shorts, and pink rubber zoris decorated with sequined daisies.

Inside the study, the air conditioner was humming, emitting a delicious chill against the rapidly rising mercury outside. Sitting at the desk, in an ugly orange, but eminently comfortable, ergonomic desk chair, she eyed the two wooden tray tables off to one side, atop which rested three stacks of paper, each weighed down with a smoothly rounded stone.

Two copies of Urania's manuscript—one clean and one marked up—plus a separate thick pile of editorial notes, Tracey recalled, from having glanced at them the previous day.

She flexed her fingers like a surgeon. Now to get cracking.

Tracey began by gathering her hair up into a metal clamp, the kind ordinarily used to hold a sheaf of paper together. That done, she stuck sharpened pencils through her hair. Not only was her hair out of her face, but a pencil was always within easy reach.

She got up and carried both copies of Urania's manuscript from the tray tables to the work surface, then fetched the pile of editorial notes. She decided to read the novel first. This way the notes wouldn't skew her judgment. It was important that she formed her own opinion.

She shoved the pile of notes aside.

Now then. Which set of manuscript pages to read?

She discovered that the only difference was that on the clean copy, someone had already typed in the scribbled changes. The marked-up copy was shunted off to the sidelines. Thus prepared, she started to read.

The title page:

EYE FOR
AN EYE

a novel by
URANIA VICKERS

Hmmm. Eye for an Eye. *So that's the title,* Tracey thought. *Not bad.*

The prologue began auspiciously enough. The opening paragraph consisted of a single sentence, and it was certainly a grabber:

The psychopath held Montana in the grip of terror.

At first Tracey thought Urania was writing about the state of Montana, but by sentence three, she realized the Montana in question was a woman.

The prologue was short and to the point. Five pages in all, it ended on a melodramatic page-turning note.

His arm whipped around Montana's throat. The blade in his other hand gleamed as he stabbed. And stabbed. And stabbed.

He thrust her limp body away from him and watched her crumple to the floor. Only then, when she twitched one last time, did the psychopath realize his mistake. He dropped the bloody blade and staggered backward.

"Aw, fuck! You're not Montana Ripley!" he sobbed. "Christ, I killed the wrong bitch!"

And then a smile crossed his face. The real Montana was still out there! He'd have another chance to experience the thrill of hunting her down. The pleasure of killing her all over again.

Tracey cocked her head. So far, so good. Nothing that a few minor changes and additions couldn't fix. She turned the page to Chapter One. The location and a date—May 21, 1986—directly beneath the chapter number, gave the action a place and time.

Tracey immersed herself in the pages. The first chapter was devoted to a royal wedding in a mythical oil emirate called Kuhrain. A young American woman, Juniper Ripley, of Parsippany, New Jersey, was marrying the crown prince. What Juniper is apparently unaware of—

"How dumb can that bimbo be?" muttered Tracey in exasperation. "I mean, hello?"

—is how many other wives the bridegroom has in his harem. And the feelings the American ambassador to Kuhrain, handsome and recently widowed, harbors for her. Instead she and the ambassador are constantly at each other's throats.

This *is supposed to be a multimillion-dollar novel*? Tracey was stunned. She couldn't believe a publishing company would throw around money like that, just on the basis of a celebrity's name. In fact, she was genuinely outraged. So far Urania Vickers's novel smacked of nothing more than your formulaic, write-by-number bodice ripper—and not even a decent one at that.

But it got worse. Much worse. Urania, she'd already discovered, wasn't capable of writing fiction. Tracey had to remind herself that she wasn't a critic. She was a ghostwriter. *Just keep reading,* she thought and forced herself to continue.

As she did, Tracey jotted down the highlight of each scene on a separate index card. She did the same for characters, noting their physical descriptions, vital statistics such as hair and eye color and age, and such salient characteristics as temperament, tendencies, likes, and dislikes. On a legal pad, she started a chart on which to keep track of the relationships among the various characters.

It was tedious going. The dialogue was stilted, the settings lacked any sense of reality, and the characters were one-dimensional and unappealing. Leading the pack in this area was Juniper Ripley herself. Instead of a heroine the reader could root for, she turned out to be spoiled, threw regular tantrums, whined constantly, felt sorry for herself, and was infuriatingly vain about her appearance.

It wasn't long before Tracey wanted to strangle the bitch. She only hoped that Urania hadn't based the character of Juniper on herself. If she had—watch out!

By the third chapter, the fictional honeymoon was over. Juniper—renamed Princess Layla of Kuhrain—was not only confined to the harem with the crown prince's other wives, but found herself a virtual prisoner in a palace over which a scheming grand vizier presided. The crown prince's other wives shunned her for being a Westerner, as well for being the prince's current favorite. But bad became worse when Juniper/Layla discovered she was pregnant—a condition the crown prince apparently found repugnant; he let it be known that he refused to set eyes on her again until after the child's birth.

Desperate, Juniper/Layla bribed a servant to smuggle out messages to the ambassador; naturally, they were intercepted.

The next several chapters were predictable. There was the requisite palace coup, during which the minions of the crown prince's ambitious half brother, aided by the grand vizier, murdered the king and imprisoned the crown prince. During this melee, Juniper/Layla seized the opportunity and made her escape by throwing a chador over her Chanel suit, its jacket pockets stuffed full of crown jewels.

What Tracey found truly amazing was that scenes which should have been highly dramatic made for painfully dull reading. And it was plain to see why. Urania, for all her theatrical flair, was unable to bring a blank page to life.

Simply put, the woman couldn't write.

Tracey did not grin, but she did have to bear it.

It's not as if I've got much choice, she reminded herself. *I took on this job—jumped at it, in fact. Plus, I was paid in advance. Now I've got to deliver.*

The sheer chutzpah of believing she could save Urania's literary career pressed down on her like a physical force.

What was I thinking? she wondered in a sudden panic. *I don't know anything about writing. I'm not even a published author. I've never sold a book in my life. Heaven help me. It's a fine mess I got myself into this time, Ollie.*

The only question was: *Now how do I get myself out?*

The answer was: *You don't.*

Tap-tap.

Tracey had no idea how long she'd been forcing herself to read and jot notes before she became aware of the soft knocks on her terrace door.

Startled, she swiveled around in her chair. She could make out a silhouette peering in through one of the panes of glass set into the upper portion of the door, but couldn't tell who it was. The blinding glare from outside was too bright. Whoever it was had to hold up a hand in a kind of salute in order to see in.

"Yes?" she called out.

The door opened just enough for a head to stick around it. It was Mark Varney. "Knock-knock?" he said tentatively. "Am I interrupting?"

"Are you kidding?" Tracey was about to blurt out that considering the numbing flatness of Urania's novel, any excuse for diversion was welcome. Just in the nick of time she reminded herself, *If it weren't for Mark, you wouldn't even have this job. The least you can do is show some gratitude.*

"Well?" she said. "Don't just stand there. Come on in."

"You're sure?" he asked.

"Pos," she replied.

He breezed in and shut the door against the heat outside.

"Like your hairdo," he commented with a wink.

Tracey's hands flew up to her head and encountered pointy pencils and the metal clamp. "Gawd, I must look a sight!"

"Seems rather efficient," he said, and smiled.

That smile.

Tracey could almost hear a musical "ding!" and see a dazzling star gleaming from Mark Varney's teeth. Then, bearing in mind that he was off limits, she gestured awkwardly at what she took to be Urania's futuristic boardroom throne.

"Please," she offered formally. "Have a seat."

He shook his head. "I was just going by. Seeing that it was almost two, I thought, 'Hey, why not chance it and pop in on the new kid? See if she wants to go and have lunch.' "

"Two o'clock?" Tracey stared at him.

"Yes. Why?" She thought she detected a note of disappointment in his tone. "Don't tell me," he said. "You've had lunch already?"

She shook her head. "As a matter of fact, no. I'm just amazed, that's all. I didn't realize it was so late."

"Oh?" One side of his mouth twisted up in a sly, sardonic grin. "Don't tell me. Time flies when you're not having fun?"

"I," Tracey pointed out primly, "never said that."

"No, but I did." He thrust his hands casually into the pockets of his loose white cotton gauze trousers and glanced around her work area at the manuscript, yellow legal pads, and stacks of index cards on which she'd been making notations. He pulled a face. "How's it coming, or shouldn't I ask?"

"You can ask, but don't hold your breath," she said. "You're not going to get a reply out of me."

He cocked an eyebrow in surprise. "Oh?"

"At least, not yet you aren't," she continued. "Mark, I've barely even started. It's much too early to jump to, er, hasty judgments."

"Hmm." He smiled with amusement.

She narrowed her eyes. "And what, may I ask, is so funny?" she demanded.

"Your diplomacy." He grinned. "You missed your calling. The State Department could well do with your skills."

She was about to say something about flattery getting him everywhere, but stopped herself in time. She didn't know what it was, but something about him begged for clever repartee. She would have to watch herself and exercise control, lest she got carried away and Urania received the wrong impression.

I can't afford to blow this opportunity, Tracey reminded herself grimly.

"About lunch," Mark said. "With what you're in for, I suggest you best eat. My advice is, keep up your energy." He smiled a touch sourly. "You're going to need it."

"And what sorts of ominous things am I in for?" Tracey inquired, gazing up at him from under her lowered lashes. Her green eyes, half hidden, were luminous, and she herself was barely aware of the effect she had on him.

"You may ask, but don't hold your breath," he retorted, giving her a dose of her own medicine. "Anyway, why don't you go fetch your bag or whatever it is women fetch when they step out? Because I'm not taking no for an answer."

"It'll just take me a few minutes to get ready," Tracey replied with a smile. "Is that okay?"

"Sure," he said. "I'll be right here."

Tracey ducked out of the room and shut the door. It was a testament to the tidal pull of his personal magnetism, that singular talent he had of focusing his entire attention upon you as if you were the only person in the entire world who mattered—forget his killer looks—that caused Tracey to forget her good intentions and Urania's laying down of the law.

Staring at the vestibule door through which Tracey had disappeared, Mark sighed to himself. *Jeez,* he thought. *She's really beautiful, without being a cookie-cutter knockout.* She was also talented and invigoratingly uncomplicated and enticing, a novel breath of fresh air compared to the studied theatricality, endless bouts of self-absorption, and unpredictable mood swings of women like Urania Vickers. *She's like a rare wildflower, young, innocent, and completely without guile. A breath of fresh air indeed.*

Oblivious to the effect she'd had on him, Tracey entered the windmill. Passing a mirror, she caught sight of her working persona and attacked her fountain of pinned-up Pebbles Flintstone hair. She discarded the pencils she had stuck through it like so many chopsticks and removed the big metal clip, then shook her hair free.

Her destination: the clothes-filled armoire. For along with the pencils and metal clip, her comfy working outfit had to go.

Pulling the T-shirt over her head, she tossed it casually onto the bed as she passed by. Then she stopped short, frowned, and backtracked a couple of paces. Did a classic double-take.

She thought she'd seen something, and sure enough, there it was. Centered on the fluffed top pillow of her freshly made bed was a thread-thin gold neck chain. Undoubtedly crafted of real gold. Nothing else glowed with such warmth. At first glance it seemed to have been casually tossed there, but upon closer inspection, Tracey could see it had been carefully arranged to resemble the profile of a cat.

The longer she looked at it, the more unmistakable that profile became. It had to have been Prometheus.

Tracey started to reach out for the chain, then stilled her hand. Prometheus was a mere child. She wondered where, and under what circumstances, he had come into its possession. Surely not through stealing! Eyeing it a moment longer, she decided she would—yes, why not?—wear it. Prometheus meant well, and while Tracey certainly couldn't accept a gift like this, especially from a child, she would do him the honor of wearing it temporarily. This way he wouldn't be insulted when she returned it. She picked up the chain, then by feel fastened the minuscule clasp behind her neck.

Discarding her knee-length shorts, she slipped into a frisky empire-waisted cabana-striped minidress with spaghetti straps. Ditched the zoris in favor of deceptively flimsy-looking red leather sandals which were a dream to walk in. Snatched up a pair of pink-lensed, white-framed, Riviera-mod sunglasses à la Bardot, grabbed her slouchy carryall, and sallied forth.

Thus having thrown herself together, she was ready for lunch. Yes, but was she ready for Mark Varney? That was the question.

"You're not frightened of heights, by any chance?" Mark Varney was steering Tracey through the narrow, snaking main drag of Oia, a pedestrian route teeming with tourists that widened or narrowed or rose or descended according to the whims of the clifftop landscape.

Tracey didn't have a chance to reply. On this broiling thoroughfare there were oncoming, on-foot traffic jams to avoid, logjams of gawkers at various shop windows to skirt, tour groups surrounding a guide holding up some sort of identification to circumvent. On rare occasions she and Mark managed to stroll side by side. Most often they ran this gauntlet in single file.

To the right was an almost unbroken, undulating wall of buildings devoted to commerce. On the caldera side, the structures gave way intermittently to the pulse-quickening view, with narrow steps leading up to rooftop tavernas or down to shaded dining terraces. Despite the abundance of tony seasonal jewelers, crafts shops, souvenir emporiums, and entrances—usually a maze of steps or a single room leading down to "Traditional Cave Houses"—every other establishment seemed to be an eatery.

"We make a sharp left turn just about . . . here," said Mark from behind her. Placing his hands on her bare shoulders, he steered her through the two-way crowds, then down several steep steps and through a cool, dark doorway.

Tracey took off her pink-lensed glasses. Tobacco smoke stung her eyes, which took a moment to adjust. When they did, she discovered they were in a half-deserted hole-in-the-wall. It did not have much to recommend it, save for an illuminated pastry cooler and the low throbbing techno beat and chimes of music. Two tables were occupied, and from the ashtrays of both, cigarette smoke rose in blue drifts.

"We go thataway." Mark pecked a pointy finger toward the back.

An opening in the far wall led out to a balcony crammed with three napkin-sized tables for two. The tiny space was seemingly suspended hundreds of feet in midair.

Tracey nearly groaned aloud. *Courage,* she told herself.

Mark held out a chair for her at the one empty table, at the extreme left end. "We lucked out." His voice seemed filtered, as though it traveled from a great distance. "As far as the view goes, these are the three best tables in Oia."

Tracey glanced leerily at the couples occupying the two other tables. At the center was a young man with whitish blond hair whom she took to be Scandinavian, and his companion, a regal, slender-necked young black woman. At the far right sat two young men.

Tracey envied them all their lack of fear.

Courage, courage, courage, she kept repeating in her head.

With a frozen expression that might have passed for a smile, she sat down gingerly, telling herself she should be grateful that at least Mark hadn't offered her the corner seat, where there was spindly blue railing on *two* sides.

The sun was blazing with a fierce intensity, and for one awful, lurching moment Tracey had the sensation that the white cubist sculpture which was Oia was trembling and tilting and beginning its long, slow descent down the sheer cliff and into the sea.

"Trace? Trace!" Mark was leaning urgently across the tiny table and shaking her arm.

Tracey started and quickly slid her glasses back on.

"What is it?" he asked. "You're white as a sheet."

The concern in his voice did it: the buildings tumbling down into the sea slid back up the cliff. Reality reasserted itself. Tracey permitted herself a long deep exhalation. Then she forced herself to look around. Sure enough, the precarious structures remained in place. All was still well with the live picture postcard clinging to its perch high above the deep blue caldera. The calamity had been but an illusion.

Mark smacked himself on the forehead. "Don't tell me," he guessed, pulling a face. "You are afraid of heights."

Tracey gave a thin smile. "I'm not particularly fond of them, no."

"And here I bring you to this, of all places." He instantly pushed his chair back and started to get up. "Come on, we're going somewhere else."

Tracey shook her head. "Sit down. It's . . . okay now. I think. Besides, I've got to learn to get over it. Especially on this island, where everything's vertical."

"Oh, shit," he exclaimed under his breath.

"What's wrong now?"

"We put you up in that damned windmill because of its proximity to the study. How thoughtless of us. It never occurred—"

"Forget it." Tracey's smile broadened. "I got around that one by having a bed made up on the ground floor. Stavros and some man brought an armoire down from the loft so I could put away my clothes."

She reached across the table and covered Mark's hand with hers. "You see? It's okay. I'm quite capable of taking care of myself."

She let go of his hand and sat back. "Anyway, the important thing is, I told Mrs. Stefanou that I couldn't possibly sleep up in the loft due to my somnambulism. So, if you want to do me a favor, don't let on that it's because I've got acrophobia. Okay?"

"No reason on earth why I should. That's your personal business. But I don't see why you have to hide it. Everybody's got a phobia of some sort. There's no shame in it."

"I know, but I'd still rather the Greek dragon lady doesn't find out."

"Aw, come on. Stefanou isn't that bad. I grant you she may come off a bit stern and humorless and efficient—"

Tracey shook her head and frowned. "Don't ask me why," she murmured, "but I wouldn't put it past her to find some subtle way to use heights to torture me."

He stared at her.

She raised both hands, then let them drop. "I know it sounds crazy and far-fetched, but humor me on this one, Mark. Please?"

"Your wish is my command. Now, I want you to feel comfortable. Are you absolutely positive you don't want to go someplace else to eat?"

"Pos." She nodded emphatically. There was something about him that inspired trust and made her feel protected. "If I have to stare down my fears, I'd rather do it with you. That is, if you don't mind. This way, should I pass out you can catch me."

He looked alarmed. "You're not going to—"

"No, no, no." She had to laugh. "Chill. It was just a manner of speech."

They both became aware of a presence materializing beside them. They looked up.

A frump of a woman with frazzled gray hair and a mannish manner had come from inside.

"Kaliméra," she muttered gruffly, setting a sealed and chilled one-liter bottle of mineral water on the table, along with two drinking glasses, and a third glass, not much bigger than a jigger, into which she tucked a little cash register receipt.

"Kaliméra," Mark returned affably. He glanced at Tracey questioningly. "Which would you rather have? Wine or beer?"

"Water will do me just fine, but thanks all the same."

He turned to the woman. "*Ena* Mythos beer," he ordered, and she shuffled off in that way peculiar to people with flat feet.

"No menus?" Tracey asked.

"All in good time," he said. He unscrewed the cap from the water bottle and filled first her glass and then his.

Tracey raised hers in a toast. "Cheers," she said, and drank thirstily. The water was deliciously cool and sweet and thirst quenching. She practically purred with contentment as she set the glass back down. "Ah. That hit the spot. Aren't you thirsty?"

He grinned. "Waiting for my brewski."

The woman returned shortly and set down another

empty drinking glass and a chilled bottle of Mythos beer which she uncapped. She added another little cash register receipt into the shot glass and went away again.

Mark picked up the empty glass with one hand and the beer bottle with the other and tilted both toward each other and poured. Tracey didn't know what to expect from Greek beer, but it looked like any beer the world over: same shade of yellow, same head of white foam. She felt curiously let down.

Mark lifted his glass in a salute. "*Giá sas!* That's Greek for 'To your health.' " He drank half of it down, then licked a little foam from his upper lip with the tip of his tongue. "Nothing like an ice-cold beer on a scorching day. Sure I can't convince you to have one?"

"I'm quite sure. Don't forget," Tracey reminded him, "for me, this is just a lunch break. I need to keep a clear head. I still have hours of reading to do."

What a treat, she thought sardonically, but kept that comment to herself. She laced her hands atop the table. "I gather this is a working lunch?"

He grinned. "All lunches with clients are working lunches. But that isn't to say that some of them aren't more enjoyable than others."

Now, what kind of answer is that? Tracey wondered. "And the boss?" she asked. "Did you clear it with our star?" It was the wrong thing to say. She regretted the words the instant they were out of her mouth.

Mark's entire demeanor changed. His posture stiffened, his voice went frosty, and there was a sudden chill in his eyes.

"We need to get something straight right away," he said with quiet intensity. "If you're asking whether or not I asked Urania's permission to take you to lunch, the answer is no. I did not."

Tracey was silent. She realized she'd gone too far.

"I try to be a good houseguest," he continued. "I go out of my way not to rock the boat. But don't misconstrue a polite guest's passivity for being a pushover. Also, I'm a big boy. There's no reason why I should have to ask Urania's permission for anything I do. She's neither my mother, my keeper, my wife, or, as they say nowadays, my life partner. She's a client. A very high-profile celebrity client, true, but a client all the same."

He drank the rest of the beer and refilled his glass with what was left in the bottle.

"So, if you're wondering what I am doing right this very instant, I can tell you. I'm minding my own business and taking lunch with another, equally important client of mine—you. Yes, you. That's our business, and if a certain person doesn't like it, that's her tough luck."

He paused, as if for a breather, and slowly turned the glass around and around on the little café table. When he spoke again, his impassioned voice was gentle.

"I realize your position in Urania's household is rather peculiar, since you are neither a guest nor a servant as such. What it boils down to is that you're employed by Urania and live on the premises. Fine. However, that does not make you her slave, nor does it mean you are required to answer to Stefanou. She's the housekeeper, for crying out loud. Listen to me, Trace. You are not—and I repeat, not—required to account for every action or event in your personal life. You're entitled to your privacy."

His demeanor underwent yet another change, and he looked as if he was back to being his relaxed old self. "There," he said, leaning an elbow on the wooden balcony railing. He cracked a smile. "Does my long-winded lecture help clear things up?"

Tracey said, "Wow, I'll say. Now, about my running off at the mouth—" She gestured awkwardly.

He waved her to silence. "Aw, forget it," he advised.

"No! I can't just forget it," Tracey countered. "I want to apologize. It was none of my business, and I was way out of line. I guess the only reason it popped out is . . . well, because Urania seems awfully possessive of you."

"Urania," he said, uttering a mirthless laugh, "is incredibly possessive about everything. Particularly of anything or anyone she does *not* possess. Take my advice—if you're not careful, she'll have you for dinner. You'll feel like you've been chewed into little pieces and spat back out."

"I—I'll certainly keep that in mind," she said, taken aback.

He held her gaze. "You'd better. Because trust me. When your usefulness is over"—with his thumb he gestured over the balcony railing—"it's *ciao*, baby. She won't hesitate to toss you to the roadside without so much as a thank-you or good-bye or it's-been-nice-knowing-you. And I'm not just referring to you, personally." Again he uttered that soft humorless laugh. "The same goes for me, along with anyone else around her who's outlived his or her immediate usefulness."

Tracey couldn't believe his outspokenness—particularly since Urania was his client.

"You make her out to be monstrous," she exclaimed.

"Yeah?" He downed what beer was left in his glass. "That," he said, "is because Urania *is* monstrous. And you want to know something really, really weird?" The bitterness in his voice had changed to something approaching admiration. "Strangely enough, that's her appeal. Yup. It's what's made Urania Vickers the star that she is."

He eyed Tracey speculatively. "You familiar with any of her movies? Or that hit TV series she was in some years back?"

Tracey shook her head apologetically, said, "Can't say that I am. Somehow I missed out on them."

"Don't worry," he assured her. "You didn't miss much. Except for the camp value, which is considerable and has gained her a certain cult following, they'd all be long forgotten. But Urania's one smart cookie. Shallow, yes. Impetuous, yes. Liable to leap before she thinks, yes. But she's a slyboots. Don't let her empty-headedness fool you. And never, ever, make the mistake of underestimating her. A lot of people in the industry have and are sorry as a result. See, we're talking the ultimate survivor."

He paused and frowned. "I'm not boring you, by any chance?"

"Boring me? God, no! I'm just wondering why you're telling me all this."

"Because you're my client too. I don't want to see you get hurt."

"Or et up and spat out in li'l bits and pieces," she joked, trying to interject a little humor.

Mark didn't crack a smile. "Believe me, I know of what I speak. Anyway . . . where were we? . . . Right. Urania's career. Sure you want to hear this?"

"Of course. Who wouldn't?" Tracey put her elbow on the table, rested her chin on her fist, and leaned forward. "I'm all ears."

"Well, Urania never once landed a decent role. She was up for quite a few, but someone else invariably got the parts—and in some cases, the Oscar. Susan Sarandon. Sharon Stone. The list goes on and on."

"I'm almost starting to feel sorry for her," Tracey murmured.

"Don't let your heart bleed prematurely," he said. They fell silent and leaned back from the table as the frump came and raised a clatter putting down another bottle of Mythos, big thick white plates, flimsy paper napkins, and cheap flatware. She uncapped the new beer and stuck yet another little receipt in the glass, then left with the empty beer bottle, holding it by sticking her index finger in the neck.

"In the beginning of her career," Mark went on, "Urania was invariably cast as the pert ingenue, but you can't get by on that forever. After a few years those parts dry up. When they did, Urania snatched whatever roles she could get her hands on, usually parts every other actress in town had been offered and turned down."

Tracey made a face. "That must have hurt."

"If it did, she never showed it. You've got to hand it to her. Urania's a pro. Given those same circumstances, any other actress would have seen her career go down the tubes. Except that Urania possesses one overwhelming trait."

"Don't tell me," Tracey said. "Ambition."

"Not just ambition. Pure unbridled, know-no-bounds ambition. If Urania's got one thing, it's stick-to-itiveness. She wants something? She's like a rottweiler. And although she may not be a rocket scientist, and her acting will never win her an Oscar, she's never been just another pretty face. When the B-movie roles dried up, she didn't hesitate to do TV. Nowadays that's common, but back in the eighties it was like announcing the demise of your career. Soon as you did guest spots on any of the crime series, bang! Everyone wrote you off as down and out."

Tracey straightened her napkin, carefully realigning her knife, fork, and spoon. "And they wrote Urania off," she guessed. "Only she was down but not out."

"You got that right. One bright young go-getter at NBC, a junior executive, recognized Urania for her camp value. He came up with the idea of doing a TV remake of—talk about heresy—*All About Eve.* Kept pestering the brass until they gave him the green light and an unrealistically minuscule budget, just so he'd go away. Urania was offered a measly fifty grand, which was a slap in the face, but all the budget allowed."

"Which she took."

"Which she took. Not because she needed the money, which she did, but because of the part, which she wanted even more desperately."

They paused as the woman came out once again, this time carrying a giant tray, which she balanced on her hip. On it was a plethora of little plates and bowls, each containing one serving of various delicacies. Tracey recognized mashed eggplant, slices of stuffed octopus, a mound of silvery freshly sauteed sardines with lemon slices, squid baked with pasta, tiny, crisp brown whitebait dredged in flour before frying, zucchini pie, baked chick peas, and more. Much, much more. The intoxicating aromas of olive oil and thyme, mint and oregano, was perfume to the palate.

Mark said, "There's your menu. Just take what you fancy."

Tracey was overwhelmed. "Oh, gosh. Everything looks so good. I wouldn't know where to begin."

"Then I tell you what. Say I pick four dishes, and you pick a different four, and we'll share. You game?"

"Brilliant!" Tracey's eyes lit up. "A real tasting menu. How did you guess I was a sucker for ethnic cuisine?"

He smiled and honed in on a plate of cuttlefish with dill and green olives. "Oh, you just seem the adventurous type."

She glanced at him. "I'll take that as a compliment."

"I meant it as one."

She started selecting dishes. "It's weird, you know?" she said. "My ex-fiancé loathed the restaurants I dragged him to. He was strictly a steak and potatoes kind of guy. Considered anything exotic"—she made quote signs with her fingers—"as the food equivalent of bungee jumping."

Tracey paused, trying to decide between a small bowl of green bean and okra stew with sour *trahana* and a bowl of potato and olive stew with tomato sauce.

"I suppose," Mark said, "that's one reason he's your ex-fiancé."

"Please." Tracey rolled her eyes. "Let's not go there. That was the least of it, believe me."

Mark went for the potato and olive stew, which made her decision easy—she took the green bean and okra. Somehow, between them, they ended up with a total of nine separate dishes.

Tracey smiled up at the woman and gestured that they'd finished making their selection. The woman inventoried their choices with a sharp-eyed glance, nodded her approval, then went off with the still heavily laden tray.

"My God," Tracey said, gazing at the tiny tabletop so crammed with little plates and bowls that their rims jutted precariously out over the edge. "How on earth are we ever going to finish all this?"

Her question was answered by soft fur brushing against her leg. She looked down.

There was one of the cats that hadn't disappeared over the winter. It was a skinny gray one with enormous yellow eyes alert for handouts. Two more cats, a black and a marmalade, were headed their way. None looked overfed.

Tracey glanced at Mark. "You don't mind awfully," she asked, "do you?"

"What? Table feeding?" He picked up a sardine by the tail and flipped it in the air.

Sure enough, the gray cat leapt up, caught it neatly between both front paws, and proceeded to chow down.

The fried sardines were half gone, and Mark and Tracey were still spooning delicacies onto their plates when the woman returned and stuffed another cash register receipt into the little glass. If she had any opinion about their cat feeding, she kept it to herself.

"Dío Marides Tighanites?" Mark said.

The woman nodded and went back inside.

"What was that all about?" Tracey asked.

"I've ordered two more portions of fried whitebait," he explained, nodding at the cats and winning Tracey's heart forever. "Otherwise we won't have any for ourselves."

"Aw," she teased. "How sweet. Who'd ever have guessed that somewhere within that cold agent's heart of yours beats a smidgen of humanity?"

"Just don't tell anyone," he laughed, leaning over the table and spooning half a portion of stuffed octopus onto her plate and taking the rest.

Bit by bit the table was clearing as the empty dishes piled up into a leaning tower. When their plates were finally heaped and the last of the serving dishes empty, the woman returned with two fragrant plates of crispy brown, flour-dredged whitebait fried in olive oil, and the inevitable cash register receipt, which she coiled up and stuck into the little glass. She cleared the table of all the empty dishes and took them away.

Mark poured himself another glass of Mythos. "The ancients had a tradition," he said. "Mead first, feast after."

"Really?" Tracey said, picking up her knife and fork and digging in. "You seem to know the oddest bits of trivia."

"Don't I just," he said cheerfully. "Actually, I know *bubkes*. I just made that up on the spot. Sounds good, though, doesn't it?"

"Why, you little—" She didn't say the word which popped to mind.

"—shit?" he chided good-naturedly. "That is what was on the tip of your tongue, isn't it?"

"I didn't say it," she replied loftily, humming and busying herself with her food.

"Well, I'll forgive you this once," he said. *"Giá sas."* He hoisted his glass, took a long draught, and smacked his lips. "Ah, nectar. What would we humans do without the miracle of fermentation?"

Tracey couldn't help herself. Sometimes her smart-alecky side seemed to have a devilish life of its own. "Well, we might have fewer social problems . . . like drunk driving and domestic violence . . . and as for health, there's always cirrhosis of the liver."

She popped a bite-size portion of stuffed octopus into her mouth. And immediately fell reverently silent. Closing her eyes, she chewed slowly, the better to absorb the various flavors. She purred even before she swallowed.

"Heaven," she pronounced ecstatically, "sheer heaven."

"Worthy of the gods?" Mark teased, raising an eyebrow.

"Worthy of the entire pantheon," she said, in an extravagance of generosity.

"Even the dizzying locale?"

"Even your doses of B.S.," she added tartly, pointing the tines of her fork at him. "For food this good, I'd almost, and I said almost, be inclined to try paragliding."

They ate in silence for a while, too busy savoring the melding flavors of earth and sea to concentrate on talk. Finally, as Tracey made headway with the giant portion on her plate—in no small part due to the cats to which she regularly tossed tidbits—she got the pre-lunch conversation back on track.

"Before this feast arrived," she said, "you were filling me in on *All About Eve*."

"Mmm." He raised a finger, signaling his mouth was full, and she waited until he finished chewing and had swallowed. He took a quick sip of beer to wash the food down. He said, "Right. *All About Eve*. The movie won Best Picture at the Academy Awards in 1950. You're familiar with the story, I take it?"

"Who isn't? It's been like forever, but if I recall correctly, it's about a big Broadway star."

"Character by the name of Margot Channing, who was played by Bette Davis in the movie classic." He nodded. "Yes."

"And a supposedly sweet young woman named Eve who insinuates herself into her life."

"Yup. Eve Harrington, a name which has become synonymous with stealing another person's position, partner, or part. In a way, you could almost say it was the precursor to later cult classics like *Valley of the Dolls*. Without the 'dolls,' of course. Or the more recent *Showgirls*, which everyone was down on, but which I actually enjoyed for its own sake. It too has steadily gained a cult audience since its release."

One of the cats meowed plaintively.

In quick succession Mark flipped a whitebait at each of the three waiting cats. They all leapt up on their hind legs to catch the food neatly in their paws, then wandered off a foot or two to scarf it down. Mark wiped the grease off his fingers on a paper napkin.

"Naturally, when Urania was offered the role," he continued, "she jumped at it. Who in her position wouldn't have? Her career seemed over. Fact is, she would have paid to do it—which, in a way, she ended up doing. She received fifty grand for starring in a two-part, four-hour, made-for-TV movie. By industry standards, you might equate that as worse than a slap in the face."

Tracey shook her head in amazement. "Nothing like a combination of insult and injury, is there?"

He shrugged his shoulders and said: "In show business, you learn to roll with the punches. Like I said before, Urania's a pro. She's had more than her share of ups and downs, and she's always managed to bounce back. What's important is that she recognized the offer for the career reviver it could be. And boy, talk about making the most of it! She threw herself into the role of Margot Channing like there was no tomorrow."

His expression was almost sad as he added, "There are times I'm convinced she's still playing that role. Now, in real life. If you've seen the remake, you'll recognize those moments."

"But I didn't see it," Tracey murmured. "Don't ask how I could have missed it."

"Not to worry." Mark's smile was wry. "I'm sure there are plenty of copies on video floating around the compound. It wouldn't surprise me if Urania stocked every guest room with an entire set of what she likes to refer to as her 'oeuvre.' I'm certain that includes the windmill."

Tracey frowned thoughtfully. "If so, the TV and VCR must be up in the loft. Anyway . . ."

"Okay." He put down his knife and fork. "To make a long story short, filming wrapped and the tape was edited. The network honchos viewed it and sat on it. And sat on it. And kept on sitting on it."

"But for heaven's sake, why? What was the point?"

"You tell me."

"How would I—"

"Exactly." He smiled grimly. "Welcome to the high-wire act called Programming. You see, they couldn't seem to decide whether what they had was good, bad, so bad that it was good, or an unmitigated disaster."

Tracey blinked in disbelief. "That sounds downright bizarre."

"It *is* downright bizarre, which is putting it mildly. In the meantime, though, Urania was in limbo. She wasn't getting any work. See, in showbiz, you're either hot or you're dead—or might as well be."

"Yes, but she'd made that TV movie—"

"Doesn't matter." He shook his head. "If you're in something that never sees daylight, that pretty much lumps you with the dead."

"So how did Urania ever make her comeback?" Tracey wanted to know.

"The way these things usually work: totally by accident. Something like a year and a half later, the network put all its chickens into one pot—a super-expensive miniseries it had pinned everything on to take the spring sweeps by storm. So what happens?"

She waited as he wet his whistle with more beer, inadvertently gaining a little foam mustache on his upper lip. Tracey decided against drawing his attention to it. For some reason she found it inordinately cute.

"What happens," he said, "is a double disaster. First, the start of production is held up for several weeks by a Screen Actors strike. That screwed up the shooting schedule badly enough, but the executives figured they could make up for lost time by rushing production."

"And did they? And more to the point, did it work?"

"Surprisingly, yes to both," Mark Varney said. "Even more surprisingly, the next six weeks progressed as smoothly as any production. Oh, there were the usual pesky problems and squabbles, but nothing major. Even in L.A. you could almost feel the relief emanating from the New York headquarters. And then, three weeks before filming was completed—wham!"

He slammed the fist of one hand into the palm of the other so suddenly that Tracey jumped.

He said, "The lead star did the unpardonable. Would you believe, he had the temerity to die in a car crash?"

Tracey stared at Mark. She didn't know him well enough to tell if he was being ironic or serious.

Then his lips curved into a sardonically crooked smile, which put her mind at rest.

"Thoughtless of him, don't you think?" Mark said. "Imagine! The very idea. Dying before completing crucial scenes that have yet to be filmed. Downright unprofessional by industry standards."

"Tell me." She eyed him narrowly. "Is everyone in Hollywood as cynical as you?"

"If you only knew." He sighed and shook his head. "The trouble is, too many people in showbiz take themselves too damn seriously. They fail to see the obvious humor . . . particularly if a situation involves them, personally. Someone once said that when you come to Hollywood, humor is always the first thing to die."

"How terribly sad. I can't imagine getting through a day without laughing at something."

"Yet it happens all the time. Believe me, all work and all play make for dull Jacks and Jills."

"I bet the star's death gave the big shots some ulcers."

Mark smiled crookedly. "Strokes is more like it. You see, the miniseries was one of those plots where they couldn't just write the star conveniently out of the script, or revise the last third, or have a substitute finish the scenes. As luck—or I should say tragedy—would have it, the entire plot revolved around that one central character."

Tracey plucked some morsels of octopus off her plate and finger-fed the cats under the table. "So what did they do?"

"First, they tried the usual tricks. Brought in writers and tried revising the plot. Attempted to fiddle with the ending. When none of that would work, they realized there was only one solution: casting a new lead. That meant reshooting all the scenes the star was in. Plus—get this—the sets they'd finished with? They'd already been torn down. Everything needed to be rebuilt from scratch."

Tracey said, "You're pulling my leg."

"Nope. As God is my witness." He held up his right hand, palm facing outward. "In Hollywood, truth is always stranger than fiction. Anyway, the execs were finally forced to face their worst nightmare. They had a Sunday and a Tuesday of two-hour sweeps-week prime time that needed filling. You know that saying, 'Nature abhors a vacuum'?"

Tracey nodded.

"Well, television abhors it even more. You can't have empty airtime, especially during sweeps week. That's when the ratings determine a network's advertising rates for the entire coming season. This is not the period for reruns. It's when all the big guns come out. All the enticing shows and hit movies and specials."

"Let me guess," Tracey said. "One of those executives suddenly remembered that *All About Eve* was still sitting on the shelf?"

"Exactly." Mark grinned. "Next thing you know, the network execs make a dash for the screening room, dust off the video, and watch it again. And you know what? Suddenly they decide it . . . isn't that bad. At any rate, it's a whole lot better than nothing, and they slot it in place of the great miniseries that wasn't."

"So it really was an accident."

"Oh, no doubt about it. I might also mention that just in case the ax would fall, those executives hurriedly sniffed around the competition for possible jobs. They were afraid that the ratings might plunge right through the floor—taking them along with 'em."

Tracey was openmouthed. "This is wild!" she exclaimed.

"No," he said quietly, "it's not. It's Hollywood and New York, where Darwinism is rampant. But wait. It gets even wilder. The day after Part One premiered? The Monday between Parts One and Two?"

"Yes? I'm listening."

"Guess where Urania spent that morning."

"Getting a pedicure? Having her hair done? Working out with her personal trainer?"

"She spent that morning in the line at Unemployment. Applying for benefits—and being besieged by autograph hounds while other unemployed folks were cursing and screaming about movie stars living on the dole."

Tracey was mortified. "Jeez, the indignity! If I'd been in her shoes, I would have died." She carefully wiped grease off each individual finger with her napkin. "But you're wrong. It isn't wild. It's nutty!"

"Even nuttier, then, was the audience response. When the overnight Nielsons came in, *All About Eve* trounced the competition. Won the time slot hands down. Want to know something nuttier yet? Part Two actually *gained* viewers, thanks to old-fashioned word of mouth. So here Urania was, on the one hand not knowing where her next paycheck was coming from, and in the meantime saving the network's ass and earning them multimillions."

"This," Tracey told him, "sounds definitely like *Twilight Zone* material."

He shrugged. "Like I said, it's Hollywood. One day Urania Vickers was out in the cold, and the next she's sizzling on the front burner. After what seemed like a lifetime of silence, her agent's phone suddenly started ringing off the hook."

Tracey shook her head. "Hot, cold; hot, cold. How on earth can anyone stand to live like that?"

"Well, it isn't for the faint of heart, that's for certain. Or for anyone who craves financial security. It takes a special breed. Someone who has a tough hide, a willingness to forgo everything else, and a vampire's hunger for stage blood. Someone who'll do anything to get a part."

Tracey said, "In other words, someone like Urania."

"Someone like Urania," he agreed. "Exactly."

The frumpy woman came out and eyed the table, checking to see if they were finished.

Mark looked at Tracey. "Dessert?" he asked.

Tracey pushed her chair back a few inches and rubbed her stomach. "No way. I don't have room for another bite. I'd burst at the seams."

"Coffee?"

"No, thanks, but you go right on ahead."

"I prefer it later. A nice *café fredo* by the pool."

"Sounds nice."

"It is nice."

Mark asked for the check by making scribbling motions on an imaginary pad. The woman nodded. Tracey noticed that even the cats were momentarily satiated, and had gone their separate ways, presumably to sleep off the feast. Such is the reassurance of a full stomach.

Mark Varney settled the bill, which was calculated from the glassful of receipts. Despite the automatic thirteen percent service charge figured into the check, he left a handsome tip.

"Because sooner or later, I know I'll be back," he told Tracey. "So, probably, will you."

Back out on Oia's main drag, the pedestrians had thinned perceptibly. It was the hottest time of the day, and a lot of the shops were closed for a few hours. They would open again later, and do a brisk evening trade. The merchants had the cruise ship and tour bus schedules down to a science; some would stay open until the last of the restaurants closed.

Tracey and Mark took their time moseying back to Urania's compound. Idly they stopped to gaze into one beguiling shopwindow after another.

"All About Eve," Tracey murmured.

Her voice feigned disinterest, while her eyes roamed over a surface of white velvet pads in a jeweler's display. They were evenly studded with rows and rows of gold rings set with lapis lazuli and other semi-precious stones. But Tracey only pretended interest in jewelry. What she was trying to fish for was information about Urania. Only then could she start to sort out the star's history into some kind of coherent chronological order. Hopefully, that might help her insofar as it could have affected her own life.

"What about *Eve*?" Mark asked.

"When was it first aired?"

"Oh, God. Back when dinosaurs roamed the earth. Lemme think . . . she followed *Eve* with that TV-remake of *What Ever Happened to Baby Jane?*"

"Another Bette Davis classic?"

"Yep. And playing the grotesque Baby Jane Hudson made her a household word. See, Urania had finally managed to find her niche. She was the bitch audiences loved to hate. From then on, she was invariably typecast. No more Baby Janes, though. Glamourpusses with claws. If you want my opinion, the reason she plays the quintessential bitch so well is because it doesn't require any acting. Urania *is* the consummate bitch."

"That still doesn't answer my question," Tracey pointed out.

"No, you're right. It doesn't. Hmmm." He looked thoughtful. "Let me work backward in time. Urania reached her peak when she was cast as the conniving, glamorous Jezzy—short for Jezebel—on that nighttime soap set in Scottsdale. It ran for—how long?"

Tracey looked at him blankly.

"Right." He chuckled and shook his head. "I keep forgetting, you're a babe in the woods. You must have barely been in your teens. I'd hazard to say nine seasons? Ten? Around there, anyway. Which means it must have gone off the air . . . oh . . . something like seven years ago. Maybe eight. Using that and *Baby Jane* as a guide, I assume that *All About Eve* was probably first shown around 'eighty-two, meaning that shooting on it must have wrapped around 'eighty."

Looking slightly puzzled, he added, "Why do you ask?"

Tracey shrugged. "I was just wondering, that's all." She moved away from the window and strolled on to the next, yet another goldsmith's, with apparent nonchalance.

Which was hardly the way she felt. Her heart had begun to thump faster, and her pulse was racing as she did some quick mental arithmetic.

Is that where I fit in? she wondered. *During Urania's year-and-a-half of limbo between finishing* All About Eve *and its premiere*? Eighteen months. *That would have given Urania plenty of time to become pregnant and have a baby in secret.*

And another thing to keep in mind:

Back then Urania hadn't exactly been a household word. She hadn't been a fraction as famous, or as readily recognizable, as the international star and celebrity that TV had since made of her. There was no reason why she couldn't have married Dad under the assumed name of Victoria Ure and gotten away with it . . . "A euro." Mark's voice intruded upon her introspection.

"What? Oh. Sorry." Tracey turned to him and gestured with feminine helplessness at the strands of gold necklaces and bracelets glittering in the window. "I was distracted . . ."

He smiled. "I was just saying, a euro for your thoughts."

My thoughts. The words triggered an instant defensive mechanism. "Oh, they're not even worth an expired coupon," Tracey said dismissively.

But she was really thinking, *If you only knew the half of it. Or, for that matter, if* I *only knew . . .*

Chapter Twenty-one

Miami, Florida

The headquarters of the Miami Police Department is a huge hulking concrete bunker. Five stories tall, its ungainly facade is clad in clay-colored tiles; more tiles—these riotously colorful, hand painted, and artist commissioned—form a huge abstract mural. Besides being in keeping with the city's offbeat architecture, the mural fulfills the law in that a certain percentage of funding for all municipal buildings is to be devoted to art—a progressive ideal which, as this structure proves, can be a double-edged sword. For the mural, despite its well-intentioned purpose of providing culture to the masses, has been known to cause headaches in bright sunshine, due to the glare reflecting off the glazed tiles.

At the moment, however, there was no danger of sun-reflected glare, for the famous Miami sun was not shining. It often doesn't in summer, being the height of the wet season. Accordingly, greenish-black thunderheads swirled low overhead and the air was thick with the smell of ozone. A zigzagging fork of lightning pulsated, lit up the eerie clouds, and crashed to earth uncomfortably close by.

Maribel, holding a manila envelope protectively against

her chest with one hand and clutching Ramón's arm with the other, said breathlessly, "I hope this friend of yours in the fraud division . . . what's his name again?"

Her heels click-clacked a triple-time staccato up the gradual incline which serves as the wheelchair-friendly access to the main entrance of police headquarters. She and Ramón were trying to outrun the fast approaching storm.

"Montague Pleasance," Ramón supplied, having to raise his voice above the rising wind which tore at their clothes and whipped Maribel's hair sideways.

"Right, Montague Pleasance." She turned her head as a dust devil of grit swirled, and she cringed against another round of lightning. Simultaneously, an earsplitting crack of thunder followed, echos booming like artillery.

"C'mon," he urged, "let's hurry before we get wet."

Despite wobbly heels, Maribel picked up a burst of speed.

"Well, I hope this Montague can do something," she half shouted. "Besides Trace being my best friend, I just hate it when crooks think they can get away with ruining people's lives! There must be some way of stopping them."

"We'll find out soon enough. I told you, if there's anything that can be done, Monty's your guy."

Ramón and Maribel burst through the front doors and into the building lobby just as the storm broke. An instant later, a fusillade of rain thrashed against the glass with hail-like fury; outside, palms were bent in the wind, fronds went flying, and an overturned garbage can rolled down the sidewalk, its contents gone with the wind.

"Whew!" Maribel exclaimed with relief. "Made it just in the nick of time."

Ray guided her past clusters of people waiting around in the lobby for the worst of the storm to pass and stopped at the reception desk. It was manned by a uniformed veteran of the MPD, a sparse cop with skin like beef jerky, red jug ears, hair mown in a bristly old-fashioned flat-top, and narrowed eyes which gave the impression they had seen everything.

Ramón said, "We have an appointment with Detectives Pleasance and Sadwith, Fraud Division."

The cop picked up his phone. "Who should I say wants to see them?"

Ramón handed him a business card. The cop held it at a distance and squinted at it, punched an extension, and spoke into the phone. When he hung up, he gave Ramón a laminated visitor's pass.

"Appreciate it if you return this on your way out. The office you're looking for is on the third floor. Elevator's over that way."

"Thanks," Ramón smiled politely. "I know the way."

They took the next available elevator up.

The Fraud Division took up a medium-size room crammed full of work stations and filing cabinets. Cops of both sexes had on civvies, with shirt sleeves rolled up to their elbows. They sat behind computer monitors or spoke into phones, or studiously searched through voluminous stacks of papers and even old-fashioned ledgers.

Off this main room was a cubbyhole of a private windowless office. Beside the open door two engraved name plates were affixed to the wall:

DET. STANLEE SADWITH
DET. MONTAGUE PLEASANCE

Ramón glanced through the open door. Curious, Maribel hopped on tiptoe behind him and peered over his shoulder. She saw two Formica work stations pushed together, facing each other. Behind one sat a small thin woman with a lively freckled face, bright amber eyes, and a Dorothy Hamill haircut. She was sipping black coffee from a paper cup while scrolling down rows of numbers on her computer screen.

Ramón tapped on the door with a knuckle. "Knock knock," he said.

The woman twisted around. "Hey, Señor Fashion Plate!" Her face lit up with pleasure, and she quickly set down her coffee. "So whatcha doin', Ray? Long time no visit."

"Far too long, Stan. I've been remiss. Forgive me?"

"You I'll forgive anything. You know that."

He grinned. "Yeah, right. Anyway, how's life been treating you?"

"Crappy, as usual," she chortled, "or did you think anything has changed?" Then, noticing Maribel craning her neck from behind him, she raised her eyebrows questioningly.

"Oh," Ramón said. "Excuse my lack of manners." He inched sideways in the cramped space. "This is Maribel Pinales, a friend of mine. Maribel, this is Detective Stanlee Sadwith."

Maribel reached around Ramón and shook the woman's hand. Stanlee's grip was firm and businesslike, and the haircut and dye job deceived. She was older than she'd first appeared, with pronounced crow's feet and a cross-hatching of wrinkles.

"Never try to pull a fast one on Stan," Ramón warned Maribel good-naturedly. "She's got a photographic memory."

Maribel smiled. "I'll keep that in mind before I perpetrate a scam."

Stanlee hooted. "Looks like you've got your hands full, Ray." She added, "It's about time."

Ignoring that, Ramón said smoothly, "And now that you've met Stan, I'd like to introduce you to the other half of the equation. Meet the scourge of racketeers, con men, money launderers, swindlers, bank hackers—you name it. A legend in his own time, the one and only Montague Pleasance."

A name like that, Maribel had this immediate mental image of an uptight, starched little British fellow with maybe a pencil-thin mustache and nasal intonations. All stiff upper lip and snooty, the kind of guy who drank Pimm's. Either that, or a WASP from way up north, the type who could have stepped right out of a Ralph Lauren ad.

Which couldn't have been further off the mark.

From behind his computer monitor, the legend in his own time launched himself sideways on his swivel chair and into view. His movements were gracefully lithe and haughty as a native cat's, and his skin was the color of pale rum. He wore his black hair in Rastafarian dreadlocks.

Maribel was totally thrown. For more reasons than one.

For starters, Montague Pleasance looked like he belonged in a reggae band, an impression reinforced by his ragged, sleeveless shirt, a crudely sewn concoction made from four or five torn-up shirts of varying patterns and colors—red, pink, lilac, lime, and white. He wore it open, like a vest, the mismatched buttons undone. Instead of pants he had a kind of batik-patterned sarong knotted around his waist. Bare feet shod in sandals. A strand of beads around his neck; another around one wrist.

Amazingly, he not only seemed utterly at ease in this very un-MPD getup, but he exuded sex appeal without even trying. Sinewy arms, abdomen muscled with the requisite six-pack, and a cool dude attitude clinched it.

"Eh, mon," he said, aiming his put-upon tone at Ramón. "Why you bodder us busy hardworkin' people? You got trouble wit' your rich clients, dat your business. We just underpaid public servants, you understand?"

Then, catching sight of Maribel, he sat up straight and grinned hugely, his teeth as white as alpine snow.

He said, "Hel-lo, pree-ty woman!" Then tilted his head sideways and looked concerned. "But Montague has to ask himself, what's a lovely lady like that doin' hangin' around wit' legal slime like that Ramón?"

"Oh, cut the nonsense, Monty," Ray said good-naturedly. And in a stage whisper to Maribel, "Don't let the phony Jamaican accent fool you. Or the patched-up po' boy clothes. His brain gives every crooked accountant nightmares."

Maribel glanced at Ramón and then back at Montague. "But he is a cop?"

He nodded. "Oh, yeah. Has the shield to prove it. As for his . . . er . . . *wardrobe*, it's generally overlooked since he sometimes volunteers to go out and do undercover work. Otherwise, you wouldn't see a guy getting away wearing skirts here at police headquarters. Unless it's a prostitute in the slammer." He paused. "Hey, Monty. You doing vice as a sideline without telling me?"

Montague took umbrage. "Sh-shoot. I wear a skirt, I look fine, mon."

"All right already," Stanlee interjected sternly. "Montague, behave yourself. Ray, don't give him any excuses to get started. We have departmental reputations to uphold."

Maribel decided then and there to put Montague's obvious interest in her to good use. He might be a lot more willing to listen and actually do something if she teased him a little. *Anything for Tracey,* she thought. Then she restrained a laugh. *As if flirting is something I've never done before.*

"Why don't you have a seat?" Montague said, indicating two banged-up wooden chairs.

Ramón held one for Maribel, then sat down in the other. She crossed her legs and angled them in Montague's direction, making no effort to pull down her miniskirt. She let one of her stiletto-heeled pumps dangle loosely from her foot. These were four-and-a-half-inch-high wonders she referred to as her chicka-chicka boom-boom heels because she knew that they were mankillers. Most guys loved to see her wearing them.

"So to what do we owe the honor of your presence, counselor?" Stanlee asked, getting down to business.

Maribel felt Montague's eyes roving her body, and she shifted in her seat slightly, exposing a little extra thigh at the same time. *I'm going to get him all hot and bothered,* she thought brazenly. *He's going to want to hear every single word I have to say.* Besides, now that she was sitting so close to him, she could see that underneath the Rasta getup Montague was an extremely handsome and virile specimen.

"Maribel told me a story that I think you'd be very interested in," Ramón said, his tone suddenly professional. "I think it's right down your alley. And she's brought a lot of paperwork with her for you to look over if you've got the time."

Maribel propped the manila envelope on her knees and tapped it as if to say, Here it is.

Stanlee looked at the envelope with narrowed eyes. "Why don't we hear what she's got to say for starters?" she said.

"Then if we think it's something Fraud would be interested in, we'll take a look at the paperwork," Montague added, smiling provocatively at Maribel.

"Sounds good," Ramón said. He turned to Maribel. "Why don't you tell them everything you told me," he said, putting an arm across the back of her chair protectively. "Don't leave out anything."

Maribel cleared her throat. "Well . . . let me see . . . where do I begin?" she said. "There's so much."

"We've got plenty of time, pretty lady," Montague said solicitously.

"Give us the high spots," Stanlee said, "then we can go from there."

"Okay," Maribel replied, taking a deep breath before launching into her story.

Though she got off to a slow start, for over the next thirty minutes the words spilled out of Maribel in a torrent, and more than once she had to slow down and reiterate in order for Stanlee and Montague to grasp what she'd said. She filled them in on what had happened to Tracey's father, emphasizing the unlikeliness of his committing suicide, the pressure being put on him by developers to sell the house in Coconut Grove, Brian's deception of Tracey, and the resale of the mortgage that Tracey hadn't known about. Stanlee and Montague interrupted her several times to ask questions, but when she mentioned Palm Coast Developers, they exchanged quick glances.

Maribel didn't miss the looks they gave one another. "Have you heard of them?" she asked.

"You bet we have," Stanlee said.

"And something about them stinks," Montague added, his demeanor serious.

"This whole thing stinks," Stanlee said, exhaling an exasperated sigh.

"Do you think you can be of any help?" Ramón asked.

Montague nodded. "Number one," he said in a serious voice, "we're going to have Sullivan's car gone over with a fine-tooth comb. I'm pretty sure that it'll still be impounded, so that shouldn't be a problem. We'll see what his car has to tell us." He looked over at Stanlee for confirmation.

She nodded emphatically and said, "And I think we'll have a long look at that paperwork you've got there before we pay a call on Mr. Brian Biggs III."

Maribel clapped her hands together. It was all she could do to keep from shouting with glee. *If only I could call Tracey right this minute,* she thought. She could hardly wait to tell her the good news. And this *was* good news. Maribel was sure of it. As sure of it as she was that Tom Sullivan hadn't committed suicide and that something very fishy was going on with Palm Coast.

She was abruptly aware of Ramón's hand gripping her shoulder. "Feel better?" he asked her, a big smile on his handsome face.

"You bet I do," she replied. "A lot better, Ray."

"Don't worry," Montague said, "if there's something to what you've told us—and personally I think there is—we'll get to the bottom of it." He turned to Stanlee. "Won't we, partner?"

Stanlee nodded. "It's going to take some time," she said, "but we'll be getting back to you soon. About the car, at any rate. Montague'll call Forensics and get them busy on that car right away." She turned to him. "I bet those guys owe you some favors, don't they, Monty?"

"You know me, don't you, Stanlee? Of course they do. I'd say they'll be working on that car by this afternoon."

"Well, we'll get out of your way," Ramón said. "Let you do your work." He turned to Maribel. "Ready?"

She nodded and rose to her feet, then stepped over to Stanlee and put out her hand. "Thank you very much," she said solemnly. "This means a lot to me and my friend."

Stanlee shook her hand. "Your friend's got a real pal in you," she said. "We could all use a friend like you. We'll do our best."

"Thanks," Maribel repeated, then she turned and approached Montague. "Thank you, too, Montague," she said, offering him her hand to shake.

Montague took the proffered hand between both of his and held it gently. "Don't you worry, pretty lady," he said. "We're *on* this." He squeezed her hand and looked up at her flirtatiously.

Maribel thrust a miniskirted thigh toward him. "I'm so grateful," she said. "I don't know how to thank you, but it's been a pleasure to meet you and I hope we meet again."

"We'd better go," Ramón said. "You'll give a call, Monty. Right?"

"You know it," Monty said, releasing Maribel's hand at last. "And sooner rather than later."

"See you later," Maribel said, her voice full of promise. She turned, to all appearances reluctantly, and followed Ramón to the office door, where she stopped and sketched a wave over her shoulder. *"Ciao."*

Chapter Twenty-two

Santorini, Greece

Tracey had been hard at work for a week, engulfing herself in the messily told story that Urania was trying to tell. The task was an arduous one, but there was at least one growing interest that made the work much easier. Actually it was more than an interest, she'd decided, but she didn't know what to call it. At least not yet. What she did know was that there was a growing bond between herself and—dare she believe it?—Mark Varney.

They had managed to steal moments to talk with each other, and these snatched bits of time had become a treasure trove to her. Another thing she was certain of was that Mark felt the same way. He hadn't said so, but she had the unmistakable feeling that their short time together was becoming increasingly important to him.

She gazed into the computer without really seeing what was on the screen. *If only I could talk to somebody about it,* she thought. *If only Maribel were here.* She knew that discussing it was probably premature, but she was excited by this new bond and felt a powerful urge to share it with her best friend.

She finally decided to shut down the computer and go to

the Mini Market. She would see if she could get hold of Maribel right now. It only took a few minutes to get ready, and off she went.

The store was in a sandy yellow building composed of two cubes, the slightly smaller one stacked atop the larger. Above the front entrance was a large sign which read MINI MARKET in English and, beneath that, in smaller letters: *Täglich Frisches Gemüse,* in German.

The entrance to the store was two steps down. She stepped inside the store and abruptly stopped short. Two masklike visages, paler than the surrounding shadows, seemed to loom in midair like ghosts.

Tracey gasped, then realized that from the sun-drenched brightness outside, she couldn't have noticed the two old crones just on the other side of the threshold.

One was seated on a bentwood chair, hands folded atop the crook of a wooden cane, while the other was standing behind her. The faces of both looked like withered apples, and they were dressed entirely in traditional island black: head coverings, long-sleeved dresses, aprons, shawls, stockings, shoes. But there the resemblance ended.

The old woman seated in the chair was scraggy and gaunt to the point of emaciation. She had milky eyes and was obviously blind. She was also dirty, her clothing caked with dust and grease. She wore her shawl like a scarf, completely wrapped around her face, the long ends trailing back over hunched shoulders. Her jaw had the lipless, collapsed look of the toothless, and the gnarled hands atop the cane showed hornlike yellow fingernails badly in need of trimming and cleaning. The hands themselves attested to someone of great age: skeins of raised blue veins showed clearly from beneath loose, nearly translucent flesh.

The woman standing behind her was younger, though not by far, but was the better dressed. Her clothes were clean and pressed and unstained. She wore a traditional scarf knotted under her chin and incongruously large, beige-framed glasses. She was staring at Tracey with disapproval, if not downright hostility. Tracey suddenly realized that it was Mrs. Stefanou's mother.

"Don't let them scare you," called out a female voice in

unaccented English. "They just look like witches. I either tell people the third one got lost and is holding up the production of *Macbeth*, or that she's out searching for the one eye they have to share between them. But there really isn't a third one, thank God." There was a chuckle in her voice. "Help you with anything?"

Relieved to hear such fluent English, Tracey approached the counter. The woman behind the cash register was young and slim, with bright clear eyes and a good-natured face. She wore her dark hair pulled back and snug Levi's and a short-sleeved, plain black top. She reached up into one of the shallow shelves behind the counter. Took down some credit-card-size plastic. Fanned a handful out on the counter like a croupier dealing cards.

"As far as phone cards go," she said, "you'll want at least one of OTE's five euros, a ten if you intend to make a couple of overseas calls. Or, if you're not a clock watcher and tend to have long chats with friends, I advise getting two tens."

Tracey stared at her with alarm. Evidently the woman had psychic powers. How else could she have divined the very reason she'd popped in?

"Oh, chill out and stop looking at me like I'm some sort of freak," the young woman said. "It's not as if I can read minds."

"Then how—"

"—did I know what you came in for?"

Tracey nodded.

"It doesn't exactly take a clairvoyant. Look, you're employed by Urania Vickers, right?"

"I . . . I guess you could call me the new secretary."

" 'Secretary'! You do mean 'administrative assistant,' don't you? I believe 'secretary' went the way of 'airline stewardess.' "

"Here I am," Tracey said, "a woman using sexist language."

The young woman smiled. "Well, I'm sure I'll be seeing you around." She held out her hand. "I'm Kathy Vasilatos, by the way."

Tracey took her hand and shook it. "And I'm Tracey Sullivan."

"Anyway, Ms. Vickers is notorious for being cheap. And that battle ax, Mrs. Stefanou? She makes sure visitors understand that they either use their own cell phones, make collect calls, or buy phone cards and use a public telephone. You wouldn't believe how many phone cards I sell to your employer's guests."

Aha! Tracey thought. *There's no one like a shopkeeper when it comes to gossip.*

"I take this to mean Urania Vickers gets lots of visitors?" Tracey inquired, her voice deceptively casual.

Kathy frowned thoughtfully. "Come to think of it," she said slowly, "not half as many as one would imagine, considering she is—or was—a major star . . . yet a hell of a lot more than she ought to have if she's trying to pull a Garbo."

"And what about family?" Tracey ventured, trying to sound vaguely disinterested.

"Hmmm." Kathy shook her head. "Strange. You've really got me there. I don't recall any relatives, and if there were some, I'm positive I would remember. It's hardly the sort of thing one forgets, someone's being related to a movie star, is it?"

Tracey shook her head.

"And I've got hearing like you wouldn't believe. I turn on the transistor radio? I can listen to music or the news, talk to a customer, ring up a batch of groceries, *and* catch what people are whispering all the way in the back. Can you believe it? All simultaneously and from up front here."

"That's amazing!"

"Not really. Try working in a Mom-and-Pop as long as I have; you'll learn all sorts of tricks to alleviate the boredom and routine. But getting back to Ms. Vickers. We can't discount the possibility that relatives of hers did come in and buy phone cards, although they didn't chat or identify themselves in any way. Most people don't. Oia's very transient. Herds come and hoards go, and new herds keep coming. Very few people stay here all summer long."

"Yes, I suppose there is that."

"Also, you've got to keep in mind that I'm on duty only half the time. Mikey minds the store the other half. I'm certain he never mentioned any relatives of Urania Vickers's coming in, but who can tell? Some things go right over men's heads. They simply aren't attuned to the same things as us. For what it's worth, why don't you drop by later, when we change shifts? You can ask him yourself."

Tracey would have liked to, but she didn't want to seem too interested. The fact that she might have a personal stake in uncovering Urania's past was nobody's business but her own.

"Aw, it's not that important," she said dismissively.

"Whatever." Kathy was disappointed, somehow let down. "Just offering, that's all. Like I always say, 'What's life without a little gossip?' Tell you what. I'll ask Mikey, and next time I see you I'll let you know what he says. That okay with you?"

That suited Tracey just fine. "That's perfect."

"Anything else I can tell you about this terribly exciting place?" she asked.

Tracey held out a hand as though to stop traffic. "Please," she moaned, "spare me. I've about reached my saturation point for the time being. Ever since I arrived here I've been on the verge of sensory overload."

"I know what you mean." Kathy laughed. "Just give it time. The longer you're here, the more ordinary this place seems."

"Really?" Tracey didn't sound the least bit convinced.

"Really. And I should know."

Tracey tilted her head to one side and frowned. "You know," she observed, speaking slowly, "there's one thing I don't quite get."

"And what's that?"

"Your English. It's incredibly good, and your vernacular's perfect. I can't detect a trace of a Greek accent."

Kathy scrunched up her face. "I should hope not. My parents emigrated to Canada when I was two. I grew up in Toronto."

"Well, that explains it, then. I take it you live here now? For good?"

"If by 'here' you mean Greece, yes. I came back after I married Mikey. You haven't met him yet."

"Mikey . . . he sounds American. Or is he Canadian?"

"Actually, he was baptized Makis, which is the Greek equivalent of Michael, or Mike."

"So he was born here in Greece?"

"Yep, just like me. Only on Zakinthos. That's over in the Ionian. Like mine, his parents also emigrated to Canada when he was a toddler. Don't ask me why, but in addition to being attracted to one another, we both felt compelled to come back here."

"And he does what?"

"At the moment, he's at home. Guarding the monsters." She pointed at the wall behind the counter with no small amount of parental pride. Tracey's eyes followed her finger. There, tacked above shallow shelves containing stacks of cigarette packs, yellow and green boxes of film, various-size batteries, disposable lighters, and the like, were several snapshots with curling corners. In one, a boy of seven or eight, wearing a Pokémon T-shirt, was trying on an adult's wraparound sunglasses. In another, his younger sister stared solemnly into the camera. Yet a third showed the two children together.

"They're adorable!"

"What you mean is, they look adorable." Kathy laughed. "Lemme tell you, they sure are a handful. Anyway, Mikey and I alternate shifts. When I'm here minding the shop, he's home with them. And when I'm home, he's here."

"That reminds me. I take it you're familiar with Prometheus?"

"You've already made Pro's acquaintance, huh?"

Tracey nodded. "Yes, I did."

"Well, I can't say I'm terribly surprised. Anyone who's here for any amount of time generally runs into him . . . or rather, he runs into them."

"What's his story?"

Kathy sighed and fixed Tracey with her soft brown velvet eyes.

"Other than he's cute as a button, terribly sweet, highly intelligent, and totally adorable? And that he absolutely drives your Mrs. Stefanou up the wall with his cats?"

"She's not my Mrs. Stefanou, I'll let you know," Tracey retorted tartly.

"Nor mine." Kathy flashed her a cockeyed grin. "Lucky us, huh? But you asked me about Pro. Hmmm. Lemme see now. Where do I start? Well, for one thing, he's a regular little spelunker. To hear him tell it, he's familiar with every cave, nook, and cranny at this end of the island."

"And is he?"

"Somehow I wouldn't doubt it. There are times when he looks like he literally crawled out from under some rock."

"I presume," Tracey inquired carefully, "that he has a home? That he's not just some poor urchin living in a cave somewhere and running loose?"

"Pro? Homeless! Good Lord, no. He has a home, all right, and quite a nice one, too. The only rub is, it's a one-parent household. Just his father, who overindulges him and spoils him rotten."

Tracey couldn't help but compare Prometheus's upbringing with her own. She, too, had come from a one-parent household. *And Dad spoiled me rotten, too,* she remembered.

"I assume," Kathy said, "that showering him with material things is intended to make up for an absentee mother. But nothing can ever do that, can it?"

"I don't think so," Tracey agreed. "So what happened to his mother? Did she die?"

Kathy snorted. "If only she had! At least that would have given Pro and his Dad some feeling of closure. But no"—she shook her head in disgust—"Momma up and packed her bags one day and left—without so much as an *adiós* or you can reach me wherever. At the time, rumor had it she had a thing going with an underage seaman from one of the cruise ships. You know, the kind that makes the rounds of several islands every five days, letting its passengers go ashore and shop in Fíra for a few hours? Seems she met the guy on a regular basis and then ran off with him at season's end."

"How awful! When did this happen?"

"Two years ago, come September."

"Poor Pro! He must have been heartbroken!"

"I imagine he still is."

"Yes, he must be," Tracey murmured. "Small wonder he's

such a friend to stray cats. He certainly has firsthand knowledge about how it feels to be deserted."

Tracey glanced toward the door and happened to catch sight of the wall clock mounted above it. "Yikes!" she exclaimed. "I'd better get going."

She swiftly counted backward seven hours. It was a good time to try Maribel in Miami. Right now, Tracey figured, her friend would just be starting in on her second mug of strong black Café Bustelo.

"I only dropped in to pick up some phone cards," Tracey said, now that she was in a rush. "I've got to get going. There's still a call I *have* to make, or else."

"Welcome to the neighborhood, Trace. I'm sure you'll find it . . . fascinating." This last was said wryly. "Don't be a stranger."

"I won't be," Tracey promised.

"Yá sas." Kathy smiled. "That's good-bye in Greek."

"Yá sas," Tracey repeated, shouldering her bag. She was hurrying out the door past the old crones when her elbow accidentally connected with the shoulder of the blind woman.

It was a mild collision, but the reaction it provoked took Tracey aback. The crone gasped and cried out louder than such a little nudge deserved. A torrent of harsh-sounding words in Greek followed.

"Sorry," Tracey murmured in a tiny embarrassed voice.

She began to tiptoe carefully the rest of the way past the crones, but a claw suddenly shot out and clutched her arm, jerking her back into the shop.

Tracey jumped. What on God's earth? She looked down into the ancient withered face. This close, the eyes weren't purely milky, after all. They were more like cooked albumen, tinted with the palest touch of blue, and were wide with premonition. Eerie. As was the trembling crooked forefinger, tipped with its dirty horn-like nail, which was pointing directly up at her. She looked like a witch out of some nightmarish fairy tale.

The hairs on the back of Tracey's neck lifted, as though by a breeze, only there was none. The skin on her arms bristled, and a cold tingling sensation rippled along her spine. The old hag was rasping Greek at her, but she had no idea what she was jabbering on about. Whatever it was, it didn't sound nice. It sounded, as a matter of fact, rather like a string of obscenities.

Or ominous curses.

Tracey tried to shake the claw off, but the nails dug deeper into her arm. And the other crone, Mrs. Stefanou's mother, had drawn back, her own clawlike hand at her breast, magnified eyes huge with alarm.

The blind crone continued rasping, her forefinger wagging, her other claw-like hand shaking Tracey's arm for emphasis.

What in blazes?

Tracey looked helplessly over her shoulder at Kathy. "What's she spouting *on* about? I barely bumped her. I realize she's old, but surely I couldn't have hurt her."

"Oh, just ignore her," Kathy advised. Then she spoke sharply to the old crone in Greek.

The old crone's toothless gums worked overtime and she lashed some words back at her.

"What is it?" Tracey wanted to know.

"Oh, nothing," Kathy advised, with a roll of her eyes. "This is a regular occurrence."

"Of what? Tourette's syndrome?"

Kathy laughed. "If only! No, she doesn't go around spouting obscenities. She thinks she's psychic."

Tracey looked at her sharply. "Is she?"

"How would I know?"

"But what did she say?"

Kathy sighed. "She says that you must leave at once. She insists that grave danger awaits you."

Despite Tracey's logical, no-nonsense approach to life, this idea gave her the willies. The ferociousness of the crone's grip, the fierceness with which she obviously believed in what she foretold, combined with the unsettling cooked egg white of her eyes, went through Tracey like a shock. She began trembling violently.

"What . . . what does she mean, 'grave danger'?"

"Oh, forget it," Kathy advised, with a dismissive gesture. "She thinks she has the Gift and can foresee the future."

She cracked a lopsided smile. "I wouldn't worry about it if I were you. Some of the old-timers believe in her, but they're a superstitious lot."

More jabber issued from the crone, the words aimed up at Tracey; it was followed by another sharp volley of a reply from Kathy in Greek.

"Now what?" Tracey wanted to know.

"I told her she's got to stop scaring my customers."

"Yes, but . . . what did she say before that?"

Kathy sighed. "Oh, you know. The usual hokum. Something about how you recently suffered loss of love and the death of someone very near and dear—"

"Stop!" Tracey whispered, feeling as though someone had walked over her grave. She was barely aware that she was trembling or that Kathy was giving her a strange look. She was engulfed by the strangeness of the surroundings and the suffocating aggressiveness of the heat. She was afraid that in another moment she was going to faint dead away.

The forefinger tipped with its crescent of black nail had stopped wagging. The crone reached into the folds of her dirty black garments. After a bit of searching, she pressed something small and light into Tracey's hand, then forced her fingers to close around it.

Another hissed barrage in Greek.

Tracey once again snapped her head in Kathy's direction. "Now what?" Her voice was soft.

"Really, Trace. I wish you wouldn't pay any attention to her. It just encourages her."

"But I want to know."

"All right. If you insist." Kathy sighed but continued reluctantly. "She says you are to wear it on your person at all times. To ward off the evil eye."

Tracey opened her fingers and looked down into the palm of her hand. Nestled there was a tiny gold charm, identical on both sides. In the center of a circle no larger than a quarter of an inch across was a rounded, bright blue glass eye with a black pupil. The thin gold border enclosing the eye had a loop at the top for stringing it through a ribbon or a chain.

"I can't take this," Tracey exclaimed. "This is gold."

"Cheap, mass market tourist junk," Kathy declared knowingly. "Trust me. They're a dime a dozen. If you want my advice, accept it. That will get her off your back. And, if you really want to make her happy, wear it around your neck." She gave a little choke of laughter. "You're going to be on this island for a while, right?"

"Y-yes."

"Well, you don't want to go through this rigmarole every time you run into her, do you? And believe me, run into her you will. Take away the tourists, and this place shrinks to nothing."

Tracey took a deep breath. *Kathy has a point,* she told herself. *Why fight it? Besides, there's no harm in it. So take the damn thing, thank the woman, and be done with it.*

"How," she inquired, "do you say 'thank you' in Greek? I've forgotten already."

Kathy smiled knowingly, and with approval. *"Efcharistó,"* she said.

"Efcharistó," Tracey told the old woman softly.

That did the trick. She let go of Tracey's arm and nodded.

Free of the viselike claw, Tracey started to leave when—

Snap. Something happened. She had no idea what. Had the light changed? Had the oxygen suddenly been sucked out of the room? Whatever it was, a rush of claustrophobia overtook her. All at once the surroundings seemed leeched of color, as though some vampiric spirit had drained them of life. Everything had somehow become drab and dull, part and parcel of some grimmer and grayer world.

Perspective, too, had undergone a major distortion. Things seemed *closer* . . . a lot nearer physically, and loomed large and tall and menacing, as if the walls and shelves were physically closing in around her.

Tracey felt like Alice in Wonderland shrinking smaller and smaller even as the two crones—in particular the blind one—were growing enormously in size. Before long, they would reach the ceiling and hover over her, pressing down upon her like some roiling, menacing cloud.

It was too much. Tracey felt trapped. Nauseated. Unable

to breathe and overwhelmed by a feeling of impending doom.

"I'm . . . outta here!" she managed to gasp hoarsely, though not without a massive shudder. She didn't hurry out so much as flee.

Escape was her only priority.

She rushed from the hallucinatory confines of the shop. Nearly tripped as she staggered out the open door. Banged her knee resoundingly against the corner of the ice cream chest, but felt no immediate pain. Escape, and escape alone, was on Tracey's mind as she stumbled up the front steps and along Oia's main drag. Her breathing was ragged, and after the dim interior of the shop, the sunlight blinded. Yet all the while, she still retained the impression that, from the door of the Mini Market, the blind crone was watching her departure.

Watching and somehow *seeing*. . . .

It was only after she had gone a good ten or twelve yards that Tracey began to slow down. Slow and then finally stop in order to catch her breath and still her madly pumping heart.

Snap! Again, it was as if some cosmic lever had been pulled. Instantly the world rearranged itself back into the familiar. The skewed perspective was suddenly gone and back to normal, and the bleached drabness had reverted to glorious living color. Buildings were once again dazzling white sugar cubes, the sky that intense pulsating blue, and the waters of the caldera just one shade lighter than indigo.

Thank heaven, Tracey thought, weak with relief. *What happened to me back there? What kind of spell was woven?*

Get a grip, she told herself. *It was all in your head. You let your imagination get the best of you.*

There was no spell cast. No sorcery or black magic. Suddenly, away from the shop and bathed in sunlight, she felt intensely foolish.

They must think me mad.

Not that she had the luxury to worry about that right at this moment. As she had told Kathy, she wasn't here on vacation. She had things to do. Work to get back to. A phone call to make. Plus, she needed to put a bit more distance between herself and that . . . that what?

That hag.

The words and image jumped unbidden into her mind, and she felt another shiver course through her. Imagination or no, one thing was clear: the blind crone had scared her badly.

Chapter Twenty-three

Miami, Florida

Late Tuesday morning at Biggs-Dimon, on the glass elevator hurtling skyward. Montague Pleasance said, "This situation? I got this feeling playing good cop–bad cop isn't the way to handle it. Not on this dude. You saw that million-dollar lobby? This view out here?"

He gestured downward.

Stanlee's eyes followed his hand. Below, the Brickell Avenue Bridge and the Miami River fell away, swiftly shrinking to HO scale.

He said, "The acres of marble downstairs? This hundred-million-dollar tower? People got this kind of money, they crap on everybody. After a while they even start believing their own shit don't stink."

"Even though it reeks to high heaven," Stanlee Sadwith groused.

"That's right. Which is why we don't give the Biggs shot any slack. We start leaning on him from the get go. Put on the pressure and keep ratcheting it up."

Stanlee held his gaze. "You enjoy chopping the big guys down to size, don't you?"

Montague shrugged and flashed a lupine grin, his teeth

gleaming against the rich rum color of his skin. His coal black hair remained in Rastafarian dreadlocks, but he'd made some major wardrobe concessions. Gone were the beaded bands he'd worn on neck and wrist, the amazing Technicolor shirt and batik sarong. They had been replaced by a resplendent violet-gray suit, pale pink dress shirt, and a silk rep tie in a pattern of pink, black, and white interlocking horse bits.

The transformation was so complete he looked like he had an appointment with the Ford Agency. Or else was headed to a fashion shoot for *GQ*.

But there was reason behind sartorial madness. He was in full-throttle battle gear, his wardrobe a way to help even out the odds. Help put him on a more equal footing while going head-to-head against the Biggses.

Clothes, the great equalizer.

As if, he thought sardonically.

The elevator chimed softly, glided to a smooth stop. The red LED light read 31. The doors of the glass pod slid soundlessly aside.

Stanlee barely gave the plush reception area a glance. The thick carpeting, glacier green desk, and butterscotch leather sofas registered as mere background and failed to impress.

There was a decorative blonde behind the reception desk. With her telephone headset and its little curved mouthpiece, her understated twinset and expertly applied makeup, she was a calculated, if not exactly inspired, bit of hiring—*Or was it casting*? wondered Stanlee—on the part of what these days was fancily referred to as the Human Resources Department, but was still thought of by the oldsters as simply Personnel.

While Stanlee made a beeline for the receptionist, Montague sauntered around, suit jacket unbuttoned, hands in trouser pockets, playing it supercool. Looking unimpressed while taking in every inch of the surroundings, eyes here, there, everywhere.

Stanlee said, "We're here to see Mr. Biggs." Using the quasi-whisper one might use in a facility of higher learning or perhaps a house of worship.

The blonde formed a professional smile. "I'm so sorry. I'm afraid Mr. Biggs is fully booked. If you'd like to leave your card?"

Stanlee smiled sweetly, took out her little leather folder, and flashed her ID. "See, it's like this." There was nothing sweet about her tone. "I'm Detective Stanlee Sadwith. And that gentleman over there? That's Detective Montague Pleasance. We're Miami P.D., Fraud Division. You want, we can play this either of two ways. Either Mr. Biggs can talk to us here, or perhaps he'd rather accompany us to police headquarters. It's your call."

The receptionist hesitated. Obviously, she was thrown for a loop. The only dealings she'd had with the police in the past were on the rare occasions when she'd had to summon *them* to eighty-six some obnoxious visitors or demonstrators.

But for the police to come and ask for Mr. Biggs! That was a new one, and it wasn't in the guidelines.

"Personally," Stanlee said in a confidential tone, "I think Mr. Biggs would be more favorably inclined toward you if you unbooked someone else and he saw us—and I mean 'toots sweet,' as we say on the force."

Caught between a rock and a hard place, the receptionist cracked. "Oh, all *right*." She punched some numbers on the keyboard and spoke softly into the microphone. Listened for a moment. Said, "Sure, Mona, I'll wait." After a minute or so, she got the word, and nodded at Stanlee. Nodded, but didn't smile. Spoke frostily as she enunciated: "Please have a seat. Mr. Biggs's secretary said she'd be right out. She'll escort you to his office."

Stanlee nodded, thanked the receptionist, and moseyed over toward Montague, who was still strolling the luxurious reception area. "Place this swanky," he was saying, sotto voce, "makes you want to move right in, doesn't it?"

Stanlee gave him a hard look. "I'm sure it's overrated."

"Ever give any thought to how many people work in snazzy offices like this one, then at five o'clock have to go home to some roach-ridden dump?"

"You work where you got to work," Stanlee said. "You live where you got to live. Besides, last I heard, home is where the heart is."

He gave her a look. "Yeah, right. Especially if it's a twenty-five-million-dollar house on Star Island. Or just some three-million-dollar condo on Fisher."

"You know the trouble with you?" she said. "You're cynical out the wazoo."

He grinned. "And you're not?"

They both gave their full attention to a gorgeous blonde who came out and glanced around. She was wearing a melon-colored Chanel suit, matching medium heels, and the kind of perfunctory, professional smile cultivated by airline cabin attendants and boutique owners the world over. Extending a hand in welcome, she walked across the expanse of carpet, saying, "Detectives Sadwith and Pleasance, I take it?"

Stanlee and Montague nodded, indicating that they were indeed the parties in question.

"I'm Mona Claymore, Mr. Biggs's executive assistant."

Montague and Stanlee each checked her out in turn as they shook hands. Mona Claymore stood five-foot-ten. Though slim, she was provocatively voluptuous in all the right places. Her designer frames were tortoiseshell, and she wore her hair pinned up, the type of woman usually confined to movies in which she kicked off her heels, flung aside her glasses, and shook loose her thick hair and let it tumble to her shoulders.

Her voice was clipped. "If you'll please follow me?"

Montague and Stanlee exchanged nods, and Mona Claymore led them down a luxurious hallway and into a vast windowless conference room.

"I'll tell Mr. Biggs that you're waiting," she said, withdrawing and shutting the door behind her.

Not five minutes went by before the Big Kahuna breezed in. "Sorry," he said, teeth flashing. "Conference call. You know how these things go."

"Actually, I don't." Montague introduced himself and Stanlee, and they sat down at the near end of the yards-long conference table, with Brian Biggs at the head, and Stanlee and Montague respectively on his left and right, facing each other.

"So you're MPD? Fraud Division?" A momentary

frown creased Brian Rutherford Biggs III's handsome, streamlined, movie-star face.

He added, as if to be certain he'd heard correctly. "You did say *fraud*?"

"That's right, sir," Stanlee replied. "Before we go any further, we should advise you that you are entitled to have an attorney present."

Brian Biggs laughed easily. "An attorney! Oh, please. Why should an attorney be necessary? You're not leveling any charges, are you?"

Stanlee shook her head. "Not charges as such, no sir. But we *would* like to ask you some questions."

He laughed again. "Ask away. Sorry to have to disappoint you, but we're as legitimate as they come. All the Biggs-Dimon family of companies are."

Stanlee kept her voice solemn but level. "I hate to disappoint you, sir, but that's not what's come to our attention."

Something in her tone gave him pause. "Oh? He raised a single eyebrow quizzically, his gaze moving from Stanlee to Montague and back again. "I'm afraid you'll have to enlighten me. We're a big company, you know. Huge. Or, as we like to say, 'We've got more divisions than Patton's army.'"

When neither of them laughed, he said, "An in-house joke, you understand."

Stanlee exchanged glances with Montague, the two of them thinking, *Here goes. Sneaky bastard's already trying to distance himself from whatever's coming.*

Like many cops partnered together, Stanlee Sadwith and Montague Pleasance were, in many respects, as close as many married couples; in fact, they were closer to each other in some ways than they were with their respective spouses, and spoke their own peculiar brand of shorthand. Half the time, even that was unnecessary. They could easily communicate without words, simply by giving each other certain looks.

"What this concerns, sir," Montague said, "is a certain piece of property one of your, how did you put it, 'family of companies,' foreclosed on."

Brian Biggs smiled, giving his head a little shake. As if they were school children who hadn't quite caught on to the most elementary lesson. "A piece of property, you say? You don't really expect me to remember every piece of property we deal with. Like I told you, we're *huge.*"

"Yeah, with more divisions than Patton's army," Montague said.

Brian swallowed, trying to ignore the sarcastic remark. "What is it you want to know?" he asked.

"We've discovered that you're a principal in a company called Palm Coast Developers," Stanlee said in an even voice. "It seems to be a part of the rest of the Biggs-Dimon family of companies."

"What of it?" Brian asked, his confident demeanor abruptly becoming more aggressive.

"The mortgage on this piece of property we're talking about, the Thomas Sullivan property in Coconut Grove, has been sold and resold a number of times," Montague said, "and is now held by Palm Coast Developers."

"Selling mortgages is a common practice, and you know it," Brian said. Irritation was creeping into his voice, and he was becoming visibly anxious. "It's done every day by everybody in the business."

"Indeed it is," Stanlee said. "We know that, sir. Sometimes we even see the extraordinary circumstances we've seen in the case of the Sullivan mortgage. That mortgage has been sold and resold so many times that the only thing we can figure out is that somebody appears to want to conceal the identity of who really holds the mortgage on the property. Tracing it to Palm Coast hasn't been easy."

Brian shrugged and held his hands out. "So what?" he said. "Happens all the time."

"Maybe so," Montague said, "but in this case, call us stupid, *sir*, but we're interested in why you'd try to do something like that." Montague smoothed his dreadlocks with a hand and looked up at the ceiling. "I mean, just linking you to Palm Coast has been like finding a needle in a haystack. Know what I mean? Why would a nice guy like you want to conceal his identity, Mr. Biggs?"

Montague paused a moment, then lowered his gaze from

the ceiling and stared directly at Brian. He enjoyed watching the big shot's wheels turn, trying to come up with an answer to his question.

"Did it have anything to do with you being engaged to Tom Sullivan's daughter?" Montague continued, deciding to make the weasel really squirm. "Uh, Tracey, I believe the young lady's name is?"

Sweat began to bead Brian Biggs's forehead, and he abruptly pushed back his chair and rose to his feet. Gone were any traces of his charm and bonhomie. "Look, unless there's anything else, I have a busy schedule."

"Please, sir. We're almost finished," Stanlee said. "Why don't you sit back down and—"

"I don't know what you're leading up to," Brian blurted, "but this is a waste of my time."

"If you'll just give us another minute, sir, we'll tell you what we're leading up to," Montague said. "And I think you'd better sit your ass back down and listen to what we have to say if you know what's good for you."

Brian felt sweat soaking his expensive custom-made Turnbull and Asser shirt, and his heart began to race. He stood there silently, his mind in a quandary as he considered his options. Finally, he decided to hear what they had to say. *It's probably nothing,* he told himself. *So far, what they know adds up to one big pile of bullshit in a court of law.*

He sat back down and planted a smile on his face. "I don't think I have to explain to you why I didn't want the girl I was seeing to know that I held the mortgage on her father's old cracker dump in Coconut Grove," he said amicably. "You know what I mean, officers. Right? She'd kick up a real fuss if she knew I was the one who had to foreclose."

Montague laughed. "Yeah, man. And she'd really raise hell if she knew you weren't just the fat cat holding the mortgage on her old man's place but also the developer who was trying to buy him out," he said. "Right?"

Without waiting for an answer, Montague went on, his words coming faster now. "And she'd probably get downright suspicious if she knew that her old man hadn't committed suicide, but had died in a car wreck after somebody had tampered with the brakes *and* the accelerator of his car. What do you think? Agree with me, sir? Don't you think she'd get a little suspicious if she found out there wasn't any brake fluid in her old man's car? And don't you agree that she'd get half crazy if she knew the accelerator had been fixed so it'd jam? Floor that car so he couldn't stop it? Because, you see, sir, that's what we've discovered looking into this, so I think Fraud's going to be giving this case to Homicide. Know what I mean, sir?"

The color had drained out of Brian's face, and he abruptly stood up. "Considering the nonsense you're talking about—the assumptions or whatever you want to call them that you're bandying about—I believe one of my attorneys should be present before I say anything else."

"That's cool, Mr. Biggs, sir," Montague said. "We got time." He cast a glance at Stanlee, and she smiled discreetly. *Bingo,* he thought. *We've got the fucker.*

Chapter Twenty-four

Santorini, Greece

As soon as Maribel heard Tracey's voice, she squealed with glee, then launched into mile-a-minute Spanglaise. "*Concha de Madre,* Trace. I'm so glad you called. I've got news for you, *cariña.* And what news. Remember me telling you about Ray? My Ramón? The fabulously sexy man I'm going out with? The lawyer?"

Tracey laughed. "How could I forget, Maribel?"

"Well, get this, *cariña,*" Maribel went on. "You know Ray knows a lot of people. All kinds of people. Rich, poor, in between. Everybody in Miami, it seems like."

Tracey wondered what in the world Maribel was getting at, but she didn't interrupt her friend because she knew that Maribel was relishing telling her tale.

"Anyway," Maribel said, "I told you how I wanted to talk to him about what happened to your dad. About the accident and everything. Or suicide or whatever it was."

Tracey was suddenly on full alert. She could hardly restrain herself from asking Maribel a barrage of questions, but she held herself back and let her friend go on with her story.

"So, I had a talk with him, and he was very interested,"

Maribel said. "I mean, like, superinterested. Ray said the whole thing sounded real fishy to him. Said it stank to the high heavens. You know, with Brian and Palm Coast and the mortgages and your dad suddenly out of the picture. And guess what?" She paused for dramatic effect.

"What?" Tracey asked, truly intrigued.

"My Ray has a friend in the police department. Wouldn't you know it? And this guy he knows works in fraud."

"Fraud?" Tracey interjected. "But what's—"

"*Cariña,* just wait," Maribel said. "Just listen to me, okay?"

"Sure," Tracey replied.

"Well, this guy in fraud is a real sharpie, Ray says. The kind of guy you can't put anything past. Very experienced. Seen it all. You know what I mean? Knows all the cons."

"I think so," Tracey said.

"He's a strange dude. African-American. Looks Rastafarian with dreadlocks and all, but he cleans up real spiffily. And he's incredibly efficient and sneaky with lots of contacts," Maribel said. "Anyway, Ray said to me, 'We're going to police headquarters and see Montague Pleasance about this.' That's the guy's name. I kid you not. Montague Pleasance. So he dragged me there with him, to police headquarters. You know, near Overtown."

"You've actually been there?" Tracey asked.

"Sí, sí, sí, cariña," Maribel said. "Met Montague Pleasance in person, and told him what I told Ray. All about your dad and everything. I told him that I didn't believe for one minute it was suicide and I didn't think you really do either."

"What . . . what did he have to say?" Tracey asked.

"They said the same thing Ray did. It stinks, Trace. Really fishy. He knows a lot of dirt about Palm Coast from what he said. So anyhow, what he planned to do for starters was go over to have a little talk with Brian and he said something about going over your dad's car with a fine-tooth comb."

"Really?" Tracey said in amazement.

"You bet, *amiga,*" Maribel said. "I don't know what happened yet, but I should find out soon. It should be very interesting."

"It is, Maribel," Tracey said. "You've got this ball rolling, that's for sure. My God, you haven't wasted a minute."

"What can I say?" Maribel replied. "I'm a busy girl. What've you been up to, may I ask? Hmmm? Something tells me there has to be an exceedingly handsome young man somewhere in the picture."

"Maribel," cried Tracey in bewildered anxiety. "Don't tell me you're psychic now too."

"Aha!" Maribel's triumphant crow trumpeted loud across the crystal-clear connection. "I knew it. I just knew it. So there *is* a handsome young man."

Tracey rolled her eyes. "Well, er, yes. But it isn't what you think. At least not yet."

"Cariña," Maribel replied in suddenly silky, worldly tones, "it's quite all right. I'm a *Latina*, remember? And if there's one thing us *Latinos* understand better than anyone, it's matters of the *corazón*. So it's perfectly excusable if you've been swept off your feet by a tall, dark, and handsome stranger—"

Tracey was beside herself with frustration. "But that's just it, Maribel," she cried. "I haven't been swept off my feet. How could I? You know that old adage of not mixing business with pleasure?"

"Business? Lemme get this straight. You did say 'business'?"

"Yes, sweetie," Tracey sighed, "that's exactly what I said."

"In other words, this Prince Charming of yours—"

"He's not my Prince Charming!"

"All right, this man, then. *Señor Mysterioso.* I take it he has a name?"

"Of course. Mark Varney."

"Then he's your . . . whatchamacallit, right? . . ."

"Yes, Maribel," Tracey said patiently. "My agent."

"Ah. So the *señor* is attracted to you."

"I can't say that he is, nor can I say that he isn't. I just don't know."

While Maribel digested this little tidbit, Tracey added, "And, as if things aren't complicated enough, the woman I work for seems to have gotten it into her head that I pose a threat to their relationship. Can you believe that? As if I'm intent upon stealing Mark out from under her."

"And are you?"

"Maribel! For Pete's sake, you know me better than that. I've never been one to break up a relationship."

"Maybe not, but ai yi yi." Maribel sounded impressed. "To think you accomplished all this in such a short time. Amazing."

"Well, that's the situation," Tracey said. "It's all rather convoluted, and I'd rather it weren't. I wish we could discuss it, but you know the situation. I did sign that confidentiality agreement I told you about. The one in which I was sworn to silence."

"Yes, but that hotshot *abogado* obviously omitted one essential clause," cracked Maribel.

"Oh? And which might that be?"

"Oh, *por favor!* Which do you think? The one prohibiting you of robbing your prima donna employer of her boy toy. What else?"

Tracey nearly dropped the telephone receiver. *Oh, shit,* she thought. *Maribel's made the connection. She knows I'm working for Urania Vickers.*

"Maribel." Tracey now spoke so quietly and evenly that, to the few who knew her intimately, it raised red flags signaling her distress and displeasure. "Exactly how much do you know about this? And where did you get your information?"

"Cariña," said Maribel defensively. "I know who your agent is. That isn't exactly a secret. Is it?"

"N-nooo . . ." Tracey admitted.

"Anyway, I got this bright idea and went online. Took a gander at the agency's Web page."

Tracey waited silently.

"And there it was, a list of the most recently published books the agency had handled. Not that I made any startling discoveries. But I saw where you could access the backlist of older books that had foreign rights still available. So I aimed my mouse and clicked." She paused. "And guess whose name and postage-stamp-size face jumped right out at me?"

Tracey pinched her brow. She didn't need to guess. She already knew. Urania Vickers. Who else could it be?

"Of course, at first I didn't put two and two together. I said to myself, 'Maribel, don't be *estúpida.* Urania Vickers? It's too much of a coincidence.' But all the same, I clicked on the air-brushed picture and up popped the covers of books she'd apparently published."

"Yes?" Tracey said. There was a brief silence from the other end, and she could practically see Maribel taking a gulp of coffee from a steaming mug.

"At any rate," Maribel said, "that was a bore, so I finally clicked on *About the Author*. Just to see what it said."

Tracey didn't respond.

"There I found a link to the site of the Official Urania Vickers Fan Club. So I thought to myself, 'Why not? There can't be any harm in it.' And I aimed my mouse and clicked."

"I see."

"And what do you suppose should suddenly pop up? Eh? Why, mention to the effect of, 'Urania Vickers divides her time between a house in Beverly Hills, an apartment in Paris, and a villa in the Greek isles.' "

"The Greek isles," murmured Tracey tonelessly. "So that's when everything fell into place."

"That's right," Maribel repeated. "That's when everything fell into place."

There was a moment of drawn-out silence. Tracey could only shake her head in wonder. *Wouldn't you know it?* she thought. *All the confidentiality agreements in the world are no match for a few clicks of a computer mouse.*

Maribel broke the silence. "Look," she said, "I hope you're not mad at me. I was curious about your agent, that's all. I had no idea he also handled Urania Vickers."

"He only represents her . . . er . . . literary endeavors. One of the big West Coast agencies, I forget which, handles all her movie and television deals."

From thousands of miles away, Tracey could hear a hiss and a clink and a gurgle: Maribel refilling her coffee mug. "So you're with Urania Vickers and no one is supposed to know," Maribel said.

Tracey emitted a pained sigh. "Shit," she said softly. "Shit, shit, *shit*. This complicates matters."

"*Querida,* look. Let's be practical. Why should it have to complicate anything?"

"Why? Because the confidentiality agreement I signed is serious business. If you tell a soul, it could have serious consequences. For starters, it could leave me open to a lawsuit."

"*Por favor*. Really," sniffed Maribel. "I thought we were *amigas*. Remember? Or has that all of a sudden changed?"

Tracey awakened to how foolish and petty her reaction must appear.

"Oh, Maribel," she blurted. "I'm being such an ass. Of course you can keep a secret. I wish I knew what came over me. Forgive me, will you?"

"Hey, it's okay," Maribel soothed. "But enough about that. I have been checking on your house. You'll be glad to know that so far, everything seems fine."

"In other words," Tracey commented dryly, "it's still standing."

"Why shouldn't it be?" Then Maribel sucked in a sharp breath. "Trace!" she exclaimed reprovingly. "You don't think—"

"Where Palm Coast Developers is concerned, I don't know what to think. I wouldn't put anything past them. Should the slightest out of the ordinary thing occur, no matter how minor, you have to tell me."

"Of course, why wouldn't I? Wait a moment. Come to think of it . . ." Maribel's voice trailed off.

"What is it?"

"Nah. Forget it."

Tracey's voice was level but firm. "Come on. You have to tell me."

"All right. Yesterday afternoon, when I swung by, there was a car parked down the street a ways, on the same side as your house. Maybe a hundred, a hundred and twenty feet down. Next to one of those vacant overgrown lots."

"The one on the corner."

"The only reason I noticed the car," Maribel was saying, "is because it was so big and shiny and brand-new. A Lincoln Town Car. Dark blue or black. If it had been a dirty old pickup, it wouldn't even have registered. Anyway, I pulled up in front of your house and parked and let myself in. Walked through the place. Saw that everything looked okay, let myself out, and locked up again. Got back in my car and drove off."

"And?" Tracey pressed.

"Well, I thought the Town Car was just parked there. The passengers out somewhere, like maybe looking over the properties or whatever."

"Yes?"

"Well, there was someone behind the wheel. Reason I didn't notice that from a distance was because of the tinted windows."

"Go on."

"Well, I headed on home. Didn't give it another thought. Then, a few blocks later, around Grapeland and Bird, I look in my rearview mirror . . ."

"And the Town Car's behind you."

"Well, I think it was the same Town Car. But I couldn't be sure. Then, heading north on Southwest Twenty-seventh Avenue, I swear, there it was again. Now three cars behind me. I was starting to get very nervous, so I made a few sharp turns where it would be obvious if I was being followed. But I wasn't. See? I told you; nada."

"So long as it stays nada." But it had Tracey worried. "I don't like this. Maybe it's better if you don't check on the house for a while."

Maribel laughed. "Oh, don't be silly," she scoffed.

"No. Don't *you* be silly." Tracey's voice was dead serious. "I mean it, Maribel. I don't trust these people. I'm holding up their development, and I'm sure they're royally pissed off."

"I'm sure they are. But I can take care of myself."

"Do. Please do. Promise me."

"*Querida,* have you ever known me to be suicidal?"

"Not that I can recall, no."

"Okay, so there you have it. Now give it a rest."

If only it were that easy.

"Oh," Maribel said, "one last thing before we hang up. Can you give me a number where you can be reached? Just in case?"

A shadow came into Tracey's face. "What would you say if I were to tell you that right now, I'm standing at a phone booth using a telephone card? Or that I've been warned against making long-distance calls from Madame's phones? Ditto about giving out Madame's number? As if I could, not knowing it offhand. But I'll go to an Internet café and e-mail you the number if you promise to use it only in the direst emergency. Okay?"

"That and e-mail will be cool," Maribel said.

Movement and footsteps from behind caught Tracey's attention. She turned her head. A middle-aged matron in a flowered dress was pacing back and forth, impatiently flourishing a phone card in her hand and scowling. The instant Tracey looked at her, she pointedly lifted her wrist and tapped the face of her watch with a corner of the card.

Tracey rolled her eyes. *More friendly natives,* she thought wryly, already able to tell the locals from the tourists by how they dressed.

She signaled that she wouldn't be much longer, which earned her another scowl. Ignoring it, she gazed past the woman, her eyes sweeping along a panoramic view of the caldera, which was then obstructed by the prisonlike buff tower adjoining Urania's compound, and followed by the wall which shielded it from curious eyes. From behind the wall, the windmill with its skeletal armature for sails, which Tracey currently called home, rose decoratively against the pulsating blue sky. Her eyes moved on, coming to rest on the Mini Market beyond. The very place from which, only minutes ago, she had made her escape.

Of course! she thought. *Why didn't I think of it sooner? Surely Kathy won't mind.*

Ducking her head back into the booth, she excitedly told Maribel, "I just had a major flash of inspiration. I think I know a number here where you can leave messages for me. I'll e-mail it to you tomorrow or the next day."

Tomorrow when, hopefully, the crones would be haunting some other place. "I'll call you back then?"

"*Bueno.*" Maribel was delighted. "*Fantástico!* We'll talk tomorrow or the next day, then?"

"Promise," Tracey said. "Bye for now."

She was barely out of the booth when the woman in the flowered dress charged past her, phone card at the ready.

Tracey ignored the rudeness. Something else had caught her attention—on the top floor of the buff-colored tower. A flicker of movement behind the grille of a tiny arched window.

Once again, she thought she saw a pale face pressed against the glass panes. But then it seemed to fade in front of her eyes like a disintegrating photograph. It was hard to tell if the face was real. She was facing into the sun, and it could easily have been an optical illusion.

She blinked, shielding her eyes against the glare with her hand. The face, if there had really been one, was gone.

Chapter Twenty-five

The screams came out of darkness, black and deep.

For a few moments she remained disoriented, suspended in that purgatory between the world of sleep and waking. Then gradually the blackness lost its intensity and her surroundings solidified. Pale moon glow filtered in through the staggered square windows that rose diagonally to the loft above.

Her racing pulse slowed as she got her bearings. It was the middle of the night, and she was in her bed in the windmill. She massaged her left wrist, as though to get her circulation going. A glance at the alarm clock told her the time: 2:22.

She recalled having read somewhere that it was during these early morning hours that the grim reaper most often came calling, knocking his scythe on the doors of the elderly and the infirm.

Certainly not the kind of thoughts to promote sweet dreams.

But Tracey was not ready to go back to sleep. She felt curiously unsettled.

Oia, sober Oia, was fast asleep. Tracey frowned to herself. Surely something had reached down through the strata of her sleep to rouse her.

Then she heard the screams.

Tracey froze as the piercing, bloodcurdling cries shattered the night. They shot chills straight into the marrow of her bones. These shrieks did not belong here in Oia's peaceful, comalike silence.

After a half minute or so, the screams stopped, but Tracey's skin continued to crawl. The howls belonged to a creature in a zoo, yet no animal she could name was capable of forming a sound of such intense fury mingled with so much pitiful, haunting pain. Surely its origin belonged confined to some maximum-security asylum, not this picture-perfect village.

In the ensuing silence, Tracey sat rigidly, listening intently, waiting for the screams to start again. She found it impossible to relax. What bothered her more than the screams themselves was that they had seemed so *close*, as if they'd originated from right outside the windmill.

Which was hogwash, she realized. How was that possible . . . unless something eerie was afoot on Oia's main drag and the residents, furtive like those of the celluloid Transylvania, battened down the hatches after dark, made signs against the evil eye, and refused to tell unsuspecting strangers what, exactly, was wrong.

But were the screams real? Or had she dreamed them in a nightmare? Already, the cognitive half of her brain was working to cast doubt upon what her ears had registered, attributing the screams to her overactive imagination and the nightmare from which she must have awakened.

Oh, forget it, she told herself. *Go back to sleep. It was nothing.*

Despite her misgivings, she forced herself to lie back down. Even so, her ears remained alert, attuned to any sound that did not belong to the night.

Could it be that I'm actually still asleep? she wondered. *That I only dreamed I woke up?*

Dreams within dreams . . .

She frowned up into the dark. Yes, it was possible. It even, in a strange, convoluted kind of way, seemed to make sense. Enough, at least, that she felt some of the tension seep out of her and let herself start to relax.

Then more noises.

"What the hell?" Tracey muttered.

They weren't screams this time, but soft, spooky laughter.

Tracey threw aside the covers and swung her legs over the edge of the bed. For a moment she sat there, both feet planted firmly on the scratchy flatweave of the Anatolian kilim. She jumped to her feet, grabbed the embroidered white cotton coverlet from the foot of the bed, and draped it around herself. Refraining from switching on a lamp, lest someone should see the light in her windows, she hurried barefoot across the cool *krokalia* and out into her foyer.

At the entrance, she paused and pressed her ear against the crack between the doorjamb and the door. Held her breath and listened carefully.

At first, silence. Then, from some distance but not too far away, came gurgles, like the sounds of a happy baby, interspersed with little girlish giggles. As quietly as possible, she slowly unlatched the deadbolt. There was a sharp snick, which sounded extremely loud to her own ears, but was probably undetectable from five feet away. Then cautiously she felt for the door handle and pressed down on it. Held her breath and opened it an inch.

The hinges, which obviously could use oiling, protested with a squeak. Why did one never notice such things during the day? But the night air was deliciously, comfortably cool. And silent. The gurgles and giggles, like the screams before them, had ceased.

She pulled the door open a few more inches, enough to stick her head out and listen. She glanced first to the left, then the right, and finally down.

Nothing seemed amiss. Stars were out in full force, spangling the sky. The moon was a white scimitar riding at a jaunty angle, and its light was pallid but sufficed. Oia's cuboid white structures glowed ghostly and pale along the crest of the cliff top. Below, the caldera was black and motionless, as though to better mirror the moon.

Tracey opened the door just wide enough to slip outside. Her heart was pounding against her ribs, urging her to go back, but she paid it no heed. She made sure the corner of the coverlet dragging behind her didn't get in the way and closed the door quietly behind her.

Click!

Something about the finality of that sound unnerved her. She lunged against the wood panels of the door, but it was too late. The sound had been the lock snapping shut.

Stifling a groan, she tried the door handle. Sure enough, she'd forgotten to disengage the automatic locking mechanism. Nor had she thought to bring her card key.

Now she was locked out.

Way to go, Sullivan, she scolded herself. *Fine gumshoe you'd make. Let's see you get out of this one.*

After mentally whacking herself over the head, she calmed down sufficiently to consider her options. There were other ways in—perhaps not into the windmill, but at least into her study. The narrow staircase chiseled out of solid rock, for instance, up which Mrs. Stefanou had led her that very first day. It began in the living room, at the rear of the alcove on the right side of the lowest level.

Yes. Then, if she spent the remainder of the night in the study, so what? She could always claim she had been burning the midnight oil and had fallen asleep at her desk. If anyone even thought to mention it. And when Iliki came to the windmill in the morning, and unlocked the door to make the bed and clean the bath, in she'd slip . . .

Indeed, it was feasible. And rang so true no one would give it a second thought.

Remarkable, how such a simple solution to a problem could compose one's nerves. Rather than feeling like a lurking spy, Tracey instantly felt empowered.

Now that she'd figured out a way back inside, the only thing she had to worry about was negotiating the steep flights of outdoor steps without tripping and killing herself. She had moved from the shelter of the doorway and started carefully forward when yet another sound stopped her dead in her tracks.

The diabolical laugh—cackly, hissing, and low—seemed to swoop down through the air from high above as though propelled by black, leathery wings. Tracey instinctively looked up, seeking its source.

At that very moment, a bright light snapped on in one of the top-floor rooms of the prisonlike tower next door. Its window, which obviously opened inward, was open to the night and any curtains had been torn aside. Tracey focused on the black shadows which danced with dervish madness up and down the walls.

Shivering, she wrapped the coverlet closer around her, though nothing could dispel the chill slithering through her. Its cause was not due to any drop of the mercury, but lay in whatever madness flitted about in that top-floor room. Without conscious thought, her hand crept beneath the coverlet and closed around the amulet dangling from around her neck. She had put the old crone's gift on the chain that Prometheus had left for her.

At this hour, in these strange surroundings, and with what she was witnessing, wearing a charm against the evil eye did not seem at all extreme.

From the window, soft cackles rose and fell, and then the figure danced its frenzied gyrations into view in the center of the room and—*snap!*—froze and remained motionless. Its arms were stretched outward, and the odd shape it assumed was dictated by the pliability of the sheet it had draped around itself from head to toe, the ends of it clutched in tensed fingers, and with that most simple and single of props, thereby rendered human and cloth into a disturbing sculpture.

Then, as though hearing some slow music only it could hear, the sculpture began to move. No mad dervish now. Rather, its movements were the slow, agonized contortions in a ghastly dance.

For some reason, the dramatic, slow-motion stretching of the fabric this way and that did more to expose a haunted, tormented soul than all the frenzied whirling and gyrating of earlier. Fueled by curiosity and an equal sense of awe, Tracey found herself drawn closer to the wall dividing the properties. The stones and cement beneath her bare feet felt cool and uneven. Despite not taking her eyes off that window to see where she was going, she moved surefootedly, miraculously without tripping.

Reaching the spot from which to best view this bizarre

performance, she stood there, mesmerized. Head tilted back as she stared upward, agog at the variety of emotions these abstract contortions could evoke. There seemed to be no limit to their power of expression. Still, Tracey sensed that rhyme and reason fueled the movements, and that they followed some particular beat. A mental tune? An emotion? Or perhaps it was a way to exorcize personal demons.

Ghostly it was, that nocturnal performance, at once repulsive and hauntingly beautiful. And Tracey was its spellbound voyeur. She felt like a Peeping Tom, yet was unable to tear her eyes away.

And in the midst of the fabric's tug-of-war, the figure behind it abruptly stilled. And remained motionless.

Then slowly, by degrees, perhaps a millimeter at a time, a shadowed face revealed itself. Just enough for one eye to peer out from behind that tautly stretched sheet.

Tracey sensed that eye seeking her out, could swear she actually felt the instant it made contact with hers.

The effect was like an electric shock.

The rest happened in such quick succession that afterward it all seemed to have been a blur. The outstretched hands whipped aside the sheet, revealing the silhouetted upper half of a figure. Whether it was male or female was difficult to determine, so fierce was its expression in the split second it was bathed in light and so quickly did it rush to the barred window and become a shadow against the stark light blazing from behind.

Instinctively Tracey shrank back, as though fearful that the manic figure was capable of summoning superhuman strength and manage to rip out the bars and fly right down at her like some bloodthirsty, Draculean bat.

The silhouette gripped the bars and howled with rage. *"How dare you? So now they've employed spies!"* It was a woman's voice, but scarcely recognizable as such, hissing and howling and spitting the way she did. Her hands, pale and clawlike in the moonlight, gripped the curlicued wrought iron.

Tracey was so taken aback by the swiftness and vehemence of the verbal attack that it was a moment before she registered that the woman's screech had been in *English*.

Not only English, but *American*-accented English, with the slightest hint of the South.

However, she had no time to digest that now. Other lights were clicking on, spilling out windows and doorways on the two terraces below.

Tracey flinched as if they were alarm sirens. *Time to make myself scarce,* she decided. She was out in the open in this spot, too exposed. Too visible from anyone below.

Meanwhile, the Fury kept ranting from the window next door, *"You know you can't keep me locked up forever!"* There came a witchlike cackle, and there was triumph in the voice of madness.

From the terrace immediately below rose a flurry of whispers, one voice sibilant, the other sandpapery: a hasty confab. Tracey caught the sound of accusations, recriminations. For some reason—most likely to draw less attention—the step and walkway lights had still not been switched on. But two thin, moving beams of light, like *Star Wars* sabers, wobbled circles on the ground. Flashlights.

Flashlights that, she remembered Mrs. Stefanou pointing out, there was no shortage of, due to potential power outages.

Suddenly a third, sharper voice joined the fray below and snapped an impatient order. Urania.

The bickering whispers abruptly ceased, followed by a whirlwind of activity on the terrace below. An elongated shadow moved into Tracey's view, grew swiftly, stretching longer and thinner until it split like a dividing paramecium. Two people, each aiming a hooded flashlight groundward, were moving swiftly, but by slightly different routes, toward the same destination: the heavy wooden door set into the wall dividing Urania's property from the one with the tower next door.

The very door that, Tracey realized with a pang, was not ten feet from where she was standing.

Then she recognized, as if they were fingerprints, the click-clack of efficient footsteps. She'd recognize them anywhere.

Mrs. Stefanou.

And in tandem with that unmistakable gait angling diagonally toward Tracey, a shadow, like black liquid flowing uphill, was surging up the steps. The only thing hiding Tracey was the low whitewashed wall beside the steps, but in a few more seconds Mrs. Stefanou would appear.

Damn!

Tracey looked around in desperation. Discovery was inevitable. There was no time to even attempt a dash for the nearest corner or shadow. *It's futile,* she thought.

But she wasn't the only one snooping about. The next instant a hand reached out from nowhere and seized her by the ankle.

Tracey's natural instinct was to scream. She opened her mouth wide, but her vocal cords refused to form so much as a squeak.

"Pssst!" The hiss was so quiet that her first thought was she'd imagined it. Then the hand tried to give her ankle a vigorous shake, but her legs were immobile.

"Miss!"

This time she knew it wasn't her imagination at work. *What the devil?*

With a supreme effort, she forced herself to look away from the beam of Mrs. Stefanou's light slithering snakelike up the steps toward her. She glanced over her shoulder and down at her foot, and could make out the pale ghost of a thin arm reaching out through a narrow gap in the low stone wall beside her. A thin short pale arm.

Prometheus?

"Miss!" The whisper, barely audible, was his, and she let his arm tug her urgently sideways against that narrow gap. With luck, it just might be wide enough for her legs to slip through.

Yes, but what was behind it? What awaited her there? A narrow ledge? An incline? Surely not a vertical drop-off. Young daredevil that he was, Prometheus would never urge her into a life-threatening situation. Or would he?

Too late, Tracey wished she had taken the time during daylight hours to have acquainted herself with the exact layout of the entire compound. But she hadn't felt the need to poke her nose into every nook and cranny.

The beam from the flashlight wobbled back and forth not two feet in front of her. She flinched. During the next sweep she would surely be spotlighted as if on a stage.

The flashlight abruptly swung in the opposite direction. Caught in its circular beam was a stocky dark figure who had already reached the heavy wooden door separating the properties. Despite his turned back, Tracey recognized him by his build.

Stavros.

Mrs. Stefanou's voice spat something hoarsely in Greek, and he mumbled a reply. Then Tracey heard the jangle of a big ring of old-fashioned keys.

Odd, she thought. *No high-tech credit card–type entries for that door . . .*

With Stavros already sorting through the keys, Mrs. Stefanou lost no time. Intent upon joining him, she swung her light around again and was back on the move, her heels clickety-clacking like the countdown to an execution.

Tracey realized her folly. She'd been sidetracked by the unfolding drama, standing there rubbernecking instead of taking the opportunity to get a move on.

I've got to hide. Now.

She flattened her hands atop the thick flat top on either side of the narrow gap and attempted to squeeze through sideways, bare feet feeling the way. Rough stucco scratched her thighs. It was a tight squeeze, but doable.

No, not doable. The tight squeeze got even tighter, until she was unable to move any farther.

The wall was holding her captive.

Damn! Tears of frustration threatened to sting her eyes. The opening was too small. She was stuck.

Oh, no, I'm not! she told herself grimly. And gritting her teeth against the pain, she forced her way on through, skinning her thighs in the process.

Not a moment too soon, either.

A second later, the miniature searchlight illuminated the very spot where she had been standing. Swept off to the right. Then swung leftward toward her.

Without hesitation she squatted and ducked her head as low as possible.

Above her, the beam of light met empty air, and in the ambient light she saw Prometheus huddled beside her, holding Zeus and grinning hugely. She thanked him with a smile and shifted slightly to get more comfortable.

A bad mistake. Too late she felt the balls of her feet dislodge some loose pebbles.

No!

She held her breath, willing the stones to stop moving, but the ledge on which she and Prometheus hunkered sloped inexorably downward. And the pebbles skittered down, before dropping over the edge and out into space.

For a moment there was complete silence. To Tracey, it seemed time was as suspended as the breath she was holding. Then the stones rained down on the projecting rooftop below, clattering as they scattered noisily.

She cringed as if in physical pain.

Urania's voice rose from below. "And what in all hell," she demanded, "was that?"

Mrs. Stefanou's footsteps had fallen silent. Her flashlight raked the section of wall from behind which the sound had originated. The beam searched along its top and sides.

So far, nothing . . .

Tracey shrank away from the gap before the light found it and streamed through, eventually dissipating out into dark infinity. She glanced searchingly at Prometheus, who held a finger to his lips, then made soothing gestures for her to calm down. Soundlessly he kissed the top of Zeus's head, then gently but firmly gave him a nudge.

Zeus gracefully jumped up and stood atop the wall, his back arched like a horseshoe, his tail raised high. His eyes reflected a greenish glow in the light of the flashlight, an eerie effect only heightened by the streak of white fur on his face.

The cat stared at Mrs. Stefanou.

Mrs. Stefanou stared back at it, her eyes narrowing. "Is that cat!" she hissed.

And uttering a curse, she swung the flashlight high and brought it down in an arc to bash Zeus, but he proved far too wily for her. Deftly avoiding the blow, he leaped down onto the path and dashed off in the direction of the windmill.

Mrs. Stefanou shook a fist angrily after Zeus, who'd stopped several yards uphill and was surveying her tauntingly. "One of these days," she swore, "I kill it!"

"Oh, for Christ's sake!" Urania snapped from below, her nightgown an agitated swirl of silk clouds. "This is no time to bother with a cat!"

Indeed it was not. The mystery woman in the tower had obviously seen Zeus getting the better of Mrs. Stefanou, and had begun cackling mad laughter.

Tracey peeped cautiously over the wall and saw that in the window of the tower the woman's hands were clamped around the curlicued bars of wrought iron, and her face was pressed right up against them.

"Think you can get me, do you?" she snorted derisively. "Seems to me you can't even catch a cat!" Another wave of crazed laughter corkscrewed into the night.

"Trying to keep me a secret! Well! Have I got news for *you*! You'd better try a little harder! Um-hum! Eyes are *watching*! Ears are *listening*!"

"Shut up!" Urania hissed. She had gone rigid and her arms were pressed to her sides, her hands balled into quivering fists. "Would one of you shut her up!" And with that she marched back inside. A slamming door echoed her sentiments.

Mrs. Stefanou reached Stavros, held her flashlight at the keyhole, and was through the instant the door was unlocked. He was on her heels. The door slammed and was locked from inside.

Tracey and Prometheus waited silently. That haunting white face was gone from the tower now. Soon, however, Tracey saw giant shadows loom up against the walls of the room behind the bars.

A chill ran up her spine when she was certain that she saw the shadow of a syringe—in giant relief—thrown up against the wall.

Silence followed, then she watched Mrs. Stefanou and Stavros emerge from the wooden gate, lock it, and return to Urania's. Prometheus nudged her then. "We can go now," he whispered.

"I'm locked out," Tracey said softly in reply. "I left my card inside, and the door locked behind me."

"I can get in," Prometheus said.

"But how?" she asked.

He shrugged and smiled. "I have my ways. You wait here. I'll come and get you when the door is open."

"Okay," she whispered.

Prometheus was gone for only a few minutes before returning. "Your door's open now," he said.

"Thank you, Prometheus," she said. "Thank you so much."

"It's okay," he said.

"Prometheus . . . do you know who lives in that tower?" she asked before going back to the windmill.

He looked at his feet and shrugged.

"Have you heard the screams from there?" she persisted.

Prometheus acted as if he hadn't heard her.

Oh, well, she thought. *He's certainly been through enough for one night.* But on the way back to the windmill, she couldn't help but wonder why the boy chose to remain silent about the tower.

Chapter Twenty-six

Tracey surveyed the wreckage in her office with the eyes of a stranger, as if it were a place she'd never seen before. Normally she tidied up every day after she'd finished work, but the last few days had proved too much for her to give any thought as to what her office looked like. All but forgotten was the night she first heard the screams, and the ensuing drama involving the tower next door.

Her every waking hour had been spent trying to pound Urania's incoherent manuscript into shape, the work complicated by having to deal with the star herself. She'd had to constantly stroke Urania's ego, while gently but firmly insisting on certain changes and explaining why they had to be made.

To her surprise, Tracey had quickly discovered that the aging actress, legendary star, and beauty was also an insecure, childlike, and very needy woman who craved acceptance, attention, and love. Her ego, fragile at best, was inextricably bound up in her manuscript, so Tracey found herself walking on eggshells, all tact and diplomacy itself, when trying to make Urania understand the importance of her changes.

Tracey would rewrite pages, then pass them on to Urania to go over, who would return them to her with felt-penned notes scrawled all over them in her childish hand.

"It's got to have my voice, darling," she'd told Tracey.

Or: "I would never use that word," she'd said. "It's so . . . vulgar."

Ditto plot and idea changes: "No, no, darling," Urania would say. "Don't you see? That's not me."

There had been revisions of Tracey's revisions, then more revisions, and yet more. Urania's capacity to dynamite her efforts seemed endless. It had taken Tracey only a short time to realize that Urania's star-size ego was the project's worst enemy.

Urania's constant interruptions and quibbling were consuming an enormous amount of time. Time they didn't have. Tracey was forging ahead despite her, determined to see this project through to the end.

Now she made neat stacks of the mountain of paperwork that cluttered her desk, filed away papers that she'd been shuffling out of the way for the last few days, and then began dusting the computer and desk—work she wouldn't allow Iliki to do. *Thank God for a reprieve,* she thought as she cleaned off the computer's dusty screen.

Yesterday Urania had marched into the office and stood over her shoulder, puffing on one of her cigarettes. "Tracey," she'd said, exhaling a plume of smoke toward the ceiling, "I have to be gone for a few days. Public appearances, you see. I know you'll have difficulty making progress without my help, but do what little you can. We'll catch up when I get back."

Tracey finished cleaning and straightening, then was gathering up several computer disks to label, when there was a knock at the door. "Hey, can you spare me a minute?" Mark asked.

"I can always spare a minute for you," she said, smiling. She sat down and looked up at him. "What's up?"

"I wanted to see if you'd like to have dinner tonight," he asked. "Just the two of us."

"That'd be great," Tracey replied. The prospect was more than thrilling to her, but she tried to keep from sounding too excited. She didn't want him to think that she was a starry-eyed teenager. "Here or out?"

"Out, for sure," Mark said with a laugh. "But casual. How's that?"

"Fine," Tracey said. "Just what the doctor ordered after being cooped up in here with Urania."

"Well, she's flown off on her broomstick," Mark said.

"You bad boy," Tracey said, laughing helplessly.

"So we ought to take advantage of her absence," he went on. "Have a little fun."

"Where's she gone?" Tracey asked.

"She's gone to Hong Kong, all expenses paid, where she is being given a nice big check to open a new shopping center."

"Shopping center?" Tracey said.

Mark nodded. "She's always running short of cash, so she takes whatever she can get, wherever she can get it."

"It must be a little . . . demeaning . . . for her," Tracey said.

"Urania takes it in stride," he said.

Tracey was saddened by the news, and the full impact of the importance of her own work on the manuscript hit home. *Urania really needs money more than I thought. And work.* She didn't have to be told that finding work was a difficult proposition for an aging actress. *It must be awful for her. Having to keep up this image without the financial security to back it up.*

"I guess we all have to do things we'd rather not do when it comes to work," he went on. "I wouldn't be here now if I hadn't promised Urania to wait until she's back to leave for the States. In the meantime, my work's piling up."

"I don't understand," Tracey said. "Why is it so important for you to be here while she's gone?"

"To keep an eye on things," he said with a grin on his face.

She returned his smile. "Meaning me?"

He nodded. "Got to make sure that manuscript gets finished, don't we?"

"She doesn't trust me, does she?" Tracey said.

"I think she's just a little paranoid right now," Mark said. "Gigs like the shopping center opening are always a reminder that the bank account's got to be constantly fed.

Anyway, I trust you, and besides, we can have a good time with her out of the way."

"But what about your work?" Tracey asked.

"Well . . ." Mark said haltingly, "I really should have gone on back to the States, but . . . well, I thought since you're here all alone that it would be a good opportunity to talk about your work and get to know you better. You're my client, too, you know." He looked at her and smiled mischievously.

"I see," Tracey said. And she thought she did, too. Mark really was as interested in her as she was in him.

"Besides, I can do a lot of my work by e-mail, faxes, and telephone calls," he said. "Which reminds me that I'd better get busy doing a bunch of e-mails right now. I might be finished in time for dinner if I get started. There's a lot to do."

"Don't let me keep you from your work," Tracey said. "Anyway, I'm going to take a break and go into town for a while."

"Good for you," he said. "I'll meet you here about eight o'clock?"

"Great," she said.

"See you later then," Mark said. He turned and left the office.

Tracey sat and stared after him. *Oh, boy,* she thought. *I don't know what I'm getting myself into, but I think I like it a lot.*

She got busy then, carefully labeling computer disks and putting them in a drawer. Afterwards, she left the office and went in search of Maria Stefanou, whom she found in the kitchen. In her hand the woman held an enormous old-fashioned key attached to a chain. When she saw Tracey come through the kitchen door, Mrs. Stefanou tried to conceal the key, but it was a fruitless effort. The key was simply too large. She averted her eyes, then placed the key on a wall hook, where several others dangled from identical hooks.

Ignoring her inexplicable behavior, Tracey said, "I'm going out today."

The woman's chin rose into the air. "Has Madame Vickers given you the day off?" she asked haughtily.

"I think that's between Madame and myself," Tracey snapped back at her.

A brief look of surprise crossed Maria Stefanou's features, but she quickly recovered her usual grim composure. "So go," she said.

Tracey went outside into the heat of the day and sought out the shade cast by the wall between the villa and the adjacent property. She sat down in a seldom used chair with a small table next to it, where she put her shoulder bag and card key. A small, barred opening in the wall that she had only seen from a distance was almost directly behind her. She turned in her seat to examine it closely. It was perhaps a foot high and wide, but she could see nothing through it, for thick vines of some sort on the opposite side of the wall completely concealed whatever lay beyond.

She closed her eyes against the sun's blinding reflection off the pool and let the cooling breeze waft over her, relieved to be away from the intense concentration that the desk required. She slumped down into the chair and spread her legs out, her body relaxing. She wasn't certain whether she'd dozed off or not or how much time had passed, but her eyes opened with a start.

Maria Stefanou stood over her, silent and menacing. "Don't forget your pager," the woman said, then she turned and marched away, disappearing into the house.

"And a good day to you, too," Tracey murmured to Maria Stefanou's receding back.

She stood up and stretched, then retrieved her shoulder bag. Putting on her sunglasses, she started to leave.

"Pssst! Miss," a hiss came from somewhere nearby.

Prometheus, she thought. *Where is he*?

She looked around but didn't see him.

"Over here, miss."

The voice was coming from somewhere near the pool, the long side that bordered the edge of the cliff. Tracey walked in that direction, skirting around the near end of the pool toward the cliff. She looked all around, but still didn't see him.

"Here," Prometheus whispered.

Tracey looked down again and saw him just over the cliff

side, hunched down in the big rocks, Zeus dangling from his arms.

"What are you doing?" Tracey asked him, looking behind her to see if anybody was watching from the villa. No one was visible, but she was unnerved by the thought.

"Come down here," Prometheus said, as if he could read her mind. "It's easy, especially since you're wearing sneakers."

Tracey hesitated a moment, then stepped off the terrace and down onto a large rock. Once there, she stepped on down to another and another, wishing that she'd left her shoulder bag inside. The height didn't bother her, as she'd thought it might, because once she was down among the rocky outcroppings, the terrain was no longer as vertical as it appeared to be from above. She reached Prometheus, and gave Zeus a few strokes. "Now," she said, "what on earth are you doing down here?"

"I know all about the caves in the cliffs," Prometheus replied. "How to get around in them. Why don't you let me show you?"

"A guided tour of the caves," Tracey said. "That would be wonderful." Then she smiled uncertainly. "At least I think it would." She wasn't sure she relished the idea of being underground.

"You'd love it," Prometheus said, cajoling her. "Come on. Let me show you. They even run around all underneath the compound where you're staying."

"They do?" she said with surprise.

He nodded. "How do you think I can slip in and out of almost anyplace anytime I want to?"

"I see," Tracey said.

"They even lead into the tower next door," Prometheus said.

Tracey looked at him with new interest, and he smiled secretively. "Well . . . why not?" she said.

"Come on," Prometheus said, "follow me. The entrance is only a few meters from here."

"What's this, Pro?" she asked him, pointing to a large, splintered round of wood in the ground. It looked ancient, as if it had been there for centuries.

"It's an old cistern," he said, looking up at her. "It's so deep they've never figured out how far down it goes," he added. He had put Zeus down, and the cat wandered on ahead of them, as if it knew where they were going.

"The cave entrance is right here," he said, pointing to a lush cascade of bright pink bougainvillea.

Tracey looked at the spot he indicated, a few feet from the cistern, but could see nothing but the mass of bougainvillea and rock. "Where?" she asked. "I don't see anything."

Prometheus laughed. "Nobody can," he said. "That's probably why they planted the vines. People used to camp out in the caves, my father says, sometimes all summer. So they sealed them up or tried to hide them."

"You mean, people lived in them?" Tracey asked incredulously.

He nodded. "Sure," he replied. "Hippies mostly, my dad says." He stood by the bougainvillea and, reaching into the mass with an arm, pulled back a clump of vines. "See?"

Tracey looked but could see nothing but rock. She climbed over the rocks for a closer look. Behind the vines she could see that there was indeed an opening, but it looked like nothing more than a crawl hole. "Oh, Pro," she said. "I don't know about this. That opening looks like it's only for little boys, not big girls like me."

"Aw, it's a cinch," he said, climbing up closer. "If you come and look, you'll see. You grab hold here"—he indicated a rocky outcrop over the opening—"and swing right in. Come look." He gestured with his hand. "You'll see."

Tracey climbed up to his side and saw that what he said was true. The opening was much larger when viewed from his perspective, ample enough to accommodate her size easily.

She turned to Prometheus. "What about getting back out?" she asked. "What I can make out, well . . . it looks like it could be pretty steep."

Prometheus shook his head. "No," he said. "There're rocks piled up, and they lead from the tunnel right up to the opening."

"But how do we see?" Tracey asked.

Prometheus smiled and pulled back a clump of bougainvillea at his side. He felt behind a rock and pulled out a large flashlight, then felt around again and pulled out a second one. They were the big square kind with a large beam. He held them up. "I'm prepared," he said. "Here's one for you and one for me. Only I'll hold them both till we're inside."

"I see," Tracey said. "Well . . . if you say so."

"And I can hide your pocketbook down in here if you want me to."

"Okay," Tracey said, unshouldering the nuisance. "You're sure it'll be okay?"

He nodded. "Nobody ever comes here but me."

She handed him the shoulder bag, and Prometheus hid it in the rocks. "Ready?" he asked.

"I'm game," Tracey said, more bravely than she felt.

"Then follow me. Once I'm inside, I'll shine my flashlight for you. Watch how I go in, then do the same thing."

Holding both of the flashlights in one hand, he scooted over the rock to the opening and slid both of his legs inside. Before Tracey knew what was happening, he disappeared. Loose rock tumbled down after him, raising a small cloud of dust, then she heard him call to her.

"Trace," he shouted, his voice sounding far away, "hang your legs inside the opening, then sort of swing down. Don't be afraid, my flashlight's on."

Tracey positioned herself where Prometheus had and swung her legs inside the opening. Lowering her head and looking down, she could see the beam of his flashlight. It lit up a pile of loose rock and dusty debris that formed a sort of ramp leading up to the opening where she sat. *Well,* she thought, *at least it's not a straight drop.*

"Lean way down," Prometheus called, "and try to sort of spider-crawl your way down."

Tracey took a deep breath and let her legs drop. She almost tumbled forward before she caught her balance and dug the heels of her sneakers into the loose rock and debris. "Whoa," she exclaimed. "So far so good." She leaned down and did something resembling a very slow spider crawl, she supposed, till she reached the cave's floor. When her feet crunched on the passageway at last, she stood up. "Whew."

"Great!" Prometheus enthused. "That was nearly perfect. Here's your flashlight."

"Thanks, Pro," Tracey said and took the proffered flashlight. She swung it in a slow arc and saw that the floor of the cave was strewn with all kinds of debris: an old sneaker, newspapers, paper cups, soda bottles, what had surely been condom packets, and such. Its walls were an uneven stone that was grayish black in places, reddish, and beige. The ceiling was low, but she had no problem standing upright.

"What do you think?" Prometheus asked. "Isn't it great?"

"It's . . . well, it's fascinating," Tracey replied. The air was cooler than that outside, of course, but it was stale and damp.

"Come on, follow me," he said, "we'll go down this way." He turned and started down the passageway straight ahead, the only way to go at this point.

Tracey followed him with a mixture of curiosity and dread. Even though Prometheus knew what he was doing, she didn't like being in this close space with its damp air, and she could only imagine the kinds of creatures that inhabited these caves.

As if to affirm her fears, she heard the skittering of tiny feet on rock. *Oh, God,* she thought, shivering involuntarily, *a mouse or something.*

"Pro," she called out. "Pro, I don't know about this. There was a mouse or something. Pro?"

"Trace, come here," he shouted back excitedly. "You've got to see this."

She could see him, only a leg actually, directly in the beam of her flashlight, just around a bend in the passageway. Taking a breath of the dank air, she moved on slowly, swinging her light back and forth, hoping to see any obstacle in her path. When she'd almost reached him, her face and hair were suddenly caught in a tangled mass.

"Pro," she shouted. "Oh, God, get me out of this." Her free hand flew up to her face and began slashing at the sticky strands, while she jerked her head from side to side, hoping to extricate herself.

"It's okay," Prometheus assured her. "Just a harmless spiderweb."

"Oh, God," she repeated. "That was so creepy. Maybe . . . maybe I should go back."

"Look at this first," he said. "It's right here, and it'll only take a minute." He indicated a spot about five feet ahead of them.

"All right," Tracey said, "but then that's it for me. I don't think I'm a born spelunker like you."

"Here," he said. "Come look."

She stepped over to the spot next to where he stood and aimed her light in the same direction as Prometheus. She could see that there was a small rounded niche in the wall of the cave that went from the floor up to, to what? Aiming her flashlight up, she saw what appeared to be a wooden ceiling. *What on earth?* she wondered.

Prometheus turned and looked at her with a smile on his face. "See? What did I tell you?"

"What *do* I see?" she asked.

"It's the escape hatch from the tower next door to the windmill," he said. "There probably used to be a ladder to get down, but it's long gone."

Tracey looked up again and ran the beam of her light slowly back and forth across warped slats. It looked like a wooden hatch, all right, but it didn't look as if it had been disturbed for years.

"But why would this be here?" she asked.

Prometheus shrugged. "My dad says that the islanders might have used them to escape invaders. The Turks, or the Venetians, or who knows what. Maybe even to sneak from house to house. Like lovers, you know?"

Tracey almost burst out laughing. These words of wisdom from the mouth of a ten-year-old. "And so there are others?"

"Oh, yes," Prometheus replied. "The passageways lead to many of them. You sure you don't want to go on and see some more?"

"I hate to disappoint you, but I think this is enough for one day," Tracey said.

He smiled widely. "That's okay. You didn't disappoint me. You're the only person that's ever been down in here with me except my dad. Okay. Let me in front of you, and I'll lead the way out."

Tracey followed him closely, her light aimed at the cave floor close to his feet. Before long she could see light coming from the entrance. On her way in, she hadn't noticed the light behind her, showing the way back out again.

Prometheus arrived at the ramp of loose rock and debris and turned to her. "Do you want me to take your flashlight out for you?"

"I think I can manage it," Tracey said. The ramp didn't look difficult.

"Okay, I'm going out."

She watched as Prometheus spider-crawled up the pile of rock. Stones slid down with his every step, but he made it to the top effortlessly. When he got there, he turned and sat down, his legs dangling down inside.

"Okay, Trace," he called. "I'll shine my light down, so you don't have to use yours."

"Okay." She started up the pile and immediately slid backward in the loose rock. "Damn," she swore. She began again, this time making certain she had a good foothold before progressing from one rock to the next. She made it to the opening without further mishap and was glad to see the sunlight and breathe the fresh air.

"Wow, Pro," she said. "That was exciting." She didn't want to tell him that she also thought it was a little creepy. Not her cup of tea at all.

"I thought you'd like it," he said, grinning.

They sat side by side on the rocks behind the cascade of bougainvillea, hidden from any eyes that might spot them on this part of the cliff side.

"By the way," Tracey said, "there's something I wanted to ask you about."

"What's that?"

"I found a gold necklace on my bed," she said. "It had carefully been laid out in the shape of a cat." She looked down at him. "I think you had something to do with that, didn't you."

Prometheus nodded and looked up at her shyly. "Yes," he said. "It was a thank-you present for saving Zeus from Mrs. Stefanou."

"That was a very extravagant necklace," she said, pulling it out from underneath her T-shirt so he could see it. "I'm not sure I should accept it. It seems awfully expensive for a young man of your age to be giving away."

"No!" Prometheus cried. "I got it from the German lady who owns the jewelry store in Oia. You know, the one where all of her nephews work for her?"

"I don't believe I do," Tracey said.

"Well, I run errands for her sometimes, so she lets me have little things sometimes. Like the necklace. I run errands for her nephews, too, only they aren't really her nephews. She just calls them that."

"Yes, but a necklace like this is not cheap, Prometheus," Tracey went on, "and I really don't deserve it for what I did."

"Yes, you do," he said defiantly. "I won't take it back. I gave it to you, Trace. Please, please, take it."

"So you really worked for it, huh?" she asked.

He looked at her earnestly. "Yes," he said. "I didn't steal it, if that's what you mean."

"I just don't want you to get into any trouble on my behalf," she said.

"I won't," Prometheus assured her.

"Well," Tracey said, "in that case, I accept the necklace and thank you very much. It's beautiful, and I'll always think of you and our cave adventure when I wear it."

"Aw," Prometheus replied, "think nothing of it, Trace. You're my friend. Case closed."

Chapter Twenty-seven

Miami, Florida

The distance between Santorini and Miami's Star Island could be measured in thousands of miles or in eight-digit millions.

Dollars, that is.

The Greek economy being the European Union's second lowest, Urania's compound was worth a mere million dollars or two—and that was due entirely to its envied caldera view.

Star Island, however, was that Miami Beach phenomenon, a perfectly oval man-made island in Biscayne Bay that was one of the most exclusive and expensive addresses in the world. It boasted its own bridge-access road leading directly off the MacArthur Causeway, and its inhabitants were very, very wealthy and wielded enormous power and influence.

The building lots were extravagantly large, and a single two-lane drive that cut across the middle of the island assured each of its homeowners a waterfront property complete with deep-water dock. At some, multidecked, multimillion-dollar yachts shone pristinely, the ultimate ornament of excess. Docked at others were more conservative sixty-foot sports fishermen, or that midlife crisis symbol, the marine version of a Ferrari: fast, sleek Magnums, Sunseekers, and Ferrettis.

The homes themselves were huge two- and three-storied affairs. Most of them were Mediterranean in style, with stuccoed walls and loggias and undulating hip roofs of red clay tiles. Multiple-car garages and motor courts accommodated a fleet of stretch limousines, and there were the inevitable servants' wings, guest houses, and tennis courts and pools.

That most precious and treasured of all possessions, privacy, was further augmented through the use of courtyards, pergolas, hedges, clever landscaping, and state-of-the-art security. Star Island was more than just a haven for a very choice few. It was, in effect, a formidable and intimidating fortress, a bastion disguised by luxury, and a social, monetary, and physical barrier between the Have-Alls and the rest of the world.

On this particular summer evening a small dinner party was being held at the Biggs estate. It was the largest by far on the island and occupied one entire tip of Star Island. Separated from the other properties by a wall of coral stone and a set of imposing estate gates, it occupied the prime spot, with the bay on three sides. Access required passing a gauntlet of private armed guards.

Once past them, however, one came face-to-face with Real Money. It was evident in the four-deck yacht, sleek as a futuristic starship, which vied for height with the transplanted full-size royal palms. It was mirrored in the big black executive helicopter which rested on its own concrete pad, prepared to whisk away its owner at a moment's notice. It was obvious in the battalion of Rolls-Royces, Bentleys, and stretch limos crowded into the tree-shaded, brick-paved motor court, and the liveried drivers and bulky bodyguards who stood in clusters, exchanging whispered gossip and jokes and sneaking smokes.

The facades of the mansion had been whipped up by a devoted follower of Addison Mizner or Marion Sims Wyeth or Maurice Fatio. They were a veritable hodgepodge of architectural styles, pulled together chiefly through the lavish use of arches into a cohesive, if frothy, whole. The heart of the house was open to the sky and at the same time closed off to the outside world: here was the cloistered sanctuary of a central courtyard where the quatrefoil-shaped swimming pool was completely hidden and edged with a perfectly shaved, calf-high boxwood hedge, which gave it the illusion of being a decorative Moorish fountain.

Inside, the owners and their guests were enjoying cocktails while lounging on the broad, down-filled sofas and oversized chairs in one of several richly appointed sitting rooms. Here, under the splendid coffered tray ceiling, closed French doors topped by oeil-de-boeuf windows kept the humidity at bay while offering a fine view out onto the landscaped courtyard on one side of the room and Biscayne Bay and the distant high-rises sprouting on the tip of South Beach on the opposite. Here, above massive, facing Renaissance fireplaces and linenfold wainscoting, the two end walls were devoted to a pair of priceless seventeenth-century Belgian tapestries. From an easel in one corner, a gilt-framed Goya prince in blue velvet and a red satin sash was posed with a songbird on his finger.

Dress for this engagement party was black tie, and the plummy-voiced gentlemen were in formal wear, puffing importantly on their Bolivar Belicoso Finos which, despite the trade embargo with Cuba, filled the humidors of this house. Brian Rutherford Biggs II most definitely presided over this gathering. Even the crown prince, Brian Rutherford Biggs III, dashing and movie star handsome, deferred to his father, at least in the presence of company.

Among the women, the younger trophy wives were thin, elaborately coiffed, and elegantly gowned, and dripped expensive jewels. The first wives—generally older and presumably wiser—were just as elaborately coiffed, and gowned, and also bedecked with magnificent jewels. No matter the size of their jewels, however, there were two suns around whom these women orbited like social satellites.

The brightest and most important was Lillian Prescott Biggs, Brian's mother, a hawk-nosed patrician WASP whose face could have adorned Mount Rushmore. She wore but a double strand of pearls and a plain gold wedding band.

The other was adorned with nothing more than her engagement ring, although it was a stunner, enormous in size and perfect in clarity. She was Georgina Kaufmann, the cool blonde of twenty-eight who would soon be Lillian's daughter-in-law. Lillian and Brian II completely approved of the match between their son and Georgina. For Georgina Kaufmann was blessed with that most essential prerequisite of true beauty in the eyes of her future in-laws: heirdom to the Kaufmann shopping mall empire. The marriage would be the modern-day equivalent of yesterday's royal matches. It assured an alliance between two real estate giants.

The women sipped vintage Cristal champagne. The men drank Oban scotch. Lillian, however, preferred bourbon. Straight, no ice.

The men talked business, basically real estate and construction costs and the market, interspersed with the latest whispered dirty joke.

The women chatted about recent charity fund-raisers, discussed the latest couture, gossiped about certain parvenus who were trying to elbow their way into their social circle and, above all, made an effort to include Georgina, a princess soon to be a social queen, in their conversation, taking her to their collective bosom.

For instance: "You were at Oscar's trunk show in Boca, weren't you, Georgina? I thought I saw you there. Well, what did *you* think of his fall collection?"

Or: "Georgina. Now *do* tell. However did you snare that hunk Lillian calls her son?" Said with a coy, sycophantic glance in Lillian's direction.

Or: "Are you having Vera Wang do your wedding gown?"

Or: "Georgina, you were a beauty queen. Why don't you settle something for us once and for all. Who do you think is the more beautiful . . . Reese Witherspoon or Cameron Diaz?"

At that moment Brian clapped his father on the shoulder. "We need to talk, Dad," he said softly.

"Can't it wait?" his father asked.

"No," Brian said. "Now."

His father cleared his throat. "If you'll excuse the two of us for a moment," he announced in fruity tones, "there is a matter father and son need to discuss. You know how it is when a young man chooses a bride. We won't be but a few minutes."

There were knowing winks and chuckles from within the cloud of fragrant blue smoke. Then Brian Rutherford Biggs *pére* rose. He was a tall, distinguished-looking man with a full head of silver hair and the charismatic presence that comes from wielding immense power.

His son quickly finished his scotch and led the way to the French doors. As the men stepped from refrigerated comfort into stifling humid heat, a servant shut the door behind them without a sound.

The lush green turf was soft underfoot and stretched to the concrete-walled parapet at the property's edge. Beyond it, the water of Biscayne Bay was smooth as a sheet of silver foil. A welcome breeze sprang up, crinkling the foil and stirring the royal palms. On the perfect carpet of grass, feathery shadows, like extravagant showgirl headdresses, mimed the swaying of the fronds overhead.

Father and son did not drape familial arms around each other's shoulders. Away from the fawning assemblage, there was no need to posture or keep up a masquerade.

"Let's take a walk," Brian said.

His father followed him across the perfectly manicured lawn toward the water's edge.

Curious about what Brian wanted to discuss, Biggs II felt a bit uneasy, but refused to show it. He took a while to saunter after his hotshot son, and kept him waiting at the retaining wall.

There, they both stared over at Miami Beach, the elder Biggs remembering the low-rise South Beach skyline the way it used to be. Now across the watery divide, outside the SoBe landmark zone on either side of where the MacArthur Causeway became Miami Beach Drive, glittering new high-rises filled the sky, and still more were under construction.

Brian Rutherford Biggs II had invested heavily when

the Art Deco craze started, and had made a killing buying up parcels outside the landmark zone, razing the old and conjuring up the new. Most wonderful of all, the rebirth of South Beach and the economy of Greater Miami had proven to be no passing fad. It had continued to this very day.

The most current windfall was all those billions upon billions of dollars flying out of South America to nest in the safe harbor of Miami's banks and real estate. Money from Brazil and Argentina and all the other chronically plagued Latin American economies.

Was it no wonder, then, that this man—and the son who stood beside him—judged beauty by its dollar value and saw the luxurious condominium towers as among the most beautiful sights he had ever laid eyes upon? "Well?" he finally asked his son. "You wanted to talk?"

Brian raised his chin and turned to his father. "It's about that property in Coconut Grove," he said.

His father continued to stare across the water. But it was useless. The magic moment had vanished. Exhaling a weary sigh, he said, "The Sullivan property?"

Brian nodded.

"You told me you wanted to take care of that. Clear any obstacles in our way," he said.

"And I'm doing exactly that," Brian said confidently. "But there's been a little . . . development that I thought you should know about. A little obstacle."

"What's the obstacle now?" he asked. "You told me this Sullivan had committed suicide."

"It's her," Brian said. "The daughter."

"If you'll recall, you rated your machismo factor so highly that you guaranteed us success if we did it your way." His glared at his son with hard eyes. "You were that certain of your lady killer prowess."

"She found out about Georgina and broke it off with me," Brian said. "Then somehow the bitch came up with the money to pay off the mortgages."

"Christ," his father spat. "So now what do you suggest? Any bright ideas?"

Brian's lips curved into an evil smile. "Yes, but it will cost us dearly. It will also distance us from this"—he signaled his displeasure by making sprinkling motions with his spatula-fingered hand, as though flinging holy water upon an invisible audience—"this messy situation."

"Yes?" There was a cunning smirk on his father's lips. He cocked his head to one side. "And how is that?"

Brian took his time, wondering how much to divulge to his father. He turned his back on the skyline across the water and resumed his leisurely stroll, hands clasped in the small of his back. He angled off diagonally, heading across to the far shore of the property, along which luxuriant plantings ensured precious privacy.

The route was a deliberate detour. He avoided his father's 164-foot, tri-deck monster of a motor yacht, with its permanent crew of eleven. There were altogether too many sets of curious eyes aboard, too many pairs of constantly pricked ears. Instead, he entered the green world created by two towering rows of clipped ficus hedges lining a narrow path. In this refreshing dim tunnel, the kelly green carpet of grass underfoot felt suddenly lusher and springier, and the air at once cooler: moist and rich and alive with earthy smells. Birds were chattering from inside the sheltering branches. From behind him he heard the trudging of his father.

At the midpoint of these verdant twin hedges, the path abruptly widened and the ficus walls curved into a perfect sheltered circle. In the center of this opening, a graceful cast-iron Mercury was poised in eternal flight, unable to deliver the scroll clutched in one hand. He was the centerpiece atop a two-tiered round fountain from which silvery sheets of water cascaded from the smaller basin into the larger. Four curved antique marble benches faced each other—or would, if the fountain in their midst did not intersect the view. This was a favored spot for hatching schemes, exchanging gossip, and planning illicit rendezvous.

Brian stopped so abruptly that his father nearly collided into him from behind.

"You were saying?" his father said irritably.

Brian raised his chin and regarded him lugubriously.

"I'm not quite certain," he said, "that I should even divulge the information I'm about to share with you. On the other hand, I have an obligation to let you know exactly what's going on since there's a lot of money involved."

"Yes," his father replied. "I understand."

"This should take care of Tracey Sullivan and keep our hands clean, even if it is expensive. Much more expensive than the old man was."

"But I thought the old man was a suicide," his father exclaimed, looking at his son intensely.

Brian smiled. "In a manner of speaking . . . yes. In any case, I don't believe that either of us is . . . ah . . . *qualified* to do what this situation calls for."

"And? . . ." His father was growing increasingly impatient.

Brian cleared his throat. "I'm going to use the same connection I used the last time. Only this time the price is a million bucks."

"A million bucks," his father gasped. "You're convinced that this connection of yours can do it?"

"I'm absolutely certain," Brian replied. "Just leave it to me and don't question the charge."

His father shrugged. "What's a million bucks anyway, considering what's at stake? We have to have that property. I'll arrange to have a briefcase filled with the necessary cash. You get hold of your contact."

He paused. "Need I remind you that your bright idea to weasel your way into a certain person's affections failed, and as a consequence has landed us in this situation?"

Brian grimaced. "You had to point that out, didn't you?" He'd hoped that his father would be proud of him for making the necessary contacts and taking care of the situation.

His father smiled grimly. "Our guests have waited quite long enough, don't you think? After all, this dinner *is* being given in honor of you and your fiancée. Or have you forgotten that this is supposed to be a joyous occasion?"

Chapter Twenty-eight

Santorini, Greece

Passing a boutique that sold bathing suits, Tracey decided to go in and have a look around. A native of Miami, she could always use a new bathing suit. The prices, she soon discovered, were outrageously expensive. *Wow,* she thought, *I guess this is an example of the new one-world economy I keep hearing about.*

After looking around a while, holding up one tempting garment after another, she decided she would spring for a bathing suit after all. *What the hell?* she asked herself. *Why not splurge for a change? I've been working like a horse.* She saw a prim but beautiful black maillot and held it up, looking at it in the light.

"For God's sake, you're not old enough for that thing," an unmistakable voice said from behind her. "Maybe you're not an exhibitionist, but you don't have to be prudish, either."

Tracey turned around. "Mark," she said, smiling at his grinning features. "I thought I wasn't going to see you till dinner."

"I got a lot of work done and decided to take a walk into town," he said. "Hoping I would run into you," he added.

Tracey felt a lump in her throat. Interest had definitely

turned into attraction, she thought. If it hadn't been there all along.

"Oh, I bet Maria Stefanou sent you to keep tabs on me," Tracey joked.

"No," Mark replied, "of course not. I saw Prometheus, and he told me you were headed into town to sightsee, so I decided to look for you. Then I spotted you through the window, and here I am." He smiled. "Mind terribly if I join you?"

"I hope Urania won't mind our . . . our doing things together, if she finds out," Tracey said.

"To tell you the truth, I don't give a damn what she says," Mark replied.

"Ah," Tracey said with a nod of her head. "So when the cat's away, the mice will play. Is that it, huh?" She looked up into his eyes.

He returned her gaze. "It's far too beautiful a day to let thoughts of Urania ruin it," he said. He looked thoughtful for a moment, then said, "Prometheus said you might take a boat trip on the caldera."

"Yes." Tracey nodded. "I thought I would."

"I've got a better idea," Mark said. He took her hand in his. "Come with me." He started toward the shop's door.

"But—but what about my bathing—" Tracey began.

"Never mind," Mark replied, gently pulling her along with him. "You won't need it where we're going."

"Where *are* we going?"

"Just follow me," Mark said mysteriously. "Let me make all the arrangements."

He was hurriedly leading her back in the direction of Urania's villa, but suddenly stopped and turned to her. "Do you have your pager with you?" he asked.

"Maria Stefanou wouldn't let me leave without it," Tracey replied.

"May I see it?"

"Sure," she said, rummaging around in her shoulder bag for it. When she found it, she held it out to him.

"Thank you," he said, taking it from her. He stepped over to the nearest garbage can and tossed it in.

"What are you doing?" Tracey cried. "Maria Stefanou will kill me."

"No, she won't," Mark said. "Just tell her you lost it. Besides, this is one surefire way to make certain that we won't be disturbed."

"She's going to be furious," Tracey said.

"Maria Stefanou may own a majority of the villa," Mark said, "but that doesn't give her any right to control your life."

"What do you mean? I thought the villa belonged to Urania."

"Maria Stefanou owns fifty-one percent. The Greek government requires Americans to go into partnership with a Greek when they buy property here, and a Greek has to be the majority owner. Santorini is considered a border territory."

"No wonder she acts like she's the boss sometimes," Tracey said.

"Yes, but like I said," Mark replied, "that doesn't give her the right to control your life."

"Well, if you say so," Tracey said.

"I say so." He smiled again.

"And you?" Tracey asked. "Did you bring a pager or cell phone?"

His smiled broadened even more. "I left them at the villa, and I'll conveniently leave them there after we're packed and ready to go."

"Packed?" Tracey said. "Ready to go? Ready to go where?"

"You'll see," Mark replied. "Just leave it to me."

With that, he tugged her along, faster now, rushing back to the villa.

At the gate that led downhill, Tracey started searching for her key card in her shoulder bag, but couldn't find it. *Where in the world?* she wondered. *I know that I had it when I went to look for Mrs. Stefanou, and I think I had it when I sat out in the shade by the wall.*

"Don't bother looking for it," Mark said. "I've got mine handy." He opened the gate, and they started the descent to the villa.

On the way down, Tracey ransacked her bag again, but the key card was not there. *Oh, boy,* she thought. *Letting Mark throw away my pager is one thing, but losing my key card is another. I don't think I'll be telling Maria Stefanou about this anytime soon.*

The little plane landed smoothly at Eleftherios Venizelos Airport, and a Mercedes taxi swept them along an almost deserted new highway into Athens. But one moment they were flying along, and the next, Tracey discovered, they were stuck in some of the worst traffic congestion she had ever seen. The new highway went only a few miles, then led straight into an old, heavily traveled road.

"I liked the old airport a whole lot better," Mark told her. "Everybody did. It was right on the shore, practically opposite the yacht harbor, and it was a lot faster into town and you'd see the Acropolis a lot sooner. Still, that aside, you can't spend time in Greece without seeing some of Athens. A lot of people don't like it because of all the traffic and noise and pollution, but it's a must. Plus, I've been in worse places."

After the relative serenity and breathtaking natural beauty of Santorini, Athens did indeed seem a raucous urban nightmare, but in her excitement Tracey found it appealing nonetheless. She'd had reservations about making the trip with Mark, but in the end her growing attraction to him had easily overcome those. Now she was glad that she'd thrown caution to the wind and dismissed any qualms she'd had, for the vibrancy of the city was infectious.

"What are those?" she asked him, pointing out the taxi window. "Those funny-looking things on the roofs everywhere."

"Solar panels and batteries," he replied. "They're all over Greece."

"I never would've imagined," Tracey said.

As they entered the city center, she was enchanted by the number of neoclassical buildings, then awestruck when she glimpsed the first true antiquity rising majestically on her right. "What is that?" she asked Mark.

"The Temple of Olympian Zeus," he said.

"And that!" she asked excitedly.

"Hadrian's Arch," Mark said. "It was built to face the Acropolis. Hadrian showing off his power."

"Oh, my God," Tracey cried. "Look, it's Melina Mercouri."

Mark nodded. "And they put the sculpture of her so that it would face Hadrian's Arch." He smiled indulgently.

They turned off the wide boulevard and began negotiating narrow side streets.

"The place we're going isn't grand or anything," Mark warned her. "It's a small, family-run pension on the edge of the Plaka, but I think you'll like it."

"I'm sure I will," Tracey replied.

The driver soon pulled up and stopped at what seemed to be a dead end on Koudrou Street. "Here we are," Mark said, opening the door. "The Doric House."

Tracey was out of the taxi before either Mark or the driver could open her door. Straight ahead she saw a narrow marble-paved lane lined with three- and four-story buildings, and on her right stood the Doric House, a neoclassical building built in the nineteenth century like many of those in the Plaka.

Mark paid the driver, and they shouldered their carry-on bags, all that they'd brought for the short stay. It was a only a few steps to the hotel and a few more up into the tiny lobby, but once inside, Tracey felt that she'd entered another, quieter era. The walls and high ceilings were painted with stylized murals, and off to her left she noticed a small breakfast room. In a lounge on her right vases were filled with fresh flowers, and a couple of guests were watching a television set.

"Mark!" called a tanned, bespectacled, gray-haired man from the other side of the desk. He came around from behind it and shook hands, then immediately turned his attention to Tracey. "And you must be Ms. Sullivan," he said, looking her up and down appreciatively.

"I am," Tracey said with a smile.

Mark quickly made introductions.

"It's wonderful to have you both here," Panos said. "And I have the rooms you requested."

"Good," Mark replied. "We'll go on up and get settled."

Panos fetched their keys from behind the desk and handed them to Mark. "I'll see you later," he said with a wink.

"It's this way," Mark said, leading Tracey up a curving staircase to the next floor, where there was a large hallway with three or four doors leading to rooms. He unlocked the door to her room and held it wide.

Tracey walked in and looked around. In a small front room was a single bed and dresser. That led into a much bigger room with a double bed, dresser, and chairs. The walls, which reached to an incredibly high ceiling, were covered with old, yellowing paper, and everything was much used, but clean. French doors opened onto a balcony.

"I told you it wasn't fancy," Mark said.

"I love it," Tracey said, making her way around the big double bed to the French doors.

She opened them and stepped out onto the balcony. "Oh, Mark," she cried, "come here."

Mark smiled knowingly and followed her out onto the balcony.

"Look," she said, pointing to her left. "Is that what I think it is?"

He nodded. "It sure is. Part of it anyway."

"The Acropolis," Tracey breathed dreamily. "I've always dreamed of seeing it."

"Well, you know what?"

"What?"

"If you hurry up and get ready real fast, there's still time to walk up there, and you can see the whole thing for yourself."

"I can't wait," she said.

"My feet are killing me!" Tracey exclaimed. "But I don't think they've ever been happier." She took a Kleenex from her shoulder bag and dabbed at the thin veil of perspiration that coated her face and neck.

Mark laughed. "It's a climb, isn't it?"

"Coming back down was almost harder than going up for me," Tracey said. "It's almost like you're up in space surrounded by nothing but air. It was worth every minute of it, though. The Parthenon is one of the few wonders of the world I've ever seen that didn't disappoint me. It's actually a lot bigger than I'd imagined."

They sat at a small table at an outdoor café in the Plaka, surrounded by vine-covered latticework. Even with the throngs of tourists that crowded the narrow, winding lanes of the old shopping area night and day, there was an air of intimacy about the setting. On the table were the ubiquitous bottles of water and two cups of *café fredo*.

She stuffed the Kleenex back into her shoulder bag and looked up. Mark sat staring at her from across the table. A smile hovered on his sensuous lips, and his eyes seemed lit from within.

Tracey held his gaze for a moment, then looked away as she felt herself blush. When she turned back, he was still staring but silent. "What are you smiling at?" she asked him in a voice that she hoped sounded casually offhand.

"You," he said. "All this." His moved his arm in an expansive arc. "I'm glad that it gives you pleasure."

Soon they were up on their feet again, strolling along the thronged lanes of the Plaka, enjoying the spectacle of the tourist shops and tavernas. Dark was descending, but they decided to have dinner later and sightsee a bit more instead. They walked from the Plaka over to the Syntagma Square vicinity, where they admired the lit-up Parliament Building, and the bizarrely but delightfully dressed guards. On they walked, admiring more of the monuments and buildings and the special magic that floodlights gave them at night. Hadrian's Arch and the Temple of Olympian Zeus, which they'd seen by day, were transformed, and the Acropolis, which they could see from several vantage points, was even more beautiful at night.

Tired at last, Mark suggested that they have dinner at the little café Panos had suggested. "It's near the hotel," he said, "so we won't have far to go to collapse after eating."

"I'm game if you are," Tracey said.

They found the café on the second floor of an ancient vine-covered house in an out-of-the-way area of the Plaka. They were seated on its expansive balcony at a candlelit table. "It doesn't look like there's a single tourist in this place," Tracey observed.

"No," Mark said. "Panos wouldn't have sent us to a

tourist trap. It looks like a nice mix of locals. Students and artists and neighborhood people."

They selected their food from an enormous tray that the waiter brought. It held several dishes, and they pointed to what they would like. Octopus in a sauce, tiny sardines fried whole, little meatballs, and a salad of cucumbers, tomatoes, onions, and fresh feta cheese. They washed it down with a red house wine.

"What did you think of that?" Mark asked her.

"Fabu!" Tracey said. "I love ethnic foods of all kinds."

Mark laughed. "My sentiments exactly," he said. "Do you want dessert?" Mark asked.

"No way," Tracey said. "Not after all that food."

"Okay. I'll get the check, and we can head back to the hotel." He signaled for the waiter and took care of the bill.

At the hotel, they stopped in the lobby to chat with Panos and pick up their keys. "How do you like Athens, Ms. Sullivan?" Panos asked her.

"I love it," Tracey told him. "I thought it was going to be dirtier and noisier from what people had told me."

Panos smiled. "We've been cleaning up for the Olympics," he said. "And people are getting smarter about pollution."

"Well, I think it's beautiful," Tracey said, meaning it.

"Good," Panos said. "I hope you two have a wonderful stay."

"We will," Mark said, leading the way upstairs.

When they reached the upper floor, they stood and stared at each other. "Do you want to come in for a little nightcap?" Mark asked. "I've got some bottled water."

Tracey laughed. "Everybody in Athens runs around with bottled water," she said. "I've got some, too. Remember? But I think I'll go straight to bed. I'm exhausted." She put the key in her door.

"Okay," Mark said, but he hesitated and didn't immediately go to his room.

Tracey turned to him and smiled shyly. "I'll see you in the morning," she said.

Mark nodded. "Sleep as late as you want to," he said. "I'm going to."

"Okay," Tracey said. She turned the key in the lock and opened the door. " 'Night, Mark," she said softly.

" 'Night, Tracey." He looked at her a moment, then reluctantly went to his door and let himself in.

Damn, he thought as the door snapped shut behind him, *if only . . . if only . . . If only what*? He wasn't sure, but he did know that he desired Tracey Sullivan, wanted her desperately, in fact. But he wasn't about to push too hard for fear that he might chase her away.

It's going to be a long, lonely night, he thought, *especially with her on the other side of that wall.* He looked at the offending wall with its fading paper and scowled. But his scowl soon turned to a smile. *We'll have tomorrow,* he told himself, *and tomorrow night. Maybe, just maybe . . .*

He shook his head and went over to the air conditioning unit to turn it on. *Best to not think about it now, Mark,* he reflected. *Don't get your hopes up too high.*

Tracey opened the French doors and stepped out onto the little balcony. In the distance she could see the ramparts of the Acropolis, flooded with light, as was the magnificent Parthenon itself. She gazed at it dreamily for a while, then turned and went back into her room. She pulled the curtains across the doors and began to undress, surprised to find that her clothing was damp. Athens was hot and humid, and she and Mark had done a lot of walking. The breezes had made it seem less torpid, and the company had been so enjoyable that she hadn't thought about personal discomfort.

She decided to close the balcony doors and turn on the air conditioner. That done, she brushed her teeth, washed her face and hands, and put on a long, well-worn T-shirt to sleep in. The bed looked inviting, and she lay down on it, switching off the light at the same time.

Closing her eyes, she waited in vain for sleep to come. In her mind's eye, she could see Mark Varney. Mark Varney of the handsome features and bright smile. Mark Varney of the courteous manners and good humor. Mark Varney, who was just beyond the wall next to her.

It was clear to Tracey that Mark felt an attraction to her.

Why else would he be treating her to this trip? It wasn't just an act of kindness, she was certain.

She tossed and turned, trying to sort out the conflicting thoughts and feelings that whirled around in her head and heart. She had to admit that she was powerfully attracted to Mark Varney. More attracted to him than she'd ever been to anyone.

She lifted her head and fluffed the pillow, then lay back down again. *But it's more than that,* she told herself. *It's much more than mere attraction.*

She looked toward the wall in the dark. *I want you,* she whispered to the wall. *I want you desperately.*

Chapter Twenty-nine

Athens, Greece

Tracey opened her eyes and was momentarily confused. *Where am I?* she wondered, sitting up and stretching. One look around answered her question. The faded wallpaper, the remnants of what had been murals on the high ceilings, and the French doors leading to the balcony brought a smile to her lips. She picked up her wristwatch and looked at the time. Eight-fifteen. She hopped out of bed quickly and slipped into a pair of shorts, opened the balcony door, and stepped outside.

Her ears were assaulted by the cacophony of car horns, motorcycle and scooter roars, buses, and the raised voices of store owners and shoppers that together formed a constant in Athens life. Her nose immediately twitched at the exhaust fumes that filled the air. Lifting her gaze, she saw that the Parthenon was still atop the Acropolis, as it had been for nearly twenty-five hundred years.

Anxious to have breakfast and begin sightseeing again, she went back into her room and quickly showered, put on a modicum of makeup, and donned fresh clothes. Wondering if Mark was up yet, she was tempted to knock on his door or call his room, but she decided not to bother him in case he was asleep. It would be nice to have breakfast with him, she thought, but eating alone wouldn't bother her, either. She couldn't stay in with this new and exciting city to explore.

So she set off down the curving stairs to the lobby, stopping on her way to look at the old framed prints of various Greek islands and ruins. Panos wasn't at the desk, but his mother, Miss Vicky, as she was known, was in the lobby to greet her.

"Good morning, Miss Sullivan," she said. "Did you sleep well?"

"Yes, thank you," Tracey replied.

"Good," Miss Vicky said, clapping her hands together. "Now. Are you ready for breakfast?"

"Oh, yes," Tracey said.

"This way, then," Miss Vicky said, gesturing toward the breakfast room. "I believe someone is waiting for you." There was a twinkle in her eye and a bounce in her step.

Tracey stepped into the room and saw Mark seated at a table for two, looking toward her. His fresh-scrubbed brightness and dark handsomeness startled her anew. He smiled, and Tracey returned it.

"Coffee or tea?" Miss Vicky asked as Tracey sat down.

"Coffee, please," Tracey said, just then noticing the other guests in the small room for the first time.

"Sleep okay?" Mark asked.

She nodded. "You?"

"Fine," he said, taking a sip of coffee.

A waitress brought Tracey's breakfast: a small pot of coffee, juice, a hard-boiled egg, a dish of oil-cured olives, and a plate with a large roll and slices of toast with an apricot spread in a little dish.

She began to eat, and Mark watched her, enjoying the way she relished the food. "What would you like to do today?" he asked. "Since we don't have much time, I thought we'd do whatever you want to."

"You know the city," Tracey replied, "so why don't I let you decide?"

"Okay," he said. "Eat all of your breakfast, because you're going to need your strength, and put on your best walking shoes."

* * *

Tracey was glad she'd taken Mark's advice. They were finally returning to the pension in the early evening. The day had flown by in a whirlwind of sightseeing, and her head was filled with the dizzying, overlapping impressions left by acres of marble ruins, ancient busts and statues and tombs and jewelry, exotic flea markets, paintings and mosaics, and icons and incense.

"What was your favorite place?" Mark asked as they walked up the steep and narrow marble sidewalk toward the Doric House.

"That's an impossible question to answer," Tracey responded. "I don't think I've ever seen more beauty in a single day. The National Archaeological Museum, the Byzantine Museum, the ancient agora, all the churches. It's a toss-up."

"Here we are," Mark said. "I bet you're exhausted."

"And exhilarated, too," Tracey said, turning to him with a happy smile.

"Good," he said. "What if we take a breather, shower, and change for a late dinner? You can nap for a while if you want to."

"Nap?" she said. "Are you kidding? While there's still so much to do and see?"

Despite her protest, Tracey did doze off after showering. She spread out on the big bed in her room, the French doors open to the sounds of the Plaka coming to life, intending to write Maribel a note on one of the many postcards she'd purchased during the day. Yet the sound of the telephone ringing loudly at her bedside awakened her a while later.

"Hello?" she said, her voice groggy.

"You're asleep," Mark said. "Do you want to forget dinner and stay in?"

"No way," Tracey cried, coming fully awake. "You're not going to get off that easy."

Mark laughed. "Is thirty minutes enough time for you to get ready?" he asked.

"Yes," she said. "Want to meet downstairs?"

"That's great," he replied. "I'll be in the lounge."

Tracey hung up the telephone and hopped out of bed. In the bathroom, she ran a brush through her hair and quickly applied makeup, a tad more than she'd wear during the daytime. She had very little choice in what to wear, and wished, too late, that she'd packed more. A navy linen sweater and white linen trousers would have to do. That and her chic navy espadrilles.

When she was dressed, she checked her appearance in the bathroom mirror one last time. "A dab more blusher," she told her reflection. She made fast work of applying it, then grabbed her key and left the room, anxious not to keep Mark waiting.

"Mind if we walk?" he asked once they were out on the marble-paved lane.

"I'd love it," Tracey replied.

The evening was warm and humid, but there was a steady breeze that felt good on the skin. The narrow sidewalks were crowded as they headed toward the bright lights of Syntagma Square with its fast-food restaurants and kiosks.

"Where're we going?" Tracey asked.

"Kolonaki," Mark said. "It's a nearby neighborhood. I think you'll like it."

It was an uphill climb to Kolonaki, and as they made the ascent, Tracey could see that they were entering a decidedly different Athens, rich and chic, with trendy boutiques and antiques shops. When they neared Kolonaki Square, she was stunned by the sight of hundreds of people gathered at tables under huge canvas awnings at sidewalk cafés that stretched for at least a couple of city blocks and then ran off paved lanes lined with exclusive shops and restaurants. These lanes ran perpendicular to the main thoroughfare.

"My God," she said, "I've never seen anything like this."

"Isn't it a wonderful sight?" Mark said. "They're nearly all Athenians, out to see and be seen. It's like this every afternoon and night in good weather."

"It's sort of like a very rich version of the Plaka, without the tourists or tourist shops," Tracey observed.

"Not unless they're looking for Gucci and Prada and

stuff like that," Mark said. "Over this way," he added, indicating a paved lane that led off between a series of cafés.

Exclusive shops and restaurants were next door to one another. Beautiful trees, many strung with tiny white lights, and luxuriant plants created a junglelike effect. Diners sat under umbrellas, basking in candlelight, and the delicious aromas emanating from the restaurants were truly wonderful.

"This is so magical," Tracey said. "Like a fantasy land."

"I'm glad you like it," Mark said. "I think it's very special. And here we are."

The restaurant was a study in high luxe postmodernism, all marble and exotic woods and glass and brass. "It's Italian," Mark said. "I hope you don't mind."

"It looks wonderful," Tracey said.

After they were seated outside at a small table, Mark ordered a bottle of Veuve Clicquot champagne, then they both had salads and seafood pasta with a very good wine, followed by tiramisu with espresso. They discussed the sights they'd seen together during dinner, but as the night wore on, the conversation became more intimate. Mark told her of his ambitions for his agency, and Tracey could see that he was committed and very hardworking. He asked her about her own ambitions after leaving Greece.

"I'm not really certain," she replied, appreciating his interest in her. "I'll go home to Miami, of course. Maybe go back to work. The station might have a job for me."

"What about your writing?" Mark asked. "You can't give it up. You're too good at it. And you're a damn good ghostwriter, to boot."

She smiled at him. "I'm glad you believe in me," she said. "It really means a lot."

"Well, it's true," he told her. He looked over at her then, his eyes holding hers. "What about the rest of your life?" he asked. "I guess you're seeing somebody?"

Tracey looked away from him, then cleared her voice and returned his gaze. "I—I was," she said, "but not anymore."

"What happened?" Mark asked. "Or am I being too nosy?"

She shook her head. "No," she said, "not at all." She shrugged. "Let's just keep it simple and say he was also seeing someone else. So I broke it off."

"Are you still hurting from it?" Mark asked softly.

"I—I guess so," Tracey said. "A little bit. What really hurt was finding out that he'd been deceiving me." She decided to tell him the whole story, and Mark sat rapt, completely focused on her, listening to every word.

"I think the hardest thing is to learn to trust myself again," Tracey concluded. "My own instincts and judgment. How could I have been so deluded?"

"If I could answer that question, I'd be a billionaire, wouldn't I?" He emitted a sigh. "When we're in love or think we're in love, we'll believe anything, won't we?"

"Absolutely," Tracey agreed.

"But you can't let that distort the way you think about yourself," Mark said. "I think you've got remarkable insight and maturity for someone your age."

Tracey laughed. "That's very charming of you to say, but I still feel like a fool."

"I would, too," he admitted, his laughter joining hers. He paid the check, and they began strolling back to the pension. In Syntagma Square, the sidewalks were thronged with people, and someone bumped against Tracey, throwing her off balance. Mark grabbed her before she fell.

"I've got you now," he said, "and I won't let go." His voice was playful, but the expression on his face was serious.

Tracey enjoyed the sensation of his body touching hers, the hard, muscled strength of his arm around her shoulders, and she didn't push him away. It felt natural and right, and she overcame her initial embarrassment.

Back at the Doric House, they stopped in the hallway outside her room. Both of his arms encircled her. She had longed to have his arms around her last night, and looking up into his dark eyes, she knew that she wanted to be with him tonight, all night long. He leaned down and kissed her lips tenderly, hugging her closer to his body, and Tracey returned his kiss, reveling in his masculine scent and his darkly tanned hardness.

He hugged her tighter, kissing her deeper, his tongue

probing and exploring, exciting her to respond in kind. His hands moved gently up and down her back, caressing her, then moved down to the firm roundness of her buttocks, stroking them tenderly and pressing them against his aroused manhood.

Tracey drew back with a sigh of pleasure, and Mark ran his lips about her ears and down her neck, his breath a soft whisper on her silken flesh. "We—we're making a scene in the hallway," she said.

"That means we have to go inside, doesn't it?" he replied. "We don't want to upset anybody." He smiled down at her.

"No," Tracey said, "we wouldn't want to do that." She reluctantly extricated herself from his arms and started to put the key in the door.

"Here," Mark said, "let me."

She gave him the key, and he unlocked the door, holding it open wide for her. Tracey stepped into the room, with Mark just behind her. He closed the door and locked it, then flipped on the light and turned around and took her in his arms again. He walked her backward into the big bedroom, his lips on hers, his hands moving up and down her back. At the bed, he stopped and hugged her to him again before slipping his hands under her linen sweater and running them lightly over her bare flesh.

Tracey's breath caught in her throat as she felt his fingers on her breasts, kneading them gently, inexorably seeking out her nipples.

"Hmmm," he murmured. "Let me undress you."

Tracey stepped back, and Mark deftly pulled her sweater off, then unhooked her brassiere. He tossed both onto a chair, then stood still, mesmerized by her splendid torso. Reaching out, he ran his fingers lightly over her breasts and down to her pelvis, then back up to her breasts, one of which he took in each hand, stroking them, thrumming her nipples with his fingers.

Tracey nearly swooned at his light touch, the thrill coursing through her body one that she'd never experienced before, not with any man. She reached over and slid her hands up under his black sweater, anxious to feel his flesh on her fingertips.

Mark obliged her by quickly slipping out of the sweater and letting it fall silently to the floor. He held her against him, and Tracey gloried at the fiery sensation of his warm, hard body against hers. Mark leaned down and kissed the cleft between her breasts, his tongue traveling to first one nipple, then the other, licking and kissing, teasing her mercilessly.

Tracey shuddered with excitement and threw her arms around him tightly, bringing her body closer to his again. Mark started to fumble with her trousers, but she reached down and undid them herself, then let them slide to the floor. She stepped out of them and slipped off her panties as Mark quickly shed his pants and jockey shorts.

Naked, they stood before one another, their hands reaching out and stroking, brushing, exploring, until he took her into his arms again, his powerful body against hers and, like hers, trembling with sensual pleasure. He eased her down onto the bed and stood over her, watching as she adjusted the pillow under her head.

Tracey looked up at his clearly defined musculature in the faint light, at his manhood which strained for satisfaction, and at the glimmer of a smile that was on his lips as his eyes took in the sight of her lovely nakedness on the bed beneath him.

Mark got on the bed then, positioning his knees between her legs, his hands trailing up and down her torso, pausing at her breasts to knead and stroke before moving on down to the mound between her thighs, where he felt her moist readiness.

Tracey trembled with desire again at the feel of him there in her most private place, and her hands reached out to hold him, to feel his sex. She heard him suck in his breath as she fondled his engorged cock and the dark, heavy globes beneath it, brushing her fingertips across and around him, tantalizing him as he had her.

He brought himself down atop her then, unable to bear the separation from her any longer, his body yearning to be as one with hers. Kissing her passionately, his breath urgent in her ears, he entered her slowly, restraining the desire to plunge into her with wanton desire, wanting to sustain their pleasure as long as possible.

Tracey gasped as she felt his manhood enter her and slowly make her body his own, her need for him urging her to thrust her pelvis to meet his, to take as much of him as possible, to envelop him in the heated warmth of her sex. She wanted him with all of her heart and soul, her body aching for him, because only he could bring her satisfaction.

As he felt her desire for him mount, Mark could restrain himself no longer and began moving with increasing speed and strength, in and out, her every movement against him exciting him more, until he plunged uncontrollably. He felt her muscles suddenly contract and then heard her start to thrash and moan beneath him, and he thrust into her in a frenzy of desire, exploding in his lust for her as she spasmed beneath him, her body contracting in wave after wave of sensual bliss.

He lay atop her, peppering her face and neck with kisses, his breath labored, and Tracey hugged him to her with all of her might, hoping never to forget this ecstatic moment. When he rolled off her at last, he held her in his arms, both silently staring into each other's eyes, as their breathing returned to normal.

"That—that was so wonderful," Mark stuttered at last, his hands stroking her back. "So, so wonderful."

Tracey nodded. "Yes," she murmured. "I—I haven't ever experienced anything like it before." And she meant it, for she'd never made love that had seemed as profound and pleasurable as this.

They talked quietly for a while, about nothing and everything, laughing, delighted in their newfound discovery of each other, each confessing that they'd slowly become attracted to one another in Santorini. Both of them were already looking forward to the next round.

"I guess I should at least get up and go get my toothbrush," Mark said later. "If you'll let me stay with you tonight, that is." His eyes twinkled with mischief.

"I don't know about that," Tracey teased. "Hanging your

toothbrush next to mine sounds an awfully lot like staking a claim."

Mark looked into her eyes. "It is," he said in a soft but definite voice.

Tracey felt an unbidden surge of pride and joy and, yes, love, run through her body at his words. *He means it,* she thought with wonder. *He really means it.*

He hugged her in his arms and kissed her again, and she responded immediately. Within moments, they were making love again, as they did on and off all night.

Mark never did make it next door to get his toothbrush.

Chapter Thirty

Miami, Florida

"Nobody's home," Cliff told Brian Biggs III. "The broad is never at home, I'm telling you."

He had just tried the door of Tracey Sullivan's house in Coconut Grove, ringing the doorbell, but not trying to enter. "It's locked up tighter than a drum," he went on. "Doesn't look like anybody's been around for a while, you ask me."

"You really think so?" Brian asked him.

"Yeah," Cliff said with a nod, "for sure. Curtains closed, some of the Bahama shutters closed, no life about the place, I'm telling you. I've seen some other chick—definitely not Tracey—come in once for a few minutes."

They were parked in a shady side street near Tracey's house, and Brian tapped both hands impatiently on the steering wheel. "Shit," he said. He started the car. "Maybe she's at work."

"Maybe." Cliff nodded. "But if she's at work, it doesn't look to me like she's been coming home to sleep."

"We'll find out," Brian said, easing the car out into the street. "We'll go over to the television station and see."

He cruised down the streets of Coconut Grove and out

onto the highway, watching the traffic but taking sidelong glances at Cliff in the seat next to him. *The guy is so fucking ordinary that he could disappear in a crowd,* he thought. *Nobody would ever be able to identify him. Tall and lanky, but not excessively so. Average weight. Average clothes. Average everything, even his fucking name. Cliff. Cliff what?* he wondered. It probably wasn't his real name, but Brian didn't ask. He wasn't sure he really wanted to know.

Brian guessed that his very ordinariness was part of Cliff's success as a hit man. The guy didn't dress in a threatening or flashy way. He wasn't the least bit scary-looking, nor was he ugly. He wasn't enormously big or powerfully built like so many of the bodyguards who sidelined as hit men, nor was he a wiry little maniac like some of the bantam-legged, crop-wielding jockeys he'd met who'd off you at a moment's notice, either. Cliff didn't look like a killer. Cliff looked like most people's next-door neighbor, which was one of the chief reasons Brian had hired him to off old man Sullivan—plus his successful track record as a hit man.

The man's ordinariness put Brian off a bit—nothing cool about the dude at all—but it also scared him a little. That, coupled with what he knew about his past. He had proof that the guy was a real killer, with many accomplishments under his belt. So Brian always felt compelled to put an extra bounce in his step around Cliff, rev up the macho factor a bit, strut his stuff, making like he wasn't just some rich guy who could afford to hire somebody to do his dirty work for him, which was exactly who he was and what he was doing, of course.

Brian pulled into the TV station parking lot and killed the engine. He got out of the car and leaned in toward Cliff. "Stay in the car," he advised. "This is my kind of turf. I know my way around here, and I'll get more accomplished, since some of these people know me. The chicks especially." He winked. "Most of 'em have the hots for me."

Cliff barked a laugh. "Listenin' to you, you'd think every chick in Miami's got the hots for you." *What a chickenshit asshole,* he thought.

Brian strutted off, acting cool for Cliff's benefit. When he returned to the car a few minutes later, some of the swagger had gone out of his step.

From Brian's expression, Cliff could tell it hadn't been a fruitful errand.

Brian got in the car and slammed the door hard. "Shit!" he cursed. "She doesn't work there anymore. Can you believe that?"

"They say where she's at?"

"Nope. No forwarding address, nothing." He backed the car out with a squeal of tires.

"Now what?" Cliff asked.

"Now we pay a visit to her best friend," Brian said. "A Hispanic chick named Maribel. She's not a fan of mine, but we'll find out what she knows. And if anybody knows where Tracey is, it's Maribel. If she'll talk."

Cliff cracked his knuckles. Smiled. "Not to worry. This Maribel? Getting her to talk'll be *my* pleasure."

Maribel answered the door and was startled to see a stranger standing there. "Yes?" she said, looking at the nondescript man without any real interest, but ready to close the door on a salesman—or worse—in a moment's notice.

"I need to talk to you," the man said. "About Tracey Sullivan."

Maribel's breath caught in her throat. *Oh, my God, has something happened to Tracey?* she wondered. "What is it?" she asked the man. "Is she okay?"

"Do you mind if I step inside?" the man asked. "It's a . . . well, it's a personal matter, see."

"You tell me if something's happened to Tracey," Maribel insisted. "And tell me now."

"No, no," the man said, "it's nothing like that." He casually pushed a foot between the door and its frame so that Maribel couldn't close it. "I need to find out where she is," he said.

Brian stepped into sight and smiled at Maribel. "Hey, Maribel," he said. "We really need to find Trace." He shrugged. "It's important, you know?"

Maribel's defenses immediately went up and her antennae were on full alert. "What do *you* need to find her for, you creep?"

"You bitch," Brian snarled.

Cliff bristled at her sarcastic tone of voice and her questioning him, but he decided it might be easier to get the information out of her if he played it real cool and put on the charm.

"Cool it," he said to Brian, then he turned back to Maribel. "I have some personal things to discuss with her, see," he said mildly. "You know, like between a man and a woman."

Maribel's eyes flashed as they traveled up and down the man again. *Tracey wouldn't have anything to do with this jerk,* she thought. *Besides, if Tracey knows him, I would know him or know all about him.*

She shook her head slowly from side to side. "You don't know Tracey," she said, "and I'm not telling you one damn thing." She cast a fierce glance in Brian's direction. "As for you, Mr. Big Shot Biggs, I wouldn't give you the time of day."

She started to close the door, but Cliff shoved his way into the apartment, nearly knocking Maribel down. "What the fuck do you think you're doing?" she cried.

Brian followed him in and began looking around the apartment, ignoring Maribel as he looked for any clue—he had no idea what exactly—as to where Tracey might be.

Cliff stared at Maribel expressionlessly. "We do this the easy way or the hard way," he said. "I want to know where Tracey Sullivan is, and you're going to tell me."

Maribel glared at him malevolently. "Who the fuck do you think I am that I'm going to tell you shit?" she sniped in her nastiest voice.

Cliff continued to stare at her, his face reddening slightly, his fists clenched at his sides. He'd really enjoy doing this bitch if he had to. "I'd hoped we could do this the easy way," he said, "but I can see that you want to make it hard."

Without any warning, his hand swung out in an arc and landed with a resounding thud against Maribel's cheek, nearly knocking her off her feet.

Brian turned and looked when she screamed. She caught her balance, then automatically threw up her hands to protect her face. "You—you bastard!" she growled. "I wouldn't tell you—"

Cliff's hand flew out again, this time landing with a thud on her other cheek. Tears sprang into Maribel's eyes as she stumbled, nearly fell, caught herself, then reached a hand up to her face. It came away with blood on it. Her nose was bleeding.

"Hey, hey, hey," Brian called to Cliff. "Look what we have here." He held up a small yellow Post-it.

"What is it?" Cliff asked.

"Goddamn you," Maribel cried. She flew toward Brian and snatched at the piece of paper. "Give me that!" she cried.

Brian laughed. "It's Tracey's telephone number. In Greece, it says. Place called Santorini. What the hell is she doing in Greece?"

"Who the fuck cares," Cliff said. "Let's go."

Brian took out his wallet and placed the Post-it in it, making a great show of it for Maribel's sake. "See you later, Maribel," he said.

"Go to hell," she said in a sneer. She watched as they left and locked the door behind them. *Por Dios,* she thought in panic. *I've got to get hold of Tracey.*

Chapter Thirty-one

Santorini, Greece

Overnight bags slung across their shoulders, Tracey and Mark entered Urania's compound with looks of rested contentment on their faces, despite the sightseeing in Athens and the lovemaking that had kept them up all hours before their morning flight.

It's going to be impossible to wipe the smile off my face, Tracey thought happily as they descended the stairs to the terrace. *And if Urania is nosy or suspicious when she gets back, I'm not going to worry about it.* Mark certainly didn't seem to be concerned about what Urania might think. He had hardly even brought her up.

The sight of Maria Stefanou, who marched out onto the terrace and stood staring at them, momentarily made Tracey's smile disappear, however. The woman appeared to be simmering with rage, and when they reached the bottom of the stairs she didn't hesitate to launch into attack mode.

"Madame has been telephoning and paging you for some time," she snapped at Mark. "Nor have you responded to me. I want to know why."

"Because," Mark replied with calm confidence, "I left

my cell phone and pager here." There was a wry smile on his face.

Maria Stefanou turned to Tracey. "And you," she said. "I have tried to page you also but was unsuccessful. Did I not make it clear that you are to have your pager on your person at all times?"

Tracey blushed and felt a bit guilty. She had simply stood by and watched as Mark had thrown her pager away. "I'm afraid I . . . I . . . must have misplaced it," she lied.

Maria Stefanou looked at her suspiciously. "That was incredibly irresponsible of you." She heaved a sigh of exasperation and redirected her gaze at Mark. "You should call Madame at once."

"Thank you," Mark said. "I will once we're settled back in." He nodded and put a hand in the small of Tracey's back and started inside. Maria Stefanou marched off in the opposite direction.

"Well," Tracey said, "I'd better go change and get busy in the office."

"And I'm going to get hold of 'Madame,' " he said, scowling in imitation of Maria Stefanou.

She had to laugh, and he drew her into his arms and kissed her. "Why don't we have lunch together in a while? Okay?"

"I'd love to," she said.

"Good. I'll see you later."

She turned and went up the stairs to the windmill, barely able to contain her newfound happiness. Inside, everything seemed to be in order. She quickly put the clothes in her overnighter away, changed into a comfortable pair of shorts and a T-shirt, and hurried into her office to get busy at the desk.

Later, when the telephone rang, she was jolted from her deep concentration on the manuscript and surprised to see that over two hours had passed. She picked up the receiver.

"It's Mark."

"Hi," she replied, a smile automatically coming to her lips.

"How's it going?" he asked.

"Very well," she said. "I'm really flying along without

any interruptions from Urania. I've made enormous progress."

"Great. Still want to meet me for lunch down by the pool?" he asked.

"Sure," she said.

"Fifteen minutes okay?"

"I'll be there," Tracey said and replaced the receiver in its cradle. *I wouldn't miss it for the world,* she thought.

She stored her changes on the computer, then went into the bathroom and washed her hands and face. Looking at her reflection in the mirror, she applied a little fresh lipstick and blusher and ran a brush through her hair. In the windmill, she opened the armoire to choose a fresh top. *Something besides a plain T-shirt,* she thought. She decided on a simple but elegant white linen shirt that she tucked inside her shorts.

They were in the pool, playfully splashing around, gleefully shouting at one another when Urania swept grandly in, laden with shopping bags of booty from her trip to Hong Kong. Stavros, who'd picked her up at the airport, had also commandeered a taxi to accommodate the vast amount of luggage and packages. He followed in her wake, and set down his enormous load on the terrace before returning to the parking area to pick up another.

Maria appeared and began carrying shopping bags inside, while Urania, a vision in lilac silk and white diamonds, descended the steps to the pool terrace in her lilac stiletto-heeled sandals. At the foot of the stairs, she paused and lit a cigarette.

Mark and Tracey caught sight of her, and their voices died as the playing stopped. They acted almost as if they were guilty children.

"Hi," Mark called to her.

Tracey looked over at her and was once again stunned by the woman's undeniable glamour and presence. "Welcome back," she said.

"Well, well, well," Urania intoned in her husky voice, click-clacking toward the pool in her sling backs. At its edge, she slipped off her sunglasses and smiled down at them saccharinely. "It's true, isn't it, darlings? When the kitty cat's away, the little mice will indeed play."

"Yes, we're having a great time," Mark replied. "How was your trip?"

"It was work," Urania said, anger creeping into her voice as her Ferrari-red lips curled dangerously. "Something that it seems only I am capable of around here."

"Listen, Urania—" Mark began as he stepped out of the pool. Water sluiced off his strong, tanned body, and he reached for a beach towel to dry off.

"No, you listen to *me*," Urania snapped at him. "I think we should have a little talk in my suite right away." Then she turned her attention to Tracey. "And as for you, Ms. Sullivan, shouldn't you be at your desk, earning your keep?"

Tracey had followed Mark out of the pool and was wrapping a beach towel around herself. "I've been—"

Mark interrupted her. "Excuse me, Tracey," he said, then looked back at Urania. "She's been working all hours," he said, "making a lot of progress on the book while you've been gone. She certainly hasn't been spending all of her time here in the pool."

"I'll talk to you inside," Urania snarled. She threw her cigarette down on the terrace, then turned and walked inside, her heels clicking angrily on the terrace.

"I'm sorry she's so angry," Tracey said.

"It's too bad," Mark said, "but it's not your fault or mine. I'll go talk to her and try to calm her down." He leaned down and kissed her. "I'll see you in a little while."

" 'Bye," Tracey said, somewhat taken aback that he'd kissed her with Urania hovering about in the villa. "And good luck."

"Don't worry. I can take care of her," Mark said, and he went on inside.

Tracey gathered up her sunglasses and paperback novel and slipped into her sandals, then headed toward the windmill. Going up the exterior steps she couldn't help but hear Urania's raised voice from inside.

When she reached the stairway to her room, Maria Stefanou's voice stopped her in her tracks.

"Ms. Sullivan," she called.

Tracey turned to face the imperious woman. "Yes?" she said.

"I suggest you mind your own business," Maria said, "and keep to yourself. You have upset Madame and that is not permitted."

"I'm sorry that Madame is upset," Tracey replied, "but I'm not her slave, Mrs. Stefanou. Nor yours." She turned and left the woman glaring at her.

I'm not taking any abuse from her, Tracey told herself, *and I'm not taking any abuse from Urania, either.* She realized with a degree of pride that she felt empowered by the growing attachment between Mark and herself. At the same time she wondered what lay ahead now that Urania had returned. *We'll see,* she thought. *In the meantime, I'll get back to work until dinnertime.*

Urania lit a cigarette, then tossed the gold lighter onto the coffee table, where it landed with a clatter. Blowing a stream of smoke into the air, she stared at Mark, who stood peering out at the caldera through the terrace doors. He was still in his bathing suit, a towel wrapped around his waist.

"I didn't mean to upset you, darling," she said, almost but not quite apologetically. "It's just that this trip was such a strain. I've been out working myself half to death to make a buck, then I come home and what do I find? You and little Miss Plain Jane playing together in the pool like young lovers."

Mark turned from the door to face her. She was stretched out on the couch looking up at him. "Why must you refer to her in such an insulting way, Urania?"

"Oh, jumping to her defense, are we?" she said, her voice tinged with sarcasm.

"It only makes you sound jealous and resentful when you degrade her that way," Mark said, "and it's certainly not flattering to you."

Urania looked down at her manicured and lacquered nails—they perfectly matched her lips—heaved a sigh, then looked back up at him. "Perhaps I am jealous," she said. "She's young and . . . well, wholesome-looking, and she certainly seems to have great appeal for you." She took a drag off her cigarette, then stubbed it out in an ashtray.

"Look, Urania," Mark said in exasperation, his voice rising slightly. "Ever since I first became your agent, I've given you moral support. Emotional support. I've done everything in my power to help your writing career." He paused as she shifted uncomfortably on the couch, then in a quieter voice he continued. "I told you I wouldn't desert you, and I meant it. But that doesn't mean that you own me."

She barked a laugh that was anything but mirthful. "Well, I didn't mean to give you the impression that I 'own' you, darling," Urania said. "And I hardly think that if I did feel that way I would've left you here to cavort with that . . . that ghost."

Mark groaned audibly. "I can see we're getting nowhere discussing this," he said in frustration. "Maybe the best thing for me to do is get out of here and get back to L.A. and tend to business. Leave the two of you here by yourselves to get this work done. I only promised to stay until you got back."

"Oh, no, Mark!" Urania cried, jumping to her feet. "You mustn't go, darling. You mustn't. What will I do without you?" She grasped him by the arms frantically. "Please, Mark. I'll be all alone here without you."

"That's not true," he said calmly. "You have Maria. And Stavros and Iliki. And Tracey, whether you like her or not, will be here. Maybe you can get more work done without me hanging around."

"Oh, God," Urania wailed, tears coming into her eyes. "How will I . . . how will I get anything done?"

"You'll manage," Mark said. "I'm sure of it. Here, sit down and let me get us both a good stiff drink."

He led her back to the couch and eased her down onto it, then crossed to the little drinks table where he put ice from the sweating silver bucket into two glasses, poured in generous dollops of vodka, and finally added a small amount of tonic. Giving them a swift stir, he took one over to Urania.

"Thank you," she said meekly. She took a sip of the drink, then quickly took another one before setting it down.

He sat down in a chair facing her. "It's really the best thing, Urania," he said reasonably. "I'll only be gone for a while. I've really been neglecting my business lately, and there're a lot of things I need to see to."

"But—but what about e-mail?" she said. "And faxes and telephones? You really don't need to be in New York or Los Angeles for business. You're simply using that as an excuse to leave here."

He shook his head. "No, that's not true," he said. "There are some things I need to take care of in person. There're a couple of editors I need to meet with in New York—"

"That's nonsense," she broke in. "Julia came from New York to see me, didn't she? Why would you need to go to New York?"

"You're hardly the typical writer, Urania," he said. "An editor might fly halfway across the globe to see you because there's a fortune involved and because it's you. But it doesn't work that way for most authors. I have to go see the editors on their behalf. Plus, there's stuff I need to see about in Los Angeles. New material that's come in from writers, meetings with producers, all sorts of things."

"I still don't see why you can't do it from here," she argued, pouting in a childlike manner.

"Don't be unreasonable," Mark replied. "You know that I wouldn't interfere with your career in any way, and I expect the same professional respect from you."

Urania took another sip of her drink. She peered down into her glass, lost in thought for a moment, then turned to him with a serious expression on her heavily made-up face. "You're right," she finally said. "I'm being terribly selfish, but I do get so lonely, darling."

"You'll have plenty to keep you busy here," Mark said. "Tracey's way ahead of you on the changes, so you'll have a lot to catch up on."

Urania's grimace of distaste was not lost on him. "Yes," she said, "Ms. Sullivan seems to work very fast indeed. And she makes my work doubly difficult."

"Maybe," Mark replied. "But remember, it's very important that you make certain the novel has your voice," he added, in an attempt to humor her. He knew that one of

Urania's chief complaints to Tracey had been that the manuscript was losing her "voice" with Tracey's changes.

She nodded. "Oh, yes," she readily agreed. "That is paramount. She certainly can't do that, wondrous though you may think she is, so I have to be very careful about that."

"That's more like it," Mark said, patting her on the shoulder.

Urania reached up and put her hand over his, clutching him tightly. "You won't be gone long, will you?" she cooed.

"I'll get back as soon as I can," he said, "but I really don't know how long it'll be."

"Please try to hurry," she said. "I'll miss you so much."

He wished that he could say the same, but he didn't feel that way and couldn't lie to her. "It won't be long," he said. "Now, I'd better go get on the telephone and see about reservations." He patted her hand and got to his feet. "You probably need a good rest after all the traveling."

"Yes, I do," Urania said. "I think I'll try to nap this afternoon."

He leaned down and kissed her chastely on the forehead. "Now, rest," he said, "and I'll see you at dinner."

He hastily left her suite and returned to his own, where he showered, dressed, and packed before making reservations to fly to New York with a three-day stopover, then on to Los Angeles. That done, he decided to get one last task finished before leaving.

Tracey sat at the computer, typing rapidly, her hair, as usual when she was working, piled in a knot atop her head with pencils stuck through it at odd angles. Her concentration was such that when Mark opened the door, knocking on it as he did so, she involuntarily jerked in her seat.

"I didn't mean to scare you," he apologized.

She turned and smiled up at him. "You didn't really," she said. "I was just lost in another world."

He put his hands on her shoulders and leaned down and kissed her. Tracey responded immediately, his warm lips more than welcome relief from the task at hand.

"Hmmm," she murmured between kisses, "you just took a shower."

"How did you know?" he whispered, his mouth seeking out her neck.

"Because you smell so good."

"So do you. I love your perfume."

"I'm not wearing any," she replied.

"I know," he said. "It's you that smells so good."

Tracey couldn't help but laugh. "That's sweet of you to say, but I'm not so sure I believe you."

Mark straightened up and smiled down at her. "Can I steal a few minutes of your time?" he asked. "I need to talk to you about something."

"Please do," Tracey said. "Anything for a break."

Mark pulled over a chair and sat down. "I'm going to leave for New York tomorrow," he said. "Then I'm going on to Los Angeles."

"Work beckons," she said. She already dreaded his leaving, but didn't want him to see her disappointment.

He nodded. "Yes. I don't know how long I'll be gone, but I'll really miss you."

"I'll miss you, too," Tracey replied. "It's—it's been so wonderful."

"And it will be again," he said. He took one of her hands in his and looked into her eyes. "Do you mind if I come up to your room tonight? I'd like to spend the night with you before I leave."

"I'd like that very much," she said, "but realistically speaking, don't you think it might be wise not to risk offending Urania on your last night here?"

"I don't want to offend her," Mark said, "but Urania has to get used to idea of *us*. Besides, we can be discreet tonight, can't we?"

Tracey felt her head nod, and she heard herself say, "Yes," almost as if some power outside herself was in control. *Anything,* she thought, *to spend the night in his arms, to feel his body next to mine, and to make love with him again before he goes.*

* * *

When Mark came to her room that night, he had a small package to give her.

"What's this?" she asked, delighted with the tiny, gift-wrapped box.

"Just something I picked up for you," he replied. "Not long after you got here."

"You've waited all this time to give it to me?" she asked.

"I wanted to wait for the right moment," Mark said. "Aren't you going to open it?"

"Of course, I am," Tracey said. She slipped the ribbon off the little package, then tore the paper off in her rush to see what he'd gotten her. When she slipped the lid off the box, she exclaimed with joy. "Oh, Mark, they're lovely. So lovely." She held the carved metal worry beads up to the light. "I'll wear them like a bracelet even if it is the men you always see with them. Always worrying the beads."

"I saw how fascinated you were with the way the men use them in Athens," he said. "I hoped you'd like them even if they are cheapies from one of the kiosks."

She leaned over and kissed him. "I love them," she said. "I'll put them on right this minute." She looped the string of metal beads around her wrist twice, and held her arm up for inspection. The beads slid down slightly. "See. They fit perfectly like this, and the metal tassel looks fabulous the way it dangles."

"Beautiful," he replied. "Like you."

She leaned over and kissed him again. "I've got to see," she said. She got up and went to the mirror over the dresser where she looked at her reflection. "Wonderful," she said, turning to face him. "I'll never take my worry beads off, even if I never learn to use them like the men do."

"Good," Mark said. "Maybe they'll protect you against all evil while I'm gone." He got up and went over to her, wrapping her in his arms and kissing her deeply. When he finally drew back, he looked into her eyes and said, "I love you, Tracey."

She didn't think she would ever tire of hearing him say those words. "I love you, too, Mark," she replied.

He kissed her again, more passionately this time, then began to exploring her ears and neck tenderly, his lips feather light against her flesh, his tongue licking at her delicately. Tracey moaned with pleasure as she felt the beginnings of a carnal stirring within. His hands stroked her back and her taut buttocks, drawing her closer to him, before caressing her breasts, which were naked beneath the T-shirt she wore.

"Let's get undressed," he whispered into her ear.

Tracey nodded, anxious to disrobe, even though she had to leave his powerful embrace.

Mark helped pull her T-shirt over her head, then untied the drawstring shorts that she had on. He drew in his breath, gazing at her in rapture when she was totally naked. He kicked off his loafers, then quickly shed his shirt and pants. When he pulled down his underpants, his already engorged penis sprang out in front of him.

Tracey reached for it, and held it in her hand, marveling over the feel of it and enjoying the gasp of pleasure that escaped Mark's lips.

"Hmm. Let's get in bed," he said, taking her by the hand and leading the way.

Tracey lay on her back, then rolled to her side when Mark lay down next to her. His hands traveled her body, gently brushing her soft skin, while his lips sought out hers, before delving to her breasts. He kissed and licked her nipples, groaning with desire as they hardened at his touch.

She pressed against his strong body, her hand going down to his manhood. Encircling it again, she felt it throb with desire for her, and the urge for him overcame her wish to take it slowly, making this night of passion last as long as possible.

"Please, Mark," she said. "I want you inside me. Now. Please."

He lifted his head from her breasts and smiled, then gently pushed her onto her back. Before Tracey knew what was happening, his head dove between her legs, his tongue flicking at the precious juices of her womanhood, while his hands slid under her buttocks, pushing her up to him.

Tracey moaned aloud and thrust herself against his hungry mouth. "Oh, my God," she rasped. "Oh, my God. Oh, oh . . ." She thought was she was going to orgasm, but before she could, Mark sat up on his knees, spread her legs wide apart, then slowly entered her even as he lay atop her.

"Awwww . . ." he groaned as his penis penetrated her wet readiness.

Tracey welcomed him with tremors of electricity that shot up and down the length of her body. When his shaft was buried deep inside her, she felt engulfed with a lust such as she had never known. He began moving in and out of her, slowly and rhythmically, and she pushed herself up to meet him, craving him as a powerful drug. When he gathered speed, she began thrashing from side to side, knowing that the inevitable spasms of orgasm were imminent.

Mark's mouth covered hers, and his arms clutched her to him harder than ever as he began plunging into her mightily. Tracey cried out helplessly as she began contracting, her body giving itself up to him entirely as she felt the waves of orgasm rock her. With a final thrust Mark's body tensed, and he let out a roar as he exploded inside her.

Panting loudly, they embraced, holding each other until their breathing returned to normal. "Oh, Tracey," he finally rasped, "I love you. I love you, love you, love you. I love you so much."

"And I love you," she said, smiling ecstatically. "I feel like I'm the luckiest woman alive."

He squeezed her tightly. "I feel the same way," he said. "I can hardly believe this is happening. That I found someone like you."

She marveled at his words, wondering if anybody else on earth had ever felt such a great love. "You have no idea what this means to me. What it makes me feel like. I feel . . . I feel like nothing could ever come between us. That nothing could ever hurt us."

"And nothing will as long as we're together," he said. "Nothing, Tracey. Our love is too powerful."

They snuggled closely, kissing, their hands unable to rest, until they fell into a deep and peaceful sleep.

Chapter Thirty-two

Urania leaned against the doorframe and stared at Tracey, a cigarette in one hand, a plume of smoke drifting toward the ceiling from her richly painted lips. Tracey had heard her footsteps, but when she didn't enter the room or say anything, she turned and gazed at her.

"Hi," she said. "Did you want something?"

Urania crossed to a chair and sat down, taking the large crystal ashtray kept there for her and putting it in her lap.

Oh, dear, Tracey thought. *Here we go again. Anything to keep me from working.* Since Mark had been gone she had gotten an enormous amount of work done, but that was despite any help from Urania, for the woman had interrupted her more than ever after his departure.

I'm really going to get it now, she thought. *She's going to chew me out as never before. Or maybe she'll even fire me this time.* Never before had she seen Urania in this quiet, seemingly reflective mode, and she felt that it must bode no good. *Maybe my latest and most radical changes to the manuscript have done it,* Tracey thought.

"I—I want," Urania began hesitantly, almost stuttering. She smashed out her cigarette in the ashtray and looked down at her nails for a moment. When she looked back up, the expression on her face seemed to Tracey to be one of embarrassment.

Urania took an audible and deep breath. "What I wanted to know, Tracey," she finally blurted out, "was if you would join me for dinner tonight."

Tracey was temporarily stunned, and it took her a minute to find her tongue. "I—I would love to, Urania," she replied.

Urania's lips curved into a tentative, perhaps even nervous, smile. "I think it's time we got to know one another better," she said, regaining her composure. "It's silly, the two of us living in the same house and working on the same project and hardly knowing each other. Don't you agree?"

Tracey nodded. "Well, yes," she said. "I do."

"I realize I've been difficult," Urania went on, "but this project is very important to me, and I'm very sensitive about it, I suppose. Plus, of course, you were a complete stranger when you got here, and that made me nervous. And . . ." Her voice trailed off, and she abruptly got up. "Well, we can talk at dinner. Okay?"

"That'd be great," Tracey said. *At least I hope so.*

"Well, I'll leave you to your work," Urania said gaily. "See you on the terrace tonight."

"Okay," Tracey said, watching her leave. *My God!* she thought. *Will wonders never cease? What's come over her?* Her spirits were considerably lifted by Urania's visit, and her mind began racing with possibilities. *Does she really want to get to know me better? Does she want to be friends?*

She thought back over the week since Mark had gone. She had assumed that her relationship with Urania would remain much the same, and it had, except for the more frequent interruptions. Tracey would work in her office for hours on end, breaking for lunch and dinner, looking forward to her exchanges with Iliki during her meals. These were always brief but friendly and, besides Prometheus's unexpected and delightful visits, virtually her only communication with anyone. She would see Maria Stefanou and Stavros moving about the house and terraces, performing their duties, but they seldom exchanged more than a nod and a glance with her.

At the end of each day, she would give Urania a batch of new pages or, more usually, leave them on the desk in Urania's office for her to pick up when she was so inclined. Before lunch the next day, the actress would invariably come into Tracey's office and slap down the work with her changes and corrections, then turn and leave with little more than a few derogatory words. The pages often resembled a bloodbath, but Tracey decided not to argue with Urania unless she had made totally nonsensical changes that simply wouldn't work. When they argued a point, Urania didn't listen to her, disregarding the wisdom of Tracey's decisions. She would insist that it be done her way, then prance out of the office.

The telephone rang, and Tracey picked it up on the second ring. "Hello," she said distractedly.

"Hey, guess who?"

"Oh, Mark," she cried. "I'm so glad you called."

"I miss you," he said. "You wouldn't believe how much."

"I miss you, too," she said. "I can't wait till you're back."

"It won't be long," Mark replied. "I'm wrapping up everything here, and will get there as soon as possible. I'm not sure exactly what day yet, but I'll try to let you know as soon as I do."

"That's wonderful," Tracey said. "Has everything gone okay?"

"Fine here. How about you?"

"I've made a lot of progress," she said. "But guess what?"

"What?"

"You won't believe it," she said. "Urania asked me to have dinner with her tonight."

"That's great," he replied. "Just be on your guard."

"I think I can take care of myself."

"I know you can," Mark replied, "but I can't help but be concerned. We both know she can be a real leech and suck the life out of you."

Tracey laughed. "That's very graphic," she said.

"Oh, hell," he said. "I've got to take a call. I'd better get going. Talk to you soon." He paused. "And Tracey?"

"Yes?"

"I love you."

"I love you, too."

She hung up the receiver and repeated his last words over and over in her head. *I love you.* Somehow their love for each other seemed unreal to her. But at the same time it gave her great and much needed comfort right now.

As the work had progressed in his absence, Tracey became increasingly lonely, and her yearning for Mark grew to a profound aching that she'd never known before. She could hardly wait for these telephone calls. He'd phoned several times, almost always speaking to Urania first, if she was in, then insisting on talking to Tracey. They were a lifesaver, but still they were no substitute for the man himself.

Here I am, she thought, *on this beautiful, magical island, with a job many writers would kill for, and I'm not happy without him.* In the evenings she would often go to bed after dinner, sometimes reading or watching an hour or so of television, more for the companionship of the voices than anything else. She seldom ventured beyond the compound's walls, always conserving her energy for the next day's work.

And now this. A call from Mark, and Urania's invitation to dinner. She found that she could hardly wait to see what "Madame" had in mind, and the remainder of the day flew by as she concentrated on the manuscript.

Cliff hated Santorini. He hated the heat and humidity. It was like Miami's, but worse, he told himself. He hated the food. It was spooky, he decided, with too many weird sauces and spices and too many disgusting fish eyes peeking up at him from plates. He hated the people, the Greeks even more than the hordes of obnoxious tourists. The Greeks, he thought, were a match for the nastiest, most aggressive and suspicious sons of bitches you'd ever find in Miami Beach. No wonder so many of them lived in New York now. They fit right in. Brash and mean and hard to con. Plus, you couldn't get any kind of information out of anybody. Even if they spoke some English—and nearly everybody did—you couldn't get much more than the time of day out of them, if that.

If he hated Santorini, he hated Oia even more. He'd never walked so much in his life. Up, down. Up, down. Always in the damn heat. It never seemed to end. Couldn't follow the chick in a car, either. No frigging cars even allowed.

But he hated the place where the chick was staying more than anything else. Straight down the hill. Behind locked gates. Walls. From up on the stupid little lane that ran through the village, there was no place—not a single frigging place—where he could get a vantage point to spy on the place without a crowd of tourists and locals around. Even then it was practically impossible to see what went on inside those walls. He'd glimpsed a sliver of pool, which made him all the more furious because the place where he was staying didn't have one. Almost none of the places in this village of the damned had one, he'd soon discovered.

But he had seen enough to know that he could pull off the job.

The pack mule of a Greek he'd spotted—the one who worked at the villa—wouldn't be a problem. If he was as stupid as he looked, Cliff thought, he wouldn't have enough sense to get in out of the rain. If there ever was any in this Godforsaken place. Besides, he seriously doubted that the pack mule and the chick ever went out anyplace together.

Even if that broad that used to be in the movies was around, she sure wasn't going to be a problem. She was a skinny bag of bones and *old*. Besides, she was likely to trip on one of her high heels and kill herself on the steps. One good shove if she got in the way, and the old bitch was history.

Cliff smiled. He'd just have to watch and wait until nightfall. He'd slip in and case the house tonight, find out who was where, what the easiest way to escape was. Hey, he might even kill her tonight.

The waiter appeared at his table. "Anything else?" he asked politely.

Cliff looked up at him. "I don't think so," he said nastily.

The waiter, choosing to ignore his tone of voice, put a check in a tiny glass and placed it on the table. Cliff took it out of the glass and looked at it. Four euros. He pulled his wallet out and made a point of riffling through it, making sure the waiter saw that it was stuffed with euros, then pulled a couple of two-euro coins out of his pocket and handed them to the waiter. Making sure he knew that he wasn't going to get a cent for giving him that Greek coffee that tasted like piss and the water that didn't have any fizz to it.

"Thank you," the waiter said, and turned and left.

Ha, Cliff thought. *The turd doesn't want to give me the satisfaction of seeing him mad.* He stood up and stretched. He walked across the lane and took another sidelong glance down the cliff toward the house. Couldn't see anything, as usual. Just another white blob on the island, mixed up with all the other white blobs, practically impossible to tell where it began and another one ended.

He looked down at his wristwatch. Time to report in to Baby Biggs in Miami, he thought. Let the little chickenshit know what was going down in Greece. A waste of time, but, hey, he was the boss, right?

He started off down the lane, indistinguishable from most of the other tourists. Sneakers—didn't the whole world wear them now?—khaki shorts and a tan polo shirt. Sunglasses and a baseball cap that had NYPD emblazoned on it. He had to laugh at that touch. He'd picked it up this morning right here in Oia. Wasn't afraid of somebody remembering a suspicious-looking dude from the States wearing a baseball cap with NYPD on it. Hell, half the kids in Greece wore them.

He'd been pleased by what he could pick up in Oia. Down the road there was a hardware store that served as a regular arsenal for someone with his talents. Wire. Rope. Duct tape. Knives. More than he would ever need to do the job. He hadn't wanted to travel with a weapon—or what airport security might see as a possible weapon—and had been a little concerned because he didn't know the terrain here. If he'd known then what he knew now, he thought, he wouldn't have worried one little bit. He didn't even need a weapon on this island, he'd decided. The landscape was a killer. The rocky cliffs. The concrete and marble steps going down them. The thousand-foot-deep caldera.

But he'd decided he liked the thin-gauge wire the lady at the local hardware store sold. He could get up close and personal with that.

The table was lit by candles in hurricane lanterns that protected them from the breeze off the caldera. It was set with beautiful china, heavy polished silver, and gleaming crystal. The thick white linen napkins were starched and ironed to perfection.

Urania was dressed and made up for dinner as if she were expecting a major director to appear at any moment. She wore a revealing white parachute silk blouse shot through with gold and matching harem pants. Diamonds glittered at her ears, at her throat, and on both wrists.

"You look . . . nice," Urania said, choosing her words carefully when Tracey joined her at the table. Her eyes assessed the younger woman voraciously, as if she wanted to remember every detail of her appearance.

Tracey felt like a poor relation in her white linen trousers and navy linen sweater, but at the same time she realized there was no way she could ever expect to look as glamorous as Urania Vickers.

"Thank you," Tracey responded with a laugh. "I didn't bring much with me to wear. Besides, my wardrobe is hopeless, I'm afraid. I mean, I don't have anything that even compares to the beautiful things I see you wear."

"It's part of the business, darling," Urania said. "I *have* to dress like this. It's expected of me, and it's become a habit of sorts. But I enjoy it anyway."

During dinner, she quizzed Tracey about her past as if she were truly interested in knowing all about her, and Tracey answered her questions as honestly as she could.

"Oh, men!" Urania had exclaimed when Tracey had given her a sketchy picture of her breakup with Brian. "So many of them are snakes in the grass, it's difficult to trust any of them, don't you think?"

"I guess so," Tracey said. "It makes me wonder about my own judgment for sure."

"You must still hurt terribly," Urania said.

"Not really," Tracey said. "In retrospect, I wonder if I was ever really in love with him."

"That does make it easier," Urania said. "But I know from experience that you must be very careful with men." She arched a brow in a gesture that seemed filled with significance, and Tracey wondered if Urania was referring to Mark.

Fortunately, she dropped the subject and went on to another, commending her on her studies at Columbia and her job at the television station.

"It's good to find work so quickly after college," she said. "If you must fiddle with college at all. Doing is everything, darling. Spending all of your time locked up in an ivory tower is a waste as far as I'm concerned, but it's probably good insurance. Even the boob tube tires of older women, and in the news end of it you can count the older women on one hand."

When Tracey tried to ask Urania questions—trying not to be too personal or seem too anxious—about her past, the actress laughed. "Darling, don't you know?" she said. "I've written an autobiography. *No Time for Tears,* it's called. You'll find everything you need to know about me in it. I'll give you a copy to read."

"I'd love that," Tracey said.

"It's not a bad read," Urania said. "It covers a lot of ground. A lot of living." She took a sip of wine, then continued. "Let's see. Thirty-some movies, one nervous breakdown, an automobile crash with resulting spinal problems that continue to plague me—the same crash that killed my first husband—weight losses and gains, alcohol and Demerol addictions and rehabs, my years of total unemployment and virtual disappearance off the face of the earth—1978 through 1983—"

The time during which I was born, Tracey thought.

"—my big comeback on television in *Saga* as Delphine Guernsey, my disastrous marriage to Egon Berger who drowned during the divorce proceedings."

She paused for a moment and lit a cigarette, then looked over at Tracey. "He's the one who was suing me for alimony. Then there are the miniseries, the made-for-TV movies, the foreign movies, the road shows and Broadway flops. And you must read about that ultimate graveyard for over-the-hill actresses: guest turns on TV shows as 'very special guest star.' Not to mention my last stay in the Betty Ford Center and my last disastrous marriage. To a loser named Peter Plante, an independent producer who got himself murdered in his car with a hooker." She exhaled a plume of smoke and looked at Tracey again. "Lovely, no?"

"Incredible," Tracey said. "Really incredible."

"But true, darling," Urania said. "Now you know why the tabloids have dubbed me the 'Merry Widow.' A car crash that killed one husband in which I was supposedly driving drunk, a pool drowning that I was purportedly responsible for, and a double murder that I allegedly committed."

Tracey stared at her in wonder. *How do you survive such tragedy,* she asked herself, *without becoming a complete basket case? It's no wonder that Urania can be such a suspicious, fractious, and unpleasant drama queen.*

"And what a vicious misnomer they stuck me with," Urania went on. "The 'Merry Widow,' indeed. The truth of the matter is, the 'Black Widow' would be much more appropriate. I was devastated by each calamity. Devastated! I had fallen in love with all of those men, and regardless of what the marriages turned into, there's still a part of me that will always love them."

"That's really sad," Tracey sympathized. "And so cruel of the press."

"Well, get used to it," Urania said, "especially if you have any fame as a writer or TV personality. They love to tear you to shreds when you're at the top, and they like nothing more than to kick you when you fall to the bottom."

"It must really hurt," Tracey said. "Even if the things they say aren't true."

"They do hurt," Urania agreed, lighting another cigarette, "and make you feel that the whole world is against you. It's a terrible, lonely feeling."

"Didn't you have any children?" Tracey ventured. "I mean, a child might have helped . . ."

Her words trailed off into silence as she saw Urania cringe as if in acute pain. This was obviously a subject that she would rather not discuss. Tracey watched her exhale smoke and look off into the distance as if thinking what to say.

Her words were soft and hesitant. "I . . . well, children simply weren't in the stars for me, darling," she finally said. Then her face abruptly brightened and a smile, whether felt or not, came to her lips. "But let's change the subject," she said.

"Fine," Tracey replied. "I didn't mean to—"

Urania waved her hand to shush her. "Never mind," she said. "I've noticed lately how you've been working yourself to death and already finished so much of the manuscript. I think you're one of the few women I've ever met who's as disciplined as I am."

"I'll take that as a compliment," Tracey said with a light laugh.

"And well you should," Urania said. "Anyway, we're ahead of schedule, so I think you should take more free time. Use the pool. Explore the island. Shop. Whatever you like."

"Thanks," Tracey said. "I've just been so wrapped up in the work that it's been hard to think about anything else."

"Well, it's time you do," Urania said. "Maybe we can venture into the village together? Get out a bit. Would you like that?"

"I'd love it," Tracey replied, somewhat amazed at the invitation.

"Good," Urania said. "You must know that I have an ulterior motive. At least partly."

"Ulterior motive?" Tracey asked. She remembered Mark's graphic warning very clearly.

"Yes," Urania said. "I'm terrified of going out alone. It's not the people who hate you that are so frightening. You know, the ones who believe you really are the evil character you played in whatever movie or TV show. They just scream oaths at you in public."

"You're kidding," Tracey said in amazement.

"No, I'm not," Urania said. "It's embarrassing for a moment, but nothing more. It's the fans who love you who are truly mortifying. They'll stop at nothing to have a piece of you. Follow you everywhere. Try to touch you, feel you. Try to steal a scarf or hat or sunglasses or whatever. Even a shoe. Can you imagine?"

"No," Tracey said truthfully. And she couldn't.

"So it's nice to have someone along," Urania said, "and now that Mark's gone—he was my protector, you know—perhaps you won't mind an occasional outing with me."

"I look forward to it," Tracey said. *Protector,* she thought. *So that's how Urania perceives him.* "But I don't know how much of a protector I can be," she added.

"You'll be fine," Urania said. "Mark never had to resort to anything physical. Just form a sort of buffer between me and them."

Tracey nodded.

Urania stared at her for a moment. "You miss him, don't you?" she said.

"Pardon?" Tracey said, as if she hadn't heard Urania's words.

"You don't need to play games with me, Tracey," Urania said. "I know you and Mark are in love—or maybe it's just lust. Whatever. He always has a kind word or two for me when he phones, then spends all of his time chatting with you."

"Well, I . . ." Tracey struggled to find the right words to use. She didn't really know how to respond to Urania.

"You don't have to discuss this with me," Urania said. "I'll let you off the hook, but let me warn you."

"Warn me of what?" Tracey asked.

"I wouldn't get mixed up with Mark if I were you," she said. "Beyond any sort of professional relationship, that is. He's been very good for me in that way, and perhaps can be for you, too. But as a lover . . . well, I would be very careful. He's drop-dead handsome and young and, from what I hear, extremely promiscuous."

Tracey looked at her with a shocked expression. Mark was obviously handsome and young, but promiscuous? She hadn't gotten that impression at all. She wondered if Urania was being truthful, and realized that the actress probably knew a lot about Mark that she didn't.

"I'll be careful," Tracey said.

"Very wise of you," Urania said. "Especially in this day and age of such danger from simply going to bed with someone."

There it is again, Tracey thought. *The bitter negativity that seems to overlay every aspect of the woman's life.* It wasn't that what Urania said wasn't true—there was no doubt but that it was. Sex could be deadly nowadays. But everything in Urania's life seemed tainted, even governed, by the negative rather than by any joy she might find in any given situation.

Urania got up from the table. "It's been nice talking to you, Tracey," she said. "I'm going to go up to my rooms now and do some work. I have to go through those pages you did today and make some phone calls to friends in Athens."

Tracey had risen also. "Thanks, Urania," she said. "I enjoyed it very much."

"You don't have to go in now, darling," Urania said. "Enjoy the night air. Take a swim if you like. Whatever. Iliki will clean up."

"Thanks, I think I will stay out a while," Tracey said.

She watched as Urania swept across the terrace toward the giant arches, a glittering apparition in white silk. Tracey turned and walked to the wall that separated the terrace from the precipitous drop down to the caldera, staring out at it for a long time. It was as alive at night as in the daytime. She watched the comings and goings of the ferries and hydrofoils and enjoyed the gaily lit cruise ships near Fíra. Slowly she began a circumnavigation of the perimeter of the terrace, looking out at the splendid view from every possible angle.

Her mind was preoccupied with the amazing events, though only sketchily filled in now, in Urania's life. Along the wall that separated the villa compound from the mysterious tower next door, her thoughts were abruptly interrupted by a loud crash. Tracey started as dirt splattered her trousers and blouse and shards of pottery bounced around her feet.

What the hell? she wondered.

She looked all around herself and saw nobody, then looked up over the wall toward what she could see beyond it. Gooseflesh rose on her arms and neck when a curtain twitched in one of the tower windows. She only saw a shift of fabric, so quick it was like the click of a camera, but she was certain that she had seen it. She stood still for a moment, then ventured forward cautiously. A huge terra-cotta pot, one of the ancient olive oil storage containers found throughout Greece, lay in pieces on the terrace. Dirt and succulent plants spread out around it in clumps.

One more step, she thought, *and I would've been hit. One more step and I could have even been killed! That pot is enormous.* She rubbed her arms with her hands. *Jesus! What's happening?* she asked herself. *I don't think this was an accident. No. Somebody deliberately aimed that damn thing at me.*

She decided she would tell Maria Stefanou about this immediately. She didn't want to disturb Urania in her rooms, and in any case, if Mrs. Stefanou failed to investigate, then she'd mention it to Urania tomorrow. She went to the kitchen, where as luck would have it, Maria Stefanou was having a cup of coffee with Iliki. She told her what had happened.

"That is impossible," Maria Stefanou replied in a nasty voice that said she didn't believe a word of what Tracey had told her.

"Then come with me to see the mess," Tracey said.

"I am having my coffee," Maria Stefanou said. "Perhaps later."

"Then you leave me no choice but to go to Madame Vickers," Tracey responded in anger.

"No," Maria Stefanou said. "You will not disturb Madame." She reluctantly got out of her chair. "Show me," she said with a great sigh and heave of her bosom.

Tracey led her outside to the terrace and pointed to the spot where the huge shards of terra-cotta and the dirt and plants that had filled the pot still lay. Undeniable proof that someone had tried to injure if not kill Tracey.

Maria Stefanou surveyed the wreckage for a moment.

"Probably the wind knocked it off the wall," she said. "Or one of the filthy cats that still roam about the island."

"I don't see how a breeze like there is tonight could have toppled something this heavy," Tracey said. "And it would have taken an army of giant cats."

"It is possible," Maria Stefanou replied.

"I don't see how," Tracey argued. "That pot with all that dirt weighed a ton."

"The breezes have been strong tonight," Maria Stefanou insisted. "I think you were too busy looking at Madame tonight at dinner to have noticed it." She turned to march back to the villa, then stopped. "Stavros will clean up the mess, Ms. Sullivan," she said. "Perhaps you should rest and forget about this little accident."

Tracey didn't bother responding to the woman.

What a viper, she thought. *I could've been killed, and she brushes it off as if nothing at all happened.*

Tracey angrily hurried up to the windmill and slammed the door behind her, still extremely agitated by what had happened. She was certain it was no coincidence that the pot had fallen when and where it did. Suddenly she realized that she was trembling, and tears came into her eyes.

She took off her shoes, then her clothes, which she hung carefully in the armoire. Slipping out of her bra and panties, she noticed something on the floor that hadn't been there before. "Oh, my God," she said aloud, dropping her underwear and rushing to the armoire.

At its base, lying on the floor, was the photograph of her father, still in its frame, his face smiling up at her. Tracey felt a chill run up her spine. Then she noticed that the big folder of information she'd brought lay on the floor near it. She picked up the photograph and looked it over, determining that it hadn't been harmed in any way. She brought it to her lips and kissed her father's image, then took it to her bedside table and set it down reverently.

What the hell is going on around here? she wondered, trying to shake the feeling of unease that had come over her.

She went back to the armoire and picked up the folder. Sitting down on the bed, she emptied it out and sorted through the material. *All here,* she decided with relief. She replaced everything in the folder, then got up and pulled a chair over to the armoire, where she replaced the folder atop it. That done, she wandered around her room, her eyes searching for anything else that might be disturbed, but she saw nothing amiss.

Then she suddenly remembered her key card. *Oh, my God,* she thought. *Whoever has it—and it could be anybody—can easily get in and out of here. Anytime.* She felt more perplexed—and afraid—than ever.

What the hell? she asked herself again, her mind reeling with questions. *And who, for God's sake? And why?*

She put on a big T-shirt that she loved to sleep in and got into bed, glancing over at her father's picture from time to time, wondering who had been in the room and for what reason. Her mind would not rest, and as she thought about it, the evening began to be frightening.

The invitation from Urania, who changes the subject when I mention children.

The huge pot that could've killed me falling from the wall next to the mysterious villa next door where someone cries in the night.

Now someone rifling through my room and leaving the only things I've hidden out in the open, exposed for anyone to see.

Jesus! she thought. *If only Mark were here. I know I'm not crazy and that these things have actually happened. What's more, I want to find out what's going on. But how?*

Suddenly she was exhausted despite, or perhaps because of, these worries. Her body and mind seemed to shut down in unison, forcing her to get out of bed, brush her teeth, wash her face, and turn out the lights. Back in the comfort of her bed, she shut her eyes. She couldn't handle anything else tonight, and she hoped that sleep would bring peace.

A cry—that unmistakably terrible, anguished cry she'd heard before—pierced the peace of the night like a wound to the heart. She bolted upright in bed, her hands clutching at her breasts, gooseflesh rising on her arms and neck.

Slipping silently out of bed, she padded over to the open

French doors and peered out. The curtains, shifting in the wind, limited her view, but she trained her eyes on the terrace below. The cry came again, more bone-chilling than ever. Her skin prickled once more, even as her heart jumped into her throat. Tears, an automatic response to the awful sound, sprang to her eyes. As she wiped at them with a fingertip, she heard footsteps and, craning her neck to get a better view, looked down to the terrace. Maria Stefanou hurried across it, flashlight in hand, its beam of light guiding her toward the heavy wooden door built into the wall.

When Maria Stefanou reached the door, Tracey heard the sound of the key turning in the lock. She watched her push open the door with a screech of hinges, then slip through to the other side. But she didn't close the door. She held it open a crack, her flashlight trained on the terrace, toward the villa.

Tracey saw why in a few moments. A man, wielding a satchel that looked like a medical bag, hurried across the terrace in the direction of the door. After he passed through to the other side, Maria Stefanou closed the door. Tracey shook her head as if to clear it of the dreamlike vision. *What's going on over there?* she asked herself.

As if responding to her thoughts, the cry came again, and Tracey's body stiffened. Its chilling sound pierced her to the very core of her being once again, and the tears returned to her eyes. *Oh, my God. I can't stand this,* she thought miserably. *It's too horrible, too sad and lonely.*

The scenario in the tower was too compelling for her to avert her gaze, however, and she saw a light come on in the top window. Behind it, she saw silhouetted figures move back and forth, back and forth. Then, the cry died down to a protracted moan that seemed to last forever, barely varying in pitch and volume, an awful reminder of the suffering that must be taking place in the tower room.

She watched and listened, patiently trying to gather any clues she could to what terrible thing was transpiring in that room. But for a long time she heard nothing more, she saw nothing more, not even a silhouette moving across the lighted space of the window, and she soon grew weary of her vigil.

She went back to bed, promising herself that tomorrow she would get to the bottom of this. Maria Stefanou might not tell her anything, and Stavros surely wouldn't. But she felt emboldened by last night's dinner with Urania, and decided that she might as well broach the subject with her. *Urania,* she told herself, *is bound to know what is happening, and she can't deny what I've seen and heard. What possible excuse could the woman come up with for such a terrible scenario? None,* she decided. *Absolutely none.*

She would have to tell her the truth.

Chapter Thirty-three

"Iliki, did you hear cries in the night?" Tracey asked the young woman at breakfast. She slathered apricot jam on a roll and took a bite out of it.

"Cry?" Iliki repeated, her brows knit in a look of consternation. "No, Ms. Sullivan. I didn't hear a thing."

Tracey looked at her. "Come on, Iliki," she said, "surely you heard something. I've heard it two different times now. Terrible cries coming from the tower next door. You must've heard it some time or other."

"Oh, no," Iliki replied, avoiding her eyes. "I sleep in the servants' quarters, in one of the cave rooms. I don't hear anything in there. It's the farthest room back in the cliff side except for a bathroom."

"And you've never heard anyone else mention this?" Tracey persisted.

Iliki shook her head. "No, Ms. Sullivan. Never." Tracey didn't know whether to believe her or not. Iliki was a wily young woman and difficult to read. Tracey suspected that she had seen and heard so many secrets in her life that prevaricating was second nature to her.

"I guess I'll have to ask Madame about it," Tracey said, wondering how Iliki would react.

"Well, you'll have to ask her another time, Ms. Sullivan," Iliki said. "She's gone this morning. She left very early."

"Oh," Tracey said. "Do you know by any chance where she went?"

Iliki nodded. "To Fíra," she said. "She went to visit old Dr. Eugenikos in the hospital there."

Tracey's ears pricked up immediately. "Oh, really," she said. "And what is wrong with him?"

"I didn't know you knew him," Iliki replied, casting a suspicious glance at her.

"I don't," Tracey replied. "I just wondered. He must be a friend of Urania's. Huh?"

"Oh, yes," Iliki said. "Friends ever since she got the villa."

"Is he sick?" Tracey asked.

"Oh, he had a car crash during the night," Iliki said. "Just up on the lane. He doesn't live far from here, but somebody, probably one of those crazy young tourists, hit him with a motorbike."

"You mean he'd been here when it happened?" Tracey asked.

"I didn't say that," Iliki said irritably. "I said he doesn't live far from here."

"Oh, I thought you meant he'd been coming or going from here when it happened," Tracey said, wondering if Iliki was being honest. "Well, it's awful, isn't it?"

"It is terrible," Iliki agreed. "Just more proof they need to do something about these reckless people that rent motorbikes and don't know how to drive them, if you ask me."

Tracey finished breakfast and started up to her office to begin work, but remembered her stolen key card. *Oh, God. I have to tell Maria Stefanou,* she thought. She took a deep breath and squared her shoulders. *I might as well get it over with,* she thought. *I have to sometime.* She went to the kitchen and asked Iliki if she knew where Mrs. Stefanou might be found.

Iliki laughed. "She's right behind you," she said. Tracey turned around, and the woman stood staring at her. *My God,* Tracey thought, *where did she come from?*

"Yes?" Maria Stefanou said. "You were looking for me?"

"My key card's been stolen," Tracey said, "and I—"

"It what?" Mrs. Stefanou cried.

"It's been stolen, I believe," Tracey repeated patiently, "and I wanted to get another one."

Mrs. Stefanou stared at her as if she thought Tracey had lost her mind. "You have thoughtlessly endangered the entire compound," she finally said. "I hope you realize that."

"I'm sorry," Tracey said, "but I can't help it if it was stolen. I've never lost a key of any kind in my life. I'll be—"

"Never mind," Maria Stefanou spat. "Wait here." She left the kitchen, and Tracey sat down in a chair to wait for her. She looked over at Iliki, hoping that the young woman would sympathize with her, but that was not the case.

Iliki shook her head and clucked her tongue. "Madame is very famous," she admonished her, "and has lots of treasures. There are bad people here like everywhere. What if the key card is in some evil person's hands this very moment?"

Tracey was almost relieved when Maria Stefanou returned with a new card.

"Here," she said, thrusting it toward Tracey.

Tracey took the proffered card from Mrs. Stefanou. "Thank you," she said.

Mrs. Stefanou stared at her silently, and Tracey left the kitchen and hurried back upstairs to her office.

By lunch, Tracey had printed out a batch of pages and was going over them when there was a knock at the door.

"Come in," she said, absorbed in her work.

"Oh, I see you're busy," Urania said. "Shall I tell Mark to call back at another time?"

Tracey looked up at her. "I'll take it now."

Urania's lips twisted into a semblance of a smile. "I thought as much," she said. "He's on line one, and when you're finished I'll be in my office. Let's have a little chat."

"Sure," Tracey said. "I won't be long."

Urania left, and Tracey pressed the button for line one and picked up the receiver. "Mark?"

"Hi," he said.

"Oh, you sound like you're next door," she said.

"You say that nearly every time I call," he said with a laugh. "But this time you're close."

"What do you mean?" Tracey asked.

"I am closer. I'm in London."

"Really?" she said. "Does that mean you're on your way back?"

"That's exactly what it means," he said. "I'm seeing a publisher here, so I'm hoping I can hop a flight to Athens today."

"Oh, I hope you can," Tracey said excitedly. "I miss you so much."

"I miss you, too, and I'm going to try," he said. "I can't guarantee it, but it's looking good. How about with you?"

"It's . . . well, it's been a little weird around here," she said.

"What do you mean?" Mark asked.

"Well, for starters," Tracey began, "a pot mysteriously fell off the wall and nearly killed me."

"What?" he asked anxiously. "Which wall? How did it happen?"

"It was on the wall near the old tower next door," Tracey explained, "and I don't have any idea how it happened. The thing weighed a ton, so the wind couldn't have done it."

"Did you see anybody around?" Mark asked.

"No," Tracey said. "Nobody. I was walking there after dinner, and it just fell and barely missed me. I don't have any idea how. It gave me the creeps, but Maria Stefanou made out like it wasn't important at all."

"That's typical," Mark said.

"But what really has me concerned is that my key card went missing, too. Misplaced, or maybe stolen."

"Jesus!" Mark exclaimed. "What the hell is going on around there?"

"I wish I knew," Tracey replied. "But I don't have a clue."

"Listen, Tracey," he said, his voice more anxious, "I don't want to sound like an alarmist, but be careful. I'll get there as soon as I can, and we'll get to the bottom of this."

"I don't mean to worry you," she said, "but I . . . well, I really don't know whether these things are connected or not. Maybe just stupid accidents, or . . . I don't know what."

"I'll get there soon," Mark said. "As fast as I can."

"That makes me feel a lot better," she replied. "I can't wait to see you. I know everything will be better then."

"I miss you," he said. "I can hardly wait to get back."

Tracey felt a surge of joy at his words. "Me, too," she said. "I think about you every minute."

"I'd better run if I'm going to try to get there today." He paused and cleared his throat. "Tracey, I . . . I want to tell you that . . . well, I love you."

The surge of joy she'd felt before was as nothing compared to the frisson of excitement that seemed to course through her entire body, thrilling her to the core of her being. "I—I love you, too, Mark," she replied.

"See you soon."

"Yes," she said, "soon."

He hung up, and she replaced the receiver in its cradle. She slumped down in her chair with a smile on her lips, her mind spinning with his words, her body still excited by their effect. She suddenly remembered that Urania was waiting for her and went to the anteroom and knocked on her office door.

"Come in," Urania called in her throaty voice.

Tracey opened the door and stepped into Urania's office.

"How's Mark?" Urania asked, putting down the pages she held and looking up at her.

"He seemed fine," Tracey said, "and very busy."

Urania stared at her for a moment, then said, "I think he really has captured your fancy. You look suspiciously like a young woman in love."

Tracey felt herself blush. "Oh, I don't know," she said, hoping that Urania would drop the subject.

"Well, I do," Urania said, "and I just hope you'll heed my warning."

Oh, no, not again, Tracey thought.

"Do you still have my book, by the way?" Urania asked. "My autobiography?"

"Yes, it's in my room," Tracey said. "Do you want it now?"

"Yes," Urania said. "I ran into Sir Hugh, the next-door neighbor. He'd like to read it, so I told him I'd lend him a copy. With all his millions, he's too damn cheap to buy a copy."

Tracey laughed. "I'll get it."

She went to the windmill, and Urania followed along behind her. Tracey retrieved the book and turned to give it to her.

Urania stood at the bedside table, holding the framed photograph of Tracey's father in her hand, staring down at it intently. Tracey felt her heart leap into her throat, and a feeling of near panic suddenly engulfed her. Urania might very well be staring at the image of a former husband . . . or lover.

"Who *is* this man?" Urania asked, still transfixed by the photograph.

"Don't you know?" Tracey ventured.

Urania shook her head and looked over at Tracey with a quizzical expression. "Why, no," she said. "Of course not. Why should I?"

Tracey took a deep breath. "It's my father."

Urania looked back down at the photograph before replacing it on the bedside table. "He's . . . oh, I'm sorry, darling . . . he *was* a very good-looking man." She looked at the photograph again, then back at Tracey. "I see a bit of him in you."

Tracey studied Urania's face for any hint that she knew the man in the photograph, but she could detect nothing that indicated she might be concealing or withholding anything. *Well, Urania* is *an actress*, she told herself, *and a pretty good one at that. Who knows? She could be playing a part this very minute, pretending not to know the man*—my father—*at all. On the other hand, she might not have ever seen him before. She might be entirely on the level.*

She wished she could pluck up the courage to simply take her hidden package from the armoire and show it to Urania, and see what her reaction to that would be, perhaps settling her questions once and for all. But she realized that doing so might not provide any answers. Urania might possibly react to her father's scrapbook in exactly the same way she'd responded to his photograph: complete composure, seemingly genuine curiosity, and impossible to read.

"I'll take that as a compliment," Tracey finally said.

"You should," Urania replied. "He was a very handsome man, and you're a very attractive young woman." She paused, looking for an ashtray, and used a decorative bowl on the dresser to put out her cigarette. She turned back to Tracey. "You loved him very much, didn't you?"

"Yes," Tracey said, nodding. "Very much."

"It's so . . . so very difficult to lose the ones we love," Urania said, her voice filled with sadness. "Whether it's death, divorce, or . . . well, any of the many other things that can take them away from us."

Tracey watched with fascination as the mask of a great tragedienne came over Urania's features, and she found it hard to believe that the profound sadness, and perhaps regret, that she saw comingled on that finely painted palette could be feigned. It appeared to be genuine, and if not, then Urania was a far better actress than she'd previously thought.

"Well," Urania said brightly, in a complete turnabout of mood and expression, "let's change this dreary subject, why don't we?"

"Yes," Tracey agreed.

"Why don't I treat us to lunch in Oia today?" she asked her. "Can you tear yourself away from your desk long enough for that?"

"I think that might be possible."

"Meet you downstairs in ten minutes," Urania said and left the room.

Tracey hurried to the bathroom and quickly applied lipstick and a hint of blusher, ran a brush through her hair, then dabbed a bit of perfume under each ear. She changed into a lightweight black sweater and matching slacks—it wouldn't do to be seen with Urania in jeans or sweats—and donned a lightweight fire-engine red leather jacket that she'd bought on sale in Miami last year. It looked great with her red Prada sports shoes, rip-offs that were comfortable but looked smart at the same time.

Taking her shoulder bag, she went down to the entrance hall to meet Urania. Maria Stefanou was coming in from the terrace and looked her up and down.

"You are going out, Ms. Sullivan?" she asked.

"Yes," Tracey said. "Urania and I are going into the village for lunch."

Mrs. Stefanou's eyes glinted with what Tracey thought was a malicious light. "I hope you will not tire Madame unnecessarily," she said, then lifted her chin in that imperious manner of hers and disappeared in the direction of the kitchen.

Urania appeared, looking every inch the aging diva. She was wearing a black sun hat with an enormous brim, aqua sweater and pants, aqua suede high-heeled miniboots, with an enormous black cashmere shawl wrapped around her dramatically. Heavy gold clinked at her ears, neck, and wrists, and huge Versace sunglasses with golden Medusas at the temples were already positioned to conceal her identity from the public.

"Ready, darling?" she cooed.

"Ready," Tracey nodded, knowing that every single resident of Santorini would know within fifteen minutes that Urania Vickers was having lunch in Oia.

As they reached the gate, Tracey took out her key card, but dropped it on the steps. When she turned and bent to retrieve it, she saw Maria Stefanou staring at her from a window before she quickly moved from view. *If looks could kill,* Tracey thought, *I would most certainly be dead.* She felt the amulet around her neck, glad that it was supposed to ward off the evil eye, even though she had to smile at her own superstitious behavior.

The day was sunny, but it was cool and a strong wind swept across the island. There were still a few tourists about, though their numbers had dwindled to a trickle, and some of the shops had already shut down until Easter.

Urania and Tracey had decided to eat at a tiny café with a breathtaking view of the caldera. In a corner sat a darkly tanned man by himself, wearing sunglasses and a baseball cap. He smiled when Tracey glanced at him, and she returned it. *A lonely tourist,* she thought. *Probably on the make, trying to pick up somebody to take out to the clubs in Fíra tonight.*

It was while she and Urania were enjoying a seafood salad that Tracey decided to broach the subject of the terrible sounds she'd heard last night from next door. She told herself that she must wait for the right opportunity to present itself before raising the question, and she didn't have to wait long.

"Sir Hugh will be leaving soon," Urania said, "and maybe I should have him over for dinner before he goes."

"He doesn't stay here all year?" Tracey asked.

"Oh, no, darling," Urania said. "Sir Hugh can't live without the sun. He has a beautiful house in Barbados, and he'll be going there in a couple of weeks, then come back here after Easter."

"Does he have a house in England, too?" Tracey asked.

"Heavens, no," Urania exclaimed. "He's a tax exile. He can only spend a few days a year there, much less have a house."

"I didn't know," Tracey said. Then after a pause, she asked. "How about the neighbors on the other side? Do they leave, too?"

Urania took a sip of water and set the glass down. Tracey could hardly see her eyes through the dark glasses that she continued to wear even though they were indoors, but she would have sworn that she detected a slight change in their focus and a minute, but discernible, stiffening in her posture.

"Know nothing about them, darling," she said offhandedly. "Oh, look! There's a huge sailboat on the caldera." She pointed with a plum-lacquered nail. "Isn't it beautiful?"

Tracey looked out at the sailboat and agreed, but she had no doubts in her mind whatsoever that Urania had deliberately changed the subject. *Well, I'm not going to let her off so easy,* Tracey told herself.

"Urania," she began, "I don't know why the neighbors—not Sir Hugh but the others—are such a mystery, but I've heard this terrible crying in the night a few times and—"

Urania Vickers blanched before her eyes. She was sure

of it. Even beneath the heavy Kabuki makeup and the woman's extraordinary composure, Tracey could see her pale as if she had seen a ghost. Urania's abilities as an actress, however, remained unaffected, and she quickly interrupted Tracey.

"Surely you must be mistaken, darling," she said in a supercilious manner. Her eyebrows arched over the sunglasses. "It's the wind in the caves, perhaps. That must be it."

"No, it's not," Tracey said, determined to get to the bottom of the matter. "I know that I've heard crying in the night, *and* I've seen Maria Stefanou going next door. Sometimes I've even seen a man with her, a doctor, I think."

Urania's expression was troubled for a moment, but rapidly became cross. "Oh, really, Tracey," she said. "You have the most extraordinary imagination. If indeed you heard or saw anything, it was probably just Maria seeing to a sick cat. You know how—"

"Maria Stefanou hates cats," Tracey said. "I know because Prometheus told me so. He's scared to death of her and actually fears for his cat if it wanders into the compound."

Urania lit a cigarette and exhaled a plume of smoke. "Well, I see you're the busy beaver," she said haughtily. "I don't know when you find the time to write when you're so busy poking your nose into other people's affairs."

Tracey was dumbfounded by Urania's reaction. Urania was trying to make her feel guilty for no good reason. *This woman is an expert manipulator,* she thought. *And she obviously finds this subject irritating. I've found out absolutely nothing, and only succeeded in making her angry in the process.*

The suntanned man who'd smiled at her still sat in his corner, sipping a cup of coffee, and seemed to avert his gaze when she looked his way. *Is he staring at me?* Tracey wondered. She couldn't tell because of his sunglasses, but decided he was shy and embarrassed, having been caught ogling.

Yet then the young man stood up and approached them. Tracey had the strong feeling that she knew the man, but she had no idea who he could be. She said, "Don't I know you? I have the feeling that we've met before."

Well, my cover's blown, he thought. *So what? Just play it cool.* He put on his friendliest smile and stuck out his hand. "I'm Ted Riphenburg."

"Ted Riphen—" Tracey frowned. She knew that she should know the name, but for a moment she didn't remember why.

He laughed. "You don't remember me, do you?" he said. Then in a more solemn voice, he said, "I—I, well, I guess there's a good reason you've forgotten me."

"Oh, my God," Tracey said, suddenly recalling who he was. She took his hand in hers and shook it. "You . . . you were a witness at my dad's . . . at his . . . accident."

"That's me, I'm afraid," Ted said.

"You—you look so different," Tracey said. "No wonder I didn't recognize you." She turned to Urania, then back to Ted.

"This is my . . . a friend," she said to him, indicating Urania. "And this is Ted," she said, looking at Urania. "He was there when my dad had his . . . his accident."

"Hi," Ted said to Urania.

She nodded and smiled tightly. "Hello," she said, then looked off toward the caldera, ignoring him.

"What happened to the jazzy clothes and all?" Tracey said, trying to deflect any attention away from Urania.

"Well, it's hell to get around this island wearing my South Beach club clothes," Ted replied with a laugh.

His manner is so different, she thought. *No wonder I didn't recognize him. And it's not just the clothes—although it's a stretch from cobraskin trousers to an NYPD baseball cap. It's that he's . . . he's so subdued. Not as flamboyant, I guess.*

"So you're here on vacation, I guess," he said.

"No, not really. I'm working for someone on the island for a few weeks." She then quickly changed the subject. "Are you on vacation?"

"No," he replied. "Actually, I've been working at a club over in Fíra this summer."

A chill suddenly went up Tracey's spine, and she felt her

stomach twist into a knot. *Ted Riphenburg just happened to be at the scene of my dad's death—his* murder*—and now he just happens to show up in Santorini? At the same time that a huge pot nearly kills me? At the same time that somebody's been in my room and been through my things?* It all added up to too many coincidences to be ignored. Not only that, but there was the radical change in his appearance and demeanor.

Tracey painted a smile on her face, trying to act as if nothing were out of the ordinary. "Really," she said. "How do you like it?"

"I like it," Ted said. "It's so beautiful, it's unreal. And there're a bunch of cool people. You know?"

"Yes," Tracey agreed. "I'm sure there are." *Brian's sent him after me.* The thought came as a thunderbolt that shook her to her core. *He's sent him here to murder me like he murdered my dad.* Her hands began to tremble, and she quickly put them in her lap where he couldn't see them.

Urania abruptly rose to her feet and withdrew a handful of euros from her handbag and placed them on the table. "Use this for lunch," she said to Tracey, "and why don't you treat Ted to something? I must rush, but you stay and enjoy yourself."

Tracey grabbed Urania's arm, getting to her feet at the same time. "Oh, no," she said. "I have to get back, too. I'll go with you."

Urania couldn't have missed the uncharacteristically demanding—perhaps even desperate—look in Tracey's eyes and clearly realized that for whatever reason she didn't want to be left alone with Ted Riphenburg. "By all means," she said. "We'll be on our way." She turned to Ted. "Lovely to meet you."

"Nice to meet you, too," Ted said in an offhand manner.

"Sorry to run," Tracey said, "but I've got to get back to work. Maybe I'll see you later."

"I hope so," Ted said. "We could have a few drinks some night."

"Great," Tracey said, feeling the tug of Urania's arm. She sketched a wave with her hand and smiled. " 'Bye."

" 'Bye," Ted said. *See you soon*, he thought. *Real soon*.

Chapter Thirty-four

Tracey would not let herself look back at Ted when she and Urania left the café. They walked briskly down the lane toward the villa.

"What was all that about, darling?" Urania asked.

"I . . . I just don't like him," Tracey said vaguely, reluctant to voice her fears to Urania. She dreaded to think what the actress's reaction might be if she thought Tracey had brought a murderer into their midst. "He tried to hit on me in Miami, and I didn't want it to happen again," she lied.

"Men," Urania huffed.

During their lunch, the sky had darkened considerably, with huge angry-looking black clouds looming over the caldera. A powerful and chilling wind was blowing across the top of the cliffs, stirring up dust and grit, and the few people who were out and about were rushing indoors to seek shelter from the rain that surely lay ahead.

Urania had to hold on to her sun hat to keep it from being blown away, and Tracey kept her sunglasses on to keep grit from getting into her eyes. When they reached the Mini Market, she was surprised to see the ancient crone still seated out front in her usual spot, despite the weather. The old woman's milky eyes seemed to search her out and focus upon her before the crone became highly agitated and a stream of incomprehensible Greek began issuing from her mouth.

"Oh, God," Urania whispered under her breath. "I can't bear that old witch."

"Hey, Trace," a woman's voice called.

Tracey turned around and saw Kathy at the Mini Market's door. "Hi, Kathy." She waved.

"You've got some messages," Kathy said.

Tracey turned to Urania, but before she could speak, Urania said, "Go on. I'm getting back to the villa. I can't stand the sight of that horrid crone."

"I'll be right back," Tracey said, but Urania was already rushing on ahead.

Tracey went into the Mini Market, trying not to pay any attention to the old crone's jabbering. She felt the tremor in her hands again, and rushed past her to the counter. "So what's the message?" she asked breathlessly.

Kathy handed her a piece of paper. "She's called several times. The last time was just a few minutes ago. Said it was really important."

Tracey looked down at the paper. It had Maribel's number on it. "Thanks a million, Kathy," she said. "I'll have to see what's up."

"You still fixed for phone cards?" Kathy asked.

"Yes," Tracey said. "I'd better call right now before this storm breaks."

"Good idea," Kathy said. "It looks like it's going to be major."

"I'll see you later then," Tracey said, "and thanks again."

"No problem, Trace."

Tracey went to the nearby telephone booth and inserted her card, then dialed Maribel's number. *Oh, God, I hope that creep doesn't pass by and see me here,* she thought. Thankfully, Maribel picked up on the first ring.

"Oh, *Dios mío,* am I glad you called," Maribel said.

"What's up?" Tracey asked, making an effort to sound as cheerful and casual as she could. She was aware of both the excitement and anxiety in Maribel's voice, but her eyes were scanning the lane to see if Ted Riphenburg was nearby.

"Didn't you get my message?" Maribel asked.

"I just got it," Tracey said.

"No, no," Maribel replied. "I called at Urania Vickers's place and left a message for you to call."

"You did?" Tracey said. "I didn't know that." She was more alarmed than ever because she knew that Maribel would only have called there in an emergency. "What—what's going on, Maribel?"

"Oh, *amiga*," she said, "everything. I don't want to upset you, but you have to know. I don't know how to—"

"What, Maribel?" Tracey interrupted. "Just slow down, Maribel, and tell me whatever it is."

"Well, first. One thing you were right about for sure," Maribel said. "Your dad did not commit suicide."

Tracey was momentarily stunned, even though she'd become certain of that. "How—how do you know this, Maribel?" she asked when she could find her voice.

"I told you about that cop, Montague Pleasance," Maribel said. "The guy that Ray knows in Fraud. Remember?"

"Yes, I remember," Tracey replied. "Of course I do. But what is it, Maribel?"

"He had your dad's car impounded and had a team go over it with a fine-tooth comb," Maribel said. "It turns out the accelerator and the brakes had been fiddled with. I don't understand how exactly, but Ray does. He knows these things. They said the car had been tampered with so that the brakes would fail and the accelerator would get stuck. Jammed, you know? It would make the car go fast and impossible to stop."

When Tracey didn't respond immediately, Maribel asked, "Trace, are you still there? What?"

Tracey swallowed. "I—I'm here," she said. A chill had run up her spine, and she felt her stomach lurch. *Oh, Jesus,* she thought. *Ted Riphenburg is the the murderer, and he's just down the road.* "This—this means it was definitely murder, doesn't it?"

"That's exactly what it means, *cariña,*" Maribel replied.

Tracey felt a sense of relief knowing that her father hadn't resorted to suicide, but at the same time, the thought that he had been murdered offered her little comfort. Quite the opposite. Especially knowing that she'd just talked to his murderer.

"They've opened an investigation," Maribel went on. "Official and all that. Not just asking questions to see what they can come up with, you know?"

"I understand," Tracey said. "I—I knew he wouldn't have committed suicide, but this . . . I don't know what to say. It gives me the creeps." She tried to speak calmly, not wanting Maribel to become unduly worried.

Maribel hesitated before continuing. "I have to tell you something else, *cariña,*" she finally said.

Tracey was so preoccupied trying to digest the information that Maribel had already imparted—and what she herself had just learned—that Maribel's latest words barely registered.

"Trace? Are you there?" Maribel asked.

"I—I'm here," she said, looking out at the black clouds looming over the caldera, then searching the lane once again. "I'm sorry. I was just thinking about what you said."

"Well, listen up," Maribel said. "Please."

"I'm listening."

"Brian and some goon came to my place. I don't know who the creep with him was. But anyway, they were looking for you."

"Me?"

"Yes. You," Maribel said emphatically. "The creep started to slap me around, trying to find out where you were, then Brian found your number stuck on my computer."

"What?" Tracey was so shocked by this news that she didn't know what to say. "But . . . but . . ."

"Listen, Trace," Maribel went on. "I'm sorry, but I couldn't help it. That bastard slapped the shit out of me, and before I knew what was happening, Brian saw your number."

"Oh, God," Tracey exclaimed, almost dropping the receiver. Her hands shook uncontrollably. "It's not your fault. Don't worry about that, Maribel. Take care of yourself, and don't worry about me. I mean, what the hell can some goon do to me? I'm halfway around the world."

"I know. I know," Maribel said, "but still . . ."

"Don't worry about me," Tracey repeated. "I'll be perfectly safe here." She hated lying to Maribel, but she felt that she had to. "Besides, the compound is so safe you wouldn't believe." She was trying to convince herself of the truth of her own words as she spoke them, but knew they were lies. *He's already been in the compound,* she thought.

"Are you sure?" Maribel asked. "I'm really worried. This guy is playing hardball, you know?"

"Maribel," Tracey said, "you don't have to worry about me. I'm just sorry you've been dragged into this . . . this mess."

"You're like my sister, *cariña,*" Maribel replied. "And don't forget it."

"I won't," Tracey said, tears coming into her eyes. She looked out at the lane again. *I've got to get off the phone,* she thought, *and get back to the villa.* "But listen, I'd better get going. A bad storm is coming, and I'm going to be caught out in it if I don't hurry home."

"Okay," Maribel said, "but promise me you'll be careful."

"I will. I promise," Tracey said. "Now I'd really better get off this phone. I'll talk to you soon."

"I love you," Maribel said. "Please call soon."

"I will," Tracey promised. "And you know I love you, too. 'Bye."

" 'Bye, *cariña.*"

Tracey hung up the receiver and removed her card from the slot. She glanced around her quickly, but didn't see Ted Riphenburg. She shoved the phone card in her shoulder bag, got her key card out, and rushed over to the compound's gate. She unlocked it and started down the steps, running down them as fast as she dared, all the while searching the compound for any sign of Ted.

The wind was so powerful that she felt it could blow her off her feet. When she reached the villa, there was no one about. She looked out at the pool terrace and the grounds, but still didn't see Ted. She would search through the villa, but didn't want to alarm Urania. She went on up to the windmill, where she changed into warm, comfortable sweats, all the while trying to come to terms with Maribel's message and the reality of Ted Riphenburg's presence on the island. Looking at her wristwatch, she saw that it was a while before dinner.

I wonder if Urania will ask me to eat with her tonight? She doubted it, since Urania had not left the café in the best of moods. *I need to talk to somebody about this,* Tracey thought. But she knew that it would probably be counterproductive to discuss it with Urania. She would be furious that Tracey had brought danger to the villa.

She thought about calling Mark's cell number, but decided that she wouldn't bother him about it. Not now. She would discuss it with him when he got here, she decided.

She realized that her body suddenly felt sluggish, and her eyelids were droopy. *Ugh! All that lunch,* she thought. *That and this warm room after the chilliness of the wind outside.* She went over to the doors and opened one a crack to let some fresh air into the room, but then decided against it.

What am I thinking? There's a killer out there somewhere, and I'm leaving the door open for him?

She noticed that Stavros had lowered the umbrellas on the pool terrace, but saw nothing that might indicate anything was amiss. She turned back and looked at her inviting bed.

A nap, she thought. *I can get some more work done before dinner. Unless . . . Mark gets here.* She smiled happily at the thought, then lay back on the pillows with a copy of the *International Herald Tribune* in hand. Her eyes fell shut before she could read more than a paragraph.

When she opened her eyes, she could see nothing but pitch blackness, and she was immediately aware of the damp chill that pervaded the room. Gooseflesh rippled up and down her arms, and she would have sworn that the hair on the nape of her neck stood straight up. Her stomach churned sickly, and tears sprang into the corners of her eyes.

The cry, she thought miserably. *That cry. Again.* Only it was more forlorn, more anguished, and more fearful than ever before.

For a moment she lay in the bed immobile, paralyzed by the pathetic sound carried on the powerful wind. When she finally forced herself to move, she rolled over and switched on the lamp at her bedside and looked down at her watch.

Oh, my God, she thought. *It's after midnight. I've slept straight through dinner.* She slipped out of bed and went to the balcony doors and opened them. The draperies fanned out like sails in a stiff breeze. *It's gotten really chilly out,* she thought, pushing the doors shut again.

Then it came again, that awful cry, even louder and more horrific than before. Tracey cringed inside and stood still at the doors, her mind in a maelstrom of conflicting emotions, before deciding to venture out onto the balcony. She opened one of the French doors, stepped gingerly outside, and looked over toward the tower beyond the wall. No movement at the iron-barred window, and no light shining from within.

She turned her gaze to the terrace below, expecting Maria Stefanou to come out of the villa, the man with the satchel following on her heels. She waited, staring at the terrace, but no one appeared.

Then the awful wail came again, carrying over the roar of the wind and the rustle of the foliage. Her heart seemed to speed up dangerously, and she felt her pulse beat a thunderous tattoo against her ear. She wanted to run from the sound, yet at the same time some contrary force urged her to offer succor to whoever was in such agony.

Tracey's eyes frantically searched the terrace below once again, but there was still no sign of Maria Stefanou and the doctor. There was no movement whatsoever except that of the windswept water in the pool, the shuddering of the closed umbrellas as gusts threatened to blow them over, bougainvillea blossoms flying past, and the decorative plants struggling to remain upright in their pots.

The awful sound came again, and tears sprang into Tracey's eyes. She wiped them away with her fingertips, and looked over toward the tower. There was still no light and no evidence of anyone moving about, either there or down below on the terrace.

I've got to do something about this, she thought, resolved. *Nobody else is, so I have to.*

With that thought—and none for her personal safety—she squared her shoulders and went back into her room. She still had her sweats on, but she had to find some shoes. *My sneakers,* she thought. She went to the armoire and got them out and sat down to lace them up.

The air was suddenly split with a crash of thunder such as she had heard never before in her life, and Tracey couldn't help but jerk. The room was abruptly lit up with an unearthly flash of lightning, and Tracey involuntarily shivered at the eerie shadows cast about the room.

She quickly finished lacing her sneakers and rushed out of her room and down the stairs. *Where do I start?* she asked herself. *How do I go about this?* She stood in the entrance hall, pondering the alternatives, then made a fast decision. *At the top of the food chain, of course,* she told herself. *And around here, that means Urania. Even if she denies any knowledge of the comings and goings next door, she was lying. So I'll start with her.*

She went to Urania's suite and knocked on the door. When there was no answer, she knocked louder. Still there was no answer. *This is no time to stand on ceremony,* Tracey thought. She opened the door wide and stepped into the room. Urania's elegantly draped bed was empty. Tracey went into the sitting room, but she was not there either. She tried the bathroom to no avail. *She must've gone out. Probably to Sir Hugh's.*

Okay, she told herself. *Next in command. Maria Stefanou.* Just the thought of approaching the woman brought a grimace of distaste to her mouth, but she had no choice. She left Urania's suite and rushed through the entrance hall and outside to the terrace.

An earth-shattering clap of thunder that sounded as if it were directly overhead brought her to a temporary standstill. She thought she could practically feel the ground move beneath her feet. The lightning that followed zigzagged above the caldera in dazzling and terrifying streaks, bringing a sickly daylight to the darkness of the night. That got her feet moving again, and fast.

Tracey dashed toward the servants' quarters, as anxious to get out of the weather as she was to find Maria Stefanou. When she got there, she didn't bother to knock on the front door, but went on in. She knew that Mrs. Stefanou and her mother, Stavros, and Iliki each had separate suites within the space, although she was unfamiliar with the layout.

She found herself in a small hall that led straight ahead, with doors on both sides. She knocked on the first one she came to, on her left. No answer. She pushed the door open and entered the room. Maria Stefanou lay supine on a bed, fully clothed. On a bed across the room, her mother was in an identical position and dressed. Tracey looked back at Maria Stefanou.

Was she asleep in her clothes? she wondered. *Or?* . . . Tracey stepped lightly toward the bed. She could see that the woman lay in an odd position.

"Mrs. Stefanou?" she called in a small voice.

There was no answer, nor was there any perceptible movement.

Tracey cleared her throat. "Mrs. Stefanou," she repeated in a louder voice.

Still no answer or movement.

Tracey took a deep breath and went to the side of the bed and looked down. *"What?"* she almost screamed, but automatically threw her hand up to her mouth to cover any sound. Maria Stefanou's hands and feet had been securely tied to the bed posts. *Oh, Jesus in heaven!* Tracey thought. *She looks like she's . . . dead!*

She forced herself to lean over and look into Maria Stefanou's immobile face for any sign of life. She could see none, but she caught movement out of the corner of her eye. Yes! The woman's diaphragm was moving rhythmically, up and down, up and down, as if she were in a deep sleep.

Tracey gasped aloud and almost cried out. *Oh, thank God,* she thought. She leaned over and began shaking her her shoulder. "Mrs. Stefanou," she said. "Mrs. Stefanou." Shake. "Mrs. Stefanou!"

The woman didn't respond. She didn't blink an eye, nor

did she make a sound. She moved only when Tracey shook her. Tracey straightened up, her eyes still on the woman, satisfying herself that she was indeed breathing. *She is breathing*, she assured herself. *So what on earth is wrong?* Then it dawned on her. *Drugs. It has to be. Somebody—whoever did this—has drugged her with something.* She looked down at her for a moment longer. *No wonder she didn't respond to the cries next door. But why would someone do this?* she wondered.

And who? A gasp escaped her throat. *Ted Riphenburg.*

She quickly checked on Maria Stefanou's mother and determined that she was in the same condition.

Suddenly it occurred to Tracey that whoever had done this might still be in the compound. *Oh, God have mercy,* she thought, feeling her stomach lurch and thinking for a moment that she might be sick. She turned around and looked toward the hallway, but she could hear or see nobody.

Looking back toward Mrs. Stefanou, she wondered how she would ever untie the expertly tied knots. They were extremely tight, and she could see that she'd never be able to undo them with her fingers alone. *I'll have to get a knife from the kitchen, but first I'd better see if I can find Stavros.* Maria Stefanou and her mother were oblivious to their confinement, and Tracey could only hope that they would be safe in the meantime.

She hurried back into the hallway and went to the next doorway, where she took a deep breath before she opened it. Stavros lay on his bed, tied up exactly as Mrs. Stefanou and her mother were. Tracey stepped over closer to the bed and saw that he, too, was breathing, but there must have been some sort of struggle, for drying blood trailed from both of his nostrils and ran down across his cheeks.

At the sight of the blood, Tracey felt bile rise in her throat, but she fought it down, determined to keep control of herself. She quickly turned and left the room, going on down the hallway to the next door. *Iliki's room,* she assumed, pushing down on the handle without a second thought. The identical scenario greeted her. Iliki was tied to the bed, out cold but breathing.

Tracey turned and left the room, then walked down the hallway to the front door. Slowly, the realization that she might be in the compound alone dawned on her, engulfing her in terror. Gooseflesh broke out on her arms and neck, and cold sweat beaded her forehead. She felt herself begin to tremble, and was sure that she couldn't keep down the bile that was rising in her throat this time. She took several deep breaths, determined not to be sick.

I've got to call the police, she thought. *Right away. Yes, I'll call the police.*

She rushed into Mrs. Stefanou's room and picked up the telephone. The instant she put the receiver to her ear she knew that the line was dead. Nevertheless, she pushed buttons, hoping that somehow she could bring the instrument to life. To no avail. She went to the front door again, wondering what to do next.

A clap of thunder made her go stiff, its crashing roar briefly paralyzing her. She opened the door to the terrace and looked out. Lightning rent the sky, and right before her eyes, the once beautiful caldera was transformed into a cauldron of hell.

Her attention was immediately diverted from it by the abrupt cannonade of rain that heaved itself in relentless wind-driven sheets, drenching her as she stood in the doorway.

Then, above the din of the wind and rain, above the rumble of thunder, she heard again the terrible cry coming from the tower next door.

Oh, God, what do I do now? Tracey asked herself, cringing from the awful sound. She looked up at the tower window but could see nothing. She could hardly see the tower itself through the downpour, but she knew that somehow she had to get there, to get to the person who needed her.

She remembered the keyboard in the kitchen, the one where Maria Stefanou had hung the big, old-fashioned key she was fairly certain would open the gate in the wall. She dashed out onto the terrace and made a beeline for the door to the entrance hall. Drenched and chilled to the bone, she hurried on to the kitchen.

There the key was, just where she'd remembered Maria

Stefanou hanging it, on the board alongside several others. She snatched it off its hook, then turned and ran to the front door, where she paused a moment before going back out into the downpour. While she caught her breath, her eyes locked on to the heavy old wooden door that served as a gate.

I wonder what I'll find on the other side?

At that moment the entrance hall was plunged into darkness. The lights had gone out. Tracey started. *Oh, no!* She turned and looked behind her, but could see nothing in the darkened house. *Is it the storm,* she wondered, *or is it . . . whoever has drugged the servants?*

Her mind raced with the possibilities, but then she remembered the numerous wall niches where old-fashioned lanterns with candles were kept. She also knew that flashlights were stashed close to every doorway leading outside. She could barely make out the shape of the giant amphora that stood in the entrance hall near the front door, but she got down on her hands and knees and felt around it.

There it is! She could feel a large, almost square flashlight. Grasping it with her hands, she took it from its hiding place behind the amphora, then stood. She turned the switch and a bright beam of light hit her directly in her eyes. *Just what I need. Blinding myself in the dark.* She aimed the beam of light outside onto the terrace and decided not to waste another moment. She put her head down and took off toward the gate through the thrashing rain.

From the balcony outside her windmill room, he watched her run. There was a smile on his face, and he could hardly keep from laughing aloud. Not that she was likely to hear him over the torrential rainfall and the rumble of the thunder. But he didn't want to risk it. No, he wanted to surprise her. Give her a real shock. Something more substantial than seeing the two old ladies, the younger one, and the pack mule tied up and out cold in the servants' quarters.

What the hell is she doing anyway? he wondered. *Running at the wall?* Probably was so scared she thought that she was headed to the gate leading out of the compound. He grinned again. When she regained her bearings, she'd find a little surprise waiting for her at the outside gate. Wouldn't be able to get her card in the lock. And wouldn't be able to get the glue out of the lock that jammed it up.

He watched her fumble with the lock on the gate leading into the compound next door. The one with the little tower. The smile suddenly disappeared from his face when he saw her open it.

Shit! he thought, already running toward the door. *Where the hell does she think she's going?*

The little Olympic Airways ATR-72 hit one air pocket after another. It was being pounded in the wind and rain as if it were no more than a toy. Several of the passengers had become hysterical and screamed at every lightning bolt or crash of thunder or sudden drop of the small aircraft.

Mark sat quietly in his seat, but he was white-knuckling it, no doubt about that. He'd been thrilled in Athens when the flight had been announced, despite the impending bad weather, but now he seriously doubted the wisdom of the airline in permitting the plane to take off for Santorini. The flight was a short one, but he wondered if they would make it.

Over the public address system, the pilot announced that they were making their final approach to the Santorini airport. Mark forced his hands to relax on the armrests, but found himself gripping them more tightly than ever when the plane suddenly lost altitude and took a sharp dip to the side.

Jesus, he thought. *I hope it doesn't end like this. I want to see Tracey again before I go.*

Chapter Thirty-five

The rain had plastered her hair to her head, and her clothes clung to her as if glued in place. The heavy wooden door opened with surprising ease, and Tracey stepped through the entry to the other side of the thick wall that separated the compounds. She pushed the door closed behind her, but didn't lock it. Now that she was on this side of the wall, she paused to catch her breath. The path to the tower, she saw in the beam of the flashlight, was of the same white marble, streaked through with gray, that she saw everywhere in Greece.

I'd better watch out, she thought, *or I'll end up on my butt.* She knew that the stone could be dangerously slick even without the soaking rain.

For the first time she looked at the little tower from this perspective, running the beam of light over it. As if to help her, another burst of lightning briefly lit the scene. The path leading to the blue door was bordered by thick foliage that had been allowed to run riot, almost taking over the marble stones. The tower itself was virtually concealed from view by the enormous bougainvillea and other vines that grew up and around it, even blocking out the lower part of the iron scrollwork that covered the windows.

There was no light from within, and Tracey took a deep

breath and walked the few steps to the door, hoping that it would be open or that the key for the gate would work its lock. She pushed her rain-soaked hair out of her eyes again and tried the door.

It's locked, damn it! she thought. She grasped the big key out of her pocket and tried it. It fit the lock perfectly, and she could feel the door give instantly.

She pushed it open and stepped through into the tower, holding her breath in trepidation. She felt her heart thudding in her chest and could swear that she could feel adrenaline rushing through her veins. Running the flashlight around the darkness, she found herself in a large room with white plastered walls and a few pieces of locally made wooden furniture. She could see framed prints hanging on the walls and peasant fabrics draped at what must be niches for closets. There was also a small kitchenette built into one wall.

Suddenly her senses were assaulted by the piercing cry. Tracey felt that her heart must have stopped beating, so close and terrifying was the sound. The beam from the flashlight wavered as her hand trembled, but she didn't miss the very narrow flight of stone stairs that angled up the far wall, disappearing to the floor above her.

She went to them immediately, before she lost her nerve, and began climbing up. The awful cry grew in volume the higher she went. The steps were extremely steep, and she kept the beam of light focused on those just ahead of her. When she reached the top of the stairs, she swept the light around. She was in a small foyer or anteroom with the ubiquitous white plaster walls and a floor of tiles identical to those downstairs. A wooden door was set into a wall almost directly in front of her.

The cries, more bone-chilling than ever in her proximity to them, issued from the thick wood as if it were mere air. Tracey reached the door and put her hand on the handle, forcing herself to take deep, even breaths. She pushed down on it.

Locked! Damn! She took the key out of her pocket again, hoping that it would work this door as well. Trying to keep her hand from shaking, she inserted it, then twisted.

The lock turned smoothly, and the door gave at once, opening a crack.

Tracey drew back from it and steeled herself. *I don't have any idea who or what is on the other side,* she told herself. *I just know I've got to help.* With that thought, she switched off the flashlight so as not to alarm whoever she would find and pushed the door open. She stepped into the room.

As she stood still, her eyes grew accustomed to the dark enough that she could make out where the windows were placed in the tower's thick walls, though they emitted only a lighter shade of blackness. The terrible cries suddenly turned to low, pitiable moans, like those of an injured animal. Tracey hated to turn on the flashlight, but there was no alternative. She aimed it at the floor and pushed the switch.

Please, Lord, she prayed, *if you're there and can hear me, give me courage now.*

She slowly lifted the flashlight, bringing the beam of light up from the tiles of the floor. Continuing in a slow and steady movement, she moved the light about the room. Like the first floor, the walls were all plastered white, and hanging on them were framed prints and pictures. In a corner the light picked out the gleam of several censers and candle holders suspended from the ceiling. They were like those used in Greek Orthodox churches, and gilded or silvered crosses replaced crystal drops. Behind them, Tracey made out several icons, some of them with silver frames that glinted. She caught her breath when a mournful Virgin Mary seemed to gaze straight back at her. A particularly morbid crucifixion begged her to remove the offending beam of light from the suffering depicted.

She jerked the light away from that corner, then caught herself, remembering to move it slowly in an effort not to cause more alarm than she had to. The moans had died down almost completely, becoming little more than gasps or wheezes, and slowly she moved the light, to her left, then to her right, then—

There! A bed draped with what looked like peasant fabrics.

She stepped quietly over to it, keeping the light aimed toward the floor once again. When she reached the side of the bed, the first thing that caught her eye was a large crucifix hanging over the center of the headboard. Averting her gaze from it, she looked down and could make out the form of someone lying there. The gasps and groans seemed almost as loud in her ears as the awful cries earlier.

Bringing the light up, she aimed it so that she let the mere edge of it illuminate the prostrate figure on the bed.

"Ohhhh noooo," Tracey moaned, jerking back away from the bed. Her hands flew to her face, as if they would protect her eyes from what she'd already seen. The flashlight fell and landed with a thud on the tile floor. Sickening bile rose in her throat, and she gagged. Cold sweat instantly broke out on her forehead, and she felt a chill run up her spine. She thought that she would surely faint, but she grasped at one of the bedposts and steadied herself, forcing herself to breathe, to try to stop the churning of her stomach and the whirlwind eddying about in her head.

When she was finally in control of herself once again, she bent down to retrieve the flashlight, her hands scrabbling around in the darkness until they found it. Picking it up, she aimed the center of the beam away from the woman on the bed as she had before, while allowing the outer perimeter of the light to barely catch her in its glow.

It's . . . Urania, Tracey thought with horror, forcing herself to look at the woman, *but . . . it's* not *Urania.*

As she watched, the woman's eyes wandered, ultimately settling on her. Tracey recognized the almost identical, exquisite bone structure, the same beautiful eyes, and the perfect nose and sensuous lips. Even the hair, she could see, had once been virtually identical, though here it was streaked through with gray. Her countenance—*Urania's countenance, but no,* not *Urania's precisely*—was beseeching. A reed-thin hand lifted from the bed in an imploring gesture, and Tracey felt tears spring unbidden into her eyes.

Oh, my God, what is going on? Who is this, and what has happened to her, and what am I going to do?

The woman's hand, with its long, thin fingers, so elegant

and so like Urania's, was still extended toward her, quivering slightly. Tracey reached out and took it in hers and held it gently. It felt chilled, yet was soft and delicate, and looking down, she saw that it was pale as ivory, as if it had never been touched by the sun.

She sat down on the side of the bed gingerly, and looked back into the woman's imploring eyes, so like Urania's, only full of pain and sorrow. "It—it . . . will be okay," she whispered soothingly, as if comforting a child. "I'm . . . I'm here, and everything will be okay."

The woman's eyes, huge and glittering in the glow from the flashlight beam, focused on Tracey, studying her face. Tracey felt overcome by shyness and slightly embarrassed, as if for some unknown reason she were especially vulnerable to this woman's penetrating gaze. She saw then what she thought was the merest hint of a smile on the woman's lips, and a look of tenderness replaced the sorrow and pain in her eyes.

Tracey smiled at her and gently patted the delicate hand, but the smile quickly faded from Tracey's features as she saw the woman's eyes suddenly focus on something beyond her and grow huge with terror. Following her gaze, Tracey turned and glimpsed a figure—a man—drawing up behind her in the darkness.

"What—who—" she began.

"Hi, Trace," the man said, his hips brushing up against her back as he stood over her.

"Ted," she gasped. "What—what are you doing here? Where did you come from?" At that moment she saw the length of thin wire dangling from his gloved hand. It was wound and knotted around small lengths of wood at each end. She felt the woman's hand tighten on her own, then felt it slip away from her. Tracey turned to look at her and saw that the woman was reaching out toward the table at the far side of her bed.

Ted abruptly jerked away from Tracey and rushed to the other side of the bed. "I wouldn't do that," he growled.

The woman began screaming, and Tracey's flashlight briefly caught the gleam of brass as the woman brought a large candlestick down against Ted's shoulder.

"What are you doing?" Tracey shouted at him, jumping up and running around the bed. "What are you—"

She was thrown backward onto the floor as his powerful arm swung around and slammed against her chest. "Awww," she grunted, as she landed against the hard tiles on the floor. She caught herself with her hands before her head banged back against them, but he had nearly knocked the wind out of her. The flashlight fell out of her hand as she lost her grip on it, but she could see its light, now a dull glow, on the floor nearby.

The woman's screaming had become a gasped choking, and that horrible sound brought Tracey struggling to her knees and scuttling across the floor to the flashlight. She grasped it and stood up, then rushed to the bedside, where Ted was hunched over the woman, twisting the ends of the wire in his hands, garroting her where she lay on the bed.

Tracey saw the gleam of horror in the old woman's eyes dull at the same moment that her delicate hands ceased struggling against Ted. Her long thin fingers fluttered birdlike for an instant, then fell to the bed. Tracey lifted the big square flashlight above her head and brought it crashing down on the back of Ted's skull. She felt the impact in her arms, and her stomach lurched when she heard the awful thud. Ted fell against the woman's body with a grunt and didn't move, but Tracey couldn't see his face. The flashlight had gone out.

Oh, God, no! she thought.

She shook it repeatedly in her hand, then pushed the on-off button again and again, but it wouldn't come back on. Frantic, she dropped the flashlight on the bed. *Oh, God, what do I do now?*

She knew that she had to get the woman help at once, if it wasn't already too late, and she had to get the police. *I have to get out of here,* she decided. *Go somewhere and call the police.* If the telephones were still out because of the storm, someone would know how to get the police for her. And an ambulance.

A crash of thunder reverberated in the tower room, and the flashes of lightning that followed it illuminated the macabre tableau on the bed. The woman's horror-stricken eyes appeared to be staring at her over Ted's shoulder. *She's dead,* Tracey thought miserably. *Surely she is.* She quickly averted her gaze and glimpsed a niche in the wall near the doorway leading to the anteroom. As in many of the niches in Urania's compound, this one held an old-fashioned lantern. *Maybe there'll be a flashlight, too,* she thought.

Tracey dashed over to the niche, hoping there would be a candle in the lantern with matches placed at its side as elsewhere. The room was plunged into darkness as the lightning ran its course, but she already had a hand on the lantern. With her free hand, she felt inside the niche for matches. *There. I've got them.*

She set the lantern back in the niche, then struck a match, holding it up to look. There wasn't a flashlight, but the lantern held a candle. Tracey lit it at once, then put the matches in her pocket. Holding the lantern high, she turned to look back into the room, but thought better of it and went on out into the anteroom.

Holding the lantern out in front of her, she looked down the steps, which curved out of sight into the depths below. *Oh, God, help me,* she thought, then she took the first step down. She stopped, her heart pumping rapidly and her pulse racing. She forced herself to take another step down, then another. Stopping again, she felt the cold sweat that drenched her forehead and the back of her neck.

Then she heard footsteps. Or did she?

Tracey froze and listened, her body beginning to tremble uncontrollably. There it was again. Yes, another footstep! She was sure of it. Coming from the bedroom.

She wanted to scream aloud and flee as fast her feet would carry her, but she was terrified to make a sound, afraid that Ted would hear her. Then she thought, *So what? He has to come this way. Down these stairs.*

With steely determination she took another step down, then another, and when she heard the footsteps again, nearer this time, she tried to look at each step as it rose to meet her feet and not think about what lay at the bottom so far below—or what was following her.

When she finally saw tile replace the wooden stairs, she knew she was home free and almost cried with relief. Across the room, she could make out the doorway, and she could hear the rain thrashing against it. She rushed toward it, holding the lantern in front of her, and had almost reached it when a hand—*his* hand—clamped on her shoulder like a vise.

The taxi hit a rut in the road and bounced so hard, it threw Mark against the back of the front seat.

"Okay?" the driver asked, his voice concerned.

"I'm all right," Mark replied. "Don't worry about me, just do the best you can." He realized that the driver wasn't at fault. The torrential rain made visibility virtually nil. The windshield wiper blades couldn't hope to compete against the rain's ferocity, and the wind was so powerful that he could feel it actually buffet the little taxi from side to side.

I'm damn lucky I could get this guy to take me to Oia, Mark thought. Most of the taxi drivers had abandoned their posts at the airport and sought shelter from the storm. Besides, they figured there would be few if any landings, so they wouldn't be losing money.

Mark wiped condensation off the door window and peered out. Judging from what little he could see, he decided they were on the final stretch into Oia, on the road of hairpin curves cut into the side of the cliff. He began to get excited about seeing Tracey, although that excitement was tempered by his anxieties over what she had told him on the telephone. Remembering their conversation, he had the strong suspicion that she'd downplayed the seriousness of the situation so as not to worry him, and now he felt more in a hurry than ever to get there.

God, I hope everything's okay, he thought fretfully. *That Tracey's okay.* Despite his being tired and wet, he wanted to get to the bottom of whatever was going on at the villa as soon as he got there. He knew that the compound might still be dark because of the outage that affected the entire island, but he wanted to make certain that she was not in any danger. And as quickly as possible.

Tracey screamed aloud and swung around without even looking, at the same time heaving the lantern with all her might. It slammed into his head.

"Bitch!" he roared, but his hand slipped off her shoulder.

She heard a thud and assumed he had fallen, but now she couldn't see where he was. The candle had been extinguished.

Disoriented in the dark, she dashed toward what she thought was the door and shrieked when heavy fabric loomed up out of the darkness and slapped against her body, engulfing her face in a fuzzy warmth.

Oh, Jesus! Where am I?

In a panic she struggled against the fabric, trying to throw it aside, then abruptly fell, brushing her elbows against plaster walls and landing hard on her knees.

She still clutched the lantern in one hand, and she began to scrabble around the floor frantically with her other hand, as if she could determine where she was by feeling the tiles beneath her. Sitting up on her knees, she tried to get her bearings. *The closet,* she thought. *It has to be.*

Even though she couldn't see, she was obviously in an enclosed space that was much darker than the big open room. She reached out with a hand, feeling around her for the long peasant cloth that she knew served as a closet door. When her fingertips brushed against it, she scooted around to face in that direction.

Cautiously, she pulled the curtain aside to try to see if anything in the big room was visible. She could just make out Ted on the floor near the door leading out of the tower. *I'll never be able to get past him and out of this place. Unless . . .*

She knew that the caves beneath the compound led into this tower, just as they did into her windmill and other places nearby. Prometheus had shown her. He had shown her, in fact, where the cave led into this very tower. *But where?* she wondered. *Where would it come out in this tower?* She'd only seen the other end, where it came in.

Think, she told herself. It would have to be down here, of course, and she hadn't seen anything but the entry and the one big room with its kitchenette against a wall. And *the closet.* Tracey almost gasped with joy. *I must be right over the cave now,* she thought. *I'm sitting where the hatch leading to it would be. Must be.*

She sat the lantern down and began moving her hands around the tile floor, feeling for any indication of a latch or ring of some sort that could be used to pull up the hatch that she was sure had to be there. Shifting her body this way and that, she tried to make certain she covered every square inch of the small space.

Then she felt it. Not a latch or ring, but a tiny gap between tiles with the distinct feel of cool air rising up toward her fingers. She traced her fingers along the gap until they came to a corner, then shifting her body again, she felt along the corner and around it. There, metal. She was sure of it. It was a heavy ring cemented into the tile.

Putting her finger through the ring, she pulled with all her might. Nothing. Then she realized that she was responsible for the hatch's immobility. Her weight was holding it down in place. She shifted all of her weight on her toes, squatting, and tried again, pulling as hard as she could. With a loud scraping of tile and wood, the hatch began to move upward.

Oh, damn, it's heavy, Tracey swore.

There was the sound of movement out in the big room, and Tracey was so startled that she almost lost her grip on the hatch and let it fall back into place. *I've got to hurry. Hurry!*

Taking a deep breath and pulling with all her might, she brought the hatch fully open with a screech of tile against tile that was deafening to her own ears. Suddenly, the fabric draped over the closet opening moved, and Tracey looked up. Ted, his form barely discernible, stood in the opening and stared down at her.

Without stopping to think, Tracey heaved the hatch toward him and then grabbed the lantern.

"Fuckin' bitch!" he cursed.

Tracey didn't stop to look. She dropped down into the impenetrable darkness into the cave. She had no idea exactly what lay beneath her or whether she had far to fall, but it didn't matter. She had to get away from this . . . this killer.

Only when she quickly thumped against rock and dirt did she know the drop had been short. "Damn," she swore breathlessly. Her right ankle sent sharp pains shooting up her leg, and her right arm was bleeding from scratches down its length. Without giving her pain a second's thought, she struggled to her feet and moved out from under the opening to the closet above.

With my luck, she thought, *that maniac is liable to drop down the hole on top of me.*

She stood with her back against the cave's wall, most of her weight on her left foot, and fished around in her pocket for the matches. *Where are they?* she wondered in panic when she didn't at first find them. Then her fingers felt them, and she pulled them out of her pocket with relief.

Thank God they're waterproof. Her clothes were still wet from the drenching she'd received earlier, but the first match she struck lit immediately. She held the lantern up and put the candle back in the holder from which it had come dislodged. Some of the glass was broken, and she sincerely hoped that it was lodged in Ted's face. She got the candle lit, then held the lantern aloft, trying to see if she could get her bearings.

To the left or the right? she wondered. She tried to think in which direction the entrance would be. *Left or right?* The one that came out at the rock near the old cistern where Prometheus had brought her in. *Left or right? Why didn't I pay more attention?* she berated herself.

From above, she heard a crash, then glanced to her left. He wasn't there, but she had the distinct feeling that he soon would be. He was probably getting the hatch out of his way. *That settles it,* she thought, taking off to her right without further ado.

She held the lantern raised and slightly ahead of her, trying to see if anything looked familiar, but nothing struck a chord. Rock and dirt and more rock and dirt. In places she had to hunch over slightly—had that been the case when she came in with Prometheus?—and in others she could walk upright. There were twists and turns she had no recollection of whatsoever. But it didn't matter. She had to get away from him. She hurried forward.

From behind her came another crash, then more cursing. She hurried on ahead, and almost cried out as her hair and face caught in a spiderweb stretched across the passageway. She furiously thrashed at it with her free hand and rubbed around her face and neck, trying to get any remnants of it off her.

On she moved, faster, hoping that she was headed in the right direction. There were other openings into the caves, that she knew, but she wasn't certain where they were or exactly what they led out to. She had to find the one that she and Prometheus had used when he brought her in.

Closer behind her, she heard falling rock and a loud thud, followed by grunts and what might have been curses. She couldn't tell. *He's tripped and fallen down,* she thought, and she speeded up her pace. *I have to keep ahead of him.*

She hurried around a bend in the passage and stubbed her right toe on a rock, nearly falling down, but she caught herself on the rocks with her free hand to break the fall. She wanted to moan and curse and cry all at the same time, but she forced herself to remain silent and endure the awful pains that shot up her leg. The ankle, and now the toe.

On she limped, the pain excruciating, wondering if she would ever come to the opening Prometheus had shown her, almost convinced at this point that she'd come in the wrong direction. Rounding another bend in the passageway, she thought she could detect a paler shade of black straight ahead of her. She was certain that she could hear the rainstorm, and the cool, stale air of the cave abruptly seemed warmer and a bit humid.

Then above the sound of the rain, she heard something else too: the footfalls of the man who was chasing after her. She heard him kick at rock and dirt, was sure she heard muttered oaths and threats.

She plunged ahead, oblivious to pain, to fear. Fifty feet, forty, thirty, twenty. She almost broke into a run, a run toward salvation and freedom, toward light and life.

There it was! The gap between the rocks that Prometheus had shown her. It was just ahead and slightly elevated, but she knew that she could easily climb up to it on the loose rubble. She lunged forward, practically throwing herself against the rocky incline, then started grasping at the outcroppings above her, pulling herself up, up, up toward the gap in the rocks.

She had just achieved the top, her head actually out in the rain, when she felt something grab her foot. *God, no! Not now!*

Mark left his luggage in the entrance hall. He found a flashlight and rushed about the house, searching for Tracey. When he determined that no one was in the villa, he went to the servants' quarters to find Maria Stefanou. She would know where everyone was. He saw the shocking tableau there, and frantically began searching the entire compound.

"Tracey!" he called out again and again. "Tracey!"

There were no responses to his urgent appeals. Frantic, he hurried out onto the pool terrace, oblivious to the lashing rain that had already soaked him to the skin, and ran the flashlight over the exterior of the compound, searching every square inch of it for any clue as to where she might be.

He could feel his heart thumping in his chest and the sweat of fear that mingled with the rain coating his skin. "Tracey!" he roared into the wind. "Tracey!"

She struggled against the hand that held her in its grip, kicking as hard as she could. Tears came into her eyes, joining with the rain which already streaked her face. She realized that the lantern was still in her hand, but she didn't know if she could use it to advantage. Twisting her torso around, she flung the lantern down into the opening. Her leg was freed at once, and she scrambled on out of the hole, bloodying her scraped knees again.

She got to her feet and at once realized that she was on a precipice looking out over the caldera, nearly a thousand feet below. For a moment she was almost overcome by wooziness and felt completely disoriented. *I've got to get moving,* she told herself. *Got to.*

She knew that she was just outside the compound's walls, practically home free, but she had to negotiate the rocks carefully and watch out for the old cistern. Then she heard him scrambling out of the cave and turned and looked.

"I'm gonna get you, Trace," he howled over the sound of the rain. "I'm gonna get you."

She turned back and, in a crouch, began negotiating the treacherous rocks, moving toward the compound's wall. When she reached the old cistern hidden in the rocks, she suddenly knew what she had to do. She squatted down and, putting all of her weight against the ancient cover on the cistern, she pushed and pushed. Surprising her, it moved easily, and she almost lost her balance and tumbled over the opening. She caught herself with her hands, then got back up into a crouch.

He was no more than ten feet behind her, and she could see him better than ever before. The rain lashed against his blood-streaked face, but he kept moving toward her with ease.

"I'm gonna kill you," he roared. "You're not gettin' away from me."

Tracey crawled around to the far side of the cistern. When she got there, she stood up to her full height and turned to face him, hoping to taunt him.

He saw her standing there, staring at him, and he took two surefooted steps, then made a lunge toward her. She could hear his labored breath and would swear that she could feel its heat against her skin. Then he began to scream as his feet left the rock, and he disappeared into the ancient cistern.

Tracey gingerly stepped closer to try to see. His hand reached out and grasped her twisted ankle. "No!" she screamed as she lost her balance and fell against the rocks. For a moment she was stunned, and he got a better grip on her ankle. Then she felt her body begin to slide over the rocks toward the cistern. She could see his one hand on her ankle and saw that the other was gripping the cistern opening.

She kicked with her free leg and hit his hand repeatedly, but his strength overcame hers. Before she hardly knew what was happening, he had pulled her over to the open cistern. His hand reached above her knee, his clutch like an iron vise. Tracey kicked and kicked, but he suddenly grabbed her free leg with the hand he'd been using to clutch the cistern. Now he was holding on to her with both his hands, and she was slipping inexorably into the cistern with him.

Oh, my God! she thought with horror. *He's going to pull me in so we both go down!*

Both of her legs were now flailing over the open cistern, and she struggled with all of her might against him. She thought her legs would be crushed from the power of his grip on her, and she tried to catch hold of the rain-slick rocks to keep from following him into the cistern and the fall to its unknown depths.

Suddenly she felt her butt go over the edge. "No! No! No!" she screamed, trying to kick with her legs and grasp hold of the rocks. She spread her arms, hoping that would stop her progress, but they simply slipped over the rocks toward the hole with the rest of her body.

Her torso began sliding over the edge and, momentarily forgetting her efforts to grasp the rocks with her arms, she began thrashing her legs with all of the strength left in her. She felt his grip loosen on one of her legs, and she began kicking him like a woman possessed. Pain shot up her leg as her foot pounded against his head, and she heard his screams as his other hand abruptly loosened its grip. He plunged to the bottom of the cistern.

Her legs were suddenly free, and she tried to grasp at the rocks. But she could feel herself slip inch by inch down into the cistern.

Why does it have to end this way? She tightened her grip on the edge of the cistern, but knew that she couldn't hold on for more than a few seconds. Trying to heave herself upward proved futile.

Just as she'd given up hope, strong hands seized her wrists and began hauling her up. *What—what the hell?* she thought. She was sure that she must already be dead or that this was some sort of dream. In another moment she was nearly all the way out of the cistern and lying on her side, gasping for air.

Strong arms stroked her and pulled her close. "Tracey," she heard. "Oh, Tracey."

Mark, she thought, knowing that she really was dead and in heaven. The arms felt so real, and the voice sounded so like his. She struggled to look up and saw his face. *Are those tears in his eyes?* she wondered. *Tears in heaven?*

Before she passed out, she had an instant of realization. She was alive, and Mark had really come at last.

Chapter Thirty-six

Miami, Florida

The sun had begun its descent in the west, and the sky was dramatically tinted in shades of violet, pink and orange. With the tangy smell of the salt water in her nostrils, the wind whipping her lustrous black hair, and Ramón at her side, Maribel couldn't have been happier. The long fire-engine red Cigarette Boat he was piloting streaked through the waters of Biscayne Bay like a torpedo.

When Ramón had called her to meet him at the marina in South Beach, she hadn't asked any questions. She knew him well enough by now to know that he had something special in mind. Now, with one hand on the wheel, he slipped an arm around her shoulders and hugged her closely to him.

"Know where we're going?" he shouted over the roar of the wind and the boat's powerful engines.

Maribel shook her head. "I don't have a clue," she replied, "and I don't really care, Ray. I'm with you, aren't I?" She smiled provocatively.

He leaned over and kissed her passionately, then turned his attention back to the water. "See that island?"

"Sure," she said. "It's Star Island."

"We're going to a little party over there," Ramón said.

"On Star Island?" Maribel's eyebrows arched above her pink-tinted sunglasses.

Ramón nodded. "Montague called me," he said. "Invited us both. Said we should be there about"—he looked down at his wristwatch—"right now."

"What's going on?" Maribel asked, but before he could respond, she guessed the answer to her question. *They're going to arrest Brian Biggs,* she thought.

"They're taking Mr. Brian Biggs III in," Ramón said with a wide grin. "He's at his parents' house at a big charity shindig. All of Miami's big shots are going to be there." He kissed her again. "What do you say to that?"

Maribel threw her arms up in the air. "Yes," she shouted. "Yes, yes, yes! This is one of the happiest days of my life." She turned to Ramón and kissed him hard on the lips.

"Thought it might be," he said. He eased off on the gas as they neared the shoreline of the baronial Biggs estate, then cut the engines to just above an idle as he began to steer as close to the seawall as possible.

There were several other small craft gathered close to the Biggses' enormous yacht, where it was docked at their private pier. Maribel stood up to get a better view. She saw that the boats carried photographers.

"Oh, ai, ai, ai, Ramón," she cried delightedly. "The press is out in full force, I see."

"Oh, yeah," he said. "You kidding? This jerk's picture's going to be on the front page of every newspaper in Florida tomorrow. They got the place staked out here and at the front gates, too. But I figured we'd have a better view from here because he's most likely going to be out here when they arrest him."

"I bet the Biggses think they're here just to try to get party shots," Maribel said. "You know, like for *Ocean Drive* magazine."

Ramón nodded. "Yeah. Serves them right."

From their vantage point, she could see that a huge white canopy was set up on the grounds of the estate. Under it, a small ensemble played Mozart that Maribel could hear above the idling boat engines. She saw white-draped tables laden with food and drinks and protected by the canopy, then scanned the dozens of elegantly dressed men and women who stood in little clumps or strolled about the beautiful lawn with cocktail glasses or champagne flutes in hand. Weaving among them, waiters in tuxedos circulated with trays laden with hors d'oeuvres and drinks.

"What a blast," Maribel said derisively. "Just the kind of party you want to miss."

"Yeah, well, the fireworks haven't started yet," Ramón said. He reached into a compartment beneath the boat's instrument panel and took out two pairs of binoculars. "We're going to need these," he said, handing one of them to her.

Maribel lifted the binoculars to her eyes, then adjusted them to focus on the party. "Wow!" she exclaimed, moving the binoculars up and down and side to side, then suddenly stopping. "I see Brian and Georgina. One shitbird and one deluded woman looking like they own the world. She's wearing a little Valentino number I saw in Bal Harbour. So bo-ring. She probably is too."

"Hey," Ramón said in an excited voice. "Look, Maribel. See the French doors up on the terrace? The ones leading into the house?"

Maribel moved her binoculars from the lawn up to the terrace. "That's Montague!" she cried. "And Stanlee's with him."

"Yeah," Ramón said. "Monty and Stanlee get the honors. They deserve it. The guy with them's from Homicide."

"Who're they talking to?" she asked Ramón, not taking her eyes away from the binoculars.

"That's the old man," he said. "*Papi* Biggs."

"Brian and Georgina don't even know what's going on," Maribel laughed. "They're too busy jawing with some of their snotty friends."

As they watched, Brian's father led the police down the terrace steps and across the expanse of lawn toward his son and Georgina. Heads started turning in their direction as the crowd became curious about the newcomers in street clothes.

"Oh, *por Dios,*" Maribel said, "Look!" She pointed, then grabbed Ramón's free hand. "Montague's taking out handcuffs. Now *everybody's* looking."

Around them, they heard the motor drives on photographers' cameras begin to whir. Flashbulbs punctuated the dimming early evening light.

"They're clapping the cuffs on him," Ramón said. "You can see the little fuck sweating from here."

Maribel jumped up and down. *"Concha de madre,"* she said. "There they go. Stanlee on one side and Montague on the other."

"Yeah. Looks like he's got no fight in him."

"I don't think he ever did," Maribel said with a sneer. "Oh, now the old man's taking Georgina up to the house. Not even walking out with his son. Taking her around to the side."

When Brian disappeared inside the house with Stanlee, Montague, and the officer from Homicide, boat engines revved up around them, and the water began to rock with the wake created by photographers rushing back to work. "Well, the party's over," Ramón said. "At least out here."

"I bet the TV stations are set up out front," Maribel said.

"They are," Ramón said, putting down his binoculars and turning to her.

She looked at him. "How do you . . . ?" she started to ask, then her words trailed off and she laughed. "You made some calls, didn't you? Damn! You are one brilliant son of a gun." She threw her arms around him and gave him a kiss.

"Anything for my baby," Ramón said, "and her friends."

"Oh, wait till I tell Tracey about this," Maribel said gleefully. "Oh, Ramón. She's going to love you for this as much as I do."

He grinned. "Think so?" he asked.

"Well . . ." Maribel began, smiling mischievously, "maybe not as much as I do." She ran her hands across his shoulders and down his back to his muscular buns. "And maybe not the same way."

"What you say we get out of here?" Ramón said. "Take a little ride to someplace private."

Maribel nodded. "Hmm," she said softly, "sounds perfect to me."

The little cove was surrounded by pine scrub that hid them from the lights of boats that passed by on their way to Jimbo's, the popular smoked-fish shack that was close by on the inlet. Ramón had killed the engine and dropped anchor, then opened a bottle of Dom Pérignon champagne that he'd stowed in an ice chest. To Maribel's surprise he'd even brought along two crystal flutes that he'd carefully wrapped and hidden in one of the boat's compartments.

"You're so thoughtful, Ray," Maribel told him. "I mean it. Thoughtful and generous."

They were seated on the boat's upholstered lounge astern. Ramón, whose arm was around her shoulders, gave her a squeeze. "What else?" he asked. "Tell me more."

Maribel laughed softly. "And smart and handsome and sexy."

He set his glass down and turned to her, embracing her in his arms and kissing her tenderly. "I'd do anything for you, Maribel," he whispered. "Anything." A hand slipped beneath her halter top, and he began stroking her breasts.

"Hmm," Maribel moaned, glad that she hadn't worn a bra, "you make me feel so good."

"Let's get you out of that thing," he said as his lips traveled down her neck to the exposed cleavage above the shocking pink top.

"Yeah," she replied. "Let's do exactly that. It's a hot night, isn't it?"

Ramón sat up and helped her wriggle out of the minuscule halter, then took off the polo shirt he was wearing. "A really hot night, baby," he said.

Maribel ran her hands over his powerful shoulders and muscular chest, then down to the bulge in his shorts. "Ahhh," she cooed. "What do we have here?"

"A present just for you," he said, sliding a hand beneath her micromini.

She heard his sharp intake of breath when he realized she wasn't wearing panties and she spread her legs for him, all the while rubbing his engorged cock through his shorts.

Ramón brushed her mound with his hand, breathing excitedly, then slipped a finger inside her and felt her wetness. Maribel gasped and clamped her thighs tightly against it, enjoying the feel of him inside her, stroking her.

"Jesus, baby," he said, "let's get naked. I can see you're ready to have a real good time."

"Oh, yes," she said. "I think you are, too."

She let Ramón unbutton her skirt and pull the zipper down, then slide it down over her legs. She'd already kicked off her shoes. He stood up then, and took off his shorts and underwear.

"Look what we have here," he said, holding his cock in his hand.

Maribel leaned forward and flicked her tongue across its head, then up the shaft, and Ramón tensed up and groaned. She took it in her mouth and began sucking on it, anxious to please this man she'd grown to desire so much. Ramón placed his hands on her head and pulled her close to him, his hips moving against her, until he was at the point of ejaculating.

"Ah, God," he said, drawing back. "You're going to make me shoot, baby."

"Not yet," Maribel said. "We've got all night."

Ramón went down on his knees and lifted her legs onto his shoulders. "Yeah, we've got all night." He began running his tongue up and down her thighs, kissing her, then his mouth sought out the sweet mound that was readily awaiting him.

When he thrust his tongue inside her, Maribel shivered with ecstasy and put her hands on his head while he licked at her juices. "Oh, Ray," she rasped, "that feels so good. Oh, God. Oh, God. You're going to make me orgasm."

Ramón took her legs off his shoulders and got to his feet. "Lie down, baby," he said, urging her to stretch out on the lounge. Positioned on his knees between her legs, he brought them up onto his shoulders again, placing his hands on the cushions beside her head.

He plunged into her then, and Maribel let out a cry of pleasure. "Oh, yes, Ray," she said. "Oh, yes, yes, yes!"

He thrust his cock in and out of her with abandon, so

excited by her desire for him that he couldn't hold back. Maribel lustily pushed herself against him, driven to heights of passion that she didn't think she'd ever felt before.

Suddenly she cried out as she felt the first orgasm begin to engulf her, and when Ramón reared back and plunged into her again, his seed exploded inside her as he bellowed. She thought she would drown in rapture as she felt their juices mingle.

Ramón proclaimed breathlessly that he loved her, over and over again, as he collapsed atop her, panting heavily. As she brought her legs down, he hugged her tightly to his sweat-soaked body and remained inside her, reluctant to leave her warmth.

"Oh, my God," Maribel said. "Oh, Ramón. You really make me feel so good. Like nobody else. Nobody."

"I know," he said. "I know. We really got something going here, don't we?"

"Uh-huh," she said. "We sure do."

He hugged her tightly, and kissed her. "And we've just started, haven't we?"

"Oh, yes," Maribel said. "The night's young."

"You said it, baby," Ramón said.

She felt his cock growing tumescent inside her again. "Oh, oh, Ray. What did I do to deserve this?" She wriggled against him.

"Just being you, Maribel," he whispered. "Just being you." He began moving inside again, slowly and rhythmically.

I think I died and went to heaven, Maribel thought as she began moving with him. *Oh, yes. This is heaven.*

Chapter Thirty-seven

Santorini, Greece

Tracey, drifting somewhere at the edges of sleep, heard the soft, distant sound of New Age trance music. Its repetitive chords and beat were like the soothing, rhythmic lapping of waves at the beach. As she fell back into a light slumber, she couldn't help but smile, remembering how at first she'd thought it odd that this hip club music was so often playing on Urania's CD system. She'd soon discovered that it wasn't a matter of Urania trying to act much younger. It was simply that she found the music soothed her nerves. Tracey found it had the same effect on her.

The music drifted back into her consciousness as she felt a cool cloth brushing lightly across her forehead. Then that same coolness traversed her cheeks, her nose, and her chin. Her eyelids fluttered open, and when she focused she found Mark sitting next to her on the bed.

Turning her head slightly, she could see Urania comfortably sprawled in a chair at the bedside, her bare feet with their scarlet toenails propped up on the bed's pristine white linen. She was smoking as she watched Mark minister to Tracey, a benign smile on her heavily painted scarlet lips.

"Oh, you're awake, darling," Urania cooed softly.

"Yes," Tracey said. "I must've dozed off again after dinner."

Mark removed the cloth from her face. "Yes, you did," he said. "Welcome back." He leaned down and kissed her lips gently.

"Hi," Tracey said, returning his kiss.

"How do you feel, darling?" Urania asked, putting her cigarette out in an ashtray.

"I feel a lot better," Tracey said. She started pushing herself up in bed with her hands, and Mark shifted the pillows behind her to support her back.

"You sure?" he asked.

"I'm positive," Tracey said, smiling. She repositioned herself, sitting almost completely upright, and settled back against the downy pillows, wincing with the assorted pains.

She'd suffered no major wounds, but nearly her entire body had been covered with scratches, and every muscle seemed to have been pulled or bruised. Now she wore nothing more than an elastic bandage around her sprained ankle. Her scratches were not bandaged but cleansed with peroxide, then covered with an antibiotic ointment twice a day. Mark insisted on performing this ritual every morning and evening.

As the shock wore off, she came to realize how lucky she was to survive the attack. The psychological wounds would take far longer to heal, but even the effect of those had been diminished by the presence of Mark and his act of saving her.

She still awoke in the middle of the night, covered with sweat, shaking from the terrifying dreams that haunted her. The cry in the night; the face of Gaia, her mother, Urania's lookalike, as she lay dead; the man, Ted—but not Ted—chasing, chasing, chasing; finally, being pulled down, down, down into the cistern. Luckily, Mark had been there when she had awakened in a tangle of sheets and held her in his arms, soothing her back to sleep.

"Are you ready to eat something else?" he asked. "You didn't have very much dinner."

Tracey shook her head. "No," she said, "but if it's not too much trouble, maybe something to drink."

"I'll get it," Urania said cheerfully. "What would you like, darling? Juice, water, soda? Anything. You just say the word."

"Just some water, Urania," she replied.

"Sparkling?"

"That's fine."

Urania slipped into her sandals and hurried out of the room.

Mark leaned down and kissed Tracey's forehead and took one of her hands in his. "Alone at last," he whispered.

Tracey smiled. "She's been like a mother hen," she said. She looked up at Mark. "Well, you've both been like mother hens."

"It's because we both love you," he said. "In very different ways."

"I love you, too," Tracey said, squeezing his hand. She was lost in thought for a moment, then cleared her throat. "Has Urania decided when she's going to have the funeral?"

"She's waiting until she's sure you feel up to it," Mark said.

"I'm okay now."

"Are you sure?"

"Yes," she replied. "Absolutely. I think I'd have been ready sooner if it hadn't been for those painkillers and tranquilizers the doctor gave me. I think that's why I haven't been very hungry. They were so powerful they turned me into a zombie."

"Maybe that's what you needed," Mark said. "I mean . . . with all the things you had to face. And all at once."

"Maybe," Tracey said, "but it feels good to be coming back to normal now. Getting them out of my system. Even if a lot of terrible things have happened, I think I can handle them better without looking at the world through a haze. Besides, I'm tired of being treated like an invalid."

"Here, Tracey," Urania said, coming back into the room. "I put a slice of lemon in it. Do you want a sip now?"

"Yes, please." Tracey took the glass from her and after a long sip set it down on the bedside table.

"Thanks, Urania."

"You're welcome," Urania said, slipping out of her sandals and propping her feet back up on the bed again.

Tracey looked over at the glamorous creature who seemed to be deriving pleasure from waiting on her. "I'm ready for the funeral," she told her in an even voice. "Mark told me you were waiting until I feel up to it, and I appreciate that."

"It's the least I could do," Urania said with a shrug. "If you really think you're up to it, then I'll arrange it. Father Apostolou has agreed to say a few words at a little Catholic cemetery nearby. Gaia . . . your mother—" Tears came into Urania's eyes and her voice choked. "—I'm sorry, darling," she said. "I still can't quite get over it."

She wiped tears away with her fingertips, and took a moment to compose herself, then continued. "Gaia was a believer, or used to be. So anyway, Father Apostolou will say a few words at the cemetery, if that's okay with you, then we can come back here for dinner. How's tomorrow?"

"I think that's perfect," Tracey said, "and I really appreciate your waiting for me, Urania." If the truth be told, Tracey did appreciate Urania's efforts on her behalf, but she felt very strange about the whole thing. Being consulted about the funeral arrangements for this woman who had been her mother only served as a reminder of the fact that she'd never known the woman at all. Had it not been for hearing her tortured cries in the night and witnessing her gruesome murder, Tracey honestly didn't know if she would have any feelings for the woman at all.

"I'll go call Father Apostolou," Urania said, "and set a time with him." She got to her feet. "Be right back."

They watched her leave the room, then Mark leaned over and kissed Tracey again. She put her arms around his neck and pulled him closer, returning his kisses. "Oh, I'm so glad you're here," she whispered fervently. "Aside from the fact that I wouldn't be alive, you make a great doctor . . . and an even better lover."

Mark grinned. "As long as I don't damage the merchandise," he said.

"No chance of that," Tracey said. "I think you're making me better and better. So much better, in fact, that I think when Urania comes back we should tell her that we're going to have an early night."

"You think your old Auntie Urania is going to believe that?"

"Not for a minute," Tracey replied with a laugh, "but she'll go make herself busy somewhere else."

"While we make ourselves busy here, right?"

"Right," she said with a nod of her head. "Very busy."

"Then I'll go head her off at the pass," he said, "and tell her that we're busy ministering to your wounds."

"You don't have to do that," Tracey said, "but I'd love it if you did."

"Be right back."

He kissed her, then got up and left the room to search for Urania. Tracey watched him go, still somewhat stunned by his Adonis looks and his love for her. *I've had some awful luck in the last year,* she told herself, *but getting to know Mark . . . to fall in love with Mark . . . makes it all seem a lot better.*

He soon was back at her beside. "Mission accomplished," he said.

"It was that easy?" she asked.

"Remarkable, isn't it?" he replied. "This whole thing has humbled the legendary Urania Vickers. And I bet it'll last at least a few more days."

Tracey smiled. "You naughty boy," she said. "Talking about my poor old auntie like that. Come here. You'll have to kiss me to make up for it."

He eased down onto the bed beside her and kissed her lips. "Gladly," he said.

The sky was overcast, and a chill wind swept over the gray landscape. Whitecaps decorated the churning sea as far as the eye could see. The funeral was held in an old Catholic graveyard in Fíra, and the tiny chapel behind the cemetery was typical of all the others on Santorini: a cerulean domed roof crowned with a cross, whitewashed plaster walls, and an ancient-looking wooden door. The priest, Father Apostolou, stood before the simple coffin with its spray of white roses, reading selections from the funeral mass, but the wind carried his words away so that nothing he said was intelligible.

Urania, Tracey, and Mark stood in a row, the household help lined up behind them. In the distance photographers with telephoto lenses were snapping away, the motor drives on their cameras making a constant whir. After word had inevitably leaked out about the murder, they had descended on the island in droves, but the local police, ever protective of Urania's privacy, were out in full force, making certain that none of them could get close to the cemetery or the compound.

Tracey could see the priest's lips move and could hear the faintest drone, but her thoughts were elsewhere. Out of the corner of her eye, she saw the tears that streaked down Urania's face, visible even behind the heavy black veil that was draped from the big black hat she wore. For Tracey, they brought back the night of the murder—a night when she had seen Urania totally unmasked for the first time since she'd met her—and the ensuing revelations.

After Mark had pulled her from the cistern, he had carried her in his arms to the wind- and rain-lashed terrace around the pool, where she had insisted he put her down. Urania had come through the gate leading out of the compound, a coat held above her head in an effort to protect herself from the deluge.

"Mark!" she cried. "What on earth?" Then she saw Tracey's dirty, torn clothes and the streaks of dirt and blood intermingled with the rain on her face and arms and legs. "My God, what's happened here, Tracey?" She stood transfixed on the terrace, staring at the two of them, ignoring the rain.

"Hurry," Mark said. "Let's get indoors. We have to get a doctor and the police."

"The police?" Urania cried as Mark ushered them both through the doorway into the entrance hall. "But—but I've just been next door at Sir Hugh's. What the hell's going on?"

Once they were indoors and lanterns had been lit, Tracey told them what had transpired in a torrent of words. Urania was horrified hearing the news and nearly collapsed upon hearing of the death in the tower. Mark retrieved Urania's cell phone from the beaded evening bag she had indicated, pushed the power button, and called a cell number only Urania and a handful of other important islanders had for the police.

Well over an hour passed before the police and emergency services personnel finally left the compound. The household staff—Stavros, Mrs. Stefanou, her mother, and Iliki—were taken to Fíra for observation in the clinic there. It was quickly determined that they had been drugged with a powerful hypnotic, but they appeared to be unharmed otherwise. The body in the tower was removed by the coroner, but Ted was left where he fell, in the old cistern, the police having decided that the cistern was virtually bottomless. They crawled over every square inch of the compound with their flashlights and finally left after taking statements and coming to the conclusion that no further danger was present.

The police had since learned that the man's real name was Frederico Paulo Salerno, and his birthplace was New York City. He lived in Miami Beach, Florida. Frederico was known to have ties to an organized crime family there, or so the Greek police had learned from Interpol.

The local police had concluded that his motive for entering the compound, incapacitating the help, and murdering the old woman, who had gotten in his way, was his desire to rape Tracey. She was the only person in the compound he knew, with the exception of Urania, whom he'd only just met, and in their "expert" opinion he was obsessed with Tracey. She was in no condition to theorize with them about the possible causes of what had happened and had remained mute.

The doctor tended to Tracey's wounds. Although primarily superficial, many of them had to be treated for possible infection. Her ankle was wrapped in an elastic bandage for support, then he gave her a tranquilizer and a painkiller and left behind bottles with the instruction that she should take at least three of each every day for the time being.

In the living room, lanterns had cast pools of light that, under normal circumstances, would have been romantic, but on that awful night they had merely added to the grotesque nature of the events. Tracey lay on a couch wrapped in a blanket, and Mark sat next to her, an arm draped protectively around her shoulder. Urania pulled a chair close to them, and sat with a tumbler of brandy in one hand and a cigarette in the other. Her hair had fallen about her face in a tangled, Medusa-like mess, and that perfect mask of a face was ravaged by anguish, her makeup tear-streaked and smeared. She looked much older suddenly, Tracey thought, and even the beautiful beaded evening gown she'd worn to Sir Hugh's dinner looked somehow tacky, its luster diminished by the night's events.

"I guess," Urania had said in her smoky voice, "that we have at least one miracle to be thankful for." A grim smile appeared on her lips as she looked over at Mark. "And that's that your plane managed to land in the storm. Tracey would be dead otherwise."

"When we left Athens, it was fine," Mark said. "I don't think we'd have taken off if they'd known what was coming, but the storm's intensity wasn't expected."

Urania took a sip of the brandy, then set it down on the table. "Tracey, are you certain you won't have some brandy, darling?"

Tracey shook her head. "I don't think so. I already feel the tranquilizer."

"I feel the one I took, too," Urania replied, "but I'm having some anyway. Mark?"

"I think I will now," he said. He gently patted Tracey's shoulder, then went over to the drinks table and poured himself a generous portion, returning to Tracey's side on the couch.

Urania stared down at her fingernails, lost in thought, but she finally looked up at Tracey. Her eyes held an infinite sadness. She cleared her throat. "I . . . I suppose I owe you an explanation," she said at last, "and this . . . well, it isn't going to be easy for either of us."

Tracey nodded. She decided to let Urania talk while she listened rather than ask questions, though her mind had been swirling with them and still was, even in her sedated condition.

"You don't have to talk about it now, Urania," Mark offered. "You might want to try to rest a while first."

Urania shook her head. "No, Mark," she said. "I couldn't possibly rest now, and besides, I want to get this out of my system."

She ground out her cigarette, lit another, and got to her feet. Slowly pacing the room, she nervously took deep drags off the cigarette. Finally, she settled back down in her chair, took a sip of brandy, and looked over at Tracey again.

"Gaia . . . the woman in the tower," she said, "was my twin sister. I'm sure you'd already guessed that if you saw her clearly. We were identical twins, right down to the little moles on our left cheekbones. We could actually pass for one another, everyone used to say. Sometimes we did, playing games, you know, and, growing up together, we were inseparable. No two sisters could ever have been closer . . . for a while at least."

Tracey's curiosity overpowered her decision to remain silent. "Did that change?" she asked. "I mean, your closeness. Did you grow apart?"

"When . . . when I started getting to be famous," Urania replied, "we saw a great deal less of each other. Not because I didn't want to, but I was always working, usually on location someplace, and besides, Gaia despised the limelight and the attention that it would have focused on her simply because of me. Or at least that's what I *thought*."

Urania took a puff off her cigarette and blew a plume of smoke toward the ceiling. "Anyway, she got married and lived in Europe for a few years during her first marriage."

"She was married more than once?" Tracey asked, her curiosity growing by the minute.

Urania nodded. "Yes. The first time around was miserable. He was an Englishman, rich and handsome, *and* a drunk and a gambler. She knew it, but she thought she could change all that. Like a fool, she thought that marriage would be a cure. Well, he made her life hell, so she finally got a divorce and came running home."

Urania stubbed her cigarette out in an ashtray and sighed.

"Did she marry again?" Tracey asked.

Urania was silent for a moment, looking back down at her fingernails. Then she took a deep breath and looked back up. "Yes," she said, exhaling. "She got married again, a while after that." Her voice held a note of exasperation.

"And what about that marriage?" Tracey asked. "Did it work out?"

"Oh . . . it . . . it *seemed* perfect," Urania replied. "On the surface. But there were . . . problems."

Before Tracey could ask another question, Mark did. "What caused her . . . condition?" he asked, careful of his words, so as not to offend. "Why was she kept over in the tower?"

Urania lit another cigarette. "She wasn't crazy, if that's what you mean," she snapped defensively.

"No," Mark said mildly, "that's not what I meant. But you have to admit that it's very strange that this woman—your twin sister—has been kept over there without anybody knowing about it."

"*I* knew," Urania cried. "Oh, did I ever." Tears came into her eyes, and she wiped them with her fingertips.

"I'm sorry, Urania," Mark said. "I didn't mean to upset you."

Urania waved off his apology with a flip of her hand. "Maria Stefanou knew, of course, and the local doctor. We've taken care of her for years and years." She paused and took another sip of brandy.

"This is just so difficult to talk about," she said, setting her brandy down. "I've kept it bottled up for so long." She paused and took a deep breath.

"Anyway, Gaia and Victor—her first husband—were driving out to their place in the country after a party in London," she said. "Victor was drunk, of course, and speeding. They had a horrible accident. It completely demolished the Land Rover. Victor walked away without a scratch, naturally, but Gaia was thrown out of the car and had severe head injuries."

"So that's why she . . . had to be cared for?" Mark asked.

"Yes," Urania said. "After the accident she got a divorce and went back to the States. She'd finally had enough of him. Anyway, she was in a London hospital for a while, but there was only so much they could do. She'd had a frontal lobe injury. For a while after she came back home, she looked and seemed just like the old Gaia. Beautiful and sweet and kind."

Tears came into Urania's eyes again, and Mark got up and retrieved some Kleenex, and handed them to her. Urania dabbed her eyes. "Thank you, darling," she said, putting out her cigarette.

Mark rejoined Tracey on the couch, putting his arm back around her.

"I'm sorry," Urania said. "I guess I've never really gotten over what happened to Gaia. It's always seemed so unfair." She took another sip of brandy, then continued. "The doctors warned me of what was in all likelihood going to happen, but I didn't believe them. Like I said, after the accident Gaia seemed herself and certainly looked as beautiful as always. But then I began to see little changes in her, personality changes."

"Like what?" Mark asked.

"Oh, they were subtle at first," Urania said. "She became a bit more subdued, less . . . lively, or alive, I suppose you would say. Then I found out that she'd started lying in ways that were totally uncharacteristic of her. She was pretending to be me with certain people, and didn't seem to have any qualms at all about it. She was going after what she wanted in a very childlike way. In fact, childlike is a good way to describe what she was becoming."

"It must've been terrible for you," Tracey said. "To watch that happen."

"It was horrid and sad," Urania said, "but there was nothing I could do but watch over her. All the doctors said the same thing. It was hopeless. Because of the frontal lobe damage, her mental abilities were deteriorating, and they would get worse. Well, I wasn't getting any work at the time. No movies. No television. Nothing. I'd been working since I was sixteen, then in my thirties the work stopped coming my way. It's as if I'd been wiped off the face of the map. So at least I could be there for Gaia more than in the past."

She sighed again, heavily, as if she were exhausted from

the effort of telling them the story, but she went on. "I suppose you can guess the rest. She got worse and worse, until I finally brought her here where she could be watched over night and day without having to be put in some awful institution. I know that she doesn't seem like a very nice sort, but Maria Stefanou's been wonderful to Gaia, and if any of the islanders know about her—and I'm certain they do—they're kind enough never to say a word."

"What about her second husband?" Tracey asked. "What happened to him?"

Urania gazed over at her and shrugged. "I don't know," she said.

"Did they have any children?" Tracey asked.

Urania looked at her with a surprised expression, but was silent for a moment. "Why would you ask a question like that?" she asked.

"I'm just curious," Tracey said.

"Well, if you must know," Urania said, exhaling a stream of smoke, "Gaia did have a child."

"And what happened to it?" Tracey asked, determined to find out as much as she could. She knew now that she and Maribel had been on to something from the very beginning.

Urania looked discomfited, her brows knitting. "I don't know that, either," she said.

"But . . . but how can that be?" Tracey asked. "Your sister had a husband and child, and you don't know what happened to them?"

Mark gently patted her shoulder, warning her that she was pressuring Urania too much, but Tracey paid no attention to him.

"Well, Tracey, darling," Urania said in a waspish tone, "it's not my fault if they vanished, is it? He took the baby and disappeared into thin air. I tried to find them as best I could—he had Gaia's little girl, after all—but I couldn't find a trace of them."

A girl! Tracey thought. She extricated herself from Mark's comforting arm and the blanket she was still wrapped in and got to her feet. "Would you mind looking at something of mine?" she asked Urania.

Urania looked at her with a curious expression. "What?" she asked. "What are you up to, Tracey?"

"I'll be right back," she said. "I want to show you something."

Before Urania or Mark could protest, she made a beeline for her room, where she retrieved the scrapbook, then went back downstairs.

Urania and Mark were quietly chatting and looked over at her when she came into the living room.

"What's this?" Mark asked her.

"I'll show you," Tracey said. She sat back down on the couch and looked over at Urania. "I told you about my father's death," she said, "but I didn't tell you about personal things of his that I found hidden after he died."

"What on earth has any of this to do with me?" Urania asked, stubbing out a cigarette.

"I could be wrong," Tracey said, "but I think you'll see." She put the scrapbook down on the coffee table, where all three of them could look at it, then opened it to the page that showed her father and the woman she assumed to be her mother.

Urania glanced at the picture without any interest, then suddenly got out of her chair and, getting down on her knees, moved the scrapbook around so that she could see the picture clearly. "Oh . . . my . . . God!" she cried out. Tears formed in her eyes again as she looked at the old photograph. "This is Gaia and Tom," she said. "Around the time they got married."

She looked up at Tracey. "Where did you get this?" she asked, her tone accusatory.

"It was in my father's scrapbook, as you can see, Urania," Tracey said.

"But—but what? . . ." Urania's voice trailed off into silence as she stared at Tracey.

Tracey took some documents from the folder in the scrapbook and held them out to Urania. "Would you look at these," she said, "and tell me what you make of them?"

Urania took them and glanced down. "Oh, Tracey," she said, "I don't see—" Then her eye caught the names on one of them. "Where did you get this?" she demanded, holding up the marriage license.

"Everything was hidden together, with my father's scrapbook," Tracey replied.

Urania looked back down at the document then back up at Tracey again, the marriage license trembling in her hand. "This . . . this has *my* name on it," she said. "Victoria Ure. My real name. Before it was changed by the studio."

For a moment, Tracey was nonplussed. She had become convinced that her father had been married to Gaia, but Urania's name was on the marriage license. It made no sense to her, and she was more confused than ever.

Urania shook her head as if to clear it. "This is Gaia's marriage license," she said in a shaky voice. "When she married Tom, she used my name. I told you that I found out she'd started pretending to be me after the accident. Remember?"

Tracey nodded.

"I found out she'd stolen my passport and birth certificate, and she used them when she married Tom. I had no idea at first. I don't know why. I don't fully understand it, but it was part of the personality change, the mental deterioration, after the accident."

"Look—look at the name-change documents," Tracey told her. "I think you'll find them interesting, too." Tracey knew the truth now, beyond a shadow of a doubt. Her head was swirling with the revelation, but she made a monumental effort to remain calm.

Urania looked back down at the documents in her hand, studying each one of them closely, before looking back up at Tracey. The expression on her face was one of utter wonder. "You . . . you're my . . . niece, aren't you?" she said at last.

"I think so," Tracey said.

Mark, who'd been watching their exchange in mute fascination, broke his silence. "What?" he exclaimed. "Tracey, did you know about this?"

Tracey shook her head. "I didn't know anything," she replied. "After Dad died, I found these things. It wasn't long before I left to come over here. I didn't know *what* to believe, but my friend, Maribel, thought that the woman in the picture looked just like Urania Vickers, the movie star."

"This is unbelievable," Mark said, looking at Tracey.

"I know," she said to Mark, before turning her attention back to Urania. "I wasn't even sure who you were when I found these, Urania," Tracey said. "I didn't even know my name and my father's had been changed."

"Your name was changed?" Mark said.

Tracey nodded.

Urania held the document in her hand. "Tracey's name was Anna Melinda Reynolds," she said. She looked over at Tracey. "You were named after our mother. The Anna, anyway." Her voice choked, and she looked back down at another document, then back up again. "Your father was Thomas Luke Reynolds. The Tom who fell in love with Gaia. Only he thought it was me."

"You mean he actually thought he was marrying Urania Vickers," Mark said incredulously.

"Yes," Urania said with a nod, "but when he fell in love with Gaia, he didn't even know who Urania Vickers was. Didn't have a clue. I remember I felt a bit insulted by it when I found out, but Tom was . . . well . . . different. He didn't care about movies and television or that sort of thing, but he loved Gaia with all his heart."

"Then why did he change his name?" Tracey asked. "And mine? And if he loved Gaia so much, why did he let you take her away?"

Urania took a deep breath. "Oh, Tracey," she said with exasperation. "It's so difficult to explain, but I'll try. I—I knew that Tom didn't know anything about Gaia's condition when he married her. Then you were born. In the meantime, Gaia began deteriorating, and Tom could see that but didn't understand it until I told him about it. He knew that eventually she was going to have to be put in some kind of institution, and he was heartbroken."

"I still don't understand why he would let you take her away," Tracey said.

"Tom was afraid of me," Urania said. "He was a little afraid of Gaia, too. You see, he thought we would try to take you away from him."

"But why would you have done that?" Tracey asked.

"It's simple," Urania said. "To please Gaia. I would've done nearly anything to make her happy, and your father was afraid that because I was famous and had money that I could get you away from him. With my name and all, the courts might have let Gaia keep you. I'd offered him money for you, but he wouldn't take it. Anyway, he wasn't happy about it, but he was willing to let Gaia go, for her own sake. He knew that I would take care of her somewhere so that she wouldn't be institutionalized. What he would *not* do was let you go."

"So that's why—" Tracey began.

"That's why he disappeared with you," Urania said. "He was afraid we'd try to take you from him. We couldn't find a trace of him. I must admit I didn't look very hard. Tom was extremely independent, his own man, and I figured that he wanted his own life—a life with you. So . . . I let it go."

Urania took a sip of brandy and set the glass back down. "I also have to confess that I didn't want any publicity about it. I didn't think it would look good for my career if there was some sort of court battle and Gaia's condition became public knowledge. Work had already dried up, like I told you, and I didn't want to jeopardize my future in any way. It was a very difficult time for me. For all of us."

Tracey stared at the woman, not knowing quite what to think. It was all too much to take in at once, and she felt conflicting emotions that threatened to overwhelm her. She could appreciate her father's love for her on the one hand, but she couldn't help but feel a fury that he'd kept this from her all those years. Had he been afraid she would want to go to her mother? To meet her at least? Was he simply trying to protect her from the pain of knowing her as she had become? And Urania. She admitted she hadn't searched very hard for them. Did she care nothing for her twin's daughter? Her own flesh and blood?

As if she could read her thoughts, Urania looked over at her. The expression on her face was tentative. "Tracey," she began in a soft voice, "I—I don't know how to say this, but . . . I'm . . . I'm truly thrilled that you've surfaced. I guess it's such a shock for us both that we don't know what to do or say, but I . . . I loved you then. You were . . . *are* . . . Gaia's daughter. I think I could love you again."

Tears came into Tracey's eyes, and she started to weep silently. Mark enveloped her in his arms. Urania, too, began to cry, and tears flowed down her cheeks. She got up and sat down on the couch next to Tracey, putting an arm around her back.

"We—we can get through this," Urania said. "Somehow, together, we can get through this and be a family again."

Chapter Thirty-eight

The graveside funeral service was short, and afterward they had an early dinner at Urania's. The priest left, and the household staff went about their business. Tracey, Mark, and Urania sat in the living room, where Urania was leafing through the scrapbook again, as she had so many times since Tracey had first brought it downstairs to show her.

The telephone rang, but no one picked it up. Maria Stefanou appeared at the archway leading into the room. "It's for you, Tracey," she said with a new respect in her voice. "It's Maribel in Miami, she says. Should I tell her to call back?"

"No," Tracey said. "I'll take it."

Maria Stefanou pushed the hold button on the remote. "Just a moment," she said, then handed Tracey the receiver.

Tracey walked out to the terrace, wondering why Maribel was calling again. She'd already told her what had happened in Miami. Tracey could only hope that she'd called just to chat. She could do without any more drama for a while. "Maribel?"

"Oh, have I got news for you, *cariña,*" Maribel said excitedly. "Celia Dunne, you know, the real estate lady in Coconut Grove?"

"Yes?" Tracey said, relieved that this was merely a matter of real estate.

"She called me and said that she'd e-mailed you, but hadn't heard anything back."

"Nobody's checked the e-mail yet," Tracey said.

"Well, anyway," Maribel said, "somebody's made an offer on your house."

"And?" Tracey said, not surprised by the news, knowing that the house would sell immediately.

"They've offered a million dollars," Maribel said.

Tracey heard the sum and remained silent for a moment.

"Are you there or did you faint?" Maribel asked gleefully.

"Call Celia back and tell her I want three," Tracey said.

"Three million dollars?" Maribel asked in amazement.

"Yes," Tracey said, "and not a penny less. And Maribel?"

"Yes?"

"Thanks a lot—for everything—but I've got to run," she said. "I love you, and I'll see you soon. Okay?"

"Okay," Maribel replied.

Tracey pushed the off button. *It's Biggs,* she thought. *No matter whose name the offer is being made in, it's Biggs. It's bound to be, but they can have it. Their son will probably never live outside prison walls again,* she thought. *That's a pretty high price for a piece of property.*

She returned to the living room.

"Everything okay?" Mark asked.

"Fine," she said. "Somebody's made an offer on the house."

"Oh," Urania said. "Oodles and oodles of money, I hope."

"A reasonable offer," Tracey replied.

"You mustn't accept whatever comes your way, Tracey, darling," Urania said authoritatively. "Perhaps you should let *me* talk to these people. I'm a very good bargainer, you know, if I do say so myself. All these years in the entertainment industry haven't been for nothing."

"It's already taken care of," Tracey said, "but thank you very much for offering." She felt the knowing pressure of Mark's hand on her thigh.

"Have it your way," Urania said in a miffed voice, "but take it from an expert. These real estate people can be thieving dogs, just like producers, and you've told me how Tom's—your father's—house is so desperately wanted by these developers. They'll see what a young innocent you are and try to rip you off."

"Oh, that reminds me," Mark said to Tracey, to get her off the hook. "I e-mailed the finished part of the manuscript to Julia Markoff. And she's really crazy about it."

"Isn't it thrilling!" Urania interjected excitedly. "She *loves* my writing, darling. Praises it to the high heavens. I'm so glad I've worked so hard rewriting all the little things you did to try to help. I know you meant well, but it's just as I thought. I didn't really need you at all. Julia says that she can hear my voice throughout. Unmistakably."

Tracey almost laughed aloud and felt the gentle squeeze that Mark gave her shoulder. Urania's response to the news was so . . . well, so Urania, she thought. Tracey knew, as did Mark, that there would be nothing for Julia Markoff to love were it not for her own very hard labor rewriting and replotting the entire novel, arguing with Urania all the way.

She smiled at Urania. "That's so wonderful," she said. "I knew you could do it, Urania."

"Thank you, darling," Urania cooed. "It *has* been a struggle, but I think . . . maybe I'll start something else since they love this one so much. Perhaps I'll do another autobiography. . . ." Her words trailed off as she became lost in thought.

"But you've already done an autobiography," Mark pointed out.

Urania turned her heavily made-up eyes on him. "Of course, darling," she said imperiously, as if she were addressing a hopeless idiot, "but now there's a whole new chapter. Chapters even! Don't you see? What with the murder and all." Her eyes became narrow slits. "And don't either one of you dare say one word to the press about anything that's happened here," she warned. "The world will get the story directly from me, and they'll have to pay a fortune for it."

She abruptly stood up. "I think I'll go to my room and

make some notes," she announced. "I'll see you later, darlings." She blew kisses in their direction. "And remember. Mum's the word." She swept out of the room.

Tracey and Mark stood at the gate, ready to start the climb up the steps to the road. Mark had returned with only one carry-on bag, which he had slung across his shoulder, and Stavros had already taken Tracey's luggage up to the tiny Smart car.

Urania left the shade of an umbrellaed table where she was working and strode to the gate. She'd ordered Maria Stefanou to bring out several legal pads and sharpened pencils and had been scribbling away in her virtually illegible hand.

"I would love to see you off at the airport," she said airily, "but I'm just a poor working girl, you know. So many expensive salaries to pay." She looked at Tracey. "And so many terrible agent's commissions." She turned her steely eyes on Mark.

"I'll keep in touch, Urania," Tracey said, "and I really hope we can get together again soon."

After a moment, the hard glint in Urania's eyes softened, and they became wistful and misty-eyed. She put her arms out and encircled Tracey with them, kissing her on both cheeks. She drew back and looked at her. "I am thrilled to have you back in my life," she said breathlessly, "and I meant it when I said that I hope we can become close friends, Tracey. Like real family."

"I do, too," Tracey said. "I look forward to it."

"Well, off you go," Urania said, "and I hope this young man takes good care of you even if I've been deserted."

Mark laughed lightly. "We'd never desert you, Urania," he said. "We'll see you soon. Just keep up the good work in the meantime and call when you need to." He leaned down and kissed her chastely.

"I will," she said. "I'll find the time. Hugh's coming over tonight, then tomorrow the two of us are off to a house party for a few days on Patmos."

Stavros held the gate open for them, and Tracey and Mark started the climb up the steps to the road, with

Stavros just ahead. They turned about halfway up and looked back down at the compound. Urania blew kisses to them, then turned and shut the gate.

"That wasn't as difficult as it could've been," Tracey said softly. "I hope she doesn't get lonely after having our company."

"I wouldn't worry about it," Mark said. "She's got the autobiography to work on, if she can sit still long enough to do it. Besides, something tells me she's already sinking her teeth into Sir Hugh Apostle."

"Do you really think so?" Tracey asked.

Mark nodded. "Dinner tonight. A house party on Patmos. Plus, he's much younger, very handsome, and rich as Croesus. I'd say he pretty much fills the bill."

"Sounds like it," Tracey said, "and I sure am glad. It makes me feel a lot less guilty about keeping her in the dark about our plans."

"If we'd told her we're getting married," Mark said, stopping and turning to her, "she'd stop at nothing to plan the whole thing."

Tracey kissed his nose. "I love the idea of running off to Las Vegas to get married after we're done in Miami," she said.

"I suspect you've got a tiny bit of your aunt in you," Mark said with a laugh. "She's done it at least twice, I think."

At the top of the hill, they paused to catch their breath while Stavros went on to the car. Suddenly, a cat appeared from out of nowhere and stopped and sat down in front of them.

"Oh, it's Zeus," Tracey cried. She leaned down and stroked the big cat's fur. Mark followed suit, giving the cat pats on its head. Tracey heard a familiar giggle from behind her, and she and Mark straightened up and turned around. Prometheus stood looking at them with a smile on his face.

"So you're leaving now, my friend?" he asked.

"Yes, Pro," she replied.

Mark ruffled the boy's hair. "We'll be back soon though," he said.

"I know you will," Prometheus replied. He leaned down

and picked up the big cat. "And Zeus and I will be waiting for you when you come to visit your aunt."

Tracey and Mark exchanged glances. "You know everything that happens on the island, don't you?" Tracey said.

"You bet, Trace," the boy said.

"Look," Tracey said. She held her necklace out for him to see. "I'll be taking part of you with me," she said, "so I won't forget you, Pro."

"I won't forget you, either, Trace," he said with solemnity. "We make a good pair."

Mark and Tracey couldn't help but laugh.

"I think we do, too, Pro," she said. She leaned down and kissed his cheek. "You'll stay out of trouble and take good care of Zeus, won't you?"

"Of course," he said. "I always take good care of Zeus." He looked up at her. "Well, I'd better go now. I've got things to do."

"Okay," Tracey said. "We'll see you soon, Pro."

"*Hasta la vista,* baby," he said, doing his flawless Arnold Schwarzenegger imitation, and took off down the road, the big cat slung across his shoulder.

"He's quite a kid," Mark said.

"He sure—"

Tracey was interrupted by a loud racket. From the Mini Market just to their left, they heard a torrent of Greek that lashed at the air like a knife. They turned to look.

The ancient crone in her dirty black clothes sat at her customary station in front of the market. She'd turned her milky gaze toward them and was gesticulating wildly with her gnarled and wrinkled hands. Kathy stepped out of the Mini Market and stood listening to her with a smile on her face.

"What's she saying?" Tracey asked.

"She wants the amulet back," Kathy said with a roll of her eyes. "She says that someone else might need it now. That it's protected you from the evil eye. It's served its purpose." She shrugged indulgently.

Despite the oddity of the request, or perhaps because of it, Tracey felt a chill rush up her spine. "Could you undo my necklace?" she asked Mark in a soft voice.

"Sure," he said.

Tracey pulled her hair up away from the nape of her neck, and Mark unhooked the necklace, then handed it to her. Tracey slipped the little amulet off. "Would you put my necklace back on now?" she asked him. "Prometheus gave me this, and I'll never part with it."

Mark took it from her and put it back around her neck, clasping it shut. "There," he said.

"Thanks," Tracey said. She walked over to the ancient woman, leaned down, took one of her hands in her own, and solemnly placed the amulet in the palm.

The old woman's fingers closed around it tightly, and she began to mumble quietly, nodding her head toward Tracey, who straightened back up and smiled at Kathy.

"She's thanking you," Kathy said. "She says you've helped her spare someone else."

"Thanks, Kathy," Tracey said. "I hope we see you again. Sometime soon."

The old woman's mumbling became louder, and she rocked slightly in her chair as her words grew in volume.

"It won't be long," Kathy said. "She says this was the first of many visits for you. That you have a new life ahead of you."

"I hope so," Tracey said. She turned and rejoined Mark, waved good-bye to Kathy, and they walked to the little car that waited for them.

"Do you believe what she says?" Mark asked.

"I want to," Tracey replied.

"I do, too," Mark said. He stopped and embraced her, then kissed her mouth. "Especially the part about the new life ahead of you."

Turn the page for a special preview of

Judith Gould's breathtaking new novel

of passion and suspense

THE PARISIAN AFFAIR

The taxi lurched to a stop in front of the new high-rise building in the East Seventies, and Allegra handed the driver a wad of singles. "Keep the change," she said, already swinging the door open and sliding across the slick vinyl seat. The instant her heels hit the pavement, she righted herself and made a dash for the building's entryway.

Normally for an appointment like this, she would have taken great care with grooming and dressing, and would have allowed plenty of time to take the trip uptown. This morning, however, it had been a mad race to shower, put on her makeup, and dress, and now she felt thrown together. Last night—closer to four a.m.—she'd forgotten to set her alarm after she and Todd had made love and didn't wake up until around nine-thirty. When she'd dashed out the apartment door, Todd was still fast asleep, snoring away without a care in the world. For a moment, she'd felt like giving him a violent shake to wake him up. But as her gaze lingered on his tousled black hair and his handsome slumbering body, her hard feelings had softened. He looked so adorable, so defenseless, and so . . . sexy.

The smartly uniformed doorman swung the mirrorlike chrome and glass door open, greeting her starchily. "Good morning, miss. How may I help you?"

"I have an appointment with Mr. Whitehead," Allegra replied.

"Please see the concierge, miss," he said, indicating the desk where she would have to be announced before going up to Hilton Whitehead's.

Allegra crossed what seemed an acre of gleaming black granite before reaching the identically uniformed concierge, who stood behind a high reception desk of polished steel and more black granite. A massive body-builder with bleached blond hair, he gave her a big smile.

"How may I help you?" he asked.

"Mr. Whitehead," Allegra replied. "I have an appointment."

The concierge nodded, then stared at her with appreciative blue eyes as he phoned the apartment. Allegra, who pretended not to notice his attention, gazed about the ultramodern lobby. It was all glass, steel, and granite, with leather-upholstered couches and chairs in seating areas on thick, plush rugs. Huge floral arrangements, primarily composed of brightly colored tropical flowers in crystal vases, decorated coffee tables and commodes.

"Go right on up," the concierge said. "It's a private elevator in the vestibule to your right. The penthouse."

"Thank you," she said to the still-staring concierge. She strode to the vestibule and found the appropriate elevator. As she pushed the button, she caught her reflection in the mirrored walls. *Well, not too bad,* she thought, *considering that I got ready in record time.* The doors slid open instantly, and she stepped in. Ascending to the sixtieth floor, she began to feel the fluttering of butterflies in her stomach.

Now that the moment had come, she began to wonder anew what Hilton Whitehead could possibly want to see her about unless it was to order a piece of jewelry. It would have to be something very special, she thought. After all, he was one of the country's richest men, and he had seen to it that she came to him rather than taking a ride downtown. It was the only thing that made sense.

She was just beginning to do a mental inventory of the largest and most precious gemstones she had in stock when the elevator came to a stop and its doors slid open with hardly a sound. She stepped into a large vestibule in which there was a magnificent commode covered in shagreen. A mirror above it was covered in the same sharkskin and reflected a huge orchid plant with its dozens of ivory blooms. At either end of the vestibule, huge modern paintings hung on walls that appeared to be covered with parchment. Before she got more than a glance at them, one of the tall, ebonized double doors to the right of the commode opened.

"Miss Sheridan?" A tall African-American man with a black patch over one eye stood at attention in the doorway. His hair was snow white, and he appeared to be at least seventy-five. He was wearing an immaculate black uniform.

"Yes," Allegra said, holding her hand out to be shaken.

Momentarily nonplused—obviously few visitors ever offered to shake his hand—the butler took it in his and shook it. "I'm Boyce, ma'am," he said. "I'll take your coat."

"Thank you, Boyce," she said, turning to let him help her out of the knee-length black cashmere cape that served as her wintertime coat for uptown business.

"If you'll follow me, please," he said.

Allegra trailed just behind the elderly gentleman, her eyes feasting on the large circular entrance hall. Its walls were entirely covered in an exotic wood, and the floors were marble. Suspended from the center of the room's high ceiling was a large Calder mobile that hung nearly to the floor, each element in a different bright color. All around the room, the walls were hung with modern paintings in gilt frames. She glimpsed two Picassos, a Leger, a Braque, and two or three others that she couldn't see long enough to identify. Boyce opened one of a pair of double doors, and they turned right and went down a hallway. After walking a short distance, Boyce stopped at yet another pair of tall double doors and knocked lightly.

"Come in," someone called.

It's Sylvie, Allegra thought, hearing the unmistakable French-accented voice.

Boyce opened the door and stepped aside for Allegra to enter. "Thank you, Boyce," she said.

He nodded. "You're welcome, ma'am."

Sylvie stood up and came around her desk to greet Allegra. "*Bonjour, chérie,*" she chirped. "I'm so glad you could come this morning." She air-kissed each of Allegra's cheeks.

"*Bonjour* to you, too," Allegra replied. "This is really some place you work."

"It is nice, isn't it?" Sylvie said. "I'll tell Mr. Whitehead you're here."

Allegra noticed the wall of glass that faced her, and immediately went over to it. "My God," she said, looking out at the view. "It's like being on top of the world up here. You can see for miles."

"Yes," Sylvie said. "Isn't it fabulous? All the way past the tip of Manhattan to Staten Island, and over to Queens and Brooklyn and Long Island. And New Jersey, of course, on the other side." She sat back down at her desk, where she picked up a telephone.

"Mr. Whitehead," Allegra heard her say, still taking in the view. "Miss Sheridan is here." After a moment, she said, "Okay."

Allegra tore her eyes away from the skyline and sat down in one of the chairs. "I hope I'm on time," she said. "I overslept."

"Oh, so you and Todd had a bit of a long night, did you?" Sylvie said with a sly smile.

"You might say that," Allegra replied.

"Good. Anyway, you're precisely on time." She looked over at Allegra. "And you look stunning, *chérie*. No one would ever believe you were up half the night. I adore your necklace. Your design, unmistakably."

"Thanks, it is," Allegra said, her fingers going to the necklace and adjusting it slightly. She'd worn a simple black cashmere long-sleeved tee shirt with a matching skirt, but the austere look was offset by the drama provided by the necklace. It was a dramatic gold, set with hundreds of tiny garnets that wrapped loosely about her neck and dangled like a long apple peel.

"Did you and Jean-Pierre have a good time? I didn't see you again after we had our talk."

Sylvie shrugged. "With Jean-Pierre it's always the same. He's like a bunny, you know? But I get the feeling that I could be an old Teddy bear and it wouldn't matter. He just goes at it like a maniac and that's that."

They both laughed.

"Sensitive type, I see," Allegra said.

"Ha!" Sylvie snorted derisively. "He can be amusing at least. And after a day of work, sometimes that is enough."

"Well, at least you get to work in a beautiful place," Allegra said, looking around. "Does Mr. Whitehead work here all the time?"

Sylvie shook her head. "Oh, no," she replied. "This is just a little home office. The company is headquartered in San Jose. He has an office here in New York, but he keeps this one as a place to get things done without any distractions."

The office door opened, and a handsome man over six feet tall entered. He had brown hair that was just beginning to gray and alert brown eyes. He was tan and lean, fit for a man approaching middle age, dressed casually in slacks and a sweater, and he smiled winningly. "You must be Allegra," he said, reaching her chair in a couple of long strides.

"Yes," she said, as she started to rise. "I am."

"Don't get up," he said, taking her hand in his and shaking it. "I'm Hilton Whitehead."

"It's a pleasure to meet you, Mr. Whitehead," she said. Somehow he wasn't what she'd expected. Perhaps it was his easy manner that surprised her, added to his casual dress and obvious charm. But then why shouldn't a billionaire look and act like him? she asked herself. Nowadays, there were a lot of rich men of the Bill Gates ilk, almost never seen dressed up and less than formal in manner.

"Hilton, please," he said. He admired her lively eyes and shiny auburn hair, her pale skin and shapely figure. She had a touch of the bohemian artist about her, something indefinable that made her all the more desirable to him.

Allegra nodded. She didn't fail to notice his interest.

He eased down in a chair next to hers and scooted around slightly so he could face her. "You must be wondering what I wanted to talk to you about."

"Yes," Allegra said. "I have to say that I'm very curious."

"Well, I apologize for the secrecy," he said. "I'm not usually so mysterious, but in this case it seemed like the best way to go about it."

"Exactly what is 'it'?" Allegra asked.

"It's like this," he said, looking her in the eye. "I've always thought that the jewelry pieces Sylvie's bought from you were beautiful. Different from the stuff you usually see in the stores. Even the best ones. It's . . . unique. Like the necklace you're wearing right now. It's like art, I guess you'd say."

"Thank you," Allegra replied. "I'll take that as a compliment."

"You should," he replied. "Anyway, Sylvie told me all about how you're a gemologist. Says you really know your stones."

Allegra nodded. "I like to think so."

He looked at her with a serious expression. "I need someone like you to do a job for me," he said.

"What kind of job?" Allegra asked.

"There's an auction coming up at Dufour in Paris. One of their Magnificent Jewelry auctions."

"I know," she said. "I have the catalogue at home, but I haven't looked at it yet."

"So you've bought there?" he asked.

"Oh, no," she said with a laugh. "I'm afraid it's a little out of my league. I get the catalogues just to look at the jewelry. To see if any of it inspires me. I also like to see the exceptional stones when they come up. Just because they can be so beautiful."

He nodded thoughtfully, then looked over at Sylvie. "I think we've found the perfect person," he said.

Sylvie smiled. "I know it."

Hilton took a deep breath and steepled his hands together. "Allegra, Dufour has an emerald ring coming up for auction, and I want that ring. It is exceptionally beautiful. A huge emerald. But it's the provenance that's really important in this case."

"That's often true," Allegra said.

"Well, it is with this ring," he said, "because it's Princess Karima who's selling it."

"Oh, I see," Allegra said. "That would automatically make it worth a lot, considering who she is."

"The point is," Hilton said, "I have to have it. It's going to be a surprise for a lady friend of mine."

Allegra knew it was irrational of her to feel disappointment, but she did. Maybe it was because a ring of such provenance was going to end up as a gift for just another rich woman. But maybe, she told herself, it was actually jealousy because she wasn't going to be the recipient of his largesse.

"The thing is," he went on, "if I bid on the ring personally, the price will go through the roof. All they have to do is hear my name, and dealers and fat cats all over the world will start trying to outbid me." He gazed into her eyes. "You understand what I'm talking about, of course."

"Oh, yes," Allegra said. "So you're looking for somebody to bid for you," she said.

"That's right," he said, "and I think you're the perfect person."

"But why not Sylvie?" she asked. She looked over but saw that Sylvie had quietly disappeared from her position behind the desk.

"Sylvie's known in the auction houses," he said. "She's bid for me before. Plus, I don't want to send just anybody into that auction."

"Why's that?"

"I want somebody who really knows stones," he said. "I want you to go to the preview and study the ring to make certain you're getting the right one."

"Don't you trust Dufour to deliver the goods? My God, you're talking about one of the world's most respected auction houses. They're over two hundred years old."

"I know," he said. "I know. But we both know that so-called 'experts' goof up all the time."

"That's for sure."

"Anyway, you know your stones, so you can make sure that the ring you get is the ring that Princess Karima is selling."

"Yes," she said with certainty, "I'm sure I could do that."

"Then would you be willing to do this for me?" he asked, looking at her hopefully.

"I . . . I think so," she said. "I have to give it some thought."

"I'm willing to pay you handsomely," he said, smiling.

"It's not just a matter of money," she said. "There's my business to consider, and quite frankly I'm having a really tough time right now." She looked him in the eye. "I'm close to going under," she admitted, "so it's not a good time for me to leave."

"I'm sorry to hear that," he said. She heard the genuine concern in his voice. "But this wouldn't take long. You would have my personal jet to take you to Paris, see the preview, bid the next day, and fly straight back with the ring. What've you got to lose? A couple of days at the most. Plus, an extra paycheck might help you save your business."

"How much did you have in mind?" she asked.

"I'm willing to pay you twenty-five thousand dollars, plus expenses," he said.

Allegra kept her face devoid expression, though her heart leapt at his figure.

"My Gulfstream V, a suite at the Ritz or wherever you prefer to stay, and all your meals with a credit card I'll give you. You'll have permission to sign on it. What do you say? Fair?" He was staring into her eyes questioningly.

She managed to retain her composure while returning his gaze, but she was performing mental calculations at the same time. The rent. The gemstone dealer. The gold and silver and platinum dealers. Jason's salary. Plus, she had to figure in what Whitehead was going to get out of her services. She knew that he needed her.

"What do you say?" he repeated.

"I can't do it for twenty-five thousand dollars."

"You can't?"

"I'll need fifty," she said, her voice unwavering and her eye contact unbroken. "In advance. I've got to pay some bills, and that'll do it."

"Fifty thousand dollars for a couple of days' work?" he said with a laugh. "In advance?"

"Take it or leave it," Allegra said. She made movements in her chair as if she was going to get up.

"No, no," he said, waving her down with his hand. "Wait just a minute there. Just a minute."

"Okay," she said. "I'll wait. But just a minute. I've got a business to run, you know. It may not be a multibillion-dollar multinational, but it's my life."

"You're something else, Allegra Sheridan," he said. He sat staring at her, his lips spread in a smile. Finally, he offered her his hand. "You've got yourself a deal."

Allegra shook his hand, trying to slow the wildly beating heart within her chest.

Sylvie, who had quietly reentered the office, began clapping her hands together lightly. "Hooray!" she exclaimed. "Now we must celebrate." On the desk, she had placed a tray that held a bottle of champagne in a silver ice bucket and three crystal flutes. "Shall I do the honors?" she asked, looking toward Hilton Whitehead

"Certainly," he said. "You will stay and have a glass of champagne with us, Allegra?"

Her stomach did a turn. After last night's drinking and the excitement of the moment, a drink was the last thing she really wanted. "Sure," she said. "I'd love a glass of champagne. But just one quick one. I really do need to get back downtown to the atelier."

"Good," Hilton said as Sylvie popped the cork.

Sylvie filled the three flutes and handed Allegra and Hilton theirs.

Hilton raised his in a toast. "To a successful venture together," he said.

"Bon chance," Sylvie chimed in.

"Give her the schedule," Hilton said, looking over at Sylvie as they sipped the champagne.

From a desk drawer, Sylvie took out a single sheet of paper and handed it to Allegra. "This is the proposed schedule," she said.

Allegra glanced down at it. The auction was a week away. *That'll give me plenty of time to get things straightened out here before I leave. Like paying bills,* she thought. "This will work for me," she said, folding it and putting it in her pocketbook.

"Is your passport current?" Hilton asked.

She nodded. "Yes."

"Good. One less detail to take care of. Sylvie will handle all of the reservations for you and take care of the details."

"That's fine," Allegra said. "Is Sylvie also going to write my check?"

Hilton laughed. "You're too much," he said, "but I like that. You're one of the more straightforward people I've met lately. You don't meet many." He looked at Sylvie. "Get a check ready for me to sign," he said, "and Allegra can take it home with her."

"Thank you," Allegra said, then took a sip of the champagne. "There is one thing we didn't discuss," she added.

"What's that?" Hilton asked.

"What if I don't place a successful bid and end up not getting the ring for you?"

"That's not going to happen," he said. In the background they could hear Sylvie typing.

"But how can you be certain of that?" she asked. "There're going to be a lot of rich men like you trying to get that ring. Princess Karima's name alone is going to make it a very hot auction. Remember the sale in Geneva a few years ago with the Duchess of Windsor's jewels?"

"I certainly do," he said. "Everything went through the roof."

"Exactly," Allegra said. "Some things went for twenty or thirty times their estimates. The same thing could happen in Paris."

"I'm sure that the same thing *will* happen in Paris," he said. "It's bound to. Princess Karima's name has the same kind of cachet that the Duchess of Windsor's had."

"That's what I mean," Allegra said. "I could lose out to somebody who's a fanatic devotee of hers. And has the money to back it up."

He shook his head. "I don't think so," he said. "I'm going to give you a letter of credit with the funds deposited and immediately available in the Citibank in Paris."

"Yes, but—"

"For a hundred million dollars," he added.

"A hundred million dollars," she repeated. She looked

down into the flute of champagne, then back up at him. "That should do it, I think."

"I think so, too," he said. "The estimate is eight to ten million."

"How many carats?"

"Thirty-four and a half, I think. I can get the catalogue if you want to see it."

"No," Allegra said. "I can take a look when I get home. I was just curious."

Sylvie rose from behind the desk and went around to Hilton. "Here's the check," she said. "It only needs your signature." She handed him a pen and winked at Allegra.

He set his champagne flute on the desk, then placed the check alongside it and signed his name. "Here you go," he said, handing it to Allegra with a smile.

She wanted nothing more than to kiss the check, but she took it and slipped inside her pocketbook. She would deposit it in her bank account as soon as she left. "Thanks, Mr. . . . Hilton."

"You're welcome," he said. "I'm sure everything's going to work out fine. I'll see you before you leave for Paris. Sylvie will let you know about that. Now, I'd better get back upstairs. I've got some things to do." He got to his feet and offered his hand again.

Allegra took it and shook firmly. "It was nice to meet you, Hilton," she said. "And thanks for this opportunity."

"Thank you, Allegra," she said. "We'll get together again soon." He turned and went to the door, thinking, *And not soon enough for me.*

When he had gone, Sylvie leaned down and air-kissed Allegra's cheeks. "*Merveilleuse, chérie. Merveilleuse.*"

"I can hardly believe this," Allegra said. "When you told me I'd be glad I came up here today, I didn't dream it would be anything like this."

"I'm glad you're pleased," Sylvie said. "I hoped you wouldn't be insulted by his proposition."

"Insulted," Allegra said. "I'm thrilled, Sylvie."

"Well, I was worried that you might think he was being rude. You know, by not buying a piece from you but asking you to do him this favor."

"Well," Allegra said with a laugh, "we can work on the piece of jewelry when I've come back from Paris with the ring." She looked thoughtful for a moment. "*If* I come back with it."

"Oh," Sylvie said with a shrug, "don't be silly, *chérie*. Of course, you'll come back with it. I'm sure there'll be no problem there. What in the world could happen?"